RUBY FEVER

By Ilona Andrews

Hidden Legacy series
BURN FOR ME
WHITE HOT
WILDFIRE
DIAMOND FIRE (novella)
SAPPHIRE FLAMES
EMERALD BLAZE
RUBY FEVER

Kate Daniels series
MAGIC BITES
MAGIC BURNS
MAGIC STRIKES
MAGIC BLEEDS
MAGIC SLAYS
MAGIC GIFTS (novella)
MAGIC RISES
MAGIC BREAKS
MAGIC SHIFTS
MAGIC BINDS
MAGIC TRIUMPHS

The Edge series
ON THE EDGE
BAYOU MOON
FATE'S EDGE
STEEL'S EDGE

ILONA ANDREWS

RUBY FEVER

A Hidden Legacy Novel

AVONBOOKS

An Imprint of HarperCollins*Publishers*

This is a work of fiction. Names, characters, places, and incidents are products of the author's imagination or are used fictitiously and are not to be construed as real. Any resemblance to actual events, locales, organizations, or persons, living or dead, is entirely coincidental.

RUBY FEVER. Copyright © 2022 by Ilona Gordon and Andrew Gordon. All rights reserved. Printed in the United States of America. No part of this book may be used or reproduced in any manner whatsoever without written permission except in the case of brief quotations embodied in critical articles and reviews. For information, address HarperCollins Publishers, 195 Broadway, New York, NY 10007.

First Avon Books mass market printing: August 2022
First Avon Books hardcover printing: August 2022

Print Edition ISBN: 978-0-06-324318-7
Digital Edition ISBN: 978-0-06-287840-3

Avon, Avon & logo, and Avon Books & logo are registered trademarks of HarperCollins Publishers in the United States of America and other countries.

HarperCollins is a registered trademark of HarperCollins Publishers in the United States of America and other countries.

FIRST EDITION

22 23 24 25 26   LSC   10 9 8 7 6 5 4 3 2 1

The war in Ukraine started when this book was in its final editing stages. It is still raging as we write this dedication. We cannot stop the war, but we can help the survivors. A quarter of this book's royalties will be donated to UN Refugee Fund.

Acknowledgments

This book marks the end of Catalina's story. It was a long time coming, and many people helped us along the way. We would like to thank Erika Tsang, our editor; Nancy Yost, our agent, and the team at NYLA; Nancy F., Mark Burkeitt, and Stephanie Mowery who copyedited the manuscript; Alivia Lopez who worked to buy us a few days of extra time when we needed it; Jill Smith and Jeaniene Frost for their infinite patience and feedback; Marian Xu for medical expertise—all errors are ours alone; our long-suffering beta readers: Loise McCoy, Chiara Prato, Francesca Virgili, Deborah Lin, M.D., Katie Heasley, Kerris Humphreys, Harriet Chow, Loredana Carini, Robin Snyder, Jessica Haluska, and especially Rossana Sasso; and finally we would like to thank our readers who followed the Baylors down a long and winding road to happily ever after.

RUBY FEVER

Prologue

Is it haunted?"

Oh, for the love of . . . "No, Arabella."

My sister squinted at the monstrosity of an estate growing closer as the SUV sped up the gently climbing driveway. "Look at all the towers. It looks haunted."

"It's not," Bern said.

"How do you know it's not haunted?" Leon asked from the back.

Because ghosts didn't exist. "Because Trudy is a nice person, I like her, and she wouldn't let us buy a haunted house."

"Yes," Arabella said, "but did you ask if it was?"

"I did, and Trudy said no." Our poor, long-suffering Realtor had answered more bizarre questions in the last couple of months than she had during her whole career.

My little sister whipped out her phone and bent her blond head over it.

The entire Baylor family was in the car with the exception of Grandma Frida and my older sister and brother-in-law. We were going to buy a house.

When I was very young, we lived in a typical suburban home. It was just the five of us: my dad, my mom, my older sister Nevada, me, and my younger sister Arabella. Then our two cousins, Bern and Leon, came to live with us because their mother wasn't worth two cents and nobody knew who their fathers were. Then Dad got sick. We sold the house to pay for his treatment and moved into a warehouse with Grandma Frida, my mother's mom. Dad died. Nevada, who was seventeen at the time, took over Baylor Investigative Agency, our family business, and she and Grandma Frida, who worked on tanks and mobile artillery for the Texas magical elite, put food on our table and clothes on our backs.

Eventually Nevada came into her magic, and we became House Baylor, one of the prominent families that boasted more than two living Primes, the highest ranked mages. Nevada fell in love and moved out, I ended up as the Head of the House, and one of my first achievements was to blow up the warehouse all of us called home. The fact that said blowing up was completely accidental did nothing to put a roof back over our heads or to decrease my guilt.

For a while we made do with an old industrial building we sort of converted into a habitable home, but all of us hated it. And our needs had changed. All of us, including my little sister, were now adults. We wanted to stay together, both because we loved each other and because House Baylor was a new House and every time we left our building, we sported lovely targets on our backs. Safety in numbers was very much true in our case. But we also desperately needed privacy.

We wanted to live together. Just not together-together.

Finding the right house in our price range had taken forever, but I had my hopes pinned on this one. I really liked it.

"I heard Realtors have to disclose if the house is haunted," Leon said.

I looked at Mom in the driver's seat. She gave me an amused smile. No help there.

"Apparently only four states require you to disclose paranormal activity," Arabella reported. "Nine states require you to notify the buyer if a death occurred on the premises. And Texas does neither."

"There were no deaths on the premises. Nobody died in the house, so it can't possibly be haunted," I told them.

"How do you know nobody died?" Leon asked.

"Because I checked the records," Bern rumbled.

"That doesn't mean anything," Arabella said.

Clearly, there were two teams in this vehicle: Team Facts and Team Facts Be Damned.

"What if they hid it?" Leon asked.

Bern gave his younger brother a look. When it came to uncovering facts, Bern had no equal. If there was a record of something and that record was at any point entered into a computer connected to the Internet, he would find it.

We had run out of driveway and came to a stop atop a low hill. Mom eyed the ten-foot wall that wrapped around the estate. Directly in front of us a short, arched tunnel cut through it, allowing entry to the inner grounds. Normally the entrance was blocked by a heavy metal gate, which right now was retracted into the wall on the left side. On the right side, enclosed within the wall's thickness, was a guardhouse.

"That's a lot of security," Mom said.

"I like it," Leon said. "If the infidels choose to storm the walls, we can unleash a rain of arrows and boiling pitch."

Ha. Ha.

Mom maneuvered our armored Chevy Tahoe through the entrance and into the front parking lot on the right side. Alessandro's silver Alfa Romeo already waited in one of the parking spots.

Everyone piled out of the car. The inner driveway, a wide paved road flanked by thick, mature oaks, unrolled straight ahead, leading south to the main house. To the right of us was a large stone-and-timber pavilion with huge windows.

Mom nodded at it. "What's that?"

"That's a wedding pavilion. The beam work inside is really pretty. I thought that if we insulated it properly, we could use it as our office building."

Leon frowned. "You mean like a *separate* office building? One where we could conduct business and then *leave* and not be at work? People have such things?"

I sighed.

"Leon," Mom said. "She and Alessandro spent the last two weeks trying to get this place inspected. She barely slept and barely ate. As I recall, none of you helped except for Bern. How about you holster that razor-sharp wit and try to be less you for the next hour?"

"Yes, ma'am." Leon stood up straight and appeared to look serious. It wouldn't last, but it was a good try. My younger cousin was twenty years old, and he showed zero interest in changing his ways. And that was fine with me. I liked Leon just the way he was.

Mom squinted at the two-story rectangular building on the other side of the main driveway. "And this?"

"'Cuartel,'" I said. "According to the listing documents."

She raised her eyebrows. "Barracks?"

"Yes. The lower level has a kitchen, a mess hall, and an armory. The upper level has room for ten beds and a bathroom with four toilet stalls and three showers."

"Hmmm."

Normally interpreting Mom's "hmmms" wasn't a problem, but right now I had no idea what she was thinking.

We strolled down the driveway. The dense wall of ornamental shrubs framed the oaks on both sides, hiding the rest of the grounds. The tree limbs reached to each other above our heads and walking down the driveway was like heading into a green tunnel.

"Nice driveway," Leon said.

"Enjoy it while you can," I told him. "It's the only straight road in the place."

"How many acres did you say this was?" Mom asked.

"Twenty-three point four," Bern said ahead of us. "Sixteen are walled in, the rest is deer-fenced."

"We'll need to continue the wall," Mom said. "Deer fence won't cut it."

"Question!" Arabella raised her hand. "If we buy this, can I get a golf cart?"

"You can buy a golf cart with your own money," Mom said.

The driveway brought us to a large forecourt in front of a two-story Mediterranean mansion.

"The main house is five thousand square feet," I said. "The bottom floor is split into two wings. Each wing has a master. Four bedrooms upstairs, all en suite."

"Four bedrooms?" Arabella asked. "So, Mom and Grandma take the downstairs, and we take the upstairs?"

To say she sounded underwhelmed would be a criminally gross understatement.

"We could do that," I said, "or we could live in the auxiliary buildings."

Arabella squinted at me. "What auxiliary buildings?"

I turned my back to the mansion and pointed with both hands to the sides.

The family turned around. On both sides of the driveway, separated by the hedges, lay a labyrinth of buildings and greenery. On the left a round tower rose three floors high. On the right, half hidden by landscaping, sat three two-story casitas, each sixteen hundred square feet, joined by a second-floor breezeway. Between them and us lay gardens, benches, gazebos, and water features. Stone paths, designed by a drunken sailor, meandered through it all, trying to connect the buildings and mostly failing.

Leon spied the tower. His eyes took on a faraway look that usually meant he was thinking of flying ships, winged whales, and space pirates. "Mine."

"It needs a bit of work," I warned.

"I don't care."

Bern took a step forward and rumbled, "I like this place." He waited for a moment to let it sink in and walked to the right, starting down a stone path toward the casitas.

"Where are you going?" Mom called.

"Home," he called out without turning.

She looked at me. "Does Runa like the casitas?"

I nodded.

My oldest cousin and my best friend were slowly but surely moving toward marriage. Runa and her siblings lived with us, and it was harder and harder to ignore Runa slinking out of Bern's room to the bathroom across the hall first thing in the morning.

I could relate. Alessandro and I slept in the same bed every night, but both of us felt awkward about him moving into my room for completely different reasons, so we settled for him staying in the side building and me keeping my window open. For him, climbing in and out of the window was infinitely preferrable to having to run the gauntlet of my family just to get to my door.

"Where am I going to stay?" Arabella asked. "Am I going to stay in one of the casitas?"

"I think they're spoken for," Mom said, watching Bern double-time it down the path. "Bern and Runa will take one and the Etterson children will take the other or others."

"There's a shack in the back, behind the main house," I told Arabella. "You can live there."

She marched around the house. Mom and I followed her along a narrow path, flanked by Texas olive trees, esperanza shrubs, still carrying the last of their bright yellow flowers, and sprawling clusters of cast-iron plants with thick green leaves.

"So Bern and Leon get their picks, and I get the leftovers," Arabella called over her shoulder.

"Yep." I nodded. "You're the youngest."

She mumbled something under her breath. Torturing her was delicious.

"What did you say this place was?" Mom asked.

"A failed resort. The first owners built the main house, Leon's tower, and the bigger casita. Then they sold it to a man who decided to make it into an ultrasecure 'rustic' hotel for Primes and Significants. His website called it 'a country retreat for the Houston elite.'"

Arabella snorted.

"He owned this place for about twelve years and built all of the auxiliary craziness. His business collapsed, and now he's trying to unload the property to settle his debts."

Nothing about this estate followed any kind of plan. To add insult to injury, the second owner thought he was handy and did a lot of the renovations and maintenance himself instead of hiring professionals. According to our building inspector, his handiness was very much in doubt.

"How much does he want for this place?" Arabella asked.

"Twenty million."

"That's out of our budget," Mom said.

"It's not if we get financing," I said. We had already put in an application through a mortgage company Connor owned, and it was approved in record time.

"We can afford to put half down," Arabella said. "But this place isn't worth twenty mil. I mean I don't even get a house. I get a shack . . ."

We turned the corner and the path opened, the greenery falling behind. A huge stone patio spread in front of us, cradling a giant Roman-style pool. Past the luxuriously large pool, the patio narrowed into a long stone path that ran down to the four-acre lake. Between the pool and the lake, on the right-hand side, stood another three-story tower.

Where Leon's tower looked like something plucked from a Norman castle, this one could have fit right into the seaside of Palm Beach. Slender, white, with covered balconies on the top two levels and a sun-deck on the roof, it had a clear vacation vibe. A narrow breezeway connected its third-floor balcony to the main house. Of all the places on the property, it was the newest and required the least amount of work to be habitable.

"Your shack," I told her.

Arabella took off across the patio.

Mom and I strolled down past the pool toward the lakeshore. An exercise track circled the water, and the roofs of three other houses poked out from the greenery at random spots along its perimeter.

"The southern entrance is there." I pointed at the other end of the lake. "We can put Grandma's motor pool in that spot, facing the road." We would have to get her a golf cart to get to it. Grandma Frida was spry, but well past seventy.

"Can we really afford this place?" Mom asked.

"Yes. If we put twenty-five percent down, we will have enough for a year's worth of business expenses and have half a million left over to renovate. We'll have to stagger the repairs and we'll need to invest in some livestock for the agricultural exemption. The place already has solar panels, so we'll be saving some money there, but we will need a yard crew and probably a maid service of some sort."

Mom bristled. "I never needed maids in my life. If you're old enough to have your own space, you're old enough to keep it clean."

"I agree, but the main house is huge, and we have the barracks and the offices. We are all going to be really busy. There will be an army of people to supervise, renovation decisions to make, and we still have our regular caseload and then there is the other business . . ."

My time was no longer completely my own. A chunk of it belonged to my family and the running of our House, but another, significantly larger part, belonged to the State of Texas and the complex entanglements its magic families created.

Arabella burst onto the third-floor balcony. "Do I like it? No. I love it!"

Mom grinned. "Well, you got her vote. Where would you and Alessandro stay?"

"Over there." I pointed to the left, where a two-story house sat by the lake. "He's probably over there right now. Do you need me to walk through the main house with you?"

Mom waved me off. "I've got it. Go check on him."

I gave her a quick hug and took the stairs from the patio to the path leading to the two-story house Alessandro and I picked out for ourselves.

Hopefully he was still there. I had texted him when we were pulling up, but he hadn't answered. He might have fallen asleep.

In our world, Primes like me packed a great deal of power. Even average magic users could unleash a lot of devastation, especially if their magic was combat grade. Nobody wanted the chaos that would happen if mages were allowed to run around unchecked. While everyone was subject to laws, when it came to mages, the civilian authorities left the enforcement of said laws to the magic community itself. The magic users of each state were governed by an assembly, which in turn answered to the National Assembly.

The National Assembly appointed a Warden to each state, a single law enforcement officer whose identity was kept confidential for obvious reasons. Wardens investigated crimes committed by the magical elite and sometimes rendered judgment. Our Warden was Linus Duncan, I served as his Deputy, and Alessandro functioned as our Sentinel. Sentinels were to Wardens what bailiffs were to judges. While Wardens investigated, Sentinels guarded them and applied force when force was required. Just like me, Alessandro was always on call, and Linus called him a lot.

To top it off, in Alessandro's mind, he was bringing only himself and his skills to this relationship, and he had thrown himself into our family business trying to contribute. He was efficient and smart, and he had raised our income by almost thirty percent, which was in part why we were able to gather money for our down payment so quickly. Only Leon earned more.

But there were only so many hours in the day. Alessandro couldn't cut his Sentinel hours, he didn't want to cut his House Baylor hours, so instead he cut his rest and ended up falling asleep in random places. A week ago, after I found him asleep on the stairs with a half-eaten fajita on his plate, I told him I would lock him out of my bedroom if he didn't stop. He swore to me he would get at least seven hours a night.

I reached the house. It was a cute two-story place, charming and just right for the two of us. The lawn in front of it was green and pretty despite winter. Houston's understanding of winter was rather limited. Shadow, my little black dog, would love this lawn. Right now, her outside consisted of a paved lot and leashed walks down more paved sidewalks bordered by a narrow strip of grass. If we bought this house, Shadow would be the queen of everything.

The front door stood ajar. I walked up the steps onto the covered porch and stepped into the foyer. All the curtains had been stripped from the windows, and the house was full of light. My steps sent echoes scurrying over the travertine floor.

The floor must've cost a fortune and the money for it clearly came from the kitchen, which needed help in the worst way. I walked into it and stopped. A dozen blood-red roses bloomed in a simple glass vase on an unfortunately large island, which I would replace as soon as I scraped enough money for it. A bottle of Giulio Ferrari rosé and two wineglasses waited on the counter by the fridge.

Alessandro had bought wine and roses for me.

I grinned.

A man I'd never seen before stepped out into the hallway on my left, his hands glowing with crimson. In the split second it took me to send a surge of magic toward the intruder, Alessandro loomed behind him like a vengeful ghost, clamped his hand over the man's mouth, and slid a knife into his side. It was a quick, precise stab, so fast I would have missed it if I hadn't been looking straight at them.

Alessandro twisted the knife. His face was calm and relaxed, his eyes focused, but not frightening. The man's eyes rolled back, and he sagged slightly against Alessandro. The man I loved picked up his target like a toddler and neatly placed him on the island, the knife still between his ribs. The vase slid off and I caught it by pure reflex.

A person had just died in front of me without making a single sound. It was both beautiful and bone-chilling.

"Arkan?" I asked.

He nodded.

Arkan was the monster in the closet, the bogeyman under our bed. A former government agent from the Russian Imperium, he'd set up shop in Canada and built a cadre of assassins around himself. He plotted, killed, and meddled with political affairs all around the globe but especially in North America. He was so dangerous, the Warden database gave him a black tag, usually reserved for dictators of small countries and heads of worldwide terrorist organizations.

Linus Duncan wanted to kill him because Arkan had stolen a sample of the Osiris serum from the United States. A century and a half ago, the discovery of the serum led to the emergence of hereditary magical talents which shaped our world. The use of the serum was now banned by an international treaty, and protecting it was one of the Wardens' highest priorities. Alessandro wanted to kill Arkan because Arkan had murdered his father. I wanted to kill him to keep Alessandro safe. We had clashed twice, and both times Arkan lost operatives and allies, but the man himself remained out of our reach and our jurisdiction.

The assassin lay motionless on our kitchen island. Arkan hadn't sent his best. He sent someone just good enough to sneak up on me, and he didn't expect this man to survive. He threw a life away just to tap us on the shoulder and say, "Lovely house. I haven't forgotten about you."

Alessandro took the vase from my hands and wrapped his arms around me, pulling me to him. "Catalina, don't let it worry you." His voice was intimate and warm. "We've got this. This is nothing."

I leaned my head against his chest. We had to deal with Arkan. Until he was eliminated as a threat, we couldn't be happy.

He would never let us alone. Last year, right after we destroyed that construct in the Pit, Arkan, who had been connected to the whole thing, sent his pet telekinetic, Xavier Secada, to warn us to back off. We told him where he could shove his offer.

Xavier hated House Baylor and particularly me with the fire of ten thousand suns. He was once a member of Connor's extended family on Connor's mother's side, but after I exposed the fact that he was actively trying to sabotage Connor and Nevada's wedding, he was kicked out. I had expected Xavier to retaliate after the Pit. He didn't. Instead, he went to Spain and attacked his former family. He didn't target the adults. No, Xavier had gone after Mia Rosa, a ten-year-old child, because she was a future Prime and the pride of her family.

If she had been a little less trained or if his power had been a little more stable, he would've killed her. She survived but spent months in the hospital. To say that Connor wanted to get his hands on Xavier's neck would be an understatement. And Arkan, who had sanctioned the entire thing, sent Mia Rosa flowers at the hospital with a card that said, "See you soon."

This was the type of opponent we were dealing with. That's who stood between us and our happiness.

"This won't happen once we move in," Alessandro said.

"I know." Our private guards were top-notch, and our security chief was exceptional.

I wouldn't let Arkan taint this house for us. No, this would be our home, and I would make it safe and warm.

"Would you like some wine?" he asked.

"No."

Alessandro's expression darkened. "This didn't quite go the way I wanted it to."

"What do you mean?"

Alessandro looked at the dead killer. "But then, maybe this is better. More honest."

He took a step back. A small box appeared in Alessandro's fingers as if by magic.

Wine, flowers, new house, jewelry box. My brain connected the puzzle pieces in a lightning-bright flash, and I caught his arm just as he started to kneel, keeping him standing. "No kneeling. Please."

He opened the box. A gold ring rested on black velvet, crowned with an oval ruby.

"This is not an heirloom," Alessandro said with grim sincerity. "I didn't take it from my family. I designed it for you and had it made. Nobody else has ever worn it and if you say no, nobody ever will."

The faceted stone glittered like a star caught in a drop of blood between us.

"I love you with all of my heart," he said. "I can't promise you a calm life, but I promise you that I will do everything in my power to make you happy. Will you marry me?"

He fell silent, and I saw uncertainty flicker in his eyes. Despite everything we'd been through, he didn't know what my answer would be. This was the part of the road where our two paths either converged or parted. One word, one tiny little word, and our lives would be irreversibly changed. The moment was so deeply intimate that it almost hurt.

I stood up on my toes, wrapped my arms around his neck, and looked into his eyes.

He waited for my answer.

I kissed him and whispered, "Yes. The answer is yes."

# Chapter 1

Six months later

Monday morning started badly and only got worse.

On my computer screen, Ruben Hale attempted to glower at me. I gave him my patented Tremaine stare. Sadly, it worked much better in person. Hard to radiate deadly intent over a video chat.

"We will not proceed until the retainer is wired into our account."

Ruben was in his late fifties, with a bronze complexion, a stocky build, and a heavy jaw. He was also a Significant. In a lot of ways, Significants were harder to deal with than Primes. Primes were like tigers, deadly but conflict averse, because when Primes fought, entire city blocks ended up incinerated. Most Primes considered it beneath them to bully lesser ranked magic users. They took for granted that they would be respected, and they had a reputation to uphold.

The Significants wanted to be Primes. Their abilities placed them above the majority of magic users, but still below that coveted top layer of power. A lot of them felt compelled to throw their weight around to ensure their special status was acknowledged, and they resented Primes, so when an opportunity to safely irritate a Prime presented itself, they pounced on it.

"You listen to me." Ruben leaned closer to the screen, giving me a stunning view of his nose hair. "I went with you for one reason only. You were cheaper than Montgomery."

"Cheaper, Mr. Hale. Not free."

This was one of Alessandro's cases. Normally he would've taken the call, but he was out hunting down Dag Gunderson, another colossal pain in his neck. An alteration mage, Dag had the ability to supercharge missiles with arcane energy. He'd used his talent to settle a personal grudge by turning ordinary hail into an arcane meteor shower and accidentally damaged a municipal building in the process.

The Texas Assembly slapped him with a fine and moved on, anticipating prompt payment. Instead of paying restitution, Gunderson proceeded to evade the authorities, unleashing random bombardments against various targets. The Assembly got fed up with trying to track him down and petitioned Linus for help, who sent Alessandro to take care of it.

The look in Ruben's eyes told me he was used to bulldozing over people to get his way. I could see why Alessandro held off on doing any actual work until his deposit cleared. As of today, it was six days past due.

"You should be grateful for the work," Ruben growled.

Raised voices filtered through the glass door and walls into my office. Someone, or probably several someones, was shouting in the conference room. Odd. I couldn't recall any large problematic meetings scheduled for today.

"Do you even know who you're talking to?" Ruben demanded.

Apparently, we reached the "how dare you" stage of negotiations. "You signed a contract, Mr. Hale. According to the terms . . ."

"Terms change."

"Not after you sign them. Perhaps you should look up the definition of a contract."

Matilda ran past my door, her long dark hair flying, her skinny ten-year-old legs flashing, as she darted by.

"You are lucky to get my business. Apparently, you don't really want it."

"Business involves compensation. What you're asking for is charity."

Ruben's eyes went wide. His nostrils flared.

Ragnar sprinted past my office. First Cornelius' daughter, and now Runa's brother was involved. What in the world was going on out there?

"Who do you think you are?" Ruben thundered.

"Significant Hale!" I snapped into my Tremaine voice. "Who I am is not in question. My identity as a Prime and Head of my House is a matter of public record. The only thing in doubt is your ability to pay. You have wasted enough of my time. Consider our agreement void."

"You . . ."

"Take a moment to think and choose your next words very carefully. I have had enough of your posturing. Do not make yourself and your family the focus of my undivided attention."

His mouth clicked shut. He sat up straighter. "Miss Baylor . . ."

"*Prime* Baylor."

"Prime . . ."

I picked up his contract and tore it in two. "Our discussion is concluded."

He stared at me, shocked.

I ended the call, went to the door, and swung it open. A wave of noise hit me. Several people screamed at once, the chorus of anger and sadness punctuated by a woman sobbing.

I marched down the hall and threw the conference door open. Eight people, four of them middle-aged, sat and crawled on the floor. Matilda and Ragnar stood to the side, looking shell-shocked.

"What's going on here?"

"She's gone!" A white man in his sixties moaned at the table, his hand over his eyes. A white woman a few years younger in a mint Chanel suit protectively draped her arms over his shoulders.

"Who is gone?" I demanded.

"Jadwiga," Matilda volunteered.

"The two of you, out into the hallway."

I ushered the kids into the hallway and shut the door behind us. "What does the first queen of Poland have to do with whatever this is?"

Ragnar stared at me in awe. "How do you even know that?"

I had no idea how I knew the name of the first Polish queen. It was just one of the random facts that occasionally got stuck in my brain.

"Jadwiga is a spider," Matilda explained. "A very special spider."

Oh no.

"Is that the Dabrowski family?"

Ragnar nodded.

Jadwiga *was* a very special spider. About the size of a pumpkin patch dwarf tarantula, she was glossy, like polished mahogany. Unlike the abdomen of a typical spider, Jadwiga's rear segment ended abruptly, as if cut in half, terminating in a hardened disk with a pattern that looked like some ancient mask. It gave her a unique hourglass shape.

That distinctive disk was found in exactly one species: the Giant Hourglass spider. It was exceedingly rare—only seven specimens had been found so far—and hideously expensive. Trefon Dabrowski, the Head of House Dabrowski, had purchased Jadwiga for the cool sum of $250,000 from a Chinese orange farmer who found it. Trefon somehow got this precious spider through customs and installed it in a luxurious terrarium at House Dabrowski's mansion to be the star of his dazzling arachnid collection, only to have it stolen one week later.

Thanks to Cornelius, our firm had earned a reputation for resolving difficult animal cases, so when House Dabrowski misplaced their spider, we seemed like a natural choice. They practically threw their money at us.

"Last I checked, we declined to take this case. Matilda, your father explicitly said that spiders required a specific arachnid mage, and both you and he specialize in birds and mammals."

Matilda raised her chin. I knew that look. I was about to be hit with a long logical argument. If I let her get going, we would be here all day.

"Not only that, but this spider was smuggled into the US. Matilda, what is the definition of smuggled?"

"Illegally brought into or taken out of a country," she said.

"*Illegally* being the key word. Neither House Baylor"—I looked at Matilda—"nor House Harrison"—I looked at Ragnar—"nor House Etterson can be complicit in the smuggling of rare, endangered species."

"Technically . . ." Matilda started.

"No."

"I felt the spider. She was scared and stressed out."

I looked at Ragnar. "Explain quickly."

"Matilda wanted to find the spider to see if she could connect with it."

"Her," Matilda said.

"Bazyli Dabrowski stole the spider from his brother. We found it and we tried to give it—her—back. They had a fight in the conference room. Trefon told Bazyli he would never see Jadwiga again and then Bazyli attacked him and tried to pry the terrarium out of his brother's hands. It fell and Jadwiga ran away into the vent."

I took a deep breath and let it out slowly. "Matilda is ten. She is allowed to be irrational and to not think through the possible consequences of her actions."

Matilda looked as if she had been slapped.

"You are sixteen years old. You're less than two years away from legally being an adult."

"We'll find it," Ragnar promised.

"How did you even get involved in this? Both of you are contractors, so neither of you have the authority to accept cases. Who signed off on this contract? Whose name is on the paperwork?"

The kids clammed up.

It couldn't have been Cornelius. He had been very uncomfortable with the entire affair. Who in the world would give a ten-year-old animal Prime and a sixteen-year-old poison Prime free rein on an illegal spider kidnapping . . .

Of course. He would be the only one who'd do it.

My phone vibrated on my desk. An unfamiliar number. I took the call.

"Deputy Baylor," a deep voice said.

In the entire state of Texas, only a handful of people knew I was the Deputy Warden. I pointed at Ragnar and Matilda and pointed to the floor to indicate I wanted them to stay there. Right there. Then I slipped into my office and shut the door.

"Yes?"

"My name is Stéphane Gregoire. I am the maître d' of the Respite."

The Respite was a French themed restaurant, very tasteful, very exclusive, catering to an elite clientele. When the movers and shakers of Houston wanted to have a private lunch to discreetly discuss business, they went to the Respite. None of them knew Linus secretly owned it.

"We've met," I reminded him. "What can I do for you?"

"There has been a murder," Mr. Gregoire said. "I've attempted to reach Prime Duncan, but he is not answering."

"Who was murdered?"

"Luciana Cabera."

Oh shit.

"Who else knows?"

"You are the second person I called. I was instructed to reach out to you if the Warden was unavailable."

"Sit tight. Close the restaurant. I'll be right there."

I hung up and dialed Linus. One ring, two, three . . .

Linus always took my calls. Night or day, anytime, he picked up on the second ring.

Four, five . . .

He always warned me if he expected to be unavailable. Alessandro and I had a meeting scheduled with him tonight. I hung up and opened the door.

Matilda and Ragnar blinked at me.

"Get the Dabrowski family out of here and find that expensive, stressed out, scared spider before she bites someone or lays eggs."

I took off down the hallway toward the exit, dialing Alessandro. He'd left this morning to hunt down Dag Gunderson. He answered instantly.

"Where are you?"

"Pulling up to the gates."

"I have an emergency," I told him.

"We'll take my car."

I cleared the building and ran out into the sunshine, dialing Leon as I walked to the gates.

"If this is about the spider . . ." Leon started.

"Spider later. Linus isn't answering his phone. I need you to drive out to his place."

"On it."

"Call me when you get there."

Alessandro's silver Alfa Romeo streaked through the gates and slid to a stop in front of me. I got in and we U-turned and sped down the driveway.

"Where to?" Alessandro asked.

"The Respite. The Speaker of the Texas State Assembly has been murdered."

# Chapter 2

$\mathcal{T}$he Respite occupied a handsome two-story building on the corner of Milam and Anita, in Midtown. There were places in Houston that glittered. This area wasn't one of them. It was a place of generic apartment complexes, karaoke bars, bistros and take-out joints. Chipotle and Starbucks lived here and enjoyed heavy foot traffic from young professionals stopping in on their way in or out of the steel and glass towers of Northeast Midtown.

The Respite masqueraded as an average midlevel restaurant. Built with red brick, it boasted large arched windows on the first level, and if you were to walk through its front door, you'd find a satisfying menu of Texas staples with a hint of French flair. Special clients didn't enter through the front door. They took the side entrance and were led up a narrow staircase to the second floor. There they had a choice of a spacious dining room with tables set far apart to ensure privacy or the patio, an open-air dining space enclosed on two sides by a wall of plants and on the third, by a stone feature wall, offering art with Old West themes, framed antique maps, and black-and-white frontier photos in case the visitors somehow forgot they were in Texas.

Luciana Cabera hung off that wall, between a group shot of some cowboys and a dreamy Dawson Dawson-Watson original of a field awash with bluebonnets.

A two-foot metal spike pinned her to the stone through her chest. A second spike protruded from her open mouth. In life, she had been a slender woman with short curly hair she styled in a modern haircut, a sly nod at male politician hairstyles. She'd smiled easily, talked with her hands, and her eyes sparkled with life.

The thing that hung on the wall was her pale, lifeless imitation. Blood drenched her beige suit. Her trademark glasses with dark green frames lay on the ground. Her dark pumps had fallen off, and her bare feet, suspended six inches above the floor, dangled limp. There was something so disturbing and vulnerable about her feet with pale green nail polish on her toes. I had never seen her without shoes. It felt wrong. I couldn't explain it, but it made my throat squeeze itself into a hard clump.

In the first few months of working for Linus, I kept telling myself that eventually I'd become desensitized to the sheer brutality of magic combat, but it'd been almost two years. I knew better now. The urge to run away, the disturbing sensation of a sinking stomach, and throat gripped in an invisible fist when I saw another body savaged by someone's power would stay with me. Always. But I had gotten better at sidestepping it so I could do my job. The gloves helped. When I put on gloves before entering a scene, some part of me took it as a signal that it was time to put away personal anxiety and fear.

Alessandro stared at the corpse. His face was dark.

When the citizens of Texas found out that the Speaker of the Assembly had been murdered, the shit would hit the fan with a terrifying intensity. The fallout from this would be catastrophic. It was our job to contain it.

The first priority was to shift this scene away from the Respite. Luciana's body would have to be discovered—she was too prominent to simply disappear—but if it was discovered here, the Respite and its staff would become the focus of a media blitz. It would cripple our ability to investigate and shining a giant searchlight straight at Linus had to be avoided at all costs.

Alessandro dialed a number. "I need a cleanup crew, highest priority. Document, remove, recreate." He gave them the Respite's address and hung up.

Sometimes our thoughts were so in sync, it was almost frightening.

I forced myself to scrutinize the body. The angle of both spikes suggested a downward trajectory. The first spike had sunk so deep into the wall that only four inches protruded. The second was barely in, nearly twenty inches of it still visible. Both spikes ended in a metal ring with a hole wide enough to feed a heavy rope through.

I didn't like this. Not at all.

Alessandro stared at the spikes, then tilted his head and looked at the concrete and glass tower a couple of blocks away to the southeast.

"Mr. Gregoire, please walk me through it," I said.

Stéphane Gregoire nodded. Of average height, he was in his mid-forties, a white clean-shaven man with a Texas tan and dark wavy hair sprinkled with grey. He wore glasses, his suit was impeccably tailored, and he seemed unperturbed despite the human decoration on the wall of his restaurant. The server next to him, a young blond woman in a black and white uniform, wasn't nearly so composed. She clenched her hands into a single fist and looked at the ground directly in front of her. I understood the urge. I would've liked to look at the ground as well.

"Madam Cabera arrived alone at two minutes past eleven. She informed me that she expected a guest," Mr. Gregoire said.

"Did she say who?"

"No. She sat at her usual table." He indicated a table eight feet away, where one of the chairs was knocked over. "Simone brought her her customary wine. She preferred to have a glass of La Scolca Gavi before the meal."

"Did she order anything?"

"Not right away. It was her custom to linger. She enjoyed sipping her wine and catching up on her work. She would usually signal the staff when she was ready to order."

I had dined here before with Linus. The Respite subscribed to the European school of hospitality. Unlike American servers, who were encouraged to approach customers repeatedly, the Respite's staff left the patrons to their own devices. They didn't ignore the customers, and a slight gesture or a glance would summon the server nearly instantly, but they didn't intrude. To interrupt a meal by offering refills or bringing the check unasked would have been the height of rudeness.

"Madam Cabera sat for about six minutes. The first missile tore into her chest, lifted her out of the chair and pinned her to the wall. The second missile hit her face. Death was instant. She didn't even have the chance to scream."

We were looking at a Prime or an upper-level Significant telekinetic. A spike fired from a weapon would have hit Luciana at a downward angle and continued in that direction, piercing the chair and likely knocking it over. We would've found her on the floor. But telekinetics almost never threw objects in a straight line across a significant distance. They threw them in a catenary curve. The object swooped down and shot back up, drawing a shallow U.

Connor had explained it to me one time when he was training us to respond to telekinetic threats. He got really technical about it, but mainly it boiled down to three reasons. One, a person who saw a missile coming toward them would naturally jump to their feet or back up. The curve ensured that the missile would still get them on the upswing, which was why Luciana now hung off the wall. Two, an object thrown by a powerful telekinetic packed a lot of kinetic force. Even if it didn't kill the target, that upswing would knock them into the air, throwing them away from where they stood and resulting in additional damage. And three, the curve felt more natural than a straight line. Telekinetics using it hit with greater accuracy. It was a hard habit to break, and a surprised telekinetic would almost always throw in a curve. If you happened to see it coming, the only way to avoid it was to drop under it as flat as you could. Luciana never saw it.

"Who else was on the patio?" Alessandro asked.

"Prime Curtis and her daughter."

House Curtis specialized in horticulture, specifically cotton, sunflowers, and corn. They would have wanted none of this. They would have calmly gotten up and left and talking to them would be useless.

"Do you have video footage?" Alessandro asked.

"The Respite does not record their guests."

That was glaringly unlike Linus. Hm. "Can you tell me exactly what Prime Cabera said to you?"

Mr. Gregoire opened his mouth and said in Luciana Cabera's voice, *"Stéphane, we meet again."*

He switched back to his own voice. "Always a pleasure, madam. Your usual table?"

"Yes, please. I'm expecting a guest." Again, a flawless female voice.

"Very well, madam."

Alessandro laughed softly.

An auditory mnemonic. Linus didn't need a CCTV. Mr. Gregoire was a perfect recording device all by his lonesome.

My phone chimed. The cleanup crew was here.

"Mr. Gregoire, our people are downstairs, please let them in."

He nodded and departed with the server in tow. Simone practically tripped over her own feet to escape.

Alessandro nodded at the tower. "What's that building?"

I glanced at my phone and pulled up a map. "HCC. Houston Community College. Do you think the roof?"

"Yes. That's where I would have set up."

I pulled up an image of a two-foot spike with a ring on the blunt end on my phone and showed it to him. It looked identical to the two sticking out of Luciana.

"A marlin spike," Alessandro said. "Used by sailors for ropework."

"Most telekinetics throw crossbow bolts or giant nail-shaped skewers. I know of only one family that throws marlin spikes."

Alessandro raised his eyebrows. "House Rogan?"

I nodded. "The telekinetic who attacked us in the Pit also used marlin spikes."

"You think it's Xavier." A dangerous light flared in Alessandro's eyes.

"I seriously doubt that Connor climbed the HCC building and hammered two giant spikes into the Speaker of the Texas Assembly. If he wanted to kill her, he would have done it quietly."

My brother-in-law's control was off the charts. If he'd wanted to kill Luciana, and I couldn't imagine that he would, he could have slit her throat with a razor blade from hundreds of yards away, or choked her with her own necklace or clothes, or sent a tiny needle through her eye, scrambling her brain. This was loud and aggressive. It had to be Xavier. I had no proof, but I knew it was him. It felt like him.

Alessandro's phone rang. He stared at it like it was a snake.

"Please excuse me. I have to take this." He walked away, speaking in Italian, too low for me to hear.

Something was going on with him, and that something wasn't good.

I looked back to the spike.

Until Arkan got to him, Xavier's magic talents were modest. When Arkan had stolen a sample of the Osiris serum years ago, putting himself on Linus Duncan's permanent hit list, he kept some of it. Once someone took the serum, its effects persisted through generations, and if any of that person's descendants tried to take it again, it would kill them. Arkan was obsessed with finding a way around that certain death, and he used Xavier as a guinea pig. Most of Arkan's test subjects died in agony, but Xavier had won the life-or-death lottery, becoming an incredibly powerful insta-Prime.

Xavier had grown up in my brother-in-law's shadow. To him, Connor, his distant cousin, was the example of everything Xavier wanted to achieve. Connor was freakishly powerful, wealthy, and respected, a war hero who was looked up to by the whole family. To someone like Xavier, with his modest telekinetic talent and craving for the finer things in life, Connor was at the apex of everything he ever hoped to achieve. Now, thanks to Arkan, he thought he had reached that height, and he flaunted his power. The spikes were a special *fuck you* to Connor.

You didn't think I was strong enough to use these. Look at me now.

Alessandro came striding up, his phone put away. He and Xavier had a score to settle. Alessandro had tried to kill Arkan for murdering his father. Xavier had hit him with a semitruck and nearly ended his life.

I looked into Alessandro's eyes and saw calculated, cold rage. Fear punched me right in the stomach. I'd spent the last six months doing everything I could to avoid the confrontation between him and Arkan, but it was coming like a runaway train, unstoppable and inevitable.

"This was sanctioned," Alessandro said.

I nodded. It had to be. For all of his craziness, Xavier worshipped the ground Arkan walked on. He wouldn't have murdered the Speaker of the Texas Assembly on his own. Arkan was behind him, holding on to his pet's leash. He pointed at a target, and Xavier bit it.

"This is so . . ." I waved my hand at the body.

"Loud," Alessandro finished with a grim look on his face.

It was unlike Arkan. He preferred to operate from the shadows. Was he sending a message? To whom? Why? Was it to someone close to Luciana?

Luciana Cabera had been a halcyon Prime. She specialized in soothing magic. Psionics incited crowds, and halcyons calmed them. Two decades ago, a riot raged inside the Ellis Unit, the most dangerous prison in Texas. The authorities sought a nonviolent solution, so they turned to the best halcyon mage in the state. Luciana walked into the prison unarmed and alone, and when the sheriffs followed her fifteen minutes later, they found the inmates sitting in rows along the hallway walls, quietly smiling. That day started her political career.

In her political life, Luciana had been aboveboard. She approached the Assembly with the attitude of a veteran middle school teacher, which meant she was stern enough to follow the procedure but flexible enough to make compromises where special treatment was required. In her day-to-day life, Luciana had run a clinic that treated people suffering from anxiety. She held a PhD in psychology from Harvard.

None of these things should have put her into Arkan's crosshairs. I needed more information. Where the hell was Linus?

My phone launched into the *Fistful of Dollars* theme. Leon. Not texting, *calling.*

I took the call. Leon's face appeared on-screen.

"I'm at Linus'. The gate is shut. I entered the code, it didn't work. I called. No answer on the phone or intercom. Also, there is this."

He switched to the other camera. The keypad by the gate glowed with yellow. It should have turned green when he put the code in.

Linus had activated the siege protocol. Shit.

"Do you want me to jump the gate?"

"No! *Do not* go inside. Leon, everything is armed. The moment you step foot in there, the turrets will shred you."

"Fine. No need to be dramatic."

"Please wait there for me."

"Inside the gates?" He opened his eyes real wide.

"Leon!"

"Don't worry. I got it."

A stray thought zinged across my mind. It was vague and formless, but very disturbing. "Can you show me the gates without touching them?"

The phone view swung and presented me with the wrought iron gates. The yard was pristine.

Alessandro looked at me. "What is it?"

"There are no bodies."

For Linus to activate a lockdown meant he either expected an attack or one had already occurred. He had answered my phone call during an attack before.

"Leon, wait for us. Please."

"I will."

He hung up.

Mr. Gregoire reappeared, leading a team of five people onto the patio, each carrying a large duffel bag. They set the bags down, pulled out hazmat suits, and put them on. An older black woman approached me. We had worked together before. I didn't know her name, but I knew Linus trusted her. She referred to herself as Team 1 Leader, and that's how I addressed her as well.

"How long and where?" I asked her.

"Ninety minutes. A warehouse on Cedar Crest Street."

She gave me the address and zipped herself into the hazmat suit. The crew converged on the body, spreading plastic sheets.

"I need a Ziploc bag and her purse," I said.

One of the techs brought the purse and the bag to me. I unzipped it and looked inside. Pack of Kleenex, a glass case, a pink brush . . . That would do. I fished the brush out, slipped it into the Ziploc bag, and waved the tech on.

I sealed the Ziploc bag. I was probably wrong, but just in case.

I turned away from the team and looked at Mr. Gregoire. "Speaker Cabera was not here today."

"Understood."

"Will Simone be a problem?" Alessandro asked.

"Not at all. I chose my people very carefully."

That left the Curtises, who would not talk for fear of being implicated,

Xavier, who should be long gone by now, and whoever Cabera was meeting. That was our best lead. Over an hour had passed since this supposed lunch meeting, and her guest never showed.

Metal clanged as one of the crew members pulled a spike out of the wall with metal forceps.

I nodded to Mr. Gregoire, and Alessandro and I hurried downstairs. We exited the restaurant and marched to Alessandro's Alfa. I would have preferred sprinting, but you never knew who was watching.

We got in. Alessandro started the engine and it roared to life.

"Linus?" he asked.

"Yes." *Please be okay. Please, please be okay.*

He put the car in gear. The Alfa streaked out of the parking lot and hurtled down the street at a breakneck speed.

Linus Duncan lived in River Oaks, the most exclusive neighborhood in Houston, full of mansions, tree-lined streets, and infuriating speed bumps. Alessandro was a speed demon, and he'd bought us an extra ten minutes on the highway. But River Oaks made it impossible to maintain any kind of speed.

Bump.

Bump.

"Merda!"

Shit was a good way to describe it. I tried the phone again. No answer.

"You think something happened to him. Something serious," Alessandro said.

"He activated the siege protocol."

"It doesn't mean he's dead. It could be a test."

I looked at him.

He shrugged. "Linus could be sitting inside that house with a timer, waiting to see how long it will take us to catch on."

"I hope you're right."

It would be just like Linus to pull something like that. But a feeling deep down in my stomach told me that something was horribly wrong. When Nevada first trained me in investigative work, she taught me to trust my instincts. If it didn't look right, it probably wasn't. If the hair on the back of your neck stood up, you needed to get the hell out of there. She taught Arabella the same thing. My younger sister called it listening to the lizard brain. I trusted my lizard brain. It kept me breathing.

My phone chimed. A text message from Ragnar.

We can't find Jadwiga. Matilda says they're nocturnal, so we'll come back tonight. We've locked the conference room and put the key on your desk.

"What is it?" Alessandro asked.

"Jadwiga."

He glanced at me.

"There is an expensive and possibly endangered spider loose in the conference room. It was smuggled into the country, stolen, recovered, and during the handoff to the current owner it escaped."

"In our conference room?"

"Yes."

"How big is this spider?"

"About a four-inch leg span."

Alessandro glanced up at the heavens. The heavens were hidden by the car roof, but I was sure the higher power had seen the silent plea for mercy in his eyes.

"I forgot to ask, how did it go with Gunderson?"

Alessandro shrugged. "We talked. I dropped him off at the Justice Center trussed up like a hog. Lenora can take it from there."

Lenora Jordan, the Harris County DA, would definitely take it from there. As Connor once put it, law and order were her gods, and she served as their devoted paladin.

We turned around the bend. Linus' gates came into view, Leon's blue Shelby GT350 parked by the keypad. Alessandro pulled in behind him.

I got out of the car and walked up to the keypad. Leon had the family version of the code, but mine was the Deputy Warden sequence. I entered it.

Leon rolled down his window. "I waited as instructed."

The gates slid open with a clang. The lights on the keypad blinked but remained a steady lemon-yellow.

I was right. Linus' house thought it was under attack. The moment an intruder crossed the property line, Linus' defense turrets would sprout out of the innocuous-looking lawn like some lethal mushrooms and pulverize the offender into a pile of smoking meat. Linus was a hephaestus mage. He built devastating weapons out of random trash and duct tape. His defense systems were second to none.

Alessandro got out of the car.

The wrought iron gates stood wide open, like the mandibles of some beast ready to grind us between its teeth. Theoretically, the system would recognize me and Alessandro. Theoretically, it wouldn't kill us. Unfortunately, we'd never tested that theory under battle conditions.

"Do we go in?" Leon asked.

"I go in," Alessandro said. "The two of you stay here."

"I don't think so," I told him.

"There is no reason for both of us to go."

"You're right. I should go by myself. It's my responsibility as the Deputy."

"It's my responsibility to protect the Deputy." Alessandro's tone said the discussion was over.

"That's why we'll go together."

Leon sighed. "I guess I'll just stay here. Watching you get inside or get turned into human hamburger meat."

I could have done without that visual.

The longer we waited, the worse things would be.

Deep breath.

I took a step toward the gates. Alessandro strode next to me and took my hand. "Slow and steady. It's a walk in the park."

We walked past the gates and down the circular driveway, keeping our pace measured. The grounds looked perfectly ordinary. No signs of battle. Nothing out of place.

No sudden movements. No holding your breath. The system had our biometrics, but biometric scanners were notoriously unreliable.

Two months ago, I'd watched Linus test one of his turrets. He'd fired at an armored car with a ballistic dummy in it. The stream of bullets cut through the armor, nearly slicing the vehicle in half. When he was done, the ballistic dummy was no more. There was just mush. Thick gelatinous mush.

Alessandro's strong warm fingers held mine. "Almost there."

Slow and steady, around the fountain in a pretty flower bed, up the stairs, to the front door. Just another day in the life of a Deputy Warden.

We stepped onto the porch. I raised my head, looking straight into the hidden camera. If Linus was inside, he would let me in.

Nothing.

If this was a test, I would turn around, go straight home, and refuse to speak with Linus until he apologized. It wouldn't matter if the sky started raining the Osiris serum. I would get a genuine, heartfelt apology.

I punched the code into the sophisticated lock and pressed my thumb against the fingerprint pad.

A distant motor whirred, followed by a metal clang.

The lock clicked.

Alessandro put his hand on the door handle.

Breathe, breathe, nice and calm.

The door swung open, and we slipped inside.

The cavernous grand foyer stretched in front of us, full of shadows. Motorized blinds blocked the windows, and the only illumination came through a stained-glass dome high above. White venetian plaster on the walls, a double staircase wrapping around another fountain directly under the dome, three empty doorways, one to the left, leading to guest bedrooms and the garage, one straight ahead, into the dining room, and the last, to the right, opening into the hallway that terminated in Linus' study.

Alessandro stepped in front of me. We stood quietly, listening, waiting. The house was as silent as a tomb except for the quiet splashing of the fountain.

Alessandro pointed to the left and slightly back, his gaze sweeping the house in front of us. I moved in that direction, into the murky corner between two columns, and pressed the hidden sensor. A section of the wall slid aside, revealing a control panel with all its lights off. I'd have to speak while facing it. My back would be presenting a great target to anyone hiding inside. Adrenaline spurred my heart rate.

I held my arm out and pushed with my magic, forcing it through the bone and muscle of my forearm. An orange glow shone through my skin, forming a circle of a braided vine with a five-point star in its center. A spot between my shoulder blades itched, expecting a bullet.

"Catalina Baylor, Deputy Warden."

The panel lit up with green, the small display flaring into life. Access granted. I exhaled and typed in my code. A prompt popped up, warning me that siege protocols were in effect. I had two choices, CANCEL, which would take me back to the previous menu, or DEACTIVATE. I chose DEACTIVATE.

The panel flashed with red. I had expected some noise, something to announce it, but the house stayed quiet. No metal clanging, no machinery moving, no sirens, only a word on the display: DISARMED.

I took my phone out and texted Leon.

Clear.

Moments ticked by.

The front door opened, and Leon strode through, carrying a SIG Sauer.

The air around Alessandro's right hand sparked with orange for a fraction of a second. An identical gun materialized in his fingers.

Leon stalked left, while Alessandro started right, toward the study. I followed Alessandro. We passed through the doorway, through the short hallway, and Alessandro walked into the study. He stopped, blocking my view, moved to the left, and motioned me in. I entered.

On the right, Pete, Linus' bodyguard, sprawled on the antique Persian rug. He'd fallen on his side in a crumpled heap with his face turned toward us. His lips were black. His eyes were open wide, milky and dead. A dark pattern of jagged lines marked his face, spreading from his eyes across his skin to his hairline.

Shock splashed me in an icy wave.

I'd known Pete for almost a year. He picked me up when Linus wanted to see me, he drove me around to my assignments when I needed it, and he would have put himself between me and any threat without hesitation. I just saw him last week. I'd brought him and Linus a cranberry tart I made. They'd shared it, and Pete told me I had to stop wasting my life on trivial things like being a Warden Deputy and dedicate myself to my true calling, which was making delicious desserts. And now he was dead.

I crouched by him. It felt like someone else was moving my body for me. Slowly, I pushed his right shoulder. Full rigor. He'd been dead longer than a few hours, but less than a day.

The network of lines on his face bulged from his skin. It looked like blood, old blood, somehow forced into a pattern and darkened to near black.

Alessandro moved next to me. His hand rested on my shoulder, the warm strength of his fingers reassuring.

Funny, protective Pete was dead. There was nothing I could do. But Linus was still missing. Until we found his body, there was still hope.

I got up.

Alessandro met my gaze. We talked without saying a word.

Okay?

Yes.

We moved across the study to the corner. I pushed my hand against the wooden panel decorating the wall and waited for the sensor to pick up my presence. A motor purred inside the walls and the wooden panel slid aside, revealing a stone shaft twelve feet across. Stone stairs wound down along the wall, wrapping around a fireman's pole that stretched to the bottom floor. A dark red smear stained the metal of the pole.

Alessandro descended the stairs, quiet as a ghost. I followed.

We went down and around, three floors deep. The stairs terminated in a wide hallway. On the left, a wire cage guarded access to the freight elevator. On the right, a massive steel door barred the way to the workshop and weapon vault. A trail of blood drops led to it. Red smudges marred the control panel on the wall to the left.

My heart was beating out of my chest. If I never saw another damn control panel again, it would be too soon.

I wiped the blood off the keys with my sleeve, punched in the code, and pressed my thumb against the fingerprint scanner.

Seconds ticked by. One, two . . .

Come on.

Three, four, five . . .

Something thudded beyond the door.

Come on!

The vault door slid aside with a heavy groan, revealing the workshop hidden behind it. The stench of old urine hit me. In front, on the floor littered with first aid supplies, Linus slumped against his workbench. A trail of dark blood stretched from his nose, staining his lips and his shirt. His eyes were shut. He looked dead.

 # Chapter 3

$\mathbf{I}$ dropped to my knees by Linus and clamped my hand on his neck. A pulse. Faint but there. I slapped his face lightly. "Linus! Linus, wake up!"

"Don't bother." Alessandro plucked a wrapper from the medical refuse on the floor and showed it to me. It was about the size of my cell phone with a label that showed a black river with an outline of a boat and a hooded boatman on it.

"What is that?"

"Styxine." Alessandro rummaged through the contents of the first aid kit that had been dumped on the floor and pulled an empty syringe out. "Last line of defense against a mental assault. You inject it, and you're dead to the world. A mental mage can't attack a mind that's not there."

"How long does it last?"

"That depends. This shit is very bad for you. Sometimes you wake up after six hours. Sometimes you wake up after three days and don't know who you are. Sometimes it lasts forever."

"What do you mean 'forever'?"

"You don't wake up. You become a vegetable. No brain functions. This packet is double the recommended dose." He frowned and held up an identical syringe. Also empty. "'*Sto vecchio rimbambito* took two of these."

Oh my God. "Is there any way to reverse this? Can we give him something to snap him out of it?"

"If such a thing exists, I don't know about it."

Whatever I did next would determine if Linus lived or died.

The fear and anxiety that gnawed on me shattered like a glass bowl dropped on the ground, exploding into sharp shards. They sliced into me in an instant of pain, and I snapped into a calm place where only logic ruled.

To Alessandro and me, Linus Duncan was the Warden of Texas. To almost everyone else in Houston, he was the former Speaker of the Assembly, a man of impeccable reputation, who despite pretending to be retired, wielded a massive amount of political influence.

The current Speaker of the Assembly had been murdered, and now the former Speaker of the Assembly was attacked in his own home and found in a catatonic state. We had to contain this at all costs, or Houston would panic.

My first priority was to get medical treatment for Linus. My second was to hide his condition. And if Linus was conscious, he would tell me to reverse the order of the two.

Leon jogged down the stairs, saw Linus, and stopped. "Okay. That's a hell of a thing."

"Anything?" Alessandro asked him.

My cousin shook his head. "No. No signs of teleportation either. Looks like whoever it was killed Pete and walked out the door. I'd like to know how they managed that with the siege protocol active."

The lockdown would've kicked in the moment Linus triggered it from the inside of the vault. He wouldn't have risked taking Styxine unless he was in immediate danger, so he got into the vault, hit the siege panic button, and injected himself as soon as he could. Even if whoever killed Pete had immediately turned around and sprinted out of the house, the turrets would've gotten them before they ever made it to the gate.

"Also, I found this."

Leon held up a Ziploc bag with a black DA Ambassador, a state-of-the-art .40 pistol from Duncan Arms. Pete's gun.

"Where did you find it?" Alessandro asked.

"Behind a column by the front door."

There was no reason for Pete's gun to be there. He always had it. It rested on his nightstand when he slept. Someone must've killed Pete, picked it up, and then hid it behind the column before going out the door.

When the siege protocol was up, Linus's turrets would ignore people with special clearance, but they would still fire on them if they carried a firearm. The attacker knew exactly how the system worked.

"The intruder had to have special clearance," I said. "Like Alessandro and I."

"Linus was betrayed," Alessandro said.

"Who do you think?" Leon asked.

I shook my head. "We can figure this out later. Right now, we have to get him out of here."

Linus couldn't die. He just couldn't.

"The house is a fortress," Leon said. "Instead of risking transporting him, let's just get a medic here."

"I had to end the siege protocol to get into the vault and to let you in. Once the system is disabled, only Linus can reactivate it."

Leon stared at me. "Define 'disabled.'"

"Right now no door in this house can be locked. Doors that are already locked will remain locked, unless someone manually unlocks them, but the front door, the gate, the vault, everything that we opened, can't be relocked. The turrets are off-line. The surveillance cameras are off-line. We are deaf, blind, and defenseless."

Linus had no human guards aside from Pete and Hera, who was currently out of the country. They were his last line of defense, one he almost never used. He relied on his automated defenses instead, and right now all of them had about as much firepower as lawn gnomes. We were sitting ducks.

"Why the hell would he do that?" Leon asked.

"Because if he isn't here to reactivate the system, he is either dead or incapacitated," I told him. "He anticipated other people entering the house, like Warden personnel, paramedics, and law enforcement. Reactivating the system would be too dangerous. It could end in a bloodbath."

Alessandro straightened. "Leon, take the lead. I'm going to carry Linus to the garage, load him into one of those suburban tanks he likes, and get him to the Compound."

"Yes, let's do that, before some random passerby strolls in to loot the mansion," Leon said.

Above us something thumped.

A pair of semiautomatic handguns leaped into Leon's fingers almost on their own. He moved to the right, behind the workbench. Alessandro scooped Linus into his arms. A USB drive clattered to the floor. I grabbed it. It was slick with blood. I put it in my pocket and wiped my bloody fingers on my T-shirt.

Alessandro carried Linus to the left, outside of line of sight from the doorway, gently lowered him to the floor, and flattened himself against the wall by the vault door. I crouched behind the workbench. From here I could see the stairs, but a person coming down the stairs wouldn't notice me right away.

The sound of unhurried steps echoed through the empty house. The notes of a familiar melody floated down. A man was coming down the stairs, humming the "Triumphal March" from *Aida* in a well-trained baritone.

Leon turned to me and mouthed, *"What the fuck?"*

The humming grew louder. A pair of long legs came into view, followed by their owner. He was in his late forties, with wavy dark hair sprinkled with grey and cut in a politician style, neat and unoffensive. His features were handsome in that generic adult-male-in-good-health way. He wore a grey summer suit.

He landed on the last step and stopped, looking into the vault.

"About time you got here, Ms. Baylor."

His voice sounded perfectly generic. No regional accent, no hint of origin. He would have been at home on any major news program.

"I was beginning to think I would have to carry the old man out myself. Needs must, I suppose."

Alessandro frowned.

The man took a step toward the vault.

"That's far enough," Alessandro said.

The man's eyes widened. "Sasha! You're here too. Fantastic. This will simplify things."

The man stopped and stared straight at us. Flames licked his chin. His face caught fire.

An illusion Prime. The only illusion Prime in my life was Augustine Montgomery, and he wouldn't have bothered with a different voice or the fire show.

The flames blazed, shockingly orange. The air smelled of smoke. The man's skin, hair, and clothes burned away, as if made of paper, turning into ash and then melting into nothing. He shook his head, flinging the last of the ash into the air. He was in his late twenties now, tall and broad-shouldered. His long legs stretched a pair of faded jeans. A blue Henley draped his muscular body.

His hair was that coveted shade of white gold people spent thousands of dollars to imitate. His skin had a golden tan, and his face wouldn't just stop traffic, it would create a pileup that would require hours to sort out. A square jaw, full lips, high cheekbones, a strong nose, and large arresting eyes, warm and inviting, a deep ultramarine under the sweep of dark blond eyebrows. He looked like a celestial being knitted from sunlight and sea spray.

Wow.

The man smiled, and it was as if the spring sun had risen after a long dark winter.

"Prince Konstantin Leonidovich Berezin, of Blood Imperial, at your service."

Berezin. As in House Berezin. The Russian Imperial Dynasty.

"Why are you here?" Alessandro's voice was ice-cold.

"Because you need help." The prince tried to sidestep Alessandro, except Alessandro moved with him, preventing him from entering the vault.

"Do we have to do this, Sasha?"

"Can I shoot him?" Leon asked me. "In the leg. I shoot him in the leg, we grab Linus and take off."

"You can't shoot him. He's related to the Russian Emperor," I told him.

"True," Konstantin said. "When His Majesty wants to motivate me, he assures me that I'm his favorite nephew. Of course, he says that to all of us."

"What do you want?" Alessandro demanded. His magic coiled about him, primed and ready.

If I beguiled a Russian prince in my capacity as a Deputy Warden, would that cause an international incident? Did it matter that he entered the house uninvited? What was the protocol here?

"It's not a question of what *I* want. It's what the Imperium wants. I am just a humble instrument of Rodina's will. And right now, that will directs me to discuss things with the Deputy Warden. So, move aside or I will move you."

Orange sparks flared around Alessandro. "Please do."

Konstantin didn't move. "I'd rather not. I'm taking great pains to be reasonable. I'm not here to brawl."

"Turn around, leave the way you came, and you'll survive. That's my reasonable offer."

Alessandro's face had snapped into an expressionless mask. His voice was measured and calm. This wasn't the Alessandro with whom I woke up every morning. This wasn't the Sentinel, who was capable and decisive. This was the Artisan giving the first and final warning. Konstantin's eyes told me he recognized who he was talking to. The charming warmth went out of him, as if an armored mental door had slammed into place.

I made it a rule to never jump off the cliff unless I knew where I would land. I had no idea what the ramifications of injuring a Russian prince would be. We could probably stop Konstantin between the three of us, but I wasn't sure we could handle the consequences.

"Hypothetically, if I shot him, who would know?" Leon asked. "I could shoot him, hide the body, I know a place, and nobody could prove anything."

The prince leaned to the side to get a better look at Leon. "We wouldn't need to prove anything. We would only need to suspect."

Linus was still unconscious. We didn't have time for this.

I stood up.

The prince gave me a dazzling smile. "There you are, Ms. Baylor. Images don't do you justice."

"The Office of the Warden greets Your Highness. You are trespassing. Please leave this house."

"We have things to discuss."

"This isn't a good time."

"I'm afraid the matter is urgent," Konstantin said. "I've been watching this house for the past three hours just to talk to you."

I had no idea if anything coming out of his mouth could be trusted. He could've been involved in the hit on Linus, or he could have nothing to do with anything. Nothing mattered right now except getting Linus out of here.

"You know who I am, so you know where to find me. Right now, you're interfering with my official duties. Leave immediately, or I will lodge a formal complaint with the Russian Embassy. I will be loud and public about it."

"That would be . . . unfortunate." Konstantin smiled again. "As I've said, I'm here to help."

"The Office of the Warden thanks the Russian Imperium for its generous offer of assistance. At this time, we have to regretfully decline. Please leave."

Konstantin sighed. "In that case, I have no choice but to respect your wishes. However, we do need to chat. Am I to understand that you wish to have this discussion at your place of business?"

Why did that sound like a threat? I needed to say something neutral that didn't obligate me to anything.

"House Baylor welcomes clients during normal business hours. If you choose to visit us, we will be delighted to extend our hospitality."

"Are you sure that's what you want?"

Alessandro took a step forward. His voice promised violence. "Leave."

Konstantin sighed and took a step back. "As you wish. I did my best. I hope neither of us has any regrets."

He turned and walked up the stairs. Alessandro followed him.

"What the hell?" Leon muttered.

"I have no idea."

Moments passed, dragging on.

Alessandro returned, picked up Linus like he weighed nothing, and slung him over his shoulder in a fireman's carry. "Let's go."

Leon took point. Alessandro followed, and I brought up the rear. In seconds, we crossed the house and moved to the garage. Four armored vehicles waited on the concrete floor. I pulled the keys to a Duncan Arms Stormer off the key rack and started the engine with the remote. The huge white SUV roared in response. Of all the custom vehicles Linus owned, this was the best armored. It could withstand a mine detonation and a full blast from one of Linus' turrets for ten seconds. Only his exo-suits provided more protection.

I got behind the wheel. Alessandro loaded Linus into the backseat.

"Do you want me to ride with you or to follow?" Leon asked.

"Follow," Alessandro said. "We may need a second vehicle."

The only reason we'd need a second vehicle was if the Stormer were disabled.

Leon opened the garage door and jogged to his Shelby Cobra. Alessandro climbed into the passenger seat. Orange magic sparked, and a Duncan Arms rifle appeared in his hands.

I guided the massive vehicle around the driveway to the gates. We turned right on the one-way street, following Leon, made a U-turn, crawled over the first speed bump, and headed out of the subdivision.

"Sasha?" I asked.

He swore in Italian, too fast for me to follow.

"Who is he really?"

"Exactly who he says he is. The second son of Grand Duke Leonid Berezin, who is the younger brother of Emperor Mikhail II."

"Alessandro, you are not giving me a lot to work with."

He glanced at me, his eyes dark. "He has two brothers. His older brother is earnest, uncomplicated, the perfect heir of a Grand Duke, not too bright, not too dumb. His younger brother is a brawler, subtle like a bull on meth. Konstantin is a hedonist, who drinks, womanizes, and parties. You see what they want you to see. These are the roles they have been assigned. It's not who they are. They are not men. They are wolves in human skin who guard the Russian throne. His presence here means the highest level of the Imperium is involved. He has a mission, and he will kill whoever interferes with it."

"Can he kill us if we interfere?"

"One-on-one, I can take him. It would be a hard fight. But it wouldn't be one-on-one. The Imperium would never send him here alone. He wasn't lying. He might just be the Emperor's favorite nephew."

"None of this sounds good."

"Yeah."

"Could he be the one who attacked Linus?"

"I doubt it. Killing a Warden would be an act of war. At the very least, it would create a massive political mess. If he'd done it, he would've distanced himself from it. Instead, he presented himself complete with a grand entrance. No, my money is on Arkan."

Before his life as an assassin kingpin, Arkan had been an agent for the Imperial Intelligence Service. The Russians let him retire instead of killing him, because they considered him too expensive to take out. Arkan had Luciana murdered, Linus had been attacked, and now a Russian prince was here with offers of assistance. All of this fit together somehow, but anything I thought up now would be pure speculation. We had to revive Linus.

We merged onto the Southwest Freeway. I picked up speed. "Is he still breathing?"

Alessandro turned around in his seat to look at Linus. "Yes."

Leon's vehicle slid behind us.

Linus had never mentioned any ties to House Berezin. As far as I knew, the Texas Warden had no interaction with the Imperium. We were a strictly domestic law enforcement agency.

I couldn't lose him. He wasn't just my mentor or my boss. He was a member of our family in everything except name. Arabella adored him, Nevada respected him, I relied on him. He was one of the cornerstones of my world. When I was in trouble, Linus would help. When I needed encouragement, he would offer it. When I needed a swift kick in the butt, he would deliver a scathing lecture.

I had taken all of this for granted. In my head, Linus was untouchable and eternal. Now he was an old man dying in the backseat of his car, and I couldn't do a thing to help him.

Someone had hurt him. That someone would pay. I would hunt them down no matter where they went.

I told my phone to call home. We needed a medical team, a security lockdown, and a family meeting.

 # Chapter 4

I walked into my office, lowered the blinds with the remote, plunging the room into shadow, sat behind my desk, and took a long, deep breath.

Linus had been installed upstairs, in one of the numerous spare bedrooms of the main house. Dr. Patel, our House physician, was with him. The medical team inserted an IV, cleaned him, and checked him for additional injuries. There were none. All the blood had come from one epic nosebleed.

The prognosis wasn't good. Linus was in a comatose, vegetative state. An MRI or CT would tell us nothing. We needed a positron emission tomography scan to evaluate his brain's metabolism. Only the PET scan could predict if Linus would recover awareness. We didn't have a PET machine on premises. Transporting Linus to a hospital was out of the question. Whoever tried to kill him might decide to finish the job, and a convoy would be a lot more vulnerable than keeping him here behind sturdy walls and constant guard.

A PET scan wouldn't help Linus. It would be strictly for our benefit. Dr. Patel recommended taking the wait-and-see approach. Linus would either come out of it or he wouldn't, and there was nothing any of us could do about it.

The Compound was on high alert. Patricia Taft, our security chief, was pulling in all off-duty personnel. In twenty minutes, the entire family would gather in the conference room across from my office. I needed to present a plan of action and I had to appear calm and unrattled.

I was very rattled. *Calm* wasn't even in my vocabulary right now.

As I sat here, Linus could be slowly dying. He could be taking his final breath right this second, and I wouldn't even know until they called me. A part of me had gone into a paranoid alert anticipating that any moment my phone would ring, and Dr. Patel would announce that Linus was gone.

What then? I didn't know, but when we all met in a few minutes, somebody was bound to ask. I would have to give them an answer. And it would have to be an honest one, because while I could lie through my teeth to the entire state of Texas, I couldn't bullshit my family.

A quiet scratching came from my door.

I swiped the tears from my eyes, got up, and opened it. Shadow slipped into the room. She was long and shaggy, with glossy black fur that curled backward and a surprisingly toothy mouth for a smallish dog.

"How did you even find me?"

Shadow wagged her tail. She was carrying a stuffed hamburger toy in her mouth. When I got upset, she would bring me her toys, and sometimes, if I didn't pay attention to her efforts, she would climb up on the furniture and try to put the toy into my mouth to make me feel better.

I petted her and went back to the computer. Shadow curled up in the dog bed next to me.

I tapped my keyboard to bring my computer back to life, took the USB out of my pocket, and plugged it in. Lines of nonsense code filled the screen. Encrypted. Of course. I took the storage stick out. I would have to let Bern mess with it.

I logged into the Warden Interface with my credentials. The system let me in, and I selected "Emergency Notification" from the menu at the top of the page.

A new window popped up, blank. Linus had walked me through this. I was supposed to type out the nature of my emergency and wait for a response.

Speaker Luciana Cabera was murdered in a restaurant during lunch. Warden Duncan was attacked in his home and took

Styxine. He is now in a vegetative state but stable and safe in my care. I suspect Arkan's involvement. Prince Konstantin Berezin has approached me in my official capacity with an unspecified offer of assistance. Please advise.

I hit enter and waited. I had no idea if a Speaker of a State Assembly had been murdered before, but knowing the volatility of House politics, this probably wasn't the first time. There were likely protocols in place to deal with dead Speakers, injured Wardens, and pushy foreign princes. Perhaps we would get some help, someone with more experience, a Warden from out of state or an agent from the National Assembly.

I got a tissue and dabbed at my eyes. If only I could stop crying, I would be okay. I wasn't sobbing. The tears just kept leaking from my eyes, squeezed out by stress and pressure. If I walked into the meeting with my eyes all red, the entire family would focus on making me feel better instead of listening to what I had to say.

I needed to sort myself out and fast. Work was a great distraction. When you couldn't deal with stress, sometimes it helped to sidestep it. I still had the Cabera murder, and I was overdue for a video call.

Agent Wahl answered immediately. "Agent Wahl."

Some people looked exactly the way they were supposed to. Linus looked like a Prime, a top-tier mage who had been at the apex of power for decades. Similarly, Agent Wahl looked like an FBI agent: severe haircut, grave expression, athletic build, and that no-nonsense look in his eyes that suggested he knew you were up to no good even if you didn't and he was not amused.

"You owe me a favor."

"Do I?"

"Yes. That little affair involving two foreign Primes and a mysterious briefcase."

"Still not ringing any bells."

"The one that was rigged to explode if they didn't open it in unison."

"Oh, that briefcase. I'd nearly forgotten the whole thing."

"Agent Wahl, it was two months ago. I dropped everything and came to your building on a Sunday. You owe the Office of the Warden a favor."

"I'm not going to like this, am I?"

"It wouldn't be a favor if you did."

He sighed. "Lay it on me."

I gave him the address of the warehouse. Our crew would be long gone by now.

"What's there?"

"Something I need you to take point on. Consider this an anonymous tip."

He gave a short chuckle and hung up.

I opened a browser and searched for Konstantin Berezin. A row of images popped up, followed by numerous links. Konstantin in a sharp dark-blue uniform with bloodred trim. Imperial Air Force. Konstantin next to his father, an older hard-faced man, both in suits and overcoats, posing for a publicity shot in the middle of a snow-strewn street, with the golden cupolas of some Russian cathedral behind them. Konstantin with his brothers, all in different military uniforms at some formal function.

One brother wore the black of the Imperial Navy and a magnanimous patient smile. The other brother, dark-haired like their father, looked like he wanted to punch somebody. Anybody. He didn't seem to care who. His deep green Army uniform fit him like a second skin. Mom would call him squared away. Konstantin stood between them with a dreamy smile, as if he had just taken a long happy nap in a hammock under some tree.

Wolves in human skin, Alessandro called them. Now one of them was here. Why?

A soft beep announced an incoming message from the Wardens. Here we go. Help was on the way. I switched to the Warden Interface and clicked the message.

Understood, Acting Warden Baylor. Permission to investigate Speaker Cabera's murder granted.
Godspeed.

Shit.

I stared at the screen.

Godspeed.

A soft knock made me raise my head. Mom stood in the doorway.

A spike of anxiety hammered into me. "Linus . . . ?"

"The same. You called the meeting in ten minutes, and the conference room is locked."

Oh. I realized I was halfway out of my chair and sat down.

Mom shut the door and sat on the couch. Her leg bothered her today. I could tell by the way she moved, slightly stiff, careful how much weight she rested on it. For most of her life, Mom was athletic, strong, and fast. During a conflict in the Balkans, her unit had been caught between two enemy groups. The few survivors ended up in a POW camp in a small town taken over by Bosnians. Mom tried to escape and lead a group of soldiers out. She was caught.

They broke her leg and put her in a hole. It was a sewer shaft that led to a short maintenance tunnel, flooded with rainwater and sewage. The only dry spot was by the wall, about three feet wide. She slept sitting up. They would open the sewer cover once a day and throw down a bag of food, and if she was lucky and quick, she caught it before it fell into the foul water.

She didn't know how long she stayed in the hole. When the camp was liberated, the military tried to fix her leg, but the damage was permanent. They gave her a handful of medals and an honorable discharge. She'd only told us about it once, to explain why her leg was damaged, and never spoke about it again.

In Mom's head, she was never fast enough. She was always compensating. If a meeting was set for noon, she would get there by 11:45 a.m.

"What's up with you?" Mom asked.

"I asked for backup," I said.

"And?"

"It's not coming."

"Did you expect it would?"

"Yes, I kind of did. I asked them for advice, and they made me the Acting Warden and wished me Godspeed."

"You got a promotion with extra responsibilities but without pay or additional benefits." Mom smiled. "I'm so proud of you. You're officially a successful adult."

"I can now order around the highest level of state law enforcement. I suppose that's a benefit."

A very dubious one. Law enforcement didn't like interference.

"In life, backup is rare. Knowing that is part of being a grown-up. Do you know what I would tell you if you were one of my soldiers?"

"What?"

"Handle your shit."

I stared at her.

"You've been with Linus over eighteen months. You've been professionally trained. You have experience, skills, and power, and you know the procedure. Treat whatever it is like any other case."

"Linus . . ."

"Linus will live or die on his own. There is nothing you can do to help him, so put him out of your mind. Concentrate on what you can do."

I looked at my desk. She wasn't wrong.

"What happens if Linus dies?" Mom asked.

"I become the Warden."

"Which you would eventually anyway. He isn't going to live forever, Catalina. None of us will. That's why there is no backup. They want to know if you're ready to do the job."

"I'm not sure I'm ready."

"In battle, when your officer dies, you don't have the luxury of asking yourself if you're ready. You assume command because you're next in line and lives will be lost if you don't. I have faith in you. So does Alessandro, and the rest of the family, and Linus. He picked you for the job. So, sweetheart, do whatever it is you need to do to get yourself right. If you need to cry, cry. If you need to go to the range, you know where the ammo is."

I got up and walked over to her. "Can I have a hug?"

Mom opened her arms, and we hugged. She kissed my hair.

I almost cried. She used to hug me like this every time my magic leaked, and someone lost themselves to obsessing over me. She would hold me and tell me that it would be okay, that with practice I would get better. Mom always believed in me without any doubt.

"You and your sisters, you three are so different, and somehow you're all the same."

"How are we the same?"

"All of you can do anything you want if only you manage to get out of your own way. You especially. You need to get out of your own head, Catalina. You overthink everything. Put yourself on rails and go forward."

"Okay," I promised.

The door swung open, and Arabella stuck her head in. "Why is the conference room locked?" She saw me and Mom. "Are you getting Mom time? What happened? Something bad happened."

"Close the door," Mom told her.

Arabella retreated and shut the door.

"Are you ready or do you need a minute?"

"I'm good."

Mom nodded. "I know. Let's go do this."

The entire family had gathered in the hallway, filling it wall to wall.

Leon, tall, lean, dark haired, with a dark tan and a white smile, leaned against the wall, because if there was a vertical surface present, my youngest cousin felt compelled to prop it up. Next to him Bern, his brother, larger, with broad shoulders, a muscular build, and hair that turned dark blond during summer and light brown in the winter, wrapped his arm around Runa. Her hair was blazing red, her eyes were green, and her skin was so pale that we all teased her about glowing in the dark. Bern carried a laptop and Runa held a tablet.

To the right, by the conference room, Arabella crossed her arms. Petite, tan, with an hourglass figure, my sister wore a black-and-white floral Jacquard dress with a crew neckline, fitted waist, and flared skirt. She paired that with black pumps. Her blond hair, which she recently toned to a cool ash shade, rested on her head in an artfully loose updo, which she called "the most popular girl in church hair." She must've had a high-profile business meeting this morning.

Behind them, Grandma Frida frowned at her phone. She was about the same height as Mom, but they couldn't be more different. Grandma Frida was slender, bird-boned, with a halo of platinum curls. Her mechanic coveralls were stained with a fresh smudge of engine grease. Mom was solid, with light brown skin, dark hair, and dark eyes, which turned distant when she measured the distance for a kill shot.

Just behind them Cornelius waited, dressed in light summer suit slacks and a grey vest that fit his trim body with custom precision. He'd rolled the sleeves of his white dress shirt up to his elbows. His blond hair was slightly ruffled. Cornelius always dressed impeccably, but no matter what he wore, unless the occasion was really formal, he managed to look effortlessly casual. Gus, his massive black-and-tan Doberman, sat by his feet. When we met Cornelius and Matilda, they'd had another Doberman, Bunny, but Bunny and Matilda were the same age and after years of faithful service and a lot of playing, Bunny was slowing down. Gus was one of the puppies he had sired, which was why Leon insisted on referring to him as Gus Bunnyson.

Patricia Taft, our security chief, stood beside Cornelius. In some ways, they were polar opposites. Cornelius was artfully disheveled and appeared nonthreatening. Everything about Patricia was precise, from her dark brown hair put away into a French braid to the beige pantsuit that complemented her brown skin. She wore the pantsuit like a uniform, and she projected confidence and authority that made people fall in line when they saw her coming.

Alessandro emerged from his office carrying a plastic container with a lid. He saw me and made a trapping motion with the container. Jadwiga. Right.

I held a key up. "I need you to form a single file line."

The family stared at me.

"You have to enter the conference room one at a time, watch where you put your feet, and check your chair."

Bern turned to Leon.

"What?" Leon batted his eyes at him in pretended innocence.

"You know what," Bern told him.

"Why?" Mom asked.

"Because a very rare spider escaped its containment in the conference room this morning. It's an endangered species. It's also worth a quarter million dollars."

"Perfect," Arabella said.

"My deepest apologies," Cornelius said, looking troubled. "I've spoken to Matilda."

"If you see the spider, please don't squish it." I unlocked the door and stood aside. "Yell, and Alessandro will trap it."

"I'll definitely yell," Runa said. "But I can't guarantee the no squishing part."

"Try," I told her.

The family filed into the conference room. I waited for a scream. No shrieks came. Alessandro crossed the hallway, the plastic container in his hands, and invited me into the conference room with a sweep of his hand. I walked in, checked my chair, and took my place at the head of the table. Alessandro sat on my right. Patricia sat on my left.

Bern set the laptop at the end of the table and tapped some keys. Connor and Nevada appeared on the screen mounted on the far wall. My brother-in-law was in his work mode, dressed in black and doing his best to loom. Connor was a large man, with dark hair and intense blue eyes, and he radiated menace like a space heater radiated warmth.

My older sister waved at us. Her honey-blond hair was braided away from her face. She wore a white dress, which meant she either was about to go out or had just come back from somewhere, because Arthur Rogan and white dresses did not mix. My nephew was thirteen months old, and we all suspected that someone had switched him with an Energizer Bunny when nobody was looking. He'd learned to walk, and as soon as he could take a couple of steps unassisted, he decided he had places to go and things to do and when that failed, he levitated things to himself. His control was a bit wobbly and sometimes his sippy cups opened in midair.

"Is the feed off?" I asked.

Runa passed the tablet to Bern. He flicked his fingers across it. "Yes."

No record of this meeting would be made.

I kept my face neutral. "At 11:02 this morning Luciana Cabera was murdered at the Respite."

The room went completely silent.

"The attacker was likely a Prime telekinetic, who impaled her with two spikes, one through the chest, one through the mouth."

I tapped my phone. The screen on the wall behind me showed Luciana Cabera pinned to the wall in all of its HD gore. I let it sink in and tapped the phone again. The image of a spike extracted from the body filled the screen.

I looked at Connor.

He raised his voice. "Jeremy, clear my schedule for the next week and find Bug."

"We suspect that the telekinetic is Xavier Secada," Alessandro said. "The weapon and the manner of the murder fits his MO."

Xavier's portrait appeared on the screen. Of average height, Xavier was lean and pretty. Some men grew more masculine in their twenties, and Xavier had done some growing up, but his face still retained a slightly androgynous beauty. The first time I saw him, five years ago, I thought he looked like a singer from a boy band. His bronze skin glowed with a perfect tan. His chestnut brown hair was cut in a flattering style, the kind that screamed, "I go to an expensive salon, and I enjoy it." His dark eyes were arrogant and cruel, and the smirk on his lips told you he had a high opinion of himself.

"That little shit," Grandma Frida said.

"Xavier's involvement means the murder was committed with Arkan's blessing," Alessandro continued. "At this point we don't know what motivated him to have the Speaker murdered. Arkan prefers to remain in the shadows and when he has to eliminate a public figure, he typically arranges an accident or makes them disappear."

"The Respite is owned by Linus," I said. "Shining a searchlight on Linus isn't convenient right now, so we moved the crime scene."

Arabella pivoted toward me. "Why? What happened to Linus?"

Mom raised her hand and made a simmer-down-now motion. "He will be fine. Don't freak out."

"What's going on?" Arabella's voice spiked. "Will somebody tell me what happened?"

"I will if you stop talking for a second." I took a deep breath. "Sometime in the last twenty-four hours, Linus was attacked in his home. Pete is dead."

Arabella sucked in a sharp breath. Sadness touched Mom's face. She and Pete had been friends. Bern looked alarmed, which almost never happened. On the laptop screen both Connor and Nevada went expressionless. My sister had picked up her husband's habit.

"Linus made it to the vault," Alessandro said. "The attacker was a mental mage, because Linus took two double doses of Styxine."

Grandma Frida whistled.

"Is he conscious?" Connor asked.

"No," I said.

"What's Styxine?" Runa asked.

"It's a mental defense drug," Connor said. "Military issue. It takes your consciousness completely off-line. The mage can't kill you if they can't sense your mind. It can render you permanently comatose, so it's a last resort."

"Can we give him something?" Arabella demanded.

"No," Mom told her. "We have to wait for him to wake up on his own."

Arabella squeezed her fists. I needed to move past the "Linus might not wake up" part.

"He activated the siege protocol, which I disabled to get him out of the vault."

"Where is he now?" Runa asked.

"In the spare bedroom upstairs in the main house," I told her.

Arabella jumped up.

Mom pointed to the table. "Sit."

My sister sat.

"Dr. Patel is with him," Mom said. "When the meeting is over, you may see him."

Alessandro leaned back in his chair. "We're going on high alert. Nobody goes anywhere without an escort or backup."

Patricia nodded. "Very well."

I looked at Bern. "Linus' house with all of its toys is defenseless unless we can bring the security system back online."

There was enough firepower under that house to topple the government of a small country.

"I'll handle it," he said.

"I'll go with him," Runa said.

Runa was a Prime venenata, a poison mage, and she loved Bern. My cousin couldn't have asked for a better bodyguard.

"Thank you," I said. "Leon, I've handed the Cabera investigation to Agent Wahl. I'd like you to shadow him. Watch him, let me know what he's doing, and keep him safe in case Arkan makes a run at him."

"Will do." Leon glanced at Runa. "Have fun bodyguarding the nerd, while I babysit the FBI."

She snorted.

I texted him the address of the warehouse and looked at Connor and Nevada. "It would really help if we had some cover story for why Linus isn't available."

"No problem," Nevada said.

Connor looked at me. "Let me know the moment you see Xavier."

As soon as this meeting ended, he would unleash Bug, his surveillance specialist, onto the city of Houston. Bug was relentless and he processed visual information at superhuman speed. Xavier didn't know it, but the moment he found himself in Bug's crosshairs, his little outing would be over.

"We have another problem," Alessandro said. "For reasons unknown as of now, the Russian Imperium has taken an interest in this situation."

I tapped my tablet and Konstantin popped onto the screen in all of his uniformed glory.

Grandma Frida sat up straighter. "Well!"

"Mother . . ." Mom growled.

"I'm old, Penelope. Not dead or blind." Grandma Frida grinned. "Besides, I always loved a man in uniform."

"For the love of God," Mom muttered.

"Who is he?" Leon wanted to know.

"Prince Konstantin Leonidovich Berezin, of Blood Imperial," I said. "Nephew of Emperor Mikhail II. Son of Grand Duke Leonid Sergeyevich Berezin, who is the Director of the Imperial Security Service."

Nobody said anything. We all just stared at Konstantin's image for a long moment.

"This is not good," Connor said.

My brother-in-law, master of the gentle understatement.

"We don't know why the Imperium has chosen this moment to become involved," I said.

"We will shortly," Alessandro said. "Meanwhile, I want to stress the risks involved."

He picked up my tablet, fiddled with it, and Augustine Montgomery appeared on the screen. He was tall and lean, with platinum-blond hair cut with razor precision and the face of a demigod. His expensive white suit fit him like a glove, and he looked at the world through a pair of thin wire glasses with amusement and slight derision.

Augustine started out as the owner of our business loan and our boss and potential enemy and ended up becoming a friend. It was friendship on his terms, but friendship, nonetheless. House Baylor and House Montgomery were allies, despite being business rivals, and the fact that Augustine and Connor had been roommates and friends in college only sealed that alliance tighter.

Alessandro nodded at the screen. "Could you describe Augustine for me?"

"Stuck up," Leon said.

"Business oriented," Bern said. "Competent."

"Ruthless," Arabella said. "But fair."

"Smart," I added. "Dangerous. Good at deception."

"Compassionate," Runa said.

We all looked at her.

"He is, to a degree. If it wasn't for him, Ragnar might not be here."

Augustine was the one who convinced me to drop everything and rush to a hospital roof in the middle of the night to pull Runa's brother off a ledge with my magic before he did something that couldn't be undone.

"Anything else?" Alessandro asked.

"Beautiful," Grandma Frida added.

Alessandro tapped the tablet. A video started on the screen showing a gym empty except for two young men. One was Augustine—tall, platinum-blond hair cut short, and a face that was just a hair short of absolute perfection.

Something was slightly off about this Augustine. He seemed younger. I couldn't put my finger on any specific detail that indicated his age. He just gave an overall impression of a man in his early twenties, just like the present-day Augustine gave an overall impression of a man in his early thirties. But it wasn't the age. It was something else.

I scrutinized the image. He was barefoot and dressed in a simple white T-shirt and dark shorts. What was it?

His opponent, a tall dark-haired man, turned and we saw his face. Connor. For a moment I didn't recognize him, but his blue eyes were unmistakable.

He looked like a different person.

This Connor had all the same features that my brother-in-law did, but the man in the video lacked Connor's trademark intensity. Connor exuded menace. The man on the screen had none of it. He held himself with relaxed ease. Pre-war Connor, before the seismic shift that turned him into Mad Rogan.

Nevada turned to Connor. "When was this?"

Connor squinted at the screen. "Day after graduation. A week before I shipped out. Where did you get this?"

"That's not important," Alessandro said.

"Yes, it is. I don't have this."

Nevada looked at Bern. "Tell me you didn't hack the MII server?"

Bern looked at her for a moment. "Of course not. That would start a war."

"You got it from De Silva," Connor said.

Nevada glanced at him. "Who's De Silva?"

"He's the one filming."

On the screen Augustine and Connor squared off.

"*Ready?*" Augustine asked.

"*Any time,*" Connor said.

Connor was enormously strong and almost as fast, and once he got going, he was capable of devastating power. Present-day Augustine was as tall as Connor, but he had to weigh fifty pounds less. If you put them side-by-side, Augustine would seem almost fragile by comparison. The idea of them sparring seemed absurd. How did this even happen? Did Augustine lose a bet?

"Today, ladies," a third male voice said off camera. *"Let's start this tea party."*

On-screen Connor grinned. *"Still waiting . . ."*

Augustine's hands came up. The muscles on his arms flexed.

The feeling of wrongness crystallized. This Augustine was larger. His shoulders were broader, his arms more muscular, his legs hard and defined. Standing across from Connor, he was only slightly leaner. Oh my God.

"Augustine was buff," Runa observed.

"He still is," I said. "He slims himself down."

Alessandro smiled at me, proud that I got there first.

"What?" Arabella asked.

"Pause it," I asked.

Alessandro tapped the tablet and the image on the screen froze.

"Look at the proportion of his shoulders to his chest. The Augustine we know has narrower shoulders, a shallower chest, and longer waist. Even the line of the shoulders is wrong. You can lose the muscle mass, but you can't alter the skeletal structure of your body. He slims himself down with his magic."

"He also gives himself two inches of height," Connor said. "Makes him look thinner."

Alessandro touched the tablet.

Augustine exploded into movement. His right fist hammered into Connor's jaw, lightning fast.

"Holy shit!" Leon said.

Connor shied back, his hands up, and Augustine delivered a vicious kick into Connor's left knee. Connor must have sensed it, because his leg came up, but Augustine still connected. The impact staggered Connor back.

"He's fast," Bern said, professional appreciation in his voice.

Both of my cousins leaned forward, focused on the screen. So did Arabella. For a moment she'd forgotten Linus. Her eyes tracked the two combatants on the screen. There was something slightly predatory in the way she watched them, like a cat watching two other cats fight.

Connor leaped back and launched a low kick that grazed Augustine's thigh. Augustine danced back. His eyes lit up. His lips stretched in a smile. *"Ow."*

Connor attacked, his arm snapping out like a sledgehammer. Augustine parried, crossing his arms, drove a front kick into Connor's left thigh, and took a vicious jab to the arm for his trouble. They danced across the gym floor, kicking, punching, and growling. It was both beautiful and terrifying to watch.

On-screen, Augustine leaped. His right leg shot out like a swinging baseball bat, aiming for Connor's head. At the last moment, Connor sidestepped, grabbed Augustine's leg, and jerked him down. They rolled on the mat.

"Nice," Bern said.

Connor locked Augustine into a half nelson for half a second. Augustine twisted his face away and rolled, landing on top of Connor. Connor bridged, throwing Augustine off, and hammered a punch to Augustine's ear. Augustine snarled and kneed Connor in the face.

The mood shifted. They were playing before, aiming kicks and punches where it wouldn't cause lasting damage. The gloves just came off. This was no longer a sparring session. This was a fight.

The view moved, bobbing closer.

"All right," the invisible De Silva called. *"On your feet. You're done."*

They ignored him, trying to outmuscle each other.

Something hissed and flame retardant foam shot over them.

The two combatants broke apart.

"What the fuck, Thushan?" Augustine snarled.

"You should thank him. You're shit on the mat." Connor wiped the blood from his nose and flung it in Augustine's direction.

"Fuck you too."

Augustine rolled to his feet. He was muscled like a gymnast. His face blurred, and he was back to a younger version of the Augustine we knew, elegant, lean, and glacial.

The video stopped.

Augustine had scammed us. When we had listed his attributes, the first thing on that list should've been "a trained killer."

I looked at Bern. "If you had to . . ."

He shook his head. "He'd kill me."

"Augustine Montgomery is a highly capable martial artist," Alessandro said. "Most high caliber illusion mages are. They assume other people's identities and enter dangerous situations, usually to gather information or to kill their target. Primes like Augustine can obscure their movements in a fight. He didn't do that here, but if it was a real fight, and he had a knife . . ."

"Connor would still beat Augustine's ass," Leon said.

My younger cousin had become a shameless Mad Rogan fanboy in middle school, and he never outgrew it. As far as Leon was concerned, Connor walked on water and ate enemy tanks for breakfast.

"He blurs," Connor said. "You think his hand is in one place, and then there is a knife pressed against your ribs, and you didn't see it get there. I wouldn't fight him hand to hand. I'd kill him from a distance. But Augustine will never do anything to hurt anyone in this room."

"Did you know?" I asked Nevada.

She nodded. "They spar sometimes."

"And you didn't tell us, why?" Mom asked.

Nevada looked sheepish. It almost never happened. "It didn't occur to me. Like Connor said, he isn't a threat. Connor and he had a moment a few years ago. It realigned Augustine's worldview."

"Trust me," Connor said. "All of his veiled threats and scary promises are bullshit. He is a friend."

"Could have fooled me," Mom said, her voice flat.

Connor grimaced. "He has issues."

"Konstantin Berezin can do everything Augustine can do and probably more," Alessandro said. "If you encounter him, treat him like a cobra. Try to stay out of striking range. He kills quickly and without hesitation."

"Agreed," Patricia said. "A cornered illusion mage can be a very challenging opponent."

In my mind, once an illusion mage was discovered, they were somehow rendered powerless. Clearly, that would be a deadly mistake to make. Being told Konstantin was lethal was one thing. Watching Augustine, whom we had all dismissed as a noncombatant, turn into a murder machine wasn't something I would forget.

"Obviously, Konstantin complicates matters," I said. "But our main priority is still protecting Linus and solving the Speaker's murder."

"On that note," Nevada said. "We have some lousy news."

"PAC?" Bern asked.

Connor looked like he'd bitten into a rotten apple. "We'll handle it."

Principal Action Consulting, or the PAC as they called themselves, recently became a very sharp thorn in House Rogan's side. Just like Connor, they offered a private army for hire and, just like Connor's army, they were led by a powerful Prime, Matthew Berry, a tagger. Taggers marked a spot in a structure and then saturated it with arcane energy until it exploded. Matthew was a one-man artillery battery.

The PAC was started by Matthew's father. Back then it had been called the Black Hurricane, and after Connor erupted onto the military scene, people kept asking them if Mad Rogan and their outfit were somehow involved. The father and son duo got tired of it and changed the name.

But the real trouble started last year. A group of archeologists was taken hostage in Pakistan, four of them American citizens. For complicated political reasons, the United States government wanted to rescue them quietly. They contacted the PAC. The father of one of the archeologists and Connor's mother's friend contacted Connor. While Berry and the government haggled, Connor went in with a small team and saved the hostages.

For no apparent reason, Berry viewed this as a flex. What should have been a business rivalry at best turned deeply personal and the younger Berry decided to wipe House Rogan off the planet's surface. If Connor's people took one side of a conflict, Berry made sure to get hired for the other. They'd clashed several times on foreign soil, and we all knew the final confrontation was coming and soon.

"Berry is massing his troops in Austin," Connor said.

Berry was headquartered in Virginia. There was no reason for his people to be in Austin, only a few hours from us. He was preparing for an offensive against Connor. Everyone here knew it, and none of us would do anything about it. Whoever made the first move would have to bear the legal ramifications. It was smarter to get attacked than to land the first blow.

Berry was a significant threat, and the timing was very coincidental. I never counted on help from Connor and Nevada, although it was always available, simply because we needed to be self-sufficient. But now we knew for sure that we had to rely on ourselves. I needed to alter our plan a bit.

"Arabella?"

She looked at me. The fury in her eyes was still there.

"Whoever tried to kill Linus will likely want to finish the job," I said.

"I hope they try. Nobody touches my family."

I supposed we all saw Linus as family. Linus treated the three of us as his granddaughters and Bern and Leon as his grandsons, and he especially doted on Arabella. He let her steal his whiskey and cigars, and sometimes she would ask him for advice. Nevada got respect and guidance, I got education and lectures, but Arabella got beaming approval. If we lost Linus, she would be inconsolable. I would be inconsolable.

"You're staying in," I told her. "You don't leave the Compound no matter what happens. You're our final line of defense."

"Fine by me."

"We're done," I said. "Everyone knows what to do."

Nevada waved and the laptop screen went dark.

I walked over to Bern and handed him the USB. "I need to know what's on it."

"Will do."

He got up, and Runa and he left. Leon sauntered out the door. Mom nodded to Arabella. My sister jumped off her chair and the two of them went out of the room.

Cornelius also rose to his feet. He'd stayed so quiet throughout the meeting, it was easy to forget he was there.

"Just a moment." I got up, went back to my office, took the Ziploc bag with Luciana's brush out of my desk drawer, and brought it back to the conference room. "I'd like you to check something for me."

"I'm all ears," he told me.

# Chapter 5

The sound of my phone pulled me away from the computer screen. I glanced at it. Linus.

Linus?!

"Yes?"

"I broke into Linus' phone," Bern said.

Damn it. "You almost gave me a heart attack."

Bern made a deep rumble that was probably a chuckle.

"Did you find anything good?"

"The last call he took was at 6:43 p.m. Sunday night. All others went to voice mail. The first of these was at 10:51 p.m. That's likely your window."

"The first call that went to voice mail, who was it from?"

"Zahra Kabani."

Zahra Kabani was the Warden of Michigan. Linus and she were working together on tracking a fugitive. He would've taken her call.

"Any progress on the security system?"

"Working on it. How's Linus?"

"Still unconscious."

"No change is better than a change for the worse."

"True. What about my USB?"

"Working on it."

He said goodbye and hung up.

I rubbed my face. Whatever happened to Linus likely happened between 6:43 p.m. and 10:51 p.m. on Sunday night. We would narrow it down even further once the coroner was done with Pete.

Pete's face crisscrossed by the dark starburst of lines surfaced from my memory. I pushed the thought aside and stared back at the screen.

Alessandro and I decided to divide and conquer. He reached out to his international contacts trying to figure out why the Russian Imperium was suddenly interested in Texas or its Warden, and I decided to work on House Cabera.

My head hummed. I should probably eat something and soon. I rummaged in my desk drawers, found a packet of jerky, tore it open with my teeth, and surveyed the fruits of my labor. For a two-hour deep dive into all things Cabera, I hadn't come up with much.

Luciana Cabera, halcyon Prime, Head of the House, fifty-six years old, widowed. For some reason I thought she was in her early sixties.

Husband, Fredrick Cabera, halcyon Prime, ten years her senior, died of cancer six years ago. Fredrick had joined House Cabera and taken his wife's last name. From what I could gather, he had been born in South Africa and had wanted to immigrate to the US. At the time the US had prohibited immigration from SA due to an Ebola outbreak. Marrying Luciana allowed him to sidestep the ban.

Daughter, Kaylee Cabera, twenty-two years old. Full-time student at Rice University, right here in Houston. Her driver's license and her IP address confirmed that she still lived at home. Kaylee either hadn't wanted to leave the nest or wasn't allowed to.

Luciana had two brothers, one uncle, three aunts, and her parents were still alive, although neither was in good health. Besides Luciana, House Cabera officially listed one other certified Prime, Luciana's elderly mother. However, Luciana's twelve-year-old niece and her seventeen-year-old nephew had both undergone preliminary trials and tested in the Prime range. Their official certification would wait until they turned eighteen. The rest of the family fell into the Significant range.

Unlike a lot of other Houses, the Caberas did not diversify their business interests. The Serenity Clinic was their primary source of income, aside from some privately held stocks. All of the adult Caberas worked for the clinic, all of them held relevant degrees or were in the process of obtaining them, and none of them had attempted to break away from the family business.

None of them had been involved in any scandals, nobody had a criminal record, and their credit reports were blissfully free of bankruptcies and large debts. They were respectably boring.

Luciana's political career was equally as boring. I couldn't find a single matter she had brought before the Assembly in the last three years that could've put her into Arkan's crosshairs. I seriously doubted he cared about House inheritance minutiae or the exact procedure for the certification of Primes in the state of Texas. All of it was local and region specific.

I tapped my pen against my lips. There was one thing that bothered me. According to Herald gossip, Kaylee Cabera was a Prime like her parents. Most Primes couldn't wait to undergo the trials. Four of Kaylee's cousins had taken the preliminary test, and while it didn't grant certification, it let the family ballpark their power range. Two of them had been designated as tentative Primes and the other two were likely Significants. House Cabera had plastered the results all over their website. I couldn't find any record of Kaylee's preliminary test or her submitting to the trials.

There were reasons for which a Prime might delay being officially recognized. Usually, they had to do with business or family considerations. For example, a House involved in a feud might postpone the trials to appear weaker than they were and surprise their opponents.

However, the Caberas didn't feud, and Kaylee was a fixture among the young House scion scene. Her Instagram and Herald told me she was a privileged child. She wore expensive clothes, drove luxury cars, dined in trendy restaurants, and hung out with people who did the same. I pulled her transcripts from Rice through the Warden Network. She ran track and was pursuing a B.A. in psychology and her grades in public speaking classes told me that if she suffered from social anxiety, she had a good handle on it.

Sometimes people deliberately hid their talents. Olivia Charles, the woman who'd killed Cornelius' wife, had been a manipulator, a mage who could impose her will on other people's bodies. She had registered as a psionic. But that scenario still required one to show up for the trials.

Something just didn't feel right. I couldn't put my finger on it, and I would have to interview Kaylee to get more information.

My phone chimed. Agent Wahl. I braced myself.

"Hello?"

"That's one hell of a favor!" Agent Wahl hissed into the phone in that way people do when they're furious but have to look calm because they have an audience.

"We're even now."

"I don't know what we are right now, Prime Baylor. This is a staged scene. What do you expect me to do with this?"

And how did he know that? Linus' crew had successfully relocated three murders during my tenure alone, all with no one the wiser. They were flawless.

"I expect you to investigate. Very loudly. It would help if you refused to answer questions, then had a press conference where you gave the bare minimum of information, and then refused to answer questions again."

"You want me to be a distraction."

"I want to be free to conduct the investigation. Besides, you enjoy press conferences. You can wear that black suit again, the one you said makes you look inscrutable but official."

"Does the Warden know about this?"

"As of now, I am the Acting Warden. The National Assembly appreciates your cooperation and understanding, Agent Wahl."

There was silence.

"Is he alive?" he asked.

"In a manner of speaking."

More silence.

"I want in," Wahl said.

"You are in. I reached out to you because I trust you. Because he trusted you. I need you to investigate the case, bring me in as a consultant, and take the credit when it's solved."

"By solved, do you mean the truth or a cover story the National Assembly finds convenient?"

"It will be a version of the truth we can both live with."

More silence.

"Fine," Wahl said. "As long as you understand that I am a fucking FBI agent, and I will not allow myself or the agency to be used to delude the public."

I could bring up the Warden Network and offer him a dozen examples of the FBI doing just that. But I needed him on my side, and I respected his ethics. They aligned with mine.

"I have every intention of solving this murder and bringing the culprit to justice. We're not going to frame anyone or let anyone go unpunished. Can you live with that?"

"I'll take it. I'm going to talk to the Cabera family."

"Can I meet you there?"

"Yes. I want to get there by five. Don't be late." He hung up.

I walked over to Alessandro's office. He leaned back in his chair, his feet on the table, a phone to his ear. I rapped my knuckles on the doorway. He winked at me.

"Love and kisses to Maya. *Ciao!*"

He hung up and grinned at me.

"Ciao?"

I had never heard him say that in a professional setting. *Ciao* was very informal, both a greeting and a goodbye, and it had originated from the Venetian dialect's *s'ciào vostro* meaning "I am your slave." The phrase wasn't meant literally; it was used more as "I'm at your service" and it was mostly said to younger people and friends and family, those you knew very well.

"What's the point of stereotypes if you can't use them to your advantage?"

"I'm so glad to hear that."

"Why?"

"Wahl called. He wants to interview the family. Kaylee, Luciana's daughter, is my age. I need the Count."

Alessandro's entire persona changed. He took his feet off the table and sat straighter in his chair, throwing one long leg over the other. His pose acquired elegance. His expression turned suave. He looked worldly, slightly jaded, yet breathtakingly handsome.

"Is this the Count you were looking for?" A light Italian accent overlaid his words like a glossy polish.

"Yes. That's the guy."

"And what will this humble Count get if he comes with you?" His voice was like velvet.

"The satisfaction of a job well done?"

"I was thinking of something more substantial."

"Like what?"

"Once this is over, we go away for a weekend to the coast. I don't care which, as long as there is clear blue water and hot weather. No meetings, no appointments, no phone."

I knew what he was asking. Whether Linus survived or not, we would do this, because it was about us alone. "Done. Will you take a kiss as a down payment?"

"I'd be a fool not to."

I walked over and leaned down. My lips touched his. I started tentative and gentle, a tease rather than a promise, just a hint of things to come. His mouth opened. I caught his breath, and my tongue brushed his ever so slightly. His hand slid into my hair, and he kissed me back, hungry but savoring every moment. We kissed while the world stood still and when we finally came up for air, I had to stop myself from reaching for his clothes.

Count Sagredo gave me a dazzling smile. "I am at your service, *tesoro mio.*"

Luciana Cabera and her daughter lived in River Oaks, less than ten minutes away from Linus on foot, in a seven-million-dollar mansion. The 8,500 square foot home sat in the middle of a manicured acre and was built in what Alessandro started calling Houston European style, meaning it was a pseudo-Mediterranean beige stucco house with a colonnade and an inexplicable round turret of brown stone that matched nothing else.

Alessandro grimaced as we pulled up to the house and parked Rhino behind a stereotypical black SUV with federal license plates. Rhino was Grandma Frida's special project, a custom armored SUV she built from the ground up. It was the most secure vehicle we had that could still pass for a somewhat civilian car.

"Snob."

He gave me a pained look. "Why does it have a turret, Catalina? Are they expecting an army of medieval knights and trebuchets?"

"You never know," I told him.

"It's a Tuscan colonnade interrupted by a Scottish turret with Tudor windows."

"You can hold on to my hand. I'll lead you in while you avert your eyes."

"No need."

My phone chimed.

"Cornelius," I told Alessandro and put the phone on speaker.

"You were right," Cornelius said. "It's recent. Less than twenty-four hours."

Damn it. I had hoped I was wrong.

"Thank you so much."

"Of course. Any time."

I said goodbye and hung up.

Alessandro was looking at me.

"Do you remember the brush I stole from Luciana's purse? I gave it to Cornelius. He took the brush and Gus to Linus' house and had Gus check the scent signatures. Luciana's scent is in the yard and in the house, and it's fresh. As the Speaker, she had unprecedented access to the Warden. They likely had many confidential meetings. He might have added her as an exception to his security system."

"When did you know?"

"I didn't. I had a feeling."

Alessandro wiggled his fingers at me. "Witchery."

"No, instincts. Once Leon called and told us that the siege protocols were active but there were no bodies, I knew that either the attack never happened, or the attacker got out unscathed. Luciana and Linus, one attack after another. It felt too coincidental. I didn't suspect her, but it didn't feel right, so I wanted to cover all of my bases."

He didn't seem surprised. Why wasn't he surprised?

"Alessandro, you have something."

"I do."

"What do you have?"

"Would you like to see it?"

"Alessandro!"

Alessandro produced his phone with an elegant flourish and offered it to me. An email from someone named Doc Giordano.

"Who is Doc Giordano?"

Alessandro nodded toward the street. "A retired brain surgeon. He's lived two houses down from Linus for the last thirty years."

"I don't remember House Giordano."

"There isn't one. Doc isn't a magic user. He's a rich old guy who worked very hard for most of his life to live at this address. He and Linus are friendly. I've chatted with him a few times."

That didn't surprise me. Alessandro had the uncanny ability to get people to like him without doing anything at all. He'd enter a room filled with strangers and in thirty seconds they would start telling him their life stories.

He was also clearly enjoying dragging this reveal out.

"Give," I demanded.

"Every day Doc walks his dogs at nine in the morning and nine in the evening like clockwork. He remembers seeing Luciana Cabera walking from the direction of Linus' home toward her house a little after 9:00 p.m. on Sunday night."

That fit right into our window. "Is he sure?"

"Very. He's in his seventies, but he is still very sharp. There's more."

"Tell me."

"There was another person with her. He didn't get a good look, because they were wearing a large hoodie, but he thinks they were young from the way they walked."

I leaned back in my seat. "Unless Luciana had hidden talents, she couldn't have killed Pete with her magic. Not if she was a true halcyon."

He nodded. "Whoever was with her is likely the killer."

"If so, why did they leave Dr. Giordano alive? He saw them."

Alessandro smiled. "Hubris."

Luciana had been a Prime. She'd dealt with other Primes on a daily basis. Her entire political career revolved around mages, and Dr. Giordano was an ordinary person. She never considered him a threat because in normal circumstances he never would be. An experienced combat magic user would've eliminated all witnesses, but Luciana wasn't used to getting her hands dirty. She walked right past Dr. Giordano, because she was so conditioned to ignore people like him, he might as well have been invisible.

We had to get him out of the city. "Where is Dr. Giordano now?"

"On vacation with his lovely spouse," Alessandro said. "On the Warden's dime. I've explained the situation to him. He's onboard."

I really loved this man.

A dark thought zinged through my brain. "She had a young person with her, Pete was killed by someone with unusual magic, and Kaylee hasn't taken the trials."

"Interesting, isn't it?" Alessandro said.

If House Cabera killed Pete and hurt Linus, I would make them pay.

"I have so many questions." I tapped my fingers on the dashboard in front of me. "Why would Luciana want to hurt Linus? Why would Arkan have her killed? Did Kaylee help her mother end Pete's life or was it one of Arkan's assassins? If it was one of Arkan's people, did he somehow force Luciana to help him gain access to Linus and did he kill her after they botched it?"

"Let's go ask them." Alessandro popped his door open. "Shall we?"

"We shall."

He got out of the car to open my door.

Normally I opened my own door unless I was wearing a gown that required management, but right now we were on display and Alessandro was in his Count Sagredo persona. He switched identities like gloves, and he was always flawlessly consistent once he assumed them. Today he wore khaki trousers, a crisp white T-shirt, and a seersucker blazer unbuttoned, with the sleeves casually rolled back to mid forearm. His shoes were blue Santoni loafers, his shades were Trussardi, and if you searched the Internet for "young Italian Prime," you'd see his picture. Probably several of them.

Kaylee was twenty-two, like me. Alessandro was the god of our adolescence, and his Instagram was the altar on which all of us prayed. I was no longer in love with that fantasy. I preferred a different Alessandro, the one who plotted like a Borgia, neutralized his enemies before they knew what hit them, and woke me up in the middle of the night to do things that made me blush when he mentioned them later. But Kaylee wasn't me.

Alessandro held out his hand. I rested my fingers in his and stepped out of the car. We strode up the three wide stairs, my beige pumps clicking quietly on the concrete. Today Alessandro was the star, and I opted for understated navy slacks, a navy silk blouse with small beige and white flowers on it, and a matching jacket with three-quarter sleeves. My makeup was natural bordering on plain, and my hair was gathered into a loose knot. Everything about me was perfectly presentable and designed to fade into the background.

The thick mahogany door swung open before either of us could ring the bell revealing a solemn-looking man dressed in black. His features echoed Luciana's, but he was slightly younger, his skin a darker shade of brown, and his hair liberally salted with grey. Julian Cabera, Luciana's younger brother.

"We've been expecting you," he said.

"My deepest condolences," Alessandro said, his face broadcasting sincerity.

"Thank you." He held out his hand toward the house. "Please."

The interior of the house was a warm shade of white, complementing the travertine floor. We followed Julian left, through a thick archway past a luxurious powder room into a study paneled in rich, warm walnut.

Built-in bookcases lined the walls between large arched windows. A vintage Moroccan rug decorated the dark brown floor. At the far end of the room, an elegant desk stood, the chair behind it glaringly empty. On the left a large fireplace took up half of the wall, and in the center of the room four people sat on the plush beige sofas and overstuffed chairs arranged around a coffee table.

Agent Wahl and a woman in a beige suit sat facing the fireplace. The woman was about his age, with tawny, warm skin, shoulder-length brown hair pushed behind her ear on the left side, and brown eyes. A tiny transparent plastic tube protruded from her ear, barely visible. A hearing aid. As far as I knew, the FBI had strict medical requirements. An agent with hearing loss had to be exceptional to be admitted.

Across from the two FBI agents, an older man and a young woman sat on the other sofa, both in black. The man looked like an older version of Julian: same nose, same mouth, same worried look in his eyes, but with a longer, leaner build. His hair, cropped short, had gone grey. Elias Cabera.

Next to him, Kaylee Cabera sat rigid, her spine perfectly straight. She was slender, with a heart-shaped face, large eyes under strong eyebrows, and full lips. Her skin was the same warm brown shade as her mother's, but she'd bleached her hair to champagne blond, a beautiful color with multi-tonal highlights that looked perfectly natural. The hair framed her face in loose waves. She'd taken the time to style it. She'd also put on makeup, not just a brush of mascara, but her entire face complete with deep plum lipstick that looked almost mahogany on her lips. It could've meant any number of things, but her eyes told me exactly what it was—defiance. Kaylee Cabera refused to be broken, and she dared anyone to try her.

Everyone except Kaylee rose as we walked in. Kaylee glanced up and saw Alessandro. Her eyes widened. For a second, she forgot to look angry and just stared.

Yes, I know exactly what that feels like.

Wahl's eyes narrowed. The female FBI agent next to him glanced at Kaylee, then at Alessandro. They'd read the room.

"My deepest apologies," Alessandro murmured, his Italian accent light and refined. "We arrived as soon as we could."

"You're just in time," Wahl assured him. He turned to the family. "This is Alessandro Sagredo, Prime antistasi, and Catalina Baylor of House Baylor. They will be consulting on this case due to its sensitive nature. Just to remind everyone, I am Agent Wahl, and this is Agent Garcia. Once again, this interview is being recorded."

"Please, sit down," Elias invited.

We sat in two overstuffed chairs. Alessandro was on my left, closer to Elias and Kaylee. She was still looking at him, and she had adjusted her pose, resting her right arm on the sofa arm to open up her body, crossing her legs, and presenting him with a flattering angle. I might have been invisible. Perfect. I sent the tendrils of my magic forward ever so gently.

Agent Wahl launched into the standard list of questions. Did Luciana have any enemies? Did she have romantic partners? What was her relationship with everyone present? Were there any recent difficulties?

Elias had taken the lead on answering. Kaylee answered only when directly spoken to and every time she opened her mouth, Alessandro offered her an encouraging smile.

My magic had skimmed the surface of Elias' mind. He didn't notice. He felt like a typical halcyon. Halcyons were crowd control mages. Like me, they couldn't afford to allow magic leakage, so they kept an iron grip on their emotions, accreting a mental shield that encased their psyche. Their minds appeared opaque and hard, almost like pearls inside an oyster's shell.

Nothing unexpected here. I moved on to Julian.

My phone vibrated. I glanced at it. A video call from Patricia.

"Excuse me," I murmured, getting up.

Everyone ignored me.

I walked into the hallway and took the call. The view from a bodycam filled the screen, showing a slight, thin-looking white man in his mid-forties. He wore dark clothes and hunched over a little, as if expecting a punch on the shoulder. Four guards surrounded him.

"I have this gentleman here," Patricia said. "He says he has an appointment."

The man looked up at the camera. The brown irises of his eyes melted into aquamarine. Konstantin. Crap.

"Is that the illusion VIP we've been expecting?" Patricia asked.

"Yes."

"I told him you were busy. He says he will wait as long as it takes. What do you want me to do?"

I did tell him to come back during business hours. I also needed to know why the hell he'd been in Linus' house.

"Is he alone?"

"Yes."

"Let him in and put him under guard. Do not injure him in any way unless he becomes aggressive, and if he does become aggressive, I need bulletproof evidence of it, because we can't afford a conflict with the Russian Imperium."

"Got it."

The iron gate blocking the entrance rolled into the wall. Konstantin smiled and started walking.

There was something disturbingly smug about that smile.

Also, his assumed identity seemed familiar somehow. Where had I seen that face before?

They cleared the wall and walked into the front yard. Konstantin stopped and looked directly at me.

"I suggest you get home as soon as possible, Ms. Baylor. The clock is ticking. Tell Sasha that this round goes to me."

What the hell did that mean? I would have to sort it out after we were done here. I hung up and returned to the study.

The atmosphere had changed while I was gone. Elias and Julian were clearly wary, while Kaylee, still fixated on Alessandro, spoke in a monotone voice.

". . . dinner around seven. I had homework, so I went to my suite. I don't know what Mom did after that. Usually, she listened to audiobooks on Sunday nights. It was her way to decompress."

I took my seat. My magic net was still in place. I skimmed Julian's mind. Another halcyon. He certainly wasn't calm—I could sense turmoil deep within the shell—but he was firmly in control. I moved on to Kaylee.

"When did you go to bed?" Agent Garcia asked.

"Around eleven. Mom was still up. I had come down to grab a Tylenol. Statistical Methods always gives me a headache."

My magic's tendrils reached for Luciana's daughter and slipped across the surface of her shell.

"When did you wake up this morning?" Agent Garcia asked.

Kaylee sighed. "Around eight."

One of my tendrils burrowed through her shell. It was so sudden, I almost jerked back. The shield on Kaylee's mind was paper-thin. Inside the shield her mind churned. It wasn't a pearl, it was a glowing coal sitting in a bed of ashes.

"My first class is at ten . . . Look, my mother was murdered and you're asking about my sleep and school schedules. What does this have to do with anything? Why aren't you out there"—she pointed at the window— "looking for whoever did this?"

Agent Wahl opened his mouth.

"Ms. Cabera," Alessandro said. "We are deeply sorry for your loss and the emotional brutality of this visit. We understand the great amount of stress you must be under."

She pivoted toward him. "I just want the killer found. I can't have my mother back, but I can have justice."

"Just a couple more questions." Alessandro offered her an apologetic smile.

"Fine. Since it's you who's asking," she said.

"Do you own a blue hoodie?"

Kaylee blinked. Her mind spun, the glow of her magic growing brighter. There was some halcyon there, but the rest was something I'd never seen before. So much power, but so little training. She reminded me of Arthur, except my nephew was thirteen months old, and she was twenty-two.

"Ummm . . . maybe? I don't remember."

"Please try," Alessandro encouraged.

"Probably. Rice's colors are grey and navy, so I might have one. My closet is like a labyrinth. I have things I haven't worn since middle school in there."

"Do you ever take walks with your mother?" Alessandro asked.

Kaylee's mind flashed with angry red. The tendril of my magic vanished, severed into nothing. Pain lashed my mind and in that brief instant, I felt the veins in my brain throb.

Kaylee Cabera was Linus' would-be assassin. And she hadn't even noticed that her magic slapped me. She killed Pete. She was the reason Linus was comatose.

How the hell did she get out of the house? Her mother had special clearance, but Kaylee didn't. Why was she alive?

The two Cabera brothers came to attention. They must've realized Alessandro was going somewhere with his questions.

Kaylee gave a jerky shrug. "My mother didn't walk, Prime Sagredo. She had a chauffeur who took her wherever she wanted to go."

Liar.

She was right there, five feet away. I could blast her mind with my song, and she would confess to everything.

Alessandro reached, took my fingers into his, and squeezed my hand. He knew me too well. Nobody in that room realized that I was on the edge of violence, but he did, and he was trying to keep me from leaping off that cliff.

Kaylee's gaze snagged on our hands. A furious spark flared in her mind.

The FBI agents leaned forward, focused on Kaylee like sharks.

Alessandro gave her his charming, irresistible smile, trying to defuse the bomb before it had a chance to explode.

I stared straight at her. *Go ahead. Target me. Hit me. Do it. Do it right now, so I can end this.* All I needed was the tiniest excuse, the smallest justification. I had the FBI right here as my witnesses. *Just a little bit of aggression, Kaylee. Take a swing, and I will make you relive Pete's death until your mind snaps like a twig.*

Alessandro locked his fingers on mine in a silent *no*. His voice was smooth, almost intimate. "Where were you between the hours of 8:00 and 10:00 p.m. last night?"

The shell on Kaylee's mind tore. A burst of magic shot out, un-
even, knotted, and powerful, like a flooded mountain stream dragging
branches and rocks as the water tore down. She'd meant to focus it on
Alessandro, but her control was sloppy, and it splashed the entire room
on its way to him. The magic smashed against my shields, burning hot,
and harmlessly dissipated. The minds of the two uncles flashed in response, their shells impregnable.

Like me!

Agent Wahl's face softened into a smile. It was one of the most disturbing things I had ever seen.

Next to him, Agent Garcia wasn't smiling. She looked ready to rip
Kaylee's head off.

"As I said . . ."

A second flood of magic smashed into Alessandro, so potent, it was
shocking. The edge of it swiped me. It was like sticking your head into
a fireplace with a fire raging inside. Her magic was attempting to do
the same thing a halcyon would, but it didn't feel like any halcyon I had
come across.

Like me. Like me! LIKE ME!

My magic bucked like a wild horse, straining my hold and trying to
splay out into wings. I gritted my teeth and kept it in check.

". . . I had homework," Kaylee said.

A third flood. She was trying to cook him, except she had no training,
so she was relying solely on power. There was no subtlety there. No skill.
Just raw impact. She smashed his mind like a hammer.

Most mental mages hid their minds behind shields. It was one of the
first things we learned. The shield was like a wall of stone. With enough
power, you could shatter your opponent's wall. Committing too much
power to an attack like that could leave you vulnerable, but you could
break through if you were strong enough.

Alessandro's mind appeared to have a wall, but if you tried chipping
at it, you realized that the wall never ended. His entire mind was a basalt
craig, a solid chunk of stone. There was no breaking through.

"I didn't take any walks." A fourth flood.

Her magic burned a painful lesion across my defenses. If Alessandro wasn't an antistasi, she wouldn't have just turned him into a happy idiot, she would've damaged his brain.

Agent Garcia turned and stared at me, outrage in her eyes.

I wanted to kill Kaylee. She hurt Linus. She hurt my family. I needed to wipe her off the face of the planet here and now, before she hurt anyone else I cared about. There was a stormy ocean inside of me, with furious waves battering the rocks and unstoppable currents swirling, and I needed to drown Kaylee in it.

Alessandro shook his head at both me and Garcia.

Another splash of magic, weaker this time. She was getting tired.

None of her attacks even fazed him. He squeezed my hand again and said, his voice smooth, almost chiding, "Are you sure you didn't go out? Perhaps a quick walk around the neighborhood? I'm here to help you, but you have to be honest with me."

Kaylee stared at him, incredulous.

Agent Wahl let out a happy sigh. "I'm so relaxed right now. I really like it here. You are a lovely person, Ms. Cabera."

Elias and Julian rose in unison.

No. We're not finished. I didn't have my turn.

"My niece is tired," Julian announced.

"Does your niece know the meaning of an assault on a federal officer?" Agent Garcia ground out.

"This interview is over," Elias said.

Agent Garcia grabbed Wahl by his arm and hauled him to his feet.

He blinked at her. "Are we leaving? Can't we stay a little bit longer?"

"No, we can't." Agent Garcia steered him to the door. "This isn't over. We'll be in touch."

Julian ushered Kaylee out of the room, while Elias stared us down. "Thank you for your visit."

Alessandro nodded, rose calmly, and I stood up with him, since he refused to let go of my hand. We headed for the front door, our fingers intertwined.

 **Chapter 6**

Getting out of that house was like stepping out of a crypt into sunshine.

Ahead Agent Garcia half-guided, half-shoved Agent Wahl into the black SUV.

He smiled at her. "You are so . . ."

"So what?"

"Forceful," he told her with a dreamy look on his face.

She grabbed him by the chin. "Victor! Look into my eyes."

He gazed at her. His eyes rolled back into his skull, and Agent Wahl slumped in his seat, unconscious.

"An enersyphon," Alessandro murmured. "That explains things."

Enersyphons, also known as magic eaters, absorbed magic, pulling it into themselves. They didn't guard against it, they fed on it, which granted them a mild immunity to a lot of mental and elemental powers. Agent Garcia just sapped the magic dancing through Wahl's brain and the shock knocked him out.

"You stopped me." I pulled my hand out of his. Our backs were to their security cameras, and I kept my voice low. "She killed Pete."

"We don't have proof."

"I don't care."

"Yes, you do. We follow the rules. That's what separates us from them. Catalina, it's the wrong time and the wrong place. I know you are angry, but if I hadn't stopped you, you would've regretted it."

"No, I wouldn't have."

"If Linus were here, he would have stopped you, too."

"Linus isn't here, because she hurt him."

He dipped his head to look at me. "This is not like you."

This was *not* like me.

That thought spun my mind around. The surge of magic inside me died.

I had endangered the investigation. If he hadn't taken my hand, Kaylee and I would be locked in a mental duel right now. She was untrained, but she was freakishly powerful.

I'd come within a hair of singing. Not only had I almost jeopardized the search for Linus' assassin, but I would have put the lives of everyone in that room in danger. This didn't happen to me. I'd been controlling my magic and my emotions since early childhood, but an untrained mental mage had managed to rile me up to the point of nearly losing it.

It wasn't Kaylee. It was Linus. He was still unconscious, and it was seriously messing with my head. I needed to get a grip right now, because if I spun out of control, I wouldn't be able to undo what would happen.

"Thank you for stopping me," I told him.

"Any time," he said.

Agent Garcia marched back to us. We started walking toward her at the same time. The more distance was between us and the watchful eyes inside the house, the better.

We met halfway.

"She attacked a federal agent and the two of you just sat there," Agent Garcia growled. "Tell me why I shouldn't get a strike team down here right now and take her into custody. Alive or dead, I don't care."

That would be a nightmare. I turned my back to the security camera, pointed at it, hiding the gesture with my body, and lowered my voice.

"You're not wrong," I said. "And your anger is justified. However, she has done much worse than that. I want to nail her to the wall, but she's involved in a much larger scheme, and I don't exactly know how. I don't know what will happen if we bring her in. Please give me time."

"Promise me you won't sweep this under the rug," Agent Garcia said. "I want your word that this doesn't become one of those House politics secrets."

"I won't and you have it."

"Seventy-two hours," Agent Garcia ground out.

"The Office of the Warden appreciates your patience," Alessandro said.

Agent Garcia squeezed her hand into a fist and relaxed it. "I'll tell you one thing. That girl is no halcyon. Her magic tastes like jagged glass."

She marched around the car, got into the driver's seat, drove off, with Wahl still unconscious, and almost collided with an armored gunmetal grey Dodge as it turned into the driveway. For a moment the two cars were at a standoff, then the Dodge reversed, giving Agent Garcia room. She peeled out of the driveway.

Alessandro frowned.

The grey Dodge slid to a stop in front of us. The driver's window rolled down, revealing a tan man in his late twenties, with light brown hair and grey eyes behind large round glasses. I'd seen him before. He was one of Lenora Jordan's Assistant DAs. Matt Something.

"No," Alessandro said.

Matt gave us an apologetic wave with his hand. "I'm merely the messenger."

Cornelius appeared at the mouth of the driveway, Gus on a leash next to him. He saw us and waved. His car was nowhere in sight. He must've walked from Linus' house.

I waved back.

"We lost Dag Gunderson," Matt said.

"How, Matt?" Alessandro growled. "I left him at your doorstep."

"Gross incompetence," Matt said cheerfully. "He's been spotted near St. Agnes Academy. We're reasonably sure he's going to bomb it. I'll fill you in on the way."

Alessandro's tone was cold. "I'm busy."

It was my turn to be reasonable. I took his hand and squeezed it. He gave me an outraged look.

"Lenora personally asked for you," Matt said. "She said she would consider it a favor."

There were a handful of people in Houston not even the strongest Houses cared to provoke. The Harris County DA was one of them. More importantly, hundreds of children were about to experience a magic meteor shower that would explode on impact.

"It's okay," I told him. "Go."

He shook his head.

"She sent a car," I told him. "I won't do anything rash without you. I promise. Look, Cornelius is over there. I'll pick him up, check on Bern and Runa, and we'll go straight home."

Alessandro swore again.

"It's fine," I told him. "There are hundreds of children in St. Agnes."

He exhaled and got into the SUV. "Drive fast, Matt."

"Always." Matt smiled at me. "Thank you for your understanding, Ms. Baylor."

The window rolled back up. The Dodge reversed and sped away.

I forgot to tell him about Konstantin. Well, crap. Not that it would change anything. He would still have had to go to apprehend Dag Gunderson. I would wait to interview the prince until he returned home.

I got into Rhino and drove it to the mouth of the driveway, where Cornelius stood.

"Would you like a lift?"

"Yes, thank you."

He opened the rear passenger door. Gus hopped onto the seat and lay down, panting. A moment later, Cornelius got into the front passenger seat, and we were off.

"What are you doing here?"

"Gus and I decided to follow Luciana's scent."

And it led them straight to her house.

"Did you learn anything from talking to the family?" Cornelius asked.

"Kaylee Cabera is not a halcyon. Alessandro and I don't know what she is. The FBI has a magic eater, and she didn't know what Kaylee is either."

"Do you think she is our killer?"

"Yes. I was five feet from her, and I had to let her go, because I can't prove it."

"Yet," Cornelius said.

"Yes," I agreed. "Yet."

"Why would the current Speaker use her daughter to try to murder the former Speaker?"

"She wasn't trying to murder the former Speaker. She tried to murder the Warden."

Cornelius tapped his chin, thinking. "Luciana is prudent. Was prudent. I would classify her as having been extremely risk averse. This was rash and ultimately, unsuccessful."

"It was certainly out of character."

"It had to be self-defense," Cornelius said. "She must have felt Linus was a danger to her or someone she loved. She was a single parent like me. Her life revolved around her child. She might not have risked retribution from the Assembly to keep her job or stay out of prison, but she would do almost anything to protect her daughter."

"Would you have killed Linus to protect Matilda?"

"Absolutely."

He hadn't even paused.

"The difference is, I wouldn't have gotten caught."

"How would you have done it?"

Cornelius smiled. "Poison would be the cleanest. Did you know that Linus keeps a kitchen towel on the door handle of his icemaker? A large rat or an ermine could grab that towel and use its body weight to open the icemaker. A single rat can easily carry a plastic bag in a pocket of its harness with enough cyanide or any number of other lethal substances to cause death within minutes. The hardest variable to control is making sure the poison is evenly spread over the ice."

"Wow."

Cornelius smiled wider.

"So, are you happy with your current position and compensation? Is there anything I can do on behalf of House Baylor to make you feel more valued?"

The smile vanished. He turned toward me. "Catalina, your family is my family. My sister and brother both feel the same. You, Arabella, and Nevada are the only older sisters Matilda will ever have. You never have to worry that I would harm any of you."

Awww.

I pulled into Linus' driveway. Cornelius' electric BMW waited in front of the garage next to one of our armored Humvees. A guard stood by Linus' front door, one of our Warden people. He held a submachine gun and was doing his best to look as conspicuous as possible. The public at large had no idea what happened to Linus and knowing Linus' ties with the military, his neighbors wouldn't find the presence of an armed guard alarming. But if Arkan was watching—and I was a hundred percent sure he was—we wanted to show that the house was well protected.

"By the way, Matilda told me that she felt the spider," I said.

"Did she?" Cornelius' eyes sparkled.

"Yes. She said the spider was a she, and she was stressed out and scared. Is it possible she is an arachnid mage?"

Cornelius smiled. "It's not that. Animal mages have degrees of power like any other magic discipline. At the very bottom of that power ladder are those who can bond with a single species. Then we start climbing up the hierarchy of zoological classification. Those with Average abilities typically can affect an order like Rodentia or Carnivora. At Significant and Prime levels, most of us are capable of affecting the entire class, meaning there are Primes specializing in Mammals, or Birds, or Reptiles. Those with remarkable power can affect more than one of these classes."

"So, an entire series? Like Amniotes?"

He smiled. "Yes."

Despite Cornelius' best attempts to downplay his power, I had seen him bond with both birds and mammals.

"But arachnids are very far removed from amniotes," I said.

He nodded again, the same quiet smile on his lips.

We would have to go all the way up, to a group that included both mammals and arachnids. "I'm sorry, my knowledge of zoological classification is lacking."

"I suspect Matilda is sensitive to the entire Nephrozoa Clade. Almost all bilateral animals fall into that group. Over a million species. Of course, whether or not she can bond with all of them remains to be seen, but even if she simply feels them, it is already enough. I cannot sense a spider, Catalina."

Cornelius was a reserved man. He wouldn't say anything else, but he didn't have to. If parental pride had a glow, I would've gone blind because he would have lit up like a miniature sun.

The doors of Linus' house opened. Runa emerged and waved me over.

"I think she wants me to talk to them."

"Gus and I will wait for you. It would be best if we travelled home together."

"Thank you," I told him and got out of the car.

Bern met me in Linus' study.

"Hey . . ." I started.

He held up the USB, put it into my hand, and he and Runa walked out and shut the double doors behind them.

Okay.

I sat down and plugged the USB into Linus' desktop. A pair of headphones waited for me, already plugged in. Whatever it was, Bern clearly didn't want it to get out.

I put the headphones on and accessed the storage stick. A single video. I clicked it.

Linus appeared on the screen sitting in the same chair I now sat.

"Hello, Catalina. This is the proverbial Things Have Gone Terribly Wrong video. I've left Bernard a nice trail of bread crumbs so I'm sure it didn't take him long to break the encryption."

My eyes watered, and I paused it. He wasn't dead yet. He was a stubborn, mean old bastard, who wouldn't kick it just because he injected himself with some stupid shit.

Damn it, Linus.

I wiped my eyes and restarted the video. On-screen, Linus raised a heavy cut-crystal glass with two fingers of whiskey in it. He sipped it and smiled. "Liquid courage. Let us get on with it."

Yes, that would be good, because otherwise I would just sit here and cry.

"My name is Linus Stuart Duncan of House Duncan. My mother's name was Fiona Duncan of House Duncan. My father's name was Vassilis

Makris. His father's name was Christos Makris. His birth name was Christos Molpe of House Molpe."

The name fell like a brick and knocked me right out of my chair and to my feet. The headphone cord came out with them and I yanked the headphones off my head and dropped them to the floor.

House Molpe. The only known siren House in existence, now extinct.

Linus was a Molpe.

He was a siren.

Linus was . . .

"Go ahead." Linus lifted his glass. "Pace for a bit. Let the implications percolate. It means exactly what you think it does."

Linus was my grandfather.

Oh my God.

My brain shoved all sorts of facts at me all at once. I circled the desk to the right, reversed, circled it to the left, and finally settled on marching back and forth in front of it, trying to chew through an avalanche of memories.

Back after the battle in the Pit, when I had sung so hard and spent so much magic trying to kill a godlike construct that I couldn't even think, Linus had found me, and he'd coaxed me back to reality. I'd asked him about it later and he told me he'd done some research, and it indicated that when sirens overextended, some of them lost their minds. They could no longer speak, only sing songs of insanity and beguiling magic. If I hadn't spoken, he had a mental Prime on standby to surge into my mind and try to guide me back.

He had "done some research." He probably called whatever close relative he knew on that side.

Wow. Wooow.

Why would a Prime of Linus' standing take such an in-depth interest in a new emerging House, especially one as odd as ours? Even before I became his Deputy, Linus was a constant presence in our lives. He found a way in through Nevada, and soon we were invited to his barbecues and fishing trips. He smoothed the way for Bernard to enter grad school. Leon practically lived in his workshop when Linus was working on new firearms. Problems we encountered sometimes vanished, as if swept away by some unseen force, a helpful watchful presence acting on our behalf behind the scenes.

He was there when we registered as a House. He was one of the two witnesses, with Connor being the other.

A memory came to me, Alessandro and I in Linus' summer mansion, Linus grilling meat for his patented fajitas, Alessandro looking at me, looking at Linus, and then murmuring to himself in Italian, "I'm such an idiot."

He knew! Siren magic leaked, and Alessandro's antistasi powers would've tagged it as a threat.

"Sonovabitch!"

I wasn't even sure which one of them I was cursing at.

I braked hard in front of the desk and leaned onto it, face-to-face with the recorded Linus.

"Fuck you." It felt good to say it out loud.

"You're probably cursing and it's fair. But if you're watching this, the situation is urgent, so let's put that part aside and move forward. I have many vital things to tell you."

I landed back into the chair. Yes. I couldn't wait to hear this. I knew all about House Duncan. It was an old Scottish House with a persistent line of hephaestus Primes. Duncans made weapons of all types and sizes. One time when Linus and I were chased and had to abandon our vehicle and everything inside it, he made a detour to a recycling center and built a gun out of scrap metal and magic. It fired the little tabs you broke off aluminum cans—there was a container of them there—and he'd killed three people with it.

Linus was an orphan. Both his father and his mother had died in a tragic car accident when he was a toddler. That was the official record.

"Angus Duncan, my grandfather, was a stubborn man, set in his ways and convinced he was always right."

You don't say. Shocking.

"He and my mother butted heads. When she was nineteen, they had a row and she left for a holiday in Greece. She met my father, who was twenty-six, handsome, and charming. They had a summer romance, and she became pregnant with me. His family pushed for marriage. My grandfather told her to come home. They had another one of their fights, over the phone this time, and the next week my mother married my father. House Duncan didn't attend the wedding."

Marrying someone because you were pissed off at your parent sounded like a recipe for disaster.

"The bloom was off that rose quickly. My parents were very different people. My mother had goals. She wanted to be someone, to challenge herself, and my father was content to float within the bubble his family had built to safeguard him. Still, two years after I was born, my mother was pregnant again, with a girl. My father's relatives demanded she abort the child."

What?

Linus' expression turned harsh. "During the First World War the region was invaded by the Russian Imperium. Katina Molpe, my father's oldest aunt, rowed her boat to one of those tiny rocky islands the Aegean is famous for, little more than a boulder sticking out of the water, and then she sang to the invading army. An entire battalion drowned trying to reach her, until enough of them managed to swim across the stormy water. You can guess what happened next."

They tore her to pieces.

The love sirens inspired wasn't truly love. It wasn't gentle or selfless. It was a burning obsession and if allowed to linger, it grew into an all-consuming need to possess. If they couldn't have the entire person, they would settle for a piece. A clump of hair. A nail. A finger. Anything would do. Katina died a horrible death to save her town. Nevada had told me this story just before our trials. A cautionary tale about the perils of siren magic.

"All Molpe carry the talent, but only women are Primes," Linus continued. "I'm probably the strongest male siren alive but I'm barely an Average, and I suspect that is only due to the magic reserve I inherited from the Duncan side. I cannot compel people the way you do. The most I can do is to predispose people to like me and to sense when mental mages try to manipulate me."

He must've felt Kaylee building up her power when she and her mother entered his study. The siren magic, however weak, gave him a warning. It was the only reason he was still breathing.

"After the war the Molpe family was hounded by every neighboring government and political faction wanting access to siren powers. A lot of Molpes died. The family had to go into hiding to save themselves. They relocated, changed their name, and made sure no more Primes were born."

Selective breeding, Molpe style. Only male children were allowed to live.

"My mother refused to give up my unborn sister. She was a hephaestus Prime, and nobody would be taking her future baby away from her. She barricaded herself in a house and called my grandfather to come and get her. He and my uncles got there one day late. My father somehow got my mother to let him in and shot her in the head."

If you want us to survive, kill your wife and your unborn daughter. Do it to save the family. It was no longer shocking to me. I had seen worse. Fear made people do terrible things. But it bothered me so much. This was my family. I came from this.

"There was a massacre," Linus said. "The Duncans retrieved me and my mother's body and returned to Scotland. They had a funeral for my mother. The official report said she died during an automobile accident while on a holiday in Greece and her husband's body was lost at sea. It was a dark time. I don't remember any of it or my parents. My first memory is getting to ride a pony by the castle walls."

I knew that his grandfather had raised him, but I had no idea how deep the wound was.

On-screen Linus leaned forward, his expression grave. "The Makris family is not to be trusted. If they ever approach you, kill as many as you must to break yourself free. They fear you because they think your existence will drag their sordid history to light. Do not look for them to find answers to your magic, do not approach them, do not correspond with them. They will stop at nothing to murder you if you come into contact with them. Do not open that door."

Wow.

"I know you have questions about your magic. I will tell you every-thing I know. Very shortly you'll be facing a crisis, if you aren't already. You've concentrated on only one aspect of your powers, but your magic is more complex than you realize. The black wings are the first mani-festation of the problem, and it will become worse in times of emotional distress . . ."

A man screamed outside, his voice dropping into a tortured gurgle.

I yanked the USB stick out of the computer, shoved it into my pocket, and ran to the window.

The outline of a twenty-foot-wide arcane circle smoked on the ground. Two corpses slumped inside it, their skin turning green, the trademark sign of Runa's work. In the center of the circle, a pile of reddish flesh steamed. Bones stuck out of it. Human bones. A teleportation mage could teleport themselves, but teleporting another person required com-plex arcane circles and a lot of preparation, and a slight miscalculation or variation in weight could make it backfire.

I dashed across the house to the front door. In the doorway, Runa and Bern were looking at the three corpses. A horrible stench rolled from the circle, like rotten fish being steamed. I had smelled a failed teleportation once before. It wasn't an odor you would ever forget.

". . . question them," Bern said.

"Bernard," Runa said.

She used his full name. He was in trouble.

"If you teleport me into the house of your enemy and give me one second, I'll kill everyone I see. Even if you shot me as soon as you saw me, you would die immediately after. I love you too much to gamble with your life and I'm responsible for the safety of everyone under this roof. I stand by my decision."

"I agree," I told them.

"See? She agrees."

"I also concur," Cornelius said, approaching from the other hallway, Gus trailing him. He must've come inside at some point. "When there is an intruder in your house with a gun, you don't shoot at their feet. You shoot to kill."

Bern sighed.

I leaned past his broad back to look at the circle. The closest green corpse had long dark hair wound around her head in a kind of crown. I knew that hair. Melanie Poirier, one of Arkan's combat mages. If Runa hadn't nuked her immediately, we would have had a hard time neutralizing her.

Arkan risked a teleportation in broad daylight. Why? His hits were usually well planned and carefully executed. This seemed rushed, almost like a knee-jerk reaction to something. What could have upset him enough . . .

It hit me like lightning. I spun around and sprinted back to the study.

"What?" Runa yelled.

I didn't answer.

I got to the study, yanked the keyboard to me, clicked the Warden Network, and typed in my login. Runa, Bern, Cornelius, and Gus ran into the room, followed by one of the Warden guards.

"What's going on?" Runa demanded.

I didn't have time to answer. The network accepted the login. The Warden interface unfolded in front of me. I accessed the databanks.

"Catalina? What happened?" Runa asked.

Ignat Orlov, alias Arkan, known associates. I scrolled through the list.

No . . .

No . . .

Trofim Smirnov.

I clicked the name. The dossier opened. The familiar face stared at me from the screen. A slender, stooped white man in his forties who looked like he was expecting a surprise punch.

Fuck.

I grabbed my phone from my pocket and called Patricia. No answer.

Bern grabbed me by the shoulders and held me still. "Explain."

It took me a second to slow my brain enough to speak. "An hour ago, Prince Berezin showed up at the Compound asking to see me. I told Patricia to let him in. He was wearing this man's face."

Runa glanced at the screen. "Who is he?"

"Trofim Smirnov. He is Arkan's Bernard."

I had studied Arkan's inner circle and I knew most of them by sight. But I had concentrated on combat operatives, people who were a threat if you spotted them in the crowd. Smirnov was a pattern cybermage. He was at his most dangerous behind a keyboard. He had been low priority. I had no idea how many lives my mistake would cost us.

They stared at me. Bern whipped his phone out and began making calls.

"Right now, Arkan thinks that his oldest friend betrayed him and defected to the Wardens, and we have him in our house. Smirnov knows too much. Arkan can't let him live. He will retaliate."

Konstantin had set us up. Arkan would stop at nothing to get his hands on Smirnov.

"Our phones are compromised," Bern announced.

"How?" Runa asked.

He shook his head. He looked ready to rip someone apart with his bare hands.

"If Arkan can capture any of us and trade us for Smirnov, it would solve all his problems," I said. "Everyone outside the Compound is a potential hostage or casualty."

"Shit," Runa said. "We can't stay here."

Runa was dangerous as hell, but all of the automated defenses were down, and none of the guards were above Average on the magic scale. If Arkan sent several heavy hitters and they attacked from different sides, there would be casualties.

We had to go. Now.

Bern turned to the Warden guard. "Get your people packed. Five minutes."

I dialed Alessandro.

The guard looked at me. They answered only to the Office of the Warden.

"Do as he says," I told him.

The guard double-timed it out of the room.

"Your call has been forwarded . . ."

Bern gently pushed me out of the way and bent over the desktop. His fingers flew over the keyboard. "Baby, I need the two laptops from the vault."

Runa turned around and ran down the stairs.

I tried Alessandro again. Straight to voice mail. Text was my only option.

Konstantin put on Smirnov's face and walked into our house.

Nothing else needed to be said. He would understand. I texted Leon, trying to explain the same thing as fast as I could.

Cornelius shook his head. "My phone is affected as well."

The computer screen blinked, and Bug appeared on-screen. Connor's surveillance specialist, lean, wiry, pale, and looking like he was taking care of ten things at once. "What do you want, weirdo?"

"Arkan hacked us," Bern said. "Phones are down, network is down, we need to warn the Compound an attack is coming."

The distracted expression evaporated from Bug's face. "On it."

Bern shut down the call, opened a new window, and started typing code.

Runa emerged from the vault carrying two laptops, Linus' black one and Bern's silver. Bern waved her on and she took off out the door.

I finished the text to Leon. I had no idea if it would even make it through. "Can you get the security system online?"

"I can trigger an emergency override, which is what I'm doing." Bern's gaze was fixed on the screen.

"What does that mean?"

"It means the vault will lock and the siege protocol will be reinstated without exceptions. We'll have three minutes to get out. If you need anything, grab it now, because nobody is getting back in. If Linus dies, we'll have to fight our way inside."

He was right. It was our best option.

A phone rang somewhere in the room. Bern and I froze for a desperate second, trying to pinpoint it.

Another muffled ring.

Inside the desk.

Bern jerked open the middle drawer. Locked. Bern grit his teeth and yanked it. Wood snapped, the drawer came free, and I grabbed the cell phone. Unlocked. I answered the call.

"Catalina!" Arabella yelled into my ear.

"How are you calling me? Whose phone is it?"

"I'm calling from a burner Connor's people brought. That phone is my emergency phone."

"Why do you have an emergency phone at Linus' house?"

"He bought it for me to use when I come over because my phone is always dead."

Of course he had.

"Anyway, not important. Mom is out."

"What?"

"She left to identify Pete's body. She took a security detail with her, three guards. We can't reach them."

"Why did she go in person?"

"Pete's son is there. Someone had to go and explain why Pete died."

Crap. Pete had been taken to a private morgue at the Woman's Hospital of Texas. Twenty-five minutes from us.

"I'll get her."

An electric crackle split the air on the other end.

"Got to go," my sister said and hung up.

I shoved the phone into my pocket.

Bern yanked the cords out of the back of the tower and picked it up.

The three of us took off for the front door. The security team was piling into an armored personnel carrier. Jean, the tall olive-skinned woman in charge, looked at me from the front passenger seat, her window down, waiting for instructions.

The use of Warden guards was strictly limited. Guarding the family of Wardens wasn't covered by their duties, so telling them to escort Bern and Runa was right out. Technically they would guard me if I ordered them to as long as I was performing an official investigation but going to get my mother wasn't a Warden matter, it was a Baylor matter.

"Go back to base and fortify," I told her.

"Yes, Acting Warden."

The last person climbed into the Warden vehicle and banged on the side. The carrier rolled out. Linus' people had a base outside of Houston. Its location was well hidden and the base itself enjoyed the full benefit of the best defensive weaponry Duncan Arms could provide. If Arkan went after them, he would regret it.

He wouldn't go after them. Why would he when what he wanted was inside the Compound.

Bern loaded the computer tower into the Humvee and got behind the wheel. The Humvee rolled up to me, windows down. "Do you need us to come with you?" Runa asked.

"No. I need you to go home and get our phones back online. Alessandro and Leon are out there, and they are deaf and mute." And Bern was the only one who could fix it.

"I'll take care of it," Bern promised.

The Humvee took off.

I ran up to Rhino and jumped into the driver's seat. Cornelius was already in the passenger seat, holding a tactical shotgun. Gus panted in the back. I reversed, peeled out of the driveway, and stopped just outside the gate.

Seconds ticked off. One, two . . . Ten . . .

The gate clanged shut. Turrets spiraled out of the ground, sparking with residual magic. A low buzz rolled through the street. The system was hot. From now on Linus' mansion would be off-limits.

Cornelius' silver BMW waited parked ten yards ahead. He must've moved it.

"Do you want me to drop you off at your car?" I asked.

"No. We'd like to ride home with you. Safety in numbers. I'll pick up my car later."

Gus made a small *woof* in agreement.

I could use all of the backup I could get. "Thank you."

I drove down the street, rolling over the speed bumps, pulled a U-turn and sped toward the Buffalo Speedway.

The Buffalo Speedway was crowded. The traffic was steady but moving at a decent speed.

"I paired the phone to the car. Your mother's phone was already in contacts under Mom," Cornelius reported.

"Call Mom."

The car's audio system obediently dialed. Ring. Ring. Ring.

"Your call has been forwarded . . ."

"Mom, I'm coming to get you. Call me."

A sign flashed.

CAUTION
CONSTRUCTION AHEAD

The car in front of me put on its brakes. The caravan of vehicles compacted, slowing down.

"Call Mom."

Ring. Ring. Ring.

LEFT LANE
CLOSED
500 FEET

"Your call has been forwarded . . ."

"Your mother is very capable," Cornelius said.

"Yes."

My mother was also a high-value target. If Arkan's crew got to her, I would give them anything they wanted to get her back.

"Could you please look up the number for Margolis Autopsy Lab at the Woman's Hospital and try that?"

"Of course." Cornelius fiddled with the phone. "Here it is."

He put the phone on speaker. Ring . . . Ring . . . *You have reached the Margolis . . .*

I waited until the tone. "This message is for Penelope Baylor. Please call me immediately." I left my new phone number and Cornelius hung up.

The traffic funneled into a single lane. We crawled past the left lane blocked off with cones and white pickup trucks.

"Of course there is construction," I said. My voice was so calm, it was almost robotic.

"Different cities are famous for different things," Cornelius said. "San Antonio is known for the River Walk and the Alamo. Austin is famous or infamous for 6th Street with its bars and shootings. We have construction and floods."

The lane narrowed, hemmed in by concrete barriers on the right. I steered Rhino with laser precision, caught between the nonexistent shoulder and the row of traffic cones.

"Catalina," Cornelius said quietly. "Your hands have gone white."

"Thank you." I eased my grip on the wheel.

"You are exceptionally calm," he observed.

"Alessandro got into a car with a man who is supposedly working for Lenora Jordan but could've been an illusion mage, because the Harris DA evidently has an emergency with strikingly convenient timing. Leon was supposed to shadow the FBI, but I didn't see any sign of him at the Cabera mansion. My mother is outside of the Compound, and none of them are answering their phones. The Compound is under attack. I can't afford anything but calm right now."

"They separated us and are hitting us one by one?" Cornelius guessed.

"That's how I would do it."

"I'll try Alessandro and Leon again." He tapped the phone.

We passed Richmond Avenue.

"No response," Cornelius reported.

If I thought about it for too long, I'd panic.

The phone lit up. An incoming call. "Accept!"

"Catalina?" Mom asked.

Finally. "Where are you?"

"I am in an office in Dr. Amandi's lab." Her voice was eerily calm. My mother had gone into that serene place she always visited just before she lined up a shot through her scope.

"Where are your guards?"

"Tyler called from the airport. His car didn't show up."

Tyler was Pete's son.

"I sent the guys to pick him up. That was an hour ago. They're not answering their phones and I can't reach the house. My phone isn't working. I am using their landline. There is an armored vehicle in the parking lot. They've been sitting there for ten minutes, and nobody has gotten out."

They'd found her.

"It's Xavier." Xavier wouldn't have passed up a chance to catch my mother. He would come in person and probably not alone. "Arkan is attacking us. Our phones are compromised."

"Ah. That explains things."

My voice was flat and calm. "Xavier will wait for you to come out, but he's impatient. He will come into the lab to get you."

"Staying put isn't an option."

"No."

I crunched through our options. The Woman's Hospital had a large campus, sprawling between Greenbriar and Fannin Street and cut off by Old Spanish Trail in the north. I was still at least fifteen minutes away. Even if she hid in the building, they would find her. And if I pulled into that parking lot, Xavier would hurl the nearest lamppost through my windshield. I had to get Mom and get out alive.

What was around the Woman's Hospital? On the east side of Fannin, it was all medical buildings. On the west side, across Greenbriar, there was . . . Yes. That would work.

"Mom, can you cross to a different building without exiting into the parking lot?"

"Hold on." I heard a door open. My mother said something. A male voice answered.

She came back on the line. "Yes."

"I need you to get away from that building and cross Greenbriar to the Office of Records. Big building shaped like a quill. Go in there and tell them that I'm coming to set up an appointment and that you are waiting for me. Don't leave the building no matter what happens. They won't help you if you step one foot outside, but they will defend the building and they won't allow anyone to take you out of there."

The Office of Records kept the database of the Houses and magic users. It was a neutral institution, incorruptible and independent of all other powers in Texas, magic and civilian. It was stewarded by the Keeper of Records, whom I'd met only once and had hoped to never meet again. Nobody in their right mind would attack the Office of Records. Xavier wasn't in his right mind, and if we were very lucky, he'd try.

Mom spoke to someone. "Okay. On my way."

The call ended.

She would have to walk south through the medical complex and then cross Greenbriar out of the view of the parking lot, and then cross another large parking lot in front of the Office of Records. Her top speed was about five miles per hour. I wanted to step on the gas and knock the cars in front of me out of the way, so I could drive faster. Instead, I carefully steered Rhino out of the construction zone and veered through traffic, fighting for every second.

The short tower of black glass thrust from the middle of a giant lot, its lines elegant and flowing, a perfect imitation of a feathered quill. The dark building of the Arena of Trials loomed ominously behind it.

I hadn't spoken to Mom since I'd called her. Her cell phone was about as useful as a brick. I had no idea if she'd made it.

Please be there.

"Do we go in together or do you want to take the car?" I asked Cornelius.

"Together," he said. "We're more vulnerable on our own."

"Agreed."

I had given him an out, and he'd refused to take it. I'd expected as much.

I pulled into the center row, as close as I could get to the entrance, but all of the front parking spots were taken, and we had a lot of distance to cover on foot. Driving up to the doors was out of the question. The Office of Records maintained a clear kill zone around their tower and driving into it immediately made you a target.

Cornelius handed me a DA Rattler, a compact submachine gun, one of Linus' special editions. He picked up a tactical shotgun, and we exited the vehicle.

Fifty yards to the building. The space between my shoulder blades vibrated with tension. I strained so hard to listen for a marlin spike whistling through the air, I almost heard it in my head.

The doors slid open in front of us. Cornelius, Gus, and I entered the cavernous lobby, and I quietly exhaled. It looked just as I remembered: black granite walls, grey granite floor with a shimmering gold inlay of a magic circle in the center, and a black granite desk to the right with a lone guard behind it. But no Mom.

Ice rolled down my spine.

The guard, a middle-aged blond woman, saw us, rose, and bowed her head. "Greetings, Prime Baylor and Significant Harrison. Please deposit your weapons on the counter. Your party is waiting in the Keeper's office, fifth floor."

She'd made it. *Phew.*

Why hadn't she stayed in the lobby?

Cornelius and I put our firearms on the counter. Cornelius nodded at Gus. "Wait."

The Doberman lay down on the floor and watched us board the elevator.

The lights above the door flickered, counting off the floors. My heart was beating too hard.

The doors slid open, and we walked into a long hallway with rows of doors branching off to both sides. At the very end, the heavy black double doors stood wide open. I made a beeline for that doorway as fast as I could without breaking into a run.

We walked into a massive round room lined from floor to ceiling with bookshelves that were crammed to capacity. A round counter guarded the entrance. A small lamp glowed on it with a warm yellow light. Behind the counter several comfortable leather couches occupied the center of the room, illuminated by a chandelier. The Keeper of Records sat on the couch to the left. Across from him, sipping tea from a small blue cup, sat my mother.

A crushing weight dropped off my shoulders and hit the floor. If it had mass, it would have broken through the wood and kept falling until it landed in the lobby.

The Keeper of Records turned to me. He was of average height, slim, and old. Time had wrinkled his brown skin, carving a road map of years around his eyes and mouth, and turned his hair white. He wore a brown three-piece suit with a copper-and-black bow tie. His expression was always welcoming, but his eyes, guarded by large glasses, stopped you in your tracks. So dark, they appeared black, they sparkled like two pieces of polished black jade.

"Prime Baylor," the Keeper said, "it's been so long. What a pleasure to see you again."

Mom looked at me. Her eyes were wide.

"Good afternoon, Keeper. Thank you for keeping my mother company. We are so sorry to trouble you."

The Keeper smiled. His teeth were white and sharp. "It's not a bother. We're always happy to visit with House Baylor, aren't we, Michael?"

Michael emerged from the shadows. He didn't stride out, he congealed, like some mythical wraith coalescing from darkness. It was probably my imagination, and he must have walked out of some niche between the bookshelves, but one moment it was just the four of us, and then suddenly there were five.

Michael nodded. In his mid-twenties, he wore a black suit with a white shirt that set off his bronze skin. His hair was black and cut short with just enough length on top to keep it from being a buzz cut. Black and grey tribal tattoos swirled over the exposed skin of his hands and neck. His face was handsome, with what people called "good bones," and his eyes were an odd color, almost yellow when the light caught his irises like the old scotch Linus liked to drink.

The Keeper turned to Cornelius. "It is wonderful to see you again, Significant Harrison."

"The pleasure is all mine," Cornelius said. "It's been a long time since my trials."

"Fifteen years, three months, and fourteen days. Should you wish to revisit your certification, our doors are always open."

Cornelius drew back slightly. "That won't be necessary."

"As you prefer."

Nobody "revisited" certification unless they thought they would test higher and up their rank. I would have to tell Nevada. Like me, she'd been convinced for years that Cornelius deliberately held back at his trials.

The Keeper steepled his fingers on his bended knee. "Now, what can the Office of Records do for House Baylor?"

Going to the Keeper of Records for information hadn't been the plan. The plan had been to grab Mom from the lobby and get the hell out of here, hoping to make it home before we got attacked. But now we were here, and he'd served Mom tea. He'd made an event out of it, and I couldn't just say, "Thanks, got to run."

Perhaps this was an opportunity. The Keeper was the expert on magic bloodlines. I could get a lot of my questions answered. But what would it cost me?

The Office of Records was one of two magic-related institutions that did not fall under my jurisdiction, the Assembly Tribunal being the other. I couldn't compel the Keeper to comply. Anything he told me was strictly voluntary and the more I asked, the higher the cost would be.

Years ago, Nevada had promised the Keeper that she would fulfill an unspecified favor in return for sparing our evil grandmother Victoria. Since I had started my apprenticeship with Evil Grandmother, she'd mentioned this favor at least ten times. Not many things kept Victoria Tremaine up at night, but this one sure did. She stressed again and again that the Office of Records balanced the favor owed by the favor given and sparing her had been a significant favor.

In any case, this was a conversation best had in private.

"I wish to discuss a confidential matter. Is there a place my mother and Significant Harrison could wait?"

"Of course. Michael, please show our guests to the Blue Room."

Michael glided across the floor without making a sound. That man made my hair stand on end.

Mom and Cornelius followed him out.

The Keeper regarded me with a smile. "Tea, Acting Warden?"

And he knew. How? The National Assembly must have notified him out of courtesy. I wondered who else had gotten that memo.

"Yes, thank you."

"Honey, milk, lemon?" the Keeper offered.

"I'll take it plain."

The Keeper nodded.

Michael reappeared with a platter supporting a single extra cup. He set the cup in front of me, poured black tea from a teapot, left the platter on the table, and took three steps back.

I sipped my tea. It was lovely and smelled of vanilla. "Delicious."

"I'm glad it suits your tastes."

This conversation would have to be structured very carefully. I couldn't obligate the Office of the Warden to something it couldn't honor. If the Keeper asked for something in return for the information, I had to be sure we could deliver it. Making an enemy of the Office of Records was not an option.

"I have two requests, one for public information and one requiring discretion. The Office of the Warden would be grateful for any assistance."

The Keeper's eyes shone for a moment, as if lit from within. "The Office of Records always welcomes an opportunity to collect a favor from the Office of the Warden, doesn't it, Michael?"

Michael looked directly at me. Like being sighted through the scope of a rifle.

"Please, make your inquiries," the Keeper invited.

"Has Kaylee Cabera ever undertaken the trials?"

"No."

"Has she undertaken any preliminary tests?"

"Yes."

Now we were in a grey area. The trials took place before witnesses. Their results were public. The nature of one's magic could be sealed, but not the rank. The results of preliminary tests remained private. They were unofficial practice runs that were published only if the family wanted them to be known.

If I asked about her specific rank, the Keeper could tell me, but the cost of that information would be high. I needed to mitigate our obligation.

"Based on those preliminary tests, does the Office of Records expect Kaylee Cabera to be certified as a Prime?"

The Keeper looked wolfish. "It would take a miracle or a crime against humanity."

Administering the Osiris serum without authorization constituted a crime against humanity. He just confirmed my suspicions. Kaylee was born with minor power and her mother had gone to Arkan to make her daughter a Prime. That's why she was untrained. That's why her magic was odd.

I took out my phone, pulled up a picture of Pete's ruined face, and placed the phone on the table. "Does the Office of Records know what type of mage could cause this kind of damage?"

The Keeper glanced at the phone. "I always liked Peter. What a shame. This was done by a mentamalleus."

"A mind hammer?"

The Keeper nodded. "They're more commonly known as false halcyons, which is not strictly accurate. The false halcyons are not a twisted branch growing from the halcyon tree; rather they are two separate trunks growing from the same root."

"How do they differ?"

"Halcyon magic attacks certain areas of the brain," the Keeper said. "Specifically, the amygdala, which assesses environmental threats, and the hypothalamus, which has the power to trigger the production of stress response hormones. Instead of initiating the making of cortisol and adrenaline, which allow us to quickly respond to threats, the affected hypothalamus sends signals for the production of dopamine and oxytocin, causing their target to enter a happy, relaxed stupor. The damage halcyons cause is temporary, and their power is effort-based."

"Meaning they consciously exert an effort to induce calm?"

"Precisely." The Keeper nodded. "The magic of a false halcyon also attacks the amygdala and hypothalamus, but primarily targets the frontal cortex, and instead of triggering hormonal responses, it permanently damages the physical structure of the brain. The attack is performed mentally, but if it succeeds, the damage to the mind is mirrored by the physical trauma to the brain. The results are predictably horrific."

The memory of being struck by Kaylee's magic was still fresh. *Like me. LIKE me.*

"Is it emotion-based?"

The Keeper smiled. "Yes. Very much so. A halcyon is calm and logical. A false halcyon is an unstable creature that throws all of themselves into their attack with the passion of an upset toddler. They commit completely, they are fueled by their emotions, and they cause irreparable damage. Like true halcyons, they can induce a temporary state of euphoria, but at the end of it, their victim loses most of their cognitive abilities."

When I had thought that Kaylee was trying to turn Alessandro into a happy idiot, I'd had no idea how accurate that thought had been.

The Keeper touched my phone gently. "In Peter's case, the dominant emotion was rage or hatred. The primary directive behind it was very simple."

"Die?"

"Yes."

What about Wahl? "What if someone was grazed by a false halcyon attack? Is there any hope of recovery?"

"Yes. Like all magic users, the false halcyons vary in power. If the accidental target was coherent after the attack, the damage is likely slight. It's much like touching a hot stove. The longer one keeps their hand in the fire, the more severe the burn will be."

I let out a breath. Wahl had been coherent. He'd been happy and smiling, but coherent.

"False halcyons are notoriously erratic," the Keeper said. "There are a handful of Houses who still practice that magic, but their members undergo very rigorous mental conditioning from an early age. It's one of the few kinds of magic considered to be undesirable due to the difficulty of controlling it. Most families took steps to breed it out."

So Kaylee awakened as a mind hammer, which Luciana would have hidden at any cost until she could get her daughter some training. The

Caberas were a noncombat House. Kaylee could be seen as either a critical asset or a huge hindrance, depending on how the rest of the relatives took it.

I could now say with 100% certainty that Kaylee had killed Pete and likely attacked Linus. It was almost elegant: first, Luciana would have put everyone at ease with her halcyon powers and then her daughter would've smashed their minds. Except Linus was a siren. His magic had warned him.

I still didn't understand how Kaylee had evaded the turrets. I would figure this out before the end.

Now I knew who and when. I still didn't know why. Did Arkan order them to do it and then tied up loose ends by killing Luciana or was this something else? I would have to figure this out on my own.

There were only a few points left to clarify.

"Hypothetically speaking," I said, "if a family had produced halcyons and only halcyons for over four generations, why would a repeat application of the Osiris serum result in an awakening of a mind hammer?"

The Keeper leaned back. "Michael, the Fata Magum, please."

Michael retrieved a box from a shelf, brought it to the Keeper, and resumed his post three steps away. The Keeper opened the ornate wooden box and took out a small six-sided die, red like crystalized blood. Greek letters were carved into the die and inlaid with ivory, one per side.

The Keeper held it up to the light and the die sparkled. A ruby?

"The fate of the mage." The Keeper showed me one side with the Greek letter Z. "Zeta. Sacrifice."

He turned the die to display a different side. "Beta. Demon."

Another turn. "Lambda. Growth. The three fates awaiting those who risk the serum. Death, distortion, or power."

Those who took the serum died, became warped by it, or gained magic, from which they then acquired wealth and power.

The Keeper held it out to me.

I reached out and he let the die fall into my palm. Six sides, three unique symbols, each occurring twice.

"Make your roll."

I let the cool smooth cube fall from my fingers. The die landed on the table, rolled and stopped. Zeta.

"Death," I said.

"This die was carved in 1865, for the second wave of Osiris recipients," the Keeper said. "Countless would-be mages held it in their hands and rolled it just like you did before making their final decision. A great many of them walked away after making their roll."

The die glinted on the table.

"Why do you think some people died and others didn't?" the Keeper asked.

"Nobody knows. It's magic, not science."

"But if you had to hazard a guess . . ."

I had read a couple of books on Magic Theory, but most of my current reading focused on practical applications. "There are five leading theories, most of them agreeing that the serum kills those without latent magical powers. Various factors have been considered, such as diet, exposure to the flu pandemic, and so on. The records from that time are understandably murky . . ."

The Keeper raised his hand and I fell silent.

"Yes, but you are a Prime, the highest rank of a magic user who has used your power since birth. I want to know what you think."

"I think that in all three cases the Osiris serum does exactly what it was designed to do. It searches for latent abilities and makes them manifest. It's not that those who die aren't capable of magic, it's that it is too powerful or too destructive, and their bodies cannot handle it. It is the same with the warped. The magic twists them because their power is too great to be contained. Perhaps those who survive intact and become mages are not the strongest, but the weakest. Nobody can predict what the die will show."

The Keeper smiled. "Exactly."

I felt like I had just passed a test.

"If we apply your theory to someone who was born without power, despite their bloodline, and chooses to roll the die, what is the serum to do? The subject has the magic of their family but is incompatible with it. So the serum must look for something other than that power, some hidden traces of other talents from other bloodlines gifted to the subject by previous generations. Perhaps these talents are too weak to express themselves, yet the secondary application of the serum helps them rise to the surface."

So, there was a false halcyon talent hiding somewhere in Kaylee's bloodline, too weak to manifest without the boost of Osiris serum. The two types of magic were closely related. It wouldn't be unusual if sometime long ago there was marriage that resulted in an offspring carrying propensity for both. Their family could have gone generations without discovering it.

It made sense. My sisters and I all had the same parents. I carried hereditary traces for both Arabella's and Nevada's powers. Ten generations from now, one of my descendants could manifest as a truthseeker and never know why. That's why genetic databases keeping track of magic bloodlines were doing such a brisk business.

"I like the way you rolled the die," the Keeper said. "You didn't blow on it, you didn't shake it or toss it. You simply let it fall. Rolling that die and truly accepting the consequences is a choice none of us in this room had to make. Our ancestors made it for us and paid a great price for it. We honor their bravery through abiding by the covenants they created. The ban on unauthorized use of the serum is such a covenant. The covenants must be upheld at any cost. Those of us who understand that fact hold our duties sacred. We don't tolerate any interference, do we, Michael?"

"No, we don't," Michael said.

 # Chapter 7

The elevator doors shut, and the cabin carried us down.

"Let's not do that again," Mom murmured.

"Agreed," Cornelius said.

"I thought you'd stay in the lobby," I murmured back.

"I tried. The Keeper came and got me in person."

An audience with the Keeper wasn't difficult to get, but I couldn't think of any occasion where he'd come down and personally invited someone up to his office.

Those of us who understand that fact hold our duties sacred.

Like the Office of Records, the Office of the Warden guarded the current social order. Both institutions had to be incorruptible, because we protected the foundations of our society. As twisted and dysfunctional as it was, it was better than the free-for-all where the strongest ruled without limitations. We'd tried that during the Time of Horrors, and it'd almost ended humanity.

The Keeper saw me as a colleague of sorts, someone who, like him, placed themselves between order and chaos. He treated me and my mother with courtesy. Sadly, courtesy didn't mean assistance. If we were attacked in the parking lot in front of the building, the Keeper and his creepy sidekick wouldn't lift a finger to help us.

We reached the lobby and collected our weapons and Gus. I handed the Rattler to Mom. She checked it, and we walked to the glass entrance together.

It was past eight. The sun was beginning to set, and the world turned dimmer. Twilight dripped into the parking lot. Twenty-foot-tall lamps, four per metal pole, had come on, flooding the parking lot with bright electric light.

"Stay here," I told her. "I'll get the car and pick you up."

I could see the calculation in Mom's eyes. I would make it faster to the protection of the armored car on my own. She would only slow me down and Cornelius and Gus would present extra targets.

"Go," she said. "I'll cover you."

I exited the doors and jogged across the parking lot. Mom and Cornelius stepped out of the lobby, close enough to duck back in, and waited.

The lane stretched in front of me. I kept moving, taking a quick inventory of the other cars. Seven or eight SUVs, several trucks, a few sedans, no doubt some of them armored. A lot of vehicles despite the hour. In the distance, a good hundred yards away from Rhino, someone had parked a food truck painted a ghastly lime green with orange letters promising "flaming tacos." A bad place to leave a food truck. If they didn't move it, it would be gone by morning.

Rhino loomed in front of me. I grabbed the door handle, swung it open, and climbed into the driver's seat. I shut the door, putting B7 ballistic armor between me and the world outside, and braced myself.

Nothing.

I started the engine. It roared, reassuringly steady. I reversed and drove toward the entrance. Mom and Cornelius started toward me.

I pulled up just outside the red line that marked the kill zone around the building. A moment and the doors swung open, and then Mom, Cornelius, and Gus were in the car. I let out a breath I hadn't known I was holding and turned left, into the next row, heading down through a corridor of parked cars toward Stadium Drive. I would only be on it for a minute. Once I made a left onto Old Spanish Trail, I could blend in with traffic.

The taco truck went airborne.

My brain refused to process what my eyes were seeing.

The truck hurtled toward us as if someone had hit it with a giant bat. It was like a movie.

Food truck. Propane. *Fire.*

We were trapped between two rows of cars.

I wrenched the wheel to my left. Rhino plowed into a red Honda. The impact yanked us forward. The taco truck flew past.

"Out!" Mom barked.

We moved. I landed on my side of Rhino. Out of the corner of my eye, I saw the taco truck stop as if it had hit an invisible wall. It turned, spinning on its axis in midair.

I sprinted down the row of cars, ducking behind them as I ran.

The taco truck smashed into Rhino. The world exploded. The blast wave picked me up and tossed me to the right, straight into a white pickup. Thunder punched my ears. My head swam. I spun around, trying to clear the transparent swirls in front of my eyes.

An orange fireball engulfed Rhino. Grandma Frida wasn't going to like that. Not one bit.

My ears stopped ringing.

The truck in front of me slid, pulled out of the way. I dashed left, across the row, ducked behind a black car and kept moving, back toward Rhino and the burning wreck.

It had to be Xavier. His talent relied on sight. He must've been hiding behind the taco truck and now he was digging through the cars, shoving them out of the way trying to find me.

I jumped to my feet, ran back toward the entrance, and ducked behind another white truck. I pressed myself against it, edged toward the row, and peeked around the bed.

At the far end of the row, Xavier stood, his arms raised in a mage pose, elbows bent, palms cradling invisible basketballs. The ground around his feet glowed with white. He had set up an arcane circle. A pair of over-the-ear headphones shielded his ears. He'd come prepared.

Connor with a simple amplification could throw a city bus around like a frisbee. Xavier had less control but almost as much power, and my siren call would do nothing. He wouldn't be able to hear me.

I chanced a second look. Another man stood next to Xavier, tall, lanky, with pale blond hair dripping onto his forehead, identical headphones protecting him from my magic. Dag Gunderson.

How was he here? Where was Alessandro? Was he dead?

A second circle, a deep magenta, ignited at Gunderson's feet. The glow flared, illuminating a wooden crate behind them, and settled into a steady glimmer.

Alessandro couldn't be dead. It would take a lot more than Gunderson to kill him. I grabbed onto that thought and used it like a life preserver to keep myself from being dragged down into panic.

Gunderson thrust his arms forward and strained, as if trying to lift an enormous weight.

My magic spiraled to them. Without my voice, my wings were my next best bet. But mesmerizing with wings alone took time. Xavier would snipe me the moment he saw me. Not to mention that they were too far away, and distance was a factor.

Gunderson snarled, the veins in his neck bulging. The arcane circle slid off the ground, tilted on its side, and hung in the empty air twenty feet above the asphalt like a curtain of magic.

What the hell . . .

Wood cracked. The crate behind Xavier snapped open, and a cloud of projectiles rose in the air.

Oh great, Xavier brought his toys.

I opened my mouth and sang. My magic snaked across the parking lot and wound around their minds, but I had no way in. I sang out, pouring power into my voice.

No effect. It was like trying to grasp a cannonball dipped in oil. It was heavy and slick, and the tendrils of my magic kept sliding off.

The projectiles shot forward, slicing through Gunderson's arcane screen, and turned into glowing magenta sparks. The shower of magic rained onto the cars like an arrow storm launched by an ancient army.

A spark punctured the truck bed next to me. I glimpsed an eight-inch nail coated in a magenta glow and dove to the side. The nail detonated with a shriek. Magic crackled above my head. I glanced back. The truck bed was a mess of twisted metal, like an aluminum can that had exploded from the inside out. All around me holes gaped in cars. Metal debris littered the parking lot.

Moving cars back and forth trying to find us would have taken too much juice. Instead, they would turn them into shrapnel bombs.

I pushed harder with my power, straining with everything I had. The shoots of my magic had wrapped so tightly around both Gunderson and Xavier that I could barely see their glow in my mind. It did nothing. I had no way in.

I'd never felt so useless.

A sad sound rose to the sky behind me, a song without words sung by a beautiful male voice. It reached into my chest, took my heart in its fist, and squeezed. The world went white in a daze. I choked on empty air.

Cornelius was singing. Oh dear God.

The song reached its crescendo and died.

My magic was still wrapped around the two attackers. I sank into it, pushing as hard as I could. The world faded, its sounds dulling, as all of my energy went into invading the two minds.

A second barrage of nails tore into the cars. Magic crackled all around me, magenta lightning dancing over the trucks and SUVs. Explosions popped like crazy firecrackers. Something hot smashed into my head, and a chunk of a side-view mirror rolled off me to the ground.

I barely noticed. My magic vines pulsed and pulsed, without any way in. If I didn't succeed, we'd die in this parking lot.

Third barrage. Something stung my legs.

I had to do something, or we wouldn't make it out of here alive. I had to chance the wings.

I hauled myself forward and looked around the rear tire. Xavier was aiming another set of nails at Gunderson's screen.

The rapid staccato of the Rattler split the night. Mom returning fire.

Gunderson jerked and stumbled to the right, clutching his shoulder. The arcane screen melted into the air.

I squeezed their minds with everything I had. I never wished for Tremaine powers, but right now I'd trade ten years of my life for just one burst of my grandmother's brain cracking magic.

Xavier bared his teeth. The vehicles in front of him slid, knocked back like Matchbox cars kicked by an angry child. A huge Tahoe at the opposite end of the row screeched and rolled to the right. Mom jumped to her feet, firing. A flaming tire shot across the lot and smashed into her. Mom flew back and crashed into a blue SUV.

Mom!

I dropped my hold on their minds, and the world reeled, my mind unable to adjust.

My mother was right there, in the open, against the car. Spikes hammered into the metal around her. She screamed, a short guttural sound.

I dashed into the open.

A cloud of bats dropped from the sky swarming between us and Xavier. Magic sputtered and nails sank into the swarm. Little furry bodies dropped to the ground.

I sprinted to Mom. She sagged against the SUV and grunted. I slid on broken glass, caught myself on a car, and landed by her. "We've got to move . . ."

A two-foot spike protruded from Mom's right thigh, pinning her to the SUV. Blood drenched her leg, soaking through her jeans. Her hands were red.

I gripped the spike and pulled. It didn't move.

"Leave me," Mom snarled.

My hands slid on my mother's blood. I grabbed my shirt, wrapped it around the spike, and pulled with everything I had.

"I said leave!"

Cornelius charged around the car. He saw the spike.

"I can't!" I told him.

He tossed the shotgun to me and gripped the spike. The muscles on his forearms bulged. Mom gasped, sucking in air.

The swarm of bats had thinned and through the gaps, I saw the glow of another magenta circle sliding upright.

Cornelius planted his foot onto the car and pulled, his back swelling, the muscles in his neck cording.

"Leave me! Go!"

Cornelius growled like an animal. Gus dashed next to me and bared his teeth.

I had a shotgun and a dog. We were too far to do any damage. The moment Xavier saw Mom, she would die, and Cornelius would die with her.

Magenta magic crackled.

The bat swarm scattered. Xavier grinned in the glow of his circle, Gunderson next to him, gripping his arm with a bloody hand. His face was a mask of pain. A car hung suspended in midair above them, poised to fly through Gunderson's magic screen.

It would land on top of Mom and Cornelius, and it would explode like a bomb. They would die. In an instant, I saw my mom's lifeless body fall to the ground, Cornelius crumpled next to her, his blue eyes glassy and blind.

No. No!

I lunged into the row. Xavier saw me, his grin turning brighter.

All of my frustration and fear exploded inside me, burning into fury. Black wings burst from my back, their edges burning with red and I screeched. It wasn't a song. It wasn't a scream. It was a screech, a terrible, awful shriek that cut like broken glass. Magic tore out of me in a dark torrent, guided by my voice like a laser and smashed into the two men. The circle around Xavier went out like a candle snuffed out by a hurricane. Gunderson's eyes rolled back into his head. He dropped to his knees, tears streaming down his face. The magenta screen vanished.

Xavier stumbled back, his face bloodless, and cried out. The car in midair wobbled, dancing back and forth.

The circle around Xavier reignited. It had protected him against most of my shriek. He stumbled inside it and straightened slowly.

The tower of the Office of Records was right behind me.

Xavier was a coward, and nothing scared him more than me gripping his mind.

A surprised telekinetic throws in a catenary curve.

I sucked in a deep breath and spread my wings, my black feathers erect, their tips glowing with red like hellish coals. I thrust my arm at him and opened my mouth.

Look at me! I'm about to scream again. Look!

Xavier howled. The car dipped, swooped down, and flew at me at an insane speed. He'd swatted at me like I was a flying cockroach about to land on his face. He'd barely even aimed, and the car was coming way too fast and way too high.

I dropped to the ground. It hurtled over my head, across the parking lot, swooping up in an arc, and smashed into the Keeper's tower, three stories up. Dark glass exploded. The car vanished into the building, leaving a ragged black hole.

Thank you, Connor.

Darkness boiled out of the hole, like the tentacles of some great nightmarish beast. Michael emerged from its center and halted at the edge of the gap. Blue lightning, too dark to be natural, forked behind him.

Xavier took a step back. Gunderson remained on his knees, oblivious. The glow of his mind was gone, its light diffused.

The darkness splayed out of the hole, streaking across the parking lot in black twisting currents. The streetlamps flickered and went out one by one.

The currents surged above us, and I felt their magic. It was horrible and ravenous. It *wanted*, it *needed*, it sought its prey. Gus whined next to me, cringing. I wrapped my arms around the dog, trying to shield him. If the darkness wanted us, it would take us. There was nothing I could do against it. I couldn't even begin to fathom how to fight it.

Michael stared at Xavier. The currents twisted toward the telekinetic.

The circle around Xavier died. He spun and sprinted away, running for his life.

The currents bit at Gunderson like striking snakes. He made no move to evade. There wasn't enough left of him to recognize the danger. They whipped around him and streaked upward.

A man-shaped sculpture made of grey dust knelt where Gunderson used to be. It collapsed and scattered into nothing.

The darkness turned toward Xavier. He was almost to the end of the parking lot. The currents shot toward him, pursuing him like a living thing, indifferent and hungry.

Xavier jumped onto a motorcycle at the edge of the parking lot.

The darkness was almost to him. The last set of lamps died.

The engine roared, and Xavier tore out of the parking lot at a reckless speed.

The darkness swirled at the edge of the lot, impacting into an invisible boundary, and streaked back to the building, withdrawn as if sucked back in. It churned around Michael and slipped behind him.

Michael looked at me. The power in his stare gripped me. I didn't know if it was a warning, irritation, or a "you're welcome." I just couldn't move.

He turned around and disappeared back into the building.

I sat in a small private waiting room just inside the ER. Gus lay by my feet. Cornelius had taken a chunk of shrapnel in his back while he was pulling the spike out, and the ER personnel adamantly refused to allow the Doberman into the room with him.

As soon as Michael had left, we pulled the spike out. Cornelius picked up my mother, and we hurried across the street to the Woman's Hospital. They took Mom first, then Cornelius a few seconds later. I called home from Arabella's emergency cell phone. The call connected and I gave them a thirty-second summary. That was all I had time for because the medical staff grabbed me and nearly dragged me into the room in the back. I didn't even get to ask about Alessandro.

At some point during the fight, broken glass had punctured my legs. My pants hung in shreds and my legs had been drenched with blood. A few fractions of an inch deeper or to the side, and I would have bled out in that parking lot. I lay there as they cleaned and irrigated my wounds and prayed that Alessandro had survived.

I couldn't lose him. I just . . .

I had this fear. It lived deep inside me like a small animal with sharp claws that had burrowed into my soul ever since I saw the recording of Arkan killing Alessandro's father. I had been afraid before, I'd been anxious before, but this fear was a whole new beast. Whenever Arkan's name was mentioned, it woke up from its hibernation and scraped me with its sharp hot claws.

Once they removed the glass and patched me up, I left the room in my hospital gown and underwear. I couldn't stay in there. The walls were closing in. The brief brush of Michael's magic kept reverberating through me, as if I had been stained by it, and that stain was now slowly fading. I needed to be somewhere in the open, where I could see people, so I'd come back to the private waiting room and found it empty except for Gus.

We'd almost died. Xavier could have killed us. Mom was hurt. Cornelius was hurt. It was a miracle that all three of us survived. A ghostly echo of Michael's magic swirled around me. I hugged myself, trying to banish it. I was at my limit, and I'd been gripping all my emotions in a tight fist of my will for so long, they were choking me.

Gus rose to his feet and put his head on my thigh. I looked into his brown eyes and almost cried.

Not yet. We weren't safe yet.

The door swung open, and Alessandro marched into the room. His expression was terrible. He looked like he would murder anyone who got in his way and not even notice.

I hugged Gus. If this was an illusion mage, Gus would know.

Alessandro saw me and stopped.

Our eyes met. There were so many things in his eyes: fear, fury, relief, and love. Not an imposter. Alessandro. My Alessandro.

He cleared the distance between us in half a second, dropped by me, and gripped my shoulders. "How bad are you hurt?"

I put my arms around him and stuck my face into the bend of his neck. His skin felt scalding. I was a Prime and the Head of a House. I should have maintained composure, but I had nothing left.

He hugged me to him, his arms strong, but his hold careful.

"Catalina, talk to me."

I couldn't. I didn't have the words to explain it. I'd thought he'd died. I almost saw my mom die. I had felt everything, Xavier's volatile power, driven by pure hatred; Gunderson's deranged glee; Cornelius' desperate song that made me want to throw myself on the ground and cry until my eyes ran dry; and, worst of all, Michael's indescribable darkness that still clung to me.

He kissed me, his lips hot on mine, and pulled me closer. "I've got you. You're safe now. *Sono qui con te*, I'm here . . ."

I squeezed myself against him and held on.

"It's okay," he murmured. "It's okay, love, it's okay . . ."

My mouth finally worked. "I thought you were dead. I thought Gunderson and Xavier killed you."

"Not in a million years. I won't leave you. I'll never leave you."

The fear clawed me.

"It's okay. I'm here . . ."

"We need to go home. We all need to go home."

"We will, *angelo mio*."

My mind finally started, like a rusted water mill forced to turn by the current. "Konstantin set us up."

"I know."

"There is a mess in front of the Office of Records."

"Leon is handling it."

"Mom's security detail . . ."

"We found them. They are alive and being treated."

He kissed me again and cradled me in his arms until Cornelius returned and the nurses wheeled my mother out in a chair.

# Chapter 8

Alessandro had brought the Vault Bus.

From the outside, the massive vehicle resembled a heavily armored truck, but inside, instead of cargo space, the bus featured two rows of seats along the walls, each with an individual harness. It could seat twenty-five, if you counted the four seats in the cab. It also weighed upward of forty thousand pounds, about the same as a fully loaded sixty-foot bus. Even Connor would need an amplification circle to lift it off the road.

As soon as Mom was done, Alessandro and our guards loaded us into the Bus, and we were off.

I rode with Alessandro in the cab while one of our guards drove.

The night outside of our windows was so dark. Deep and stifling despite the streetlights and the glow of storefronts and windows.

Alessandro took my hand. I held on to him. We rode in silence for a long time.

"Talk to me," he said finally.

"It's my fault."

He raised his eyebrows.

"I should have told you about Konstantin as soon as it happened." He would have known instantly whose skin Konstantin was wearing and would have anticipated the shitstorm that would follow. "Failing that, I should have identified his disguise. I'm supposed to be smarter than this."

"You were in the middle of an interrogation with an unstable mental mage. I, on the other hand, abandoned you and left to run a political errand. Had I stayed, the outcome of tonight would've been much different."

"What happened with that?"

He shook his head. "We went to the school. Gunderson had mysteriously disappeared, then reappeared by a post office. We went there. He was gone again. Then came a sighting half a mile away. Again, we were too late. I checked the surveillance footage at the post office. The camera should have caught him according to eyewitnesses, but it didn't. I realized I've been chasing an illusion mage, and not a very powerful one at that."

A Prime would have shown up on the security footage as the person he was mimicking, but a lower-level mage didn't have enough juice.

"I tried to call you and got voice mail. Then I tried the Compound, and the call wouldn't go through. I borrowed Matt's phone and called the Compound again. No answer. I called Linus' house, then Bern . . ." He shrugged. "Finally, the light dawned. I shut off the phone and went home. I was pulling into the driveway when you called from the ER."

"Arkan got to Gunderson?" I guessed.

"Most likely. Nothing in our background on either Gunderson or Arkan shows a link between the two. Arkan saw an opportunity, and Xavier must've taken it for him. The way Gunderson got out of the lockup suggests a telekinetic interfered."

"Did Bern restore the phones?"

"Partially. He got the Compound landline working. He was still working on the system when I left. Leon got home about the same time I did. The FBI agents were hit on their way from Cabera's house to their office."

Damn it. "Is he hurt?"

"He says he isn't."

Knowing Leon, that meant nothing. His arm could be cut off and he would tell you he was "fine."

"Are Wahl and Garcia okay?"

"They are alive, but according to Leon, 'not happy.'"

Ugh. "Why go after the FBI?"

Alessandro gave me a dark look. "He's trying to cut off access to Smirnov."

"He isn't sure if the FBI knows anything, so he tried to kill them just in case?"

"That would be my guess."

"They're federal agents. He doesn't strike me as a stupid man."

"Smirnov must know something. Something so big that Arkan is desperate to keep it quiet."

I looked at him. "What could it be?"

"It concerns Konstantin. I'm following a trail of bread crumbs." He faced me. "Catalina, I promise you I will find out."

"I know."

I leaned back in my seat. We'd gotten hit on every front. The buck stopped with me.

"Blaming yourself is the easiest thing," Alessandro said. "Coming up with a plan is much harder."

I knew he wasn't telepathic, but sometimes I had my doubts.

"I got complacent."

"We. We got complacent. Do you understand how cybersecurity works? Could you write code to deal with a network security breach?"

"No."

"That's Bern's job. A job he is very good at. I had an even simpler job, one job, to protect the Acting Warden. I left that job because I judged that doing a favor for Lenora Jordan was in our House's best interest. You can't micromanage everyone. You must delegate. You have done that. All of us knew what we had to do. We got outclassed."

"Not for long." I gritted my teeth. Magic stirred inside me. Normally it was like a clear geyser bubbling up to the surface any time I lifted the lid. This time it felt different. Vengeful. Vicious.

He leaned over, brushed a tear off my cheek, took my hand, and kissed it.

"I'm not sad," I told him.

"I know. You're crying because you're angry."

I leaned against him. "Are you angry?"

Orange sparks flared in his eyes. He wrapped his arm around my shoulders and squeezed me to him. His magic wound around us, violent and charged with power. It didn't feel like anger. It felt like wrath.

"Very," he said.

I laid my head on his shoulder. "Good. Let's be angry together."

The hill around the Compound was pitted with large holes, as if someone had tossed a handful of grenades about. A crushed metal wreck that might have once been a vehicle smoked slightly on one side of the road. On the other side, three other wrecks, crumpled and smashed like discarded Coke cans, formed a modern art installation dedicated to House warfare—one on its side, one upside down, and a third torn in half.

Arabella must've been furious. There was plenty of that to go around lately.

Patricia met us at the main house, flanked by a medical team and my younger sister. The moment the Bus doors slid open Arabella bounded inside.

"Mom!"

"I'm fine," Mom answered. "It's minor. Don't freak out."

"You smell like blood and smoke!"

I turned to Patricia. "Casualties?"

"None on our side." She turned and pointed to the left.

A row of bodies lay on the ground, sealed in body bags. One, two . . . Nine. An enormous metal club, covered with dark stains, rested next to them. Connor had given it to Arabella for her eighteenth birthday. That explained the ruined vehicles. Good. I was afraid she might have stomped on them. The last time she went on a stomping spree, she cut her monster foot, and after she reverted to human form, we had a devil of a time making her get the tetanus shot.

"Arkan deployed a pyrokinetic and a psionic, backed by a few professional killers," Patricia reported. "Your sister informed me that she would handle it. She did."

It would have taken a better psionic than anyone Arkan had to panic Arabella. When she raged out, there was no room in her for anything except fury. Trying to induce fear would have just pissed her off more.

Alessandro finished helping my mom out of the Bus and handed her off to the medical team. His phone rang.

His face snapped into a harsh mask. He took the call and walked away. Italian again, too low for me to hear clearly.

The dead bodies lay in a neat row, like matchsticks in a box.

"What about the three guards who went out with my mother?" I asked.

Patricia's face was a professional mask. "An SUV rammed into them on Sam Houston Tollway at ninety miles per hour. The vehicle rolled. The first responders had to use the jaws of life to get them out. Katrina is fine, except for the concussion. Mohan has a broken leg, but Lex is in the ICU in critical condition."

Lex, tall, funny guy with an easy smile and a sprinkling of freckles on his broad face. He had gotten married six months ago. His wife was pregnant.

Nausea came, sudden and overwhelming. I felt so ill.

My sister had to kill nine people today. My mother had a hole in her leg. Cornelius had needed eighteen stitches and I was bandaged like a mummy. I had no idea how injured Leon was. Lex was in the ICU clinging to life. Both the Office of Records and the Harris County DA were involved in this mess, not to mention the FBI, which "was not happy." I knew exactly whom to blame for all of it. Anger wrapped around my head like a vise and squeezed.

"Where is he?" I asked through clenched teeth.

"In the armory."

I turned and marched back the way we'd come, heading to the wall, and left, to the squat building that served as our armory. Patricia tried to keep up with me. Her legs were longer, but I was younger and a lot madder.

"Prime Sagredo was extremely specific that no harm can come to the Prince."

"I won't kill him. He'll just wish he was dead."

"Catalina . . ."

I pushed the armory door open and barreled inside. The armory was a bunker, a rectangular concrete box of a building bathed in harsh electric light. Metal cages lined the walls in neat rows. Most held weapons. One held Konstantin. There were no guards. Patricia had locked him in and watched him remotely.

He looked the way he'd looked when I first met him in Linus' house: blond, blue-eyed, breathtaking. A picture of urbane elegance with sunlit charm.

I stormed toward the cage. My magic whipped inside me, bucking and straining to break free.

Konstantin gazed at me from inside the cage, a small smile on his lips. "I tried to warn you."

My anger was threatening what little restraints I had left. He was a threat. People I loved were hurt because of him. I had to kill him now, so nobody else would get hurt.

"I never wanted any of this to happen."

"Bullshit. This is exactly what you wanted to happen. You set us up. You made Arkan think that his best friend betrayed him and asked us for asylum. You knew Arkan would retaliate. You ensured that he and the Office of the Warden would collide."

My voice was rising. Magic vibrated in it. I hadn't aimed it at Konstantin, not yet, but I was so angry. Somewhere deep inside a voice warned me that this wasn't me, but the flood of magic inside me drowned it.

"You started a war, which my House will have to fight. You made us bleed."

"You left me no choice."

"Oh, that's good. I'll remember that phrase for when your family comes looking for you."

Patricia stepped forward. "Catalina . . ."

Black wings tore out of my back, the tips of my feathers bright red. I hissed at her. Patricia stumbled back and jerked the phone to her ear. "We need you in the armory! Right now!"

I turned toward Konstantin. He stared at me, open-mouthed. Alarm flickered in his eyes.

"Now, your Royal Highness . . ." My voice wasn't the beguiling song of a siren. This was the voice of a monster, harsh and suffused with power and menace. "Tell me again how it was all my fault."

Alessandro sprinted into the armory, picked me up, and carried me toward the door.

"Put me down!" I snarled into his face.

"No. Not until you're yourself again."

How dare he? I hissed at him.

"My point exactly." He carried me outside and called over his shoulder. "That door stays shut. Nobody goes in unless I'm with them."

"Put me down!" Struggling against him was like trying to stop a train.

He kept carrying me up the driveway past the Bus. We caught up with Arabella.

Her eyes widened. "What?"

I hissed at her.

"Your sister is a bit upset," Alessandro told her.

I beat my wings, but my feathers had no substance.

He kept going, through the main house, past the kitchen, the living room, out the back door. The pool glinted in front of us, reflecting the moonlight. He took another step and jumped. Water washed over us and closed over my head.

I sank like a stone into the cool depths.

He let go and I clawed blindly, kicking and flailing, until my brain finally realized my feet touched the bottom of the pool. I straightened and realized I was standing in four feet of water.

The water drained from my hair, hot, almost boiling. The rage drained down with it.

I took a long shuddering breath.

The sky above me was studded with stars, their light cold and soothing. I let myself fall on my back. The water picked me up and cradled me, soft and gentle. I floated as the last traces of heat and anger washed away, dissolving. The wounds on my legs burned.

"How did you know?" I whispered.

"Linus told me. He said that if you ever get out of control when your wings turn black, salt water would help."

"I hate him."

"You don't mean that."

"He didn't even have the guts to tell me in person. He left a recording on a USB."

I pulled the USB out of my pocket and showed it to him.

"That probably shouldn't be in the water." He plucked it from my fingers and placed it on the coping.

"He's my grandfather and I hate him. You knew he was my grandfather and I hate you too."

"You don't mean that either."

"Why didn't you tell me?"

"It wasn't my place to tell."

The stars winked at us.

"You can't kill Konstantin, Catalina. You would bring the entire weight of the Russian Imperium down on our House."

"My mother almost died."

"I know. You still can't kill him. If you do, everything that happened today will be a pleasant memory compared to what follows. The Imperium trained Arkan. They taught him everything he knows before they turned him loose. They have others like him."

Alessandro . . . The source of my fear and worry. Now he was trying to keep me from killing the man who hurt us. I had to nip this in the bud. I let my legs sink, swung myself upright, and turned to him.

He was in the water up to his chest. His skin glistened. His wet brown hair clung to his head in short locks, and his eyes were molten honey.

Oh . . .

Oh wow.

Mine.

We looked at each other across the water. I smiled at him. He blinked, his eyes stunned.

I sank a little. My hair swirled around me. I tilted my head and turned slowly. He reached for me, but I kicked away, floating just out of his grasp.

Come away from the wall, Alessandro. Swim through the water to me. We can stay here together forever, just us, the water, and the stars. You will be mine, all mine. Only mine.

He shook his head. "Now I know why so many sailors drowned."

I laughed softly.

Alessandro studied my face. His gaze slid over my eyes, my mouth . . . I had to lure him in.

I submerged, letting the water float my hair, brushed it back, and resurfaced. He reached for me again, but I slid away. Little amber lights swirled in his eyes.

"How are you feeling?" he asked. "Still full of homicidal rage?"

"I'm going to kill Konstantin," I told him. "And then I will kill Arkan. You will help me kill Konstantin, won't you?"

"No."

"Alessandro . . . You know you want to."

"No. We are not killing Konstantin."

"Why do you have to be so unreasonable?"

"I'm the only reasonable person in this pool. This isn't you. Not the real you."

I leaned back and looked at the moon. "You keep saying that. 'It's not like you, Catalina. You don't mean that, Catalina. This isn't you, Catalina.' This is me. The real me. The one who loves you. I would do anything for you, Alessandro. Stay here with me."

He lunged across the water. His warm hand locked on my right wrist, and he pulled me to him and spun me around, trapping me between the pool wall and his body.

He'd caught me. I looked up at him and smiled.

"There are stars in your eyes," he whispered.

"We don't have to leave," I told him. "We can just stay here forever."

He grabbed me and kissed me. It wasn't just a kiss, it was almost an assault, a mad crazy claiming, born from lust, need, worry, and most of all love. I wrapped my legs around him and sank my hands into his wet hair. He was hard like a rock, and he was gripping me to him with those strong arms. My whole body sang.

He kissed me again, his tongue thrusting into my mouth. Delicious shivers ran through me. I closed my eyes. I wanted him so much . . .

We were moving. Water was draining from me, and my magic drained down with it.

He was carrying me out of the pool.

"Traitor!" I hissed.

His voice was almost a growl. "We can't stay in the pool. I'm only human."

We were halfway up the pool stairs.

My magic thrust a fantasy in front of me: the dark pool, the moon above, the silver light reflecting on the placid surface, and Alessandro's body floating next to me, his final expression frozen on his face. I was smiling. He was all mine. He would never leave.

No! I ripped the vision apart in my mind. I would never hurt him.

Unstoppable forces clashed inside me like two opposing waves, and everything went black.

 # Chapter 9

I woke up in my own bed.

The bedroom was shrouded in a comfortable gloom. The newly installed roller shades blocked most of the light, but the morning sun slipped in around their edges, setting them aglow. I checked the clock. 6:34 a.m. Barely past sunrise.

I raised my head. Shadow padded over the covers and licked my hand. I hugged her to me and sat up.

The covers next to me were rumpled, but Alessandro wasn't there.

The memory of me smiling in my vision popped in my head like a soap bubble. I petted Shadow's furry head. What if I hadn't really blacked out? What if . . .

The door swung open, and Alessandro walked in.

"Hey," he said.

"Did I do anything to you last night? Are you okay? Did I hurt you?"

He crossed the room, leaned one knee on the bed, dipped his head, and kissed me. A few months ago, I had tasted artisanal mead at a medieval fair. It was sweet with notes of berries and honey without a trace of alcohol taste in it. I kept sipping it, and after I drank half a flagon, I tried to pick up my fork and missed. My body wasn't my own anymore. That kiss was just like that, deceptively light, but intoxicating. He had hijacked me.

I opened my eyes and gently pushed away from him. "Did I hurt you?"

He sighed. "No. To my greatest regret, you didn't do anything at all to me last night. You did pass out and scare the hell out of me, but the doc said you were fine."

I landed back on my pillow. He sat on the bed, feet over the edge.

"What's happening with everything?" I asked him.

"We are in complete lockdown. Linus hasn't woken up, the prince is safe in his cage, and I'm keeping track of Arkan's movements. He is funneling his operatives into Houston but so far, he hasn't moved. Your USB is with Bern. He thinks it will work once it dries out."

"Mom . . ."

"Is recovering well and she asked me to pass on a message. She would like you to stop worrying about it and drive on."

I rolled my eyes. Driving on. Right.

I didn't always understand what motivated the people around me. I didn't even understand my own emotions half of the time, but I knew my magic. I knew how it worked and what it could do. Last night it betrayed me. How the hell was I supposed to drive on after that?

"Bug found surveillance footage from the parking lot," Alessandro said. "I watched it. It's . . . interesting. I particularly liked the black wings and the screeching."

His tone was light, but his eyes told me he plotted murder. If he ever got his hands on Xavier, he'd tear him apart.

"Something is happening to me. I don't understand it. I almost drowned you in the pool last night."

"Not even close."

"Alessandro, you don't understand. A part of me wanted to keep you in that pool no matter what it took. I think I'm dangerous. I . . ."

"I wasn't in any danger last night."

I blinked at him.

"Your magic doesn't work on me. Also, I'm big and strong, and an excellent swimmer."

"You don't get it," I told him. "How were you not afraid?"

"Oh I was. I was mortally afraid of being caught by your entire family while having sex in the pool."

"That's not what I mean."

"After everything calms down, we should test your theory."

"Alessandro . . ."

"We can pick up right where we left off. We'll pick a night when everyone is away from the house. We'll climb into the pool, and you can do your best to drown me. I promise, you can have me all to yourself. All of me."

"You're not going to take this seriously, are you?"

His voice lost all humor. "The woman I love was attacked last night. Her mother was injured, we have a Russian royal locked in the armory, and my father's killer declared open war on us. I'm taking everything seriously."

"Did you see Gunderson's face after I screamed?"

He nodded.

"When Grandma Victoria cracks a human mind, there are pieces left. They glow in my mind's vision. Very weakly but still there."

"Gunderson's mind didn't glow?" he guessed.

"No. It was a black hole. It's like I snuffed him out of existence." I pulled my knees to my chest. "I'm scared."

He wrapped his arms around me. I leaned into him.

"What did you feel just before you screamed?"

He wasn't asking just to comfort me. His grandfather was a terrible person, but he'd made sure that Alessandro had a superb education when it came to magic theory. He was an expert in all aspects of mental magic.

"Mom was hurt and bleeding. I knew that the next hit would kill her and Cornelius. I just . . . I wanted to shove Xavier and Gunderson."

"To shove?"

"Have you ever seen little kids fight? Eventually one of them loses it and just shoves the other to the ground to make them stop."

"Were you angry?"

"Yes. Mostly I was scared that Mom and Cornelius would die."

"And Konstantin? Did you want to shove him, too?"

"He forced this confrontation on us. Did you see all those bodies? Arabella had to kill nine people. We all take it for granted, but she is probably the most sensitive of all of us. Things bother her deeply. She thinks about them for days. I don't even know how deeply this damaged her. She's my little sister, and I was supposed to protect her from this crap, except that I can't."

"I think we're safe," he said.

I glanced at him.

"You're worried you might hurt us, but you are still you even when your black wings are out. You didn't hurt me in the pool. Your magic was pouring out like a flame, but you never targeted me. You just flirted and tried to seduce me, and then pouted."

I pushed away from him. "Pouted?"

"Mhm."

"I was hissing in your face. How is that pouting?"

"Your hissing was endearing."

I put my hands over my face. He was impossible.

"The point is, you don't blindly lash out, Catalina. You're striking out at people you perceive as a threat to your loved ones. Whatever it is breaking through, let it. It needs to come out."

"You really think so?"

He nodded. "I'm not saying this in my capacity as your devoted fiancé but as an antistasi Prime. You hold yourself on a very tight leash. It is atypical for a mental Prime to be that controlled constantly. The threat level has escalated, and so did your response to it. I don't think you can effectively suppress it, but you do need to recalibrate."

And the only way to recalibrate would be to practice this new power until I could learn to control it.

"So what, choose a target and hope for the best?"

"Yes."

"What if it gets out of control?"

"I will help you. I promise."

"Okay," I said.

We sat together for a few moments.

"I suppose we have to sort out the mess with Konstantin," I said.

Alessandro grimaced. "Unfortunately, we can't keep him in a cage indefinitely. As much as I would enjoy it."

I scooted off the bed. "Why does he call you Sasha?"

"He knows I don't like it."

"And how does he know that?"

"Because he is my fourth cousin," Alessandro said. "He keeps reminding me, as if I will forget. Family. Can't live with them, can't strangle them. It's terrible."

Someone, probably Patricia, set up two chairs in front of Konstantin's cage. I took one. Alessandro sat in the other, tossing one long leg over the other and looking every inch an Italian aristocrat.

We had briefly stopped at the office to write a contract. I had asked him about the cousin thing on the way, but he avoided it. He didn't refuse to answer, he just changed the subject. That was okay. He would tell me eventually. I could recite his genealogy down to his great-great-grandparents. There were no Russians there anywhere. It was all Sagredo and British mental mages.

Konstantin studied us through the bars. He looked stunning. If the night in the cage affected him, he would never let us know.

"I'm glad we're finally in control of ourselves," the prince said.

I didn't take the bait. I just looked at him.

"Shut up and listen," Alessandro told him. "I'll keep it brief, and you can fill in the gaps."

Konstantin gave him a go-ahead wave, a gesture at once elegant and dismissive. Arrogant jerk.

"We know that as of last year, Arkan refined the last two samples of the Osiris serum, achieving a stability rate of twenty percent," Alessandro said.

Linus had been livid when he'd found out. Up until last year, Arkan's modified serum killed the majority of his volunteers. Now they had a roughly one in five chance of surviving with their bodies intact and new latent powers activated.

"Arkan is building a network of allies by secretly supplying the serum to Houses with failed vectors and duds. He had been very careful in his selection, but last summer he got greedy. He gifted a sample to House Dolgorukov. Aleksei Antonovich Dolgorukov is the current Minister of Defense. Arkan wanted to buy a future favor."

Arkan was screwing around with a family in the highest strata of Russian society. He must have been sure the serum wouldn't kill its recipient, except his chances of success were still only twenty percent. It was a huge risk. His arrogance was getting the best of him.

"House Dolgorukov has two magic bloodlines," Alessandro continued. "Pattern and precognition. The two work together, making the Dolgorukovs excellent strategists. Inna Dolgorukov, the eldest of three scions of the House, was born without magic, a fact House Dolgorukov went to great lengths to hide for seventeen years. How am I doing so far?"

"Wonderfully," Konstantin told him, his voice dry.

Of course they would hide it. Primes married for magic, and they liked the guarantee that their children would be as powerful as their parents. Without powers, Inna's odds of marrying someone in her social circle were nil. She'd spend her life on the sidelines, pitied and feeling useless, while her relatives wielded power and influence.

Not only that, but her very existence put the future of her family in doubt. In the eyes of the magic elite, she was an indicator that something went terribly wrong with the genetics of House Dolgorukov. If her parents could produce a dud, so could her siblings. Instead of a sure bet, marrying into House Dolgorukov would suddenly become a gamble.

"But that's not all there is, is it?" Alessandro said. "You like genealogy, Konstantin. Remind me, how are your family and House Dolgorukov connected?"

"Inna's mother is my aunt," the prince said in a flat voice.

"On which side?" Alessandro crooned.

"On my father's," Konstantin said.

Oh shit. Inna's mother was the sister of the czar. Inna's lack of powers didn't just mar her House. It tainted the Imperial dynasty.

"At seventeen, the odds of her manifesting powers are basically nonexistent," I thought out loud. "Sooner or later, she would have to get married, and the Imperial family would likely kill her to keep her lack of powers secret. That's why her parents went to Arkan for the serum. They were desperate."

"You think the worst of us," Konstantin said. "Inna was going to have a quiet life away from the public eye."

"No." I shook my head. "No matter how quietly she lived, her genes would always be a threat. The dynasty must appear bulletproof. One carefully worded article during a time of crisis, and suddenly there is a fatal flaw in the bloodline of House Berezin. Killing her would be cleaner. A convenient accident during this quiet life, in some remote place—a wrecked car, an unfortunate fall from a horse, a drowning. Nobody can prove that she had no magic by examining her corpse."

Konstantin leaned forward. "That's the second time you surprised me since we've met, Ms. Baylor."

Oh, you haven't seen anything yet.

I glanced at Alessandro. "What happened? Did Arkan's serum kill her?"

"Not right away. She survived the exposure and got her magic."

"What was she?"

Alessandro smiled without any humor. "Prime venenata. A very strong, very unstable venenata."

Dear God, the serum had given her Runa's talent. She could poison an entire city block in minutes.

"Nobody in House Dolgorukov knew how to handle a venenata," Alessandro continued. "Especially since Inna had no training. They tried to find the right tutor. Meanwhile, Inna had to hide her powers and pretend that everything was fine. The Dowager Empress is fond of socials. Inna, one of her favorite grandchildren, was always invited. During the last Spring Social in March, Inna took offense to something Duchess Minkina said to her. Her powers spun out of control."

Oh no.

"She killed three women on the spot, critically poisoned seven others, and would have killed everyone present if Konstantin's mother hadn't put a bullet into her niece's brain two seconds after the first victim hit the ground."

Yep, that was about the only way to stop a venenata. When they got going, you killed them, usually from a distance, or you died.

"The Dowager was grateful but most displeased," Alessandro said. "We all know how much she enjoys her get-togethers."

Konstantin's face displayed all the emotion of a stone wall. "You seem remarkably well-informed, Sasha. I see the charming Italian orphan thing still works for you."

He'd put an emphasis on the word *orphan*.

Alessandro's eyes narrowed. This was about to get ugly.

"How is your mother?" Alessandro asked, his voice light. "From what I've heard, the murder of her niece was traumatic for her."

"Quite well and fully recovered. It was regrettable but necessary. Her quick thinking and actions saved many lives. Unlike *some* mothers, she always puts the welfare of children, hers and others, before her own needs."

Alessandro's mother had done nothing to take care of him and his sisters or to protect him from the wrath of his grandfather when Alessandro tried to become the breadwinner. He had to pretend to be a rich Prime while his family secretly suffered in poverty, so he could marry a rich heiress. His entire adolescence was a giant marital advertisement, and his mother had encouraged him to put himself out there. It was a source of pain to him.

Alessandro smiled. "Aunt Zina was always very caring unless the matters of state dictated otherwise. It's a rare mother who could murder her oldest son's fiancée with her own hands. Poor Liudmilla. She never saw it coming."

Ouch. Who the hell was Liudmilla, and how many women had Konstantin's mother murdered? Was it a hobby of hers?

Konstantin leaned forward. His face changed somehow, his features sharpening, his jaw growing more square. His eyes lost their warm glow, turning uncaring and frightening. He stared at Alessandro with the unblinking focus of a predator sizing up his next meal.

"See that?" Alessandro told me. "Remember that. That's his real face. He isn't mad that I know. He's angry because I said it in front of you. They get touchy when their dirty laundry is aired in front of outsiders."

The fury in Konstantin's eyes vanished. In a blink, he was charming again. The tiny hairs on the back of my neck stood on end.

"Like I said," the prince quipped, "our aunts take pity on him because he is handsome and impoverished. I'll plug that leak when I get home."

"You called your Russian aunts?" I looked at Alessandro.

"Oh, he hasn't told you." Konstantin smiled. "He's my third cousin."

"Fourth," I corrected.

Konstantin frowned, counting on his fingers. "Oh well. Your English genealogy is confusing, and blood is blood. How is my many-times-removed Aunt Lilian, by the way? Still cowering whenever your grandfather raises his voice?"

Orange sparks flared in Alessandro's eyes.

The tension was so thick, you could cut it with a knife and make a sandwich. I raised my right index finger. "Question: Does Arkan realize that the Imperium knows that he supplied that serum?"

Konstantin leaned back. "No. He had taken pains to cover up his tracks. Even the Dolgorukovs didn't fully realize who they were dealing with until the serum changed hands."

All this time I was wondering what would cause a man as cautious as Arkan to suddenly attack us on all fronts without any regard for the consequences. He was terrified that once Smirnov started talking, the Russians would realize who was behind Inna's death. He was willing to risk a fight with the Wardens, the FBI, and the State of Texas just to avoid facing the Russian Imperium. Well, that mystery was solved.

"The Imperium sent you to dismantle Arkan's murder club," Alessandro said to Konstantin. "They already had issues with some of the assassinations he sanctioned, and the Inna incident was the last straw."

"He crossed the line," Konstantin said. "He was a tame wolf we released back into the forest. As long as he stayed there, we wouldn't hunt him. He took it upon himself to break into our pasture, kill our sheep, and crap all over our yard. Now we will put him down."

Wow.

"When did you kill Smirnov?" Alessandro asked.

"Three months ago."

And he had assumed Smirnov's identity and strolled right into Arkan's inner circle.

"How did you compensate for not being a pattern mage?" I asked.

"Patterns are logic," Konstantin said. "I was trained in logical thinking from a very young age. Call it the benefit of an excellent Russian education."

"Also, Arkan is paranoid," Alessandro added. "He compartmentalizes a lot of the work. Smirnov was in charge of his cybersecurity. Since the network is set up, it pretty much runs itself. Smirnov's main value was in being Arkan's sounding board. They play chess and bounce ideas back and forth."

"Which I quite enjoyed," the prince said. "Playing chess with a rabid tiger while plotting to topple governments and kill important people. I'll remember that bit fondly."

Konstantin had managed to impersonate one of Arkan's closest associates, a man Arkan knew for years. He lived in Arkan's compound, he talked to him every day, he played chess with him, and Arkan never had any idea that one of his oldest friends was counterfeit. It wasn't just crazy impressive, it was deeply disturbing.

Konstantin looked at Alessandro. "Arkan is a popular man. Everyone wants his head on their wall. The Imperium wants him because he presumed to meddle with us. Your National Assembly wants him because he stole their serum, and now he's peddling it like a kolachi vendor, embarrassing them further. Linus Duncan wants him because Arkan outplayed him and wounded his pride. You want him because he killed your father. Ms. Baylor wants him because she is secretly afraid he might kill you."

The hidden fear deep inside me woke up and clawed me. I had no idea how Konstantin had seen through me, but somehow, he had. Yes, Arkan was ruthless, unstoppable, and powerful. He inspired fear, and it was well earned. Only an idiot wouldn't be afraid of him. But that's not what created that hot knot inside me. If Alessandro had a choice of killing Arkan at the cost of his own life or walking away, I wasn't sure which path he would take, and that terrified me more than Arkan himself.

Konstantin leaned back and I saw the flash of his true face for a split second. "I don't want to take down Arkan. I want to dismantle everything he's built. I want him to lose his security, his position in society, his money, his people, and finally, his life. He dared to upset my mother."

Not "he caused the death of my cousin." *He dared to upset my mother.* Inna was only seventeen years old, a victim as much as she was the villain in this story, yet in Konstantin's mind her death was regrettable but almost incidental, while the anguish of his mother had to be addressed. When people showed you where their priorities lay, it was a good idea to keep it in mind.

"Funny you should mention it." The voice of Victoria Tremaine's granddaughter came out of my mouth on its own. "Right now, my mother is resting upstairs because Arkan's pet telekinetic impaled a two-foot-long spike in her thigh. You caused this."

Konstantin raised his eyebrows. "I nudged you out of your complacency. Your conflict with Arkan was inevitable. You haven't taken overt action so far because Arkan never gave you an excuse. Now you have it."

"It wasn't your nudge to make."

A muscle in his cheek jerked. I was looking at him as if he were a cockroach to be crushed under my feet and my face was wearing the trademark Tremaine arrogance. He clearly wasn't used to being on the receiving end of a sneer.

"I'm here to offer you the assistance of the Imperium. You won't get a better chance to win this."

I tilted my chin up slightly, so I could look down on him. "I don't need your assistance. In a minute I'll open my wings and then you'll fall to your knees. You will crawl across your cage to me, begging for me to keep talking to you. You will tell me all of your secrets. You'll follow me around like a gentle lamb, and when I'm done with you and we dump you in front of the Russian Embassy, you will weep and try to end your life because I'm no longer in it."

I let my green wings out and let him see a tiny hint of them. Konstantin stared and shook his head.

"Shall we begin?" I asked.

"I'm not easily broken."

True. Illusion was a mental discipline.

I channeled Victoria and scoffed. "You're not the strongest illusion mage I've met."

Technically, it was hard to tell who would win between him and Augustine, but he didn't need to know that.

"The Imperium will retaliate."

"I don't care. You hurt my mother. I'm a Baylor, Your Highness, but I am also a Tremaine. We do not forgive."

Konstantin glanced at Alessandro. "You should tell her that it's not in her best interests or yours, Sasha."

The Artisan tilted his head with clinical detachment. "I'm the Sentinel of the Texas Warden. I evaluate threats and eliminate them. You are a threat, Konstantin. Your presence here endangers the Warden. Handing you off to the embassy solves all my problems. As long as you're alive and uninjured, they will do very little. You will recover. It will take you a long time and you'll keep trying to kill yourself out of sheer desperation, but you will recover."

"Let's see what you've found in Arkan's files." I fluttered my feathers.

"What are your terms?" Konstantin asked.

I took the folder and passed it to him together with a pen. He opened it and scanned the contents and read out loud:

"The Russian Imperium surrenders all claims on the life and freedom of Ignat Orlov, otherwise known as Arkan, to Alessandro Sagredo. Alessandro Sagredo will have the sole, exclusive right to kill Ignat Orlov. A breach of this clause nullifies this contract."

"Which part isn't clear?" I asked.

"You have a guardian angel," Konstantin said to Alessandro. "Too bad she is wasted on a sinner like you."

"The angel can be kind, but the sinner is not," Alessandro told him.

"I'll keep that in mind."

"You do that."

Konstantin tapped the contract with his fingertips. "To summarize, I'm confined to the grounds of this estate. I'm forbidden from taking any action against Arkan myself or through my subordinates without the express consent of one of you. I'm precluded from endangering any member of your family. And finally, I'm expected to render aid to the best of my ability at your request. And I can't kill Arkan, even if an opportunity to do so presents itself."

"Yes," I told him.

"And you want me to sign it?"

"No. I want you to seal it."

I had done some research of my own. Members of the Imperial family tasked with special missions carried a seal which they affixed to formal documents. This seal put the reputation of the entire family behind the contract. It wasn't foolproof, but it was as close as we could get to the Emperor's word. According to Alessandro, Konstantin would have one.

"This will require a phone call," Konstantin said.

Alessandro passed a cell phone to Konstantin through the bars.

"I'll need a bit of privacy."

"You have the whole cage." It was petty but I enjoyed it.

Konstantin shook his head, rose, and walked to the far side of the cage. He dialed the number and spoke in a quiet urgent Russian. We waited. Minutes crawled by. In the ensuing pause, my brain finally started working to full capacity.

"I think we need help," I murmured to Alessandro.

"Who do you have in mind?"

I told him. "Just in case."

He laughed softly under his breath. "Your mother is going to love it."

Konstantin disconnected the call, reached into his shirt, and pulled a necklace from around his neck, a simple rectangle of silver hanging on a matching chain. The rectangular pendant slid apart under the pressure of his fingers. He took the top half and pressed it under his signature line. A red stamp with Cyrillic script winding around a double-headed eagle marked the paper. He signed his name with a flourish and grinned at Alessandro.

"Congratulations, Sasha. You will have your revenge. I get his body though. After you're done with it, of course."

Alessandro smiled like a wolf grinning at the moon in the middle of a dark forest and keyed the code into the cage's lock. "Agreed."

My phone rang. An unlisted number. I took the call.

"I'll be brief," Arkan said on the other end. "Release Trofim Smirnov, and your sisters will survive the day."

I went right back to my Tremaine voice. "What a coincidence. I've just finalized the contract spelling out what happens to your corpse. So good of you to call after it was done."

Konstantin slipped out of the cage, moving in complete silence. Alessandro grabbed the manila folder, scribbled something on the back of it, and held it up.

Provoke.

Yes, yes, I know.

No matter how many operatives we took out, as long as Arkan remained at his base in Canada, he was unreachable. Going into Canada to get him required cooperation between the two governments and an international warrant. Linus had tried, but nobody wanted to tell Canada the real reason we were going after Arkan. The moment news of the stolen serum reached the Canadian government, there would be a diplomatic explosion of international proportions. The United States couldn't afford to lose face. Without the serum, our reasoning for arresting Arkan was thin, and Canada wasn't wild about letting a team of dangerous combat Primes across their borders to apprehend one of their citizens.

We had to make Arkan come to us.

"This is your last chance to save your family," Arkan said. I knew what he sounded like from videos but hearing him over the phone sent shivers down my spine. He had a voice that cut across your senses like a knife.

"You seem to be under the impression that you hold a trump card in these negotiations," I said.

Konstantin grabbed the folder and the pen, wrote something on it, and held it up. *Get him out of Canada.*

Thank you, Prince Obvious, I would've never thought of that.

I kept going. "You are mistaken, Mr. Orlov. You are not even invited to the table. We have reached an agreement with Mr. Smirnov. He's proving exceedingly useful. We have secured the cooperation of the federal government. Your threats are hollow."

Konstantin started writing something else. Alessandro grabbed the folder and tried to pull it away from him. They struggled over it in a silent tug-of-war.

"The FBI won't help you. The Wardens won't help you. After my people walk away from the burning ruin of your home, they may show up to recover the bodies." He was hammering each word in like nails into my imaginary coffin.

Alessandro grabbed the middle of the folder and ripped it in half. The prince and my fiancé frantically scribbled on their chunks.

"You're driven by patriotism. You think what you're doing is noble because you're still a naïve, arrogant child. Your country will use you and throw you away when you no longer serve a purpose."

I needed to convince him that the only way he could win would be by showing up himself. We had seriously thinned his ranks over the past year. He was suffering a heavy personnel shortage. I'd hit him on that.

"Your reward will be a row of headstones. You're fond of Sagredo. Think of what it would be like to never hear his voice again. How will you fill that ragged hole where your mother used to be?"

Alessandro and Konstantin jerked their folder up at the same time like judges raising their scorecards at a figure skating competition. Alessandro had written *5 Primes left,* and Konstantin's paper said *Lost 1/3 of his operatives.*

I reached over, plucked the two halves of the folder from their fingers, and threw them over my shoulder.

"That was a splendid speech," I said into the phone. "Mr. Orlov, we both know why you're wasting your air and my time. You're down to five Primes, Malchenko, Sanders, Krause, Buller, and Xavier, who, as we both know, is a potential liability. Your roster of Significants suffered heavy losses. Even if you field everyone at the same time and Sanders brings his sons, I still have no problem countering you. Since you and I started this little dance, you haven't won a single skirmish, and that was before I had access to Smirnov. When all of your agents are gone and you have no one left to hide behind, killing you will be easy like swatting a fly."

Konstantin and Alessandro stared at me.

"Let me be blunt: I'm not doing this because I'm trying to keep my country safe. I could ignore that you murdered my fiancé's father. I could even ignore your little serum scheme, but you had the audacity to send killers into my new home. You've made yourself into an obstacle. I will remove you from my path, the way I would remove a pile of crap a stray dog left on my lawn, and then I will live happily ever after, content that nobody will remember your name."

He hung up.

Konstantin laughed, his eyes sparkling. "You called him a pile of dog shit to his face. I love it."

Alessandro gave me an odd look. "'You sent killers to my house'?"

He was asking me if it still bothered me. "If he thinks we're doing this 'for God and country,' he'll keep trying to intimidate me to knock me off course. I had to make it personal. He knows people with a personal vendetta are difficult to stop. You taught him that."

An alarm wailed outside. We were under attack.

The two men charged to the door. I grabbed the Imperial contract, tossed it into Konstantin's cage, and locked it. I didn't want to take any chances it would get ruined in whatever fight I would run into. I wasted another precious second on keying the code into the nearest gun cage. The lock turned green, I pulled the door open, grabbed a DA Ambassador, slapped a magazine into it, and sprinted to the door.

Both Alessandro and Konstantin were already gone.

The alarm cut off in midnote.

The grounds were eerily still. The north gate was to my right, the main house and a long driveway leading to it to my left. There should have been people running to their stations, noise, even gunfire, but there was nothing. The Compound was silent. I was alone.

What the hell was this?

Magic shifted high above me. I looked up. A black hole gaped above the north gate and another, identical hole punctured the air above the main house. Twin summoner portals.

The two holes writhed in unison and collapsed on themselves. Whatever had been summoned must've already crawled out.

A shot popped, echoing through the buildings. Mom just sniped someone from her crow's nest atop the main house's roof.

They were going after my family and Linus.

I ran toward the main house.

Another shot.

A third rifle shot.

Mom was a one shot–one kill sniper. Either she was killing multiple targets, or she was shooting at something huge.

I moved off the main driveway onto a side path, hidden by the decorative shrubs, and sprinted, the Ambassador heavy in my hand.

There was no return fire. No screams, no growls, nothing. Every hair I had stood on end.

The path curved and spat me out into the open right by Leon's tower. The main driveway widened here, connecting to a huge paver patio. At the other end of the patio, stairs led up to the main house.

People sprawled on the stairs, unmoving. Our guards, Patricia . . . I saw a wave of blond hair. Arabella lay at the top of the stairs, curled into a fetal ball, her blond hair fanning over her face.

Panic stabbed me.

I forced myself to stand still and look carefully. A faintly fluorescent indigo dust shifted on the pavers, like very fine glitter. It covered the entire patio. The front of Leon's tower shimmered with it. If he was alive, he was trapped in the tower.

I had seen this before.

I took another step and saw it, an eight-foot-tall plant in the center of the patio, anchored by a twisted mass of dark green roots. A tire-size flower bloomed atop the braided stem. It resembled a monstrous mum, with rows and rows of indigo petals rimmed in cornflower blue at the edges. A whirl of tentacles, flashing with the same pale blue, stretched from the plant, trying to wrap around Runa. She stood with her feet apart, arms bent at the elbows, palms up. The air around her was emerald green. Sweat drenched her forehead.

The flower pulsed. The outer whorls of petals rolled down and into the stem and the new whorls opened at the center, sending a burst of indigo pollen into the air. It touched the green air around Runa, turned grey, and fell to the ground. The tentacles slid, trying to wrap around her and failing.

The nightbloom, a strange creature midway between a plant and an animal. They grew in the arcane realm, crawling across the landscape and sending puffs of poisonous pollen in the air. The pollen put their prey to sleep, slowly killing them, and eventually the nightbloom would make its way to them and root in their bodies, sucking up the nutrients.

We had about forty minutes to administer the antidote or everyone affected would die.

Don't think about Arabella. Focus on the flower.

I raised my gun. The flower and Runa were intertwined. No clear shot except at the blossom. I sighted the flower, and squeezed the trigger, sending a two-shot burst at the bloom. The flower didn't even jerk.

"Run!" Runa squeezed out. "Run now!"

Something shiny winked at me through the gaps in the flower's roots. Something tall.

I took a step back.

A man emerged from behind the nightbloom. Over seven feet tall, he was built like a linebacker. Thin strands of nacre crystal wrapped over every inch of him, forming a semblance of a medieval suit of armor. He looked like he was wearing full plate shaped from long sheets of chopstick-thin, multifaceted icicles. The crystal mesh sheathed him from head to toe, thickening in some places, woven and braided in the others. Even his face was completely protected, the nacre strands twisting into a barbute helmet with a single slit of clear crystal over his eyes. The armor fit him like a glove.

Dato Buller. Prime armamagus, the Crystal Knight. Arkan had thrown one of his precious five at us. *Oh shit.*

Buller saw me.

I fired, squeezing the trigger. The bullets smashed into the helmet and slid to the ground.

He flicked his arm. A thin razor-sharp blade made from a single crystal slid from his forearm. Death was coming for me.

A sniper rifle cracked. I saw the bullet strike—it smashed into his head, jerking him a bit, and fell to the ground, flattened.

A firestorm erupted from Leon's tower, a weird noise halfway between a deafening vacuum cleaner and a high-powered drill—the M134 minigun. Leon was trying to help me.

The stream of bullets staggered Buller. He leaned into it like a man fighting a strong wind.

I dashed around the clump of greenery. Singing would do no good. My wings wouldn't work. Within his armor, Buller was deaf and impervious to mental magic. It was ballistic resistant, it maintained a temperature of exactly twenty-four degrees Celsius, and it somehow generated its own breathable air. It was a bulletproof spacesuit he could alter on the fly, and he was about to murder me.

The bushes went flying. A crystal blade emerged. Buller bore down on me like a nightmare come to life.

I scrambled through the brush to the main driveway. He was only feet behind me.

I burst through the hedges onto the main driveway and straight into Alessandro. He grabbed me by my shoulder and shoved me behind him. An unfamiliar man who was probably Konstantin in a new shape caught me and pulled me out of the way.

Buller carved his way through a hedge and loomed in front of us, a faceless knight ready to slaughter.

Orange sparks flared around Alessandro's hand and coalesced into a short sword.

Buller struck. The crystal sword sliced through the air. Alessandro leaned out of the way and sliced across Buller's forearm. It wasn't a lash. He'd planted the knife onto the crystal bracer and rolled his wrist, cutting a half crescent through it. Before Buller moved to counter, Alessandro caught the knife on the other side of his arm and sliced upward. Buller whipped around, but Alessandro clamped his hand on the bracer and ripped it away.

How?

The Crystal Knight howled, his voice muffled. Blood drenched his right arm from mid-forearm to his fingers. Muscle glistened under the blood, as if Alessandro had skinned his hand.

Buller flicked a second crystal blade onto his left arm and stabbed at Alessandro, crystals flowing over his injured right hand. Alessandro dropped under the thrust, sliced at Buller's leading leg, and tore another bloody chunk of crystal free.

Buller screamed and kicked at him in a frantic frenzy. Alessandro had nowhere to go. He braced, took the kick, rolled across the driveway, and sprang to his feet. A trickle of blood wet his lips. He flicked it off and started toward Buller.

The armamagus took a small step back.

The crystal armor was like a ballistic vest—it stopped a fast projectile but not the comparatively slow knife.

I needed a blade.

I whipped around and saw a boot knife in Konstantin's hand. It looked like one of ours. He must've taken it off somebody.

"Knife!"

He blinked at me.

"Give me your knife!"

He held it out to me. "This is unwise . . ."

I grabbed it off his palm.

Buller was a whirlwind of crystal blades. Alessandro floated around him, carving pieces off.

I was a siren through my father but also magus Sagittarius through my mother. I only got a little bit of it. She never missed while my magic helped me stab my opponent in the most vulnerable spot. It required two things to activate: a blade and a target. I had both.

Magic zinged through my palm and pulled me toward Buller. I swayed from foot to foot, looking for an opening.

Buller slashed at Alessandro. Sparks pulsed, and a heavy modern replica of a falcata on my sword wall popped into his left hand. Instead of dodging, Alessandro blocked the vertical slash, knocking the arm aside, and carved a cut on Buller's helmet. Blood swelled.

My magic pulled me. I darted behind Buller and lashed across his back. It was like slicing through a thick bunch of fiber-optic cables. The blade sank in with an odd crunch. Buller whipped around toward me. His crystal sword grazed my arm, drawing a hot line of pain across my shoulder, and then Alessandro carved a three-inch ribbon off his side.

We moved around him, slicing, slashing, cutting, just as we'd practiced hundreds of times against every conceivable practice construct and mech Linus could throw at us. We bled him cut by cut, like two wolves fighting a bear.

Buller raged. He had been invulnerable for so long, and now we hurt him again and again, and the pain and fury had driven him mad. Blood drenched his crystal armor. He kept trying to regrow it, but we had ripped too much of it away. Chunks of raw muscle wept blood through the gaps. The crystal crawled, trying to seal the gashes, but it was slow, and we kept opening more.

My face was splattered with blood, and I didn't know whose. My arm was getting tired, the exertion of making deep cuts gnawing at it. He couldn't keep this up forever, but neither could we.

Buller charged Alessandro, throwing everything into his assault. Alessandro dodged. Our eyes met for a quarter of the second, and I knew this was my shot.

Alessandro let go of his falcata. The orange glow dropped a riot shield into his hand, and he jerked it up. Buller hammered at it. The sword cut through the reinforced polycarbonate like it was butter. Instead of shying back, Alessandro braced. Buller smelled blood in the water. In a strength vs strength clash, Alessandro would lose, and Buller knew it. He rained blows onto the shield, hacking off chunks of it, locked onto Alessandro with the instinct of a predator sensing wounded prey.

Alessandro stumbled.

Buller pounded on the remnants of the shield.

I slipped my knife through a narrow gap into his liver.

He didn't notice.

I pulled the blade free and stabbed him again, fast, driving the blade into his flesh over and over like an icepick, flinging blood each time I pulled it out.

Buller jerked, arching his back.

Alessandro dropped the stub of the shield and leaped up. A ten-inch karambit knife shaped like a double-edged tiger claw flashed in his hand. He sliced at Buller's throat.

The Crystal Knight fell to his knees. A muffled gurgle escaped his mouth, the sound of his last moments skittering away. He collapsed on his side. The crystal armor melted, leaving a dead man on our driveway. He was large, muscular, and pale, with sparse light brown hair cut short and a weak chin he'd tried to cover up with a goatee. His body was a patchwork of gaping wounds and missing skin.

I heaved a long breath. Konstantin was looking at me like he had seen some alien monster.

Alessandro's right shoulder was bloody. I rushed to him. He met me halfway.

"Are you hurt?" I asked.

"It's a scratch."

A strange hissing noise came from the main house.

Runa.

I turned around.

The nightbloom flailed as if stabbed with a high-voltage wire. Its roots sagged. Its bloom drooped backward, toward us, its petals turning a dull brown and going limp. The flower shuddered. Green fuzz sprouted on the petals. The nightbloom swayed and collapsed, sagging into a liquefying mess of vegetation and rotting fluid, revealing Runa, her right hand extended, her fingers covered with plant gore.

She stared at her fingers in disgust, shook her hand, and said, "Twenty-three minutes since full bloom."

We had seventeen minutes to administer the antidote. I turned around and sprinted to the infirmary.

The family was back in the conference room. Everyone was in the exact same seats they had taken twenty-four hours ago, but nobody looked the same. We looked like we had gotten caught in an air raid and hadn't quite made it to shelter in time.

Alessandro sat on my right and Konstantin, back in his Berezin persona, on my left. The fight with the Crystal Knight had come at a cost. Both Alessandro and I were cut up. Once the adrenaline wore off, the pain set in. I must've taken a hit to my back, because everything from the left shoulder blade down to my waist felt like one giant bruise. Alessandro must've gotten hurt as well, but he showed no signs of it.

Bern had bags under his eyes, and they weren't clutches, they were totes. He was chugging a Red Bull and staring at his laptop. Next to him, Runa nursed an iced coffee, her expression grim. Halle, her sister, slumped in the chair next to her, with her face on the table. Past Halle,

Ragnar had the pinched look and wide eyes of someone who was trying his absolute best to stay awake.

Arkan had hit us with a two-prong attack. It started with three armored vehicles pulling up to the house. Buller got out of the first one and generated his armor. We had expected Buller to show up sooner or later, and the plan always was that Arabella would deal with him. No matter how indestructible he was, there was still a human being in all that armor and after my sister was done venting her frustration, he wouldn't pose a threat. Predictably, once he popped up on the security feed, Arabella ran out of the main house heading to the front gate.

Unfortunately, Arkan's Prime summoner, Maya Krause, had opened two portals, one right above the main house and the other at the north gate, and dropped two nightblooms. The sentries at the north gate went down instantly and so did my sister and her strike support team.

Runa happened to be in her siblings' casita. She heard the siren, accessed the security feed, saw Arabella asleep and Buller strolling in, told her siblings to stay put until the fight was over, and ran out there to fight. Halle and Ragnar obeyed her precisely, meaning the moment she killed the nightbloom, they raced out of the house to help detoxify everyone.

Venenata mages detoxified by either poisoning their patient with something that would kill the pathogen or by drawing the poison into themselves and metabolizing it. Even though we had cans of nightbloom antidote, time was a factor. The Etterson kids exhausted themselves trying to save everyone. Poor Ragnar looked like he wasn't sure where he was or what he was doing here.

To my right, Arabella watched Konstantin with silent hatred. I had brought her up to speed as soon as she woke up, and she zeroed in on Konstantin as the reason for Mom's wound and everything that followed. That's when Arabella was at her most dangerous, when she didn't say anything and just seethed.

Konstantin and Alessandro had run to the north gate during the attack, missing Buller by moments. Alessandro torched the first nightbloom with his favorite tactical flamethrower. Konstantin changed shape into one of our guards and went after Krause, but she had fled as soon as she dropped those portals. Once the nightbloom was dead, Alessandro doubled back and ran into Buller and me.

Grandma Frida tapped her fingers on the table, watching Mom who sat across from her. Mom looked paler today, her bronze skin tinted with grey. Grandma Frida told me Mom wasn't taking her pain medication. The attack had caught Grandma Frida in the motor pool, up to her elbow inside her latest mobile artillery project. The security protocol dictated that she and the three-person guard team protected the south gate, which was exactly what she did.

Leon sat by Grandma Frida. His arms, exposed by his T-shirt, sported hair-thin pale slashes that looked like old scars. Whatever attacked the FBI had gotten him after all. Dr. Patel told me he wasn't sure they would go away or when. It was definitely making him sick, which was why he'd been asleep in his tower when the nightbloom seed landed on our patio. He'd tried shooting it and Buller, and none of it did any good, not even the minigun. Now he brooded, heartbroken because he felt useless.

The door swung open, and Cornelius entered, his expression grave. Matilda was next, her long dark hair gathered into a ponytail. She was carrying a fluffy Himalayan cat, whose full name was Go Mi Nam and who usually answered to "Kitty." Patricia Taft was the last to enter, carrying a trash can. Some people had a stronger reaction to night-bloom than others.

Matilda walked over to Ragnar and deposited the cat on his lap. Ragnar blinked at her, startled.

"Comfort," Matilda explained.

Go Mi Nam dutifully purred like a runaway bulldozer.

"Do I not get comfort?" Leon asked sadly.

Matilda walked around the table, hugged him gently, and patted his hair as if he was a dog. "It will be okay. You can shoot people next time."

Everyone was finally here.

First things first.

"Family, Prince Berezin." I nodded at Konstantin.

"Konstantin, please," Konstantin said with a charming smile.

The family glowered back.

"Konstantin represents the Russian Imperium. He will be helping us with this matter," I said.

Arabella took the metal spoon out of Runa's drink and bent it.

I explained the prince, the contract, Smirnov, and everything surrounding it.

Nobody said anything.

"Do you know who attacked Linus?" Arabella demanded.

"Yes," I told her.

"Did you do anything about it?"

"No."

The outrage on my sister's face was so stark, I almost asked Alessandro to summon a shield for me.

"Catalina!" Arabella snarled.

"It's Kaylee Cabera, and I don't know how she fits into this yet."

"I do," Konstantin volunteered.

I pivoted to him.

"Kaylee was a dud," Konstantin said. "Luciana was facing a lot of pressure from the family to select an official successor and it couldn't be Kaylee. Of course, you are already aware of the connection between Arkan and Luciana."

Alessandro waved him on.

"Luciana contacted Arkan to fix the problem and so he did. Kaylee survived and became one of his mutant Primes. Unfortunately, someone alerted Duncan to the matter, and he went after her. Luciana realized the Warden was making circles around her daughter and getting closer with every pass, so she appealed to Arkan to kill him. He refused."

"Why?" Leon asked.

"The Warden of Texas is a risky target," Alessandro answered. "He probably wasn't sure he could handle the fallout."

"Luciana took her monster child and did it anyway," Konstantin said. "And to top it off, she failed to seal the deal. Arkan went into a rage, threw some things, and once he calmed down, decided that he needed to do damage control. He ordered Xavier to kill her and to make it public."

"And he had her killed at Linus' restaurant," I thought out loud. "As a kind of peace offering. 'Look, she tried to murder you, and I punished her in retaliation.'"

"Exactly." Konstantin nodded.

In Arkan's mind, this probably made Linus and him square somehow. And the Russian prince had seen an opening to bring Arkan down. This matter put the Wardens and Arkan on a collision course, so he gave us both a little push. I had put most of this together already, but it was nice to have a confirmation.

"I want her dead," Arabella stated, her voice flat.

"Not as much as me," I told her. "I'd like to rip her throat out." I made the squeezing motion with my hand. "Then she couldn't hurt us anymore. It would be reassuring."

Everyone looked at me. Apparently, I must've said something surprising.

"Unfortunately, there is the small matter of the oath of office," I said. "I'm the Acting Warden. I have . . . obligations."

"Screw obligations." Arabella punched the table. It quaked a little.

"We will arrest her," Alessandro told her. "If she resists, we will neutralize her one way or another."

Arabella pinched her lips together, her mouth a hard flat line.

"We are on full lockdown going forward," I said. "Arkan is coming. Do we need to get the kids out?"

"No," Ragnar said.

Halle raised her head off the table. "Absolutely not. We're not leaving. This is our home."

I looked at Cornelius.

"I will remain here," Matilda announced.

"It seems like the most prudent course of action," Cornelius said.

Patricia grabbed her trash can, stepped out into the hallway, and shut the door.

We all silently looked at each other until the retching sounds stopped and she came back in.

"Sending the children out creates an opportunity for hostages," Patricia said.

"Then the kids will stay," I said. "What about Regina?"

"My wife is still with her cousin in Lyon," Patricia said. "She isn't due back for another week. I've let them know about the situation and asked her to not cut her trip short."

I could imagine how that had gone. Knowing Regina, she would've wanted to be on the next plane to Houston.

"Where are we with our phones?" Mom asked.

Everyone looked at Bernard. He reached under the table and produced a large box filled with neatly stacked phones, each labeled with a name. Leon took his phone out and passed the box around the table.

"This won't happen again," Bernard said.

"Is there a plan for this Arkan situation?" Arabella asked.

"Konstantin provided us with a breakdown of Arkan's finances. He has squirreled away a big chunk of money stateside. We take it away from him," I said. I knew an FBI agent who would be overjoyed to help.

Alessandro spoke, his voice tinted with detachment, as if he were discussing a chore. "He has a mole in the Harris County DA's office."

Leon whistled.

I'd cursed when I found out.

"There are other informants as well, but that one is the most important," Alessandro said.

"Are you going to expose him?" Arabella asked.

"No. I'm going to take care of him personally," the Artisan said.

There was an awful finality in his voice. I had forgotten how angry he was.

Arabella smiled. "I like that part."

I turned to Leon. "What exactly happened with the FBI?"

Leon shrugged. "Nothing much."

I waited.

He sighed. "I followed them to the Caberas."

"I didn't see you."

"You weren't supposed to see me. You said 'shadow.' You didn't say 'make yourself seen.'"

He had a point.

"Arkan's people hit us on the Justice Park Drive," Leon continued.

"Literally forty-five seconds from the FBI field office. An enerkinetic and some other weird shithead. The enerkinetic lit up their vehicle with projectiles. It blew up a little bit . . ."

"Define a little bit," Mom said.

"Driver's side door blew off and the engine flew out and landed on their SUV's roof. It crushed the top of the car but didn't fall all the way through." Leon raised his hand and tilted it side to side. "Halfway in, halfway out type of thing. Of course, the windows shattered because the roof came down."

"Cheap-assed armored glass," Grandma Frida opined. "That's government contract work for you."

I killed a groan.

"I dropped the enerkinetic, but the other asshole snuck up from the opposite side. He shot bursts of this glowing crap, looked like seaweed, stung like a jellyfish, and things got serious when it wrapped around the car and the metal started smoking."

"Where were the FBI agents at this point?" Mom growled.

"Inside the car."

Oh no.

"It took me a second to find him," Leon said. "The car was smoking, and the fumes made it difficult to see and breathe, and then the seaweed kind of contracted, and there was a crunchy noise, so it was hard to hear."

Arabella put her head on the table, face down.

"Then he tried to shoot that shit at me, and I saw the direction it was coming from, and the rest is history." Leon grinned.

"What happened to the FBI agents breathing in toxic fumes while trapped in a car that was being crushed?" Alessandro asked.

"I pulled them out. Agent Garcia was mostly okay. Wahl wasn't breathing, so I did CPR until the FBI guys ran out of the building and helped."

"That's my boy!" Grandma Frida said.

I stared at him.

"What?" He raised his arms. "He was breathing fine when I left. They put one of those masks on his face and he kept taking it off to curse. All is well that ended well. And now I've got cool scars. Chicks dig scars."

"Such a fascinating family," Konstantin said.

He didn't know the half of it.

"Okay," I said. "We all know what we're doing. Arabella, you are guarding, I'm going to deal with Arkan's accounts, Alessandro and Konstantin will go after the mole."

"What about us?" Ragnar asked.

"You recuperate. We don't know when we will get attacked again."

"Before we adjourn," Cornelius said. "Has anyone seen the spider?"

"There is a spider?" Konstantin asked.

Arabella opened her eyes wide. "Yes, very large, very venomous."

Bern tapped his laptop. The security feed from the office hallway ignited on the screen on the wall. On it, Jadwiga leisurely made her way across the carpet and scurried into Arabella's office. The timestamp said 03:41 a.m.

"Well, she's still alive," Cornelius said.

"She's in there." Matilda pointed at the side wall. "I will try to coax her out when it's quiet."

"I want to stress that an attack can come at any time," I said. "He will throw everything he can at us. Nevada and Connor are dealing with Matthew Berry and his PAC mercenaries. The government is pretending that this problem doesn't exist. The National Assembly is trying to manage the death of its Speaker. We are on our own."

Everyone nodded. Nobody seemed alarmed or surprised. They just accepted it. Somewhere along the line in the last three or four years, House Baylor had become a combat House. If Arkan thought his blitz would break us, he was in for a lot of disappointment.

"You should make some of those little sandwiches with Hawaiian rolls and leftover pork tenderloin," Grandma Frida told me. "So your mother won't starve in her crow's nest."

The conference room emptied.

Leon paused by Alessandro on his way out. "How did you know about Buller being vulnerable to knives?"

"Watched a recording of him fighting a praelia once," Alessandro said.

Mages with the praelia talent summoned weapons and amplified them with their magic. They were usually called warrior mages and they were hell in a fight at close range.

"The praelia had a glowing katana," Alessandro said. "It did nothing. Toward the end of the fight, he ran out of juice and his sword disappeared. Buller grabbed him by the throat, and the mage pulled out a knife and tried to force it through the armor. He was pushing it in and it looked like it hit home, because Buller went berserk and stomped the guy to death."

"Nice find," Leon said and left.

It was just Arabella, Alessandro, and me.

"Are you okay?" I asked her.

"How much time did I have left when you revived me?" she asked.

"Twelve minutes," I told her. "You were the first one Halle detoxified."

Arabella gave me a brooding look.

"I'm sorry," I told her.

"I'm tired of bad shit happening."

"Me too."

She sighed and pushed to her feet. "I'm going to go . . . do things."

She left the room and shut the door behind her. Alessandro and I looked at each other.

"Explain the Cousin Sasha thing to me, please. How are you involved with the Imperium?"

He sighed. "How much do you remember about the change of the Russian dynasty?"

"Not that much. In 1916, the power balance in the First World War shifted in favor of Russia. The German Empire suffered heavy casualties and decided to assassinate Czar Nicholas II. I think they bombed his family's motorcade during Easter. Only Anastasia and Alexei survived because they were not in the two front cars."

"That's right." Alessandro nodded. "The murder created a vacuum. Alexei was too young and too sick to take the throne. The Imperium was in the middle of a war and required a strong hand. They offered the crown to a half-dozen people, but everyone refused."

I had no idea the Russians had to play musical chairs with the throne of the largest empire on the European Continent. The history textbooks I'd read glossed over that part. Of course, in Texas the history of Texas took up more space in the textbook than the entirety of the rest of Western Civilization combined.

"What happened then?" I asked.

"Russia scrambled to find someone who was both suitable and willing to accept the crown. They chose Michael Berezin, who'd spearheaded the Russian offensive against the German Empire. Michael Berezin became Michael I, and his entire family rallied around him to make sure he survived. The country depended on it. They faced a war from the outside and civil unrest from the inside. Communists were still agitating the workers in large cities. They were mostly failing because by killing Nicholas II, Germany made him into a martyr. The Russians wanted a new monarch and they wanted payback."

"That explains volumes about how Konstantin thinks. Family against the world."

"Exactly. Michael I had a younger brother, Boris. He was an antistasi mage, like his mother, and a Communist sympathizer. He thought that Russia would be better off without the monarchy, so he conspired with his Communist cell to assassinate his brother. The Okhrana, the Imperial secret police, had planted an operative in the cell to keep an eye on him. The plot was exposed."

"Plots often are."

"Michael I couldn't bear to kill his baby brother, so Boris was stripped of his titles and holdings and exiled instead. He ended up in the UK, where he bought a false identity, and married into a merchant family, the Winstons, who were willing to look past wobbly birth certificates and passports to add an upper-range Significant to their gene pool."

"Your mother's family."

He nodded. "My great-grandfather was a very bitter man. He spent his life trying to regain his titles and status."

"I thought you said he was a Communist."

"That was before he became poor." Alessandro laughed softly. "My grandfather was obsessed with titles as well, which is why my mother ended up in an arranged marriage to my father."

His mother was a lower-level Significant antistasi. He'd told me before that she had the magic, but not the power or the training to use it.

"My maternal grandfather arranged that marriage for the title, my mother went along with it because she liked my father and wanted to escape her family, my father thought she was beautiful and they would make powerful children, and my paternal grandfather got a dowry out of it. Everyone benefited."

His eyes were dark. Eleven years after his parents walked down the aisle, Arkan murdered Marcello Sagredo, and Alessandro's life would never be the same.

I stood up and wrapped my arms around him. He sighed, quietly exhaling tension.

"Does the Imperium want you back?" I asked.

"It's not me I worry about. Konstantin is dangerous."

"I know. I will be careful."

His phone chimed. He took it out of his pocket and looked at it. "Arkan pulled Sanders out of Alaska."

Sanders was bad news. Of all the Primes in Arkan's arsenal, he gave me the biggest dollop of anxiety.

Alessandro got up and kissed me. "I have to make a call."

"I have to let a Russian prince know exactly where he stands."

He held up his hand. We gave each other a quiet high five and headed out of the conference room, he to his office and I to the front door.

Konstantin sat on a stone bench outside our office building, exactly where I asked him to be after the meeting. A line of our guard dogs stretched from him. They approached one by one, led by their handlers, so they could memorize his scent. I wanted him properly tagged before he and Alessandro went out.

The sky couldn't decide if it wanted to be overcast or flooded with sunshine, and the wind kept pushing the clouds back and forth. As I stepped outside, the clouds overhead slid aside and a ray of golden sunshine broke through and spilled onto Konstantin, setting his hair and skin aglow. He looked like an angel. Not one of those untouchable regal angels, but one suffused with warmth. It truly was a movie moment.

I half expected him to turn to me in slow motion as a sappy soundtrack kicked in.

Konstantin held out his hand as Ranger, a huge German shepherd, sniffed him. *"Kakoy horoshiy pios."*

"Do you like dogs?"

He nodded. "They are honest creatures. Unlike us."

He would know.

The prince turned to me and smiled.

Wow.

"I didn't realize you were good with a blade," he said.

"There are many things about me you don't realize." And I would keep it that way.

"I am beginning to see that."

The way he was looking at me . . . It was a little much.

"Why didn't Arkan target Smirnov? He knew we had him. It was logical that he would be in the armory, and yet Buller walked right past it."

Konstantin regarded me with his stunning aquamarine eyes. "Arkan lacks objectivity. He is sentimental, and he places value on friendships. Let's take Xavier. He is undisciplined, volatile, and impulsive. Everything Arkan detests. But for reasons known only to him, he likes Xavier. He sees him as an apprentice of sorts. He lets him get away with things that would get most of his other agents terminated. In American terms, he plays favorites. Smirnov was the favorite. They met in basic training. They were both plucked out of it by Imperial Security, and they went through Miasorubka together. The Meat Grinder. Intense combat training. I suppose your SEAL program might be similar, except that SEAL candidates can quit and rarely die in training. People fed to Miasorubka die quite often."

"What will happen when Arkan realizes you killed Smirnov?"

Konstantin grinned. "I imagine he will face the sky and howl like a wolf. I wish I could see it."

He could call Arkan anytime and tell him that his best friend was dead. Yes, that would change the nature of the bait, but I was sure when Arkan found out that Konstantin murdered Smirnov, he would move heaven and earth to punish him. Konstantin was saving it for just the right moment.

The dog pack retreated, led away by their handlers.

"You are out of dogs."

"Not quite."

I clicked my tongue. The bushes to my left rustled, and Shadow emerged into the open. My dog did not like strangers. She was very good at not being seen when she didn't want to be.

The prince blinked.

I scooped her up and pointed to Konstantin. "Bad."

Shadow let out a quiet woof.

"Yes, we don't like him. Bad, bad."

"Is that a dachshund mixed with something? Scottish terrier, perhaps?"

"That's not important," I told him.

Shadow growled, picking up on the hostility in my voice. I set her down. She woofed one more time to let him know she meant business and wagged her tail. As I straightened, I saw two big shapes coming down the shaded path between the trees, a slender, short human between them. A fourth shadow trotted alongside, almost comically small in comparison. They moved silently, the shadows of the tree canopy sliding over their fur.

Amusement sparked in Konstantin's eyes. "Now I have met everyone. Am I free to wander?"

"Not yet."

"Is there more? Perhaps a miniature attack poodle or a valiant chihuahua?"

"Something like that." I nodded in the direction of the path.

Konstantin turned to see and clicked his mouth shut.

Several years ago, the military attempted to apply magic and genetic engineering to make hyperintelligent bears. They planned to use them in combat, how or why I could never understand. The program had been discontinued but some of its animal combatants remained. Sgt. Teddy was one of them. An enormous Kodiak, he stood at five feet three inches tall on all fours and ten and a half feet tall when he reared. He weighed over fifteen hundred pounds. His paws were bigger than my head and could crack a human skull like a walnut with one swipe. His claws were almost six inches long and his teeth would give you nightmares.

Despite all of that, Sgt. Teddy was a pacifist. He preferred human company to living in the wild, and he liked kids. Next to him ten-year-old Matilda looked tiny, like a waifish toddler. The sixty-pound golden retriever trailing them was like a six-week-old puppy.

The creature strolling on the other side of Matilda was anything but a pacifist. The first thing you noticed was his color. His fur was a striking indigo blue, so vivid, it seemed unreal, a color that should have belonged to some exotic bird, not a massive feline predator. Two and a half feet tall at the shoulder, six and a half feet long, he strode forward on huge paws hiding sickle claws. His muscular body was reminiscent of a tiger, but the fringe of tentacles around his neck left no doubt that Zeus was not a creature born on Earth.

The two beasts approached. Zeus halted two feet from Konstantin, leaned forward, and sniffed, his eyes flashing turquoise.

The Russian prince held very still.

His face realigned itself very subtly. He was almost impossibly beautiful now.

"We haven't been properly introduced," he said to Matilda. "I am Prince Konstantin Berezin. Who do I have the honor of addressing?"

"I'm Matilda Harrison, of House Harrison."

"It is a pleasure, Matilda." He bowed his head. "I'm very sorry my actions led to your father being injured. It was not my intention to include him in this affair. I ask your forgiveness and hope you will allow me to make amends."

Wow. He read Matilda in a split second. Most people wouldn't talk to a ten-year-old that way, but somehow, he figured out that Matilda was an adult in a child's body.

"Are you a real prince?"

"Yes. My uncle is the emperor, and he often tells me that I'm his favorite nephew."

Matilda considered this. "Are you?"

"I suspect my uncle tells that to all of his nephews when he wants us to do something for him."

She raised her chin. "I accept your apology. Sgt. Teddy thinks you smell like a bear."

He nodded. "My House has a long affinity with bears. You might say we're practically family."

And what the hell did that mean?

Matilda squinted at him, then turned to me. "The scent has been acquired."

"Thank you, Matilda."

"Clearly, I'm in *The Jungle Book*," Konstantin said. "I have met the wolves, the bear, and the panther."

"Don't worry, there's no python."

He gave me an odd look. "I already met her."

"What?" I asked.

"Never mind. I was being frivolous."

"Being frivolous is not a good idea," Matilda said. "My father tells me that killing is an inevitable part of being a Prime. If you break the rules, I will kill you."

"Consider me properly warned." Konstantin nodded.

The golden retriever trotted forward and sat, staring at Konstantin with a happy canine grin.

"This is Rooster," Matilda said. "She will be your watcher."

"Of all the dogs available to you, you chose to assign me a golden retriever?" Konstantin's eyebrows rose a fraction of an inch.

"Please change shape, Your Highness," Matilda said.

Konstantin's face blurred, and Alessandro sat in his place. It was a perfect impersonation, down to the narrow cut on Alessandro's chin, which he got fighting Buller.

Rooster exploded into barks. She wasn't just loud. She was deafening.

"Dear God," Konstantin yelled over the noise, "it's like being punched in the eardrums."

"Change back, please," Matilda ordered.

Konstantin reappeared. Rooster fell silent and panted at him.

"Rooster barks at 112 decibels," Matilda informed him. "She can continue to bark for hours without straining herself. If you change shape, she will bark. If you attempt to escape, she will bark. If you try to separate from her in any way . . ."

"She will bark?" Konstantin asked.

"Yes. If she barks for longer than one minute, the electronic sensor in her collar will send an alert. Cutting the collar or removing it will also trigger an alert." Matilda stared at him. "If anything happens to Rooster or her collar, I will know. I will come. I will bring friends. I hope we understand each other."

"Crystal clear," he told her.

"Please follow me now," Matilda told him. "I've been asked to familiarize you with the layout of the Compound."

"I'd be delighted," he told her.

The two of them walked down the path, flanked by a bear and an arcane tentacled tiger. Rooster trotted after them, her gaze fixed on Konstantin.

Patricia came out of the office and stood beside me. "Is that wise?"

"We can't contain him, and we can't keep him locked up. Might as well let him wander, supervised."

Patricia sighed. "We are being watched."

"We knew that."

"No, Arkan kept an eye on us. They'd buzz us with a drone once in a while or put some cameras on random trees just outside the property line, which we would find and take down. Now he has two active watch posts. One is on Orduna's ranch, watching our front gate, and the other is on the Reading property, watching our driveway. They have us under 24-hour surveillance."

"It can't be helped. It can be an advantage in certain circumstances."

Patricia nodded. "Also, I've been approached."

"Stick or carrot?"

"The stick for now. They're trying to blackmail me. Walk away or else."

"Regina?"

Patricia nodded again. She was our knight in shining armor, who made sure our guard force acted as a unit. Without her, we would be dead in the water. Her wife was hiding a secret. Regina was Patricia's weakness. Of course they would zero in on her.

"Have you told her?"

"Yes."

"How do the two of you feel about that?"

Patricia smiled, her light British accent crisp. "We are not in the habit of rolling over."

I let out an internal breath.

"We didn't meet under the best of circumstances," Patricia said.

"True."

When Patricia had walked into our office two years ago, our defenses were in shambles and her reputation was in tatters. She was practically unhireable by most House standards, but we were desperate, and she came highly recommended by Sgt. Heart, one of Connor's veteran operatives, a scary and competent man whom everyone held in a very high regard. Especially Mom. In the past year their romance had progressed from discreet meetings and Mom casually mentioning that "Benjiro called" to full on dinners in public and chilling together in the pool. They were on the cusp of making it official, and all of us were in favor of it. Patricia couldn't have come with a better recommendation.

Patricia faced me. "This is home now. We like it here."

"I'm glad."

Patricia laughed softly.

"If we do survive this, you will be in high demand," I said.

She raised her eyebrows at me.

"A security chief who held off Arkan. Whatever stains and blotches are on your record will be wiped clean. Houses will fall over their feet trying to hire you. You could write your own ticket."

"You realize it's not in your best interests to point this out?"

"Yes, but it is fair."

"Then you better think of a way to keep me here, Prime Baylor." Her tone suggested it wouldn't be very hard.

"I'll put it on my list," I told her.

# Chapter 10

I paced back and forth, trying to match the speed of my body to the speed of my brain. I had notified most of our allies and most of the probable high-risk targets that we were under attack and declined a dozen offers of assistance. Cornelius' sister and brother were in DC on business, in the public eye and well protected. My disaster of an aunt had been pulled off the street in Mexico by a private security firm. They would sit on her until the danger passed.

I had tried Wahl's cell, but the call went straight to voice mail, which likely meant the FBI agent was still recuperating.

I also had a long and grueling conversation regarding logistics and compensation with the man who would help us make sure Arkan went deaf and blind. It was like swimming in a very small pool with a very large shark. It was so bad, I texted Arabella two-thirds of the way through and let her take over the bargaining.

Alessandro and Konstantin had left an hour ago. They would neutralize Arkan's mole in the DA's office. I wasn't sure what would happen next. Arkan could hit us as soon as he realized his agent had been compromised, or he could wait and gather all of his forces for one decisive assault. Alessandro promised to video call during the meeting. If an attack came, it would be soon.

I had a nagging feeling that I had overlooked something. What was it? What hole did I fail to plug?

"If you keep doing this, I'll have to replace the rug," Bern informed me.

He sat at a horseshoe-shaped desk, with an array of monitors arranged around him. When we lived in the warehouse, all of his equipment had been contained in the small room we called the Hut of Evil. Since we'd moved, he had upgraded to a full-blown Lair. The computer lab now occupied the entire first floor of a short tower we had built to Bern's specifications. The horseshoe desk and the space around it took up most of the floor, with the gaming room featuring a row of computers and gaming chairs separated off to the side by a glass wall. A small fridge stuffed with drinks and a couch on which Runa right now napped completed the furnishings. Bern ruled over his kingdom like an ancient despot, and his tone suggested that he had judged my pacing to be a capital offense.

He'd asked me to come, but when I got there, I was presented with his back and some furious typing.

"What am I forgetting?" I asked him.

"Food. Sleep."

"Haha. When was the last time you slept?"

"That's not relevant. Okay. You may look."

I came over and stood by his chair. A black screen greeted me with some indecipherable code.

"Honey?" Bern said.

Runa pulled herself off the couch and stumbled over to us.

Bern raised his right hand and very deliberately pressed the Enter key.

Code blossomed on the screen, scrolling at dizzying speed. The display went dark.

"I love it," Runa said. She leaned over, hugged Bern, and kissed his cheek.

Bern smiled.

Runa turned around and went back to her couch.

"What am I looking at?" I asked him.

"I crashed Arkan's network," Bern said.

We looked at the dark screen.

"Do you think he's screaming right now?" I asked.

Bern gave me another smile.

We looked at the screen some more.

My cousin typed a quick sequence. "I have something for you."

A large monitor directly above us showed the inside of an armored car. Alessandro was in the driver's seat. The dark-haired woman next to him wore the tactical uniform of our guards. I didn't recognize her.

The woman said something in Russian in Konstantin's voice.

"How am I seeing this?"

Bern paused the video. "A hidden dashboard cam. All of our vehicles have them."

I wasn't aware of that upgrade. "Since when?"

"Since two months ago."

"Shouldn't I have approved something like that?"

"I approved it," Bern said. "As the Chief of Surveillance and Cyber Security."

"Chief of what now?"

"Surveillance and Cyber Security. That's how I'm written into our incorporation papers. This is a good security measure."

"Can I disable the camera in my vehicle?"

"Yes."

He left it at that. Fine, I would ask Grandma Frida. Ten to one she had installed them in the first place. Right now, I had bigger fish to fry.

"Are you spying on Alessandro?"

"No, I'm spying on the prince."

"How old is this recording?" I asked.

"Half an hour."

"I never took you for a man willing to play second fiddle," Konstantin said in English. "You were raised to lead your House, the crumbling ruin that it is. You are a man who would rather captain a sinking ship that's yours than be a sailor on a luxury liner."

"You serve the throne. You will never sit on it." Alessandro's voice was flat and quiet.

"But I wasn't raised with an expectation of leading. You were, Count Sagredo. She is the Head of her House, issuing orders, making decisions, and what does that make you? A loyal bodyguard? A pretty face in her bed?"

You asshole.

"It has to chafe a bit, trading your independence and your birthright for a seat at her table. You know they only listen to you because she's there. They tolerate you as long as you make her happy. Not quite the loving family you always wanted."

Alessandro didn't answer. Did it actually bother him? Is that the way he saw it?

"If you have a fight, they'll always take her side. If you break up, they'll line up to kick you on your way out the door. The only way to secure your position is though children, but we both know the compatibility isn't there."

Anxiety squeezed me. I wanted to have children. Not now, but eventually. I wanted to have Alessandro's children. I didn't give a crap what kind of powers they might have. I just loved him, and I would love our children. They would be smart and funny like him. They might have his eyes and his smile. And in my selfish little love, I never wondered how he felt about it. His bloodline was so long. His entire childhood was about learning to protect and preserve it. He was always expected to pass his powers to the next generation.

What if our children weren't antistasi?

"Maybe all of that is true," Alessandro said. "However, her mother is an excellent shot, and yet all of the former boyfriends and girlfriends of her children are still breathing despite their many sins. What did you think when your mother strangled Liudmilla in that hotel room? How did your perfect older brother take it?"

Konstantin's smile widened and he bared his teeth at Alessandro. It bothered him. Alessandro's thrust had hit home.

"My mother loves us unconditionally," Konstantin said. "She wishes only the best for us, and she will take sins upon herself for our benefit. Can you say the same? More importantly, can you do the same?"

Alessandro turned his head to glance at him.

"What can you offer her, really?"

"Whatever you are thinking, stop thinking it," Alessandro told him.

Konstantin smiled. "Recently I've had an occasion to visit the Siberian diamond mines. They have a saying there. 'A man who finds a diamond never gets to keep it.' Thank you for finding this diamond, Sasha."

Alessandro pulled into the parking lot in front of the new Justice Center, parked, and looked at the prince. I almost took a step back. He'd gone into his Artisan mode, and his face was so cold.

"This isn't the Imperium, Konstantin. And she isn't a rock, she is a person. You've grown accustomed to thinking everything belongs to your family including people. It's a bad habit. In this country people have freedom and a choice. Whatever choice she makes, I'll help her realize it. If someone decides to block her path, I will remove them."

Konstantin gave a theatrical shiver. "Very menacing."

"1547."

"Is that supposed to mean something?" Konstantin raised his eyebrows, but his pose shifted slightly.

"The code to the little wooden cabin your parents use in Berekhino when the pressure becomes too much and they want to hide and fish on Oka River. Consider your next move carefully."

The screen went dark.

"I've looked up the Liudmilla incident," Bern said. "Konstantin's older brother had a fiancée who hung herself in her hotel room while on holiday with her family. She had a history of 'mental instability' according to Russian press. Make of that what you will."

I crossed my arms and stared at the screen.

"The way he talks about you suggests he's thought about this. It's not a spur-of-the-moment thing."

"Yep," Runa said from the couch. "He watches you."

"I caught that." Prince Berezin had developed an unhealthy interest in me. No, it was more likely that the Russian Imperium developed an interest in me, which was bad any way you looked at it. I would have to figure out a good way to discourage it. Permanently.

A door slammed shut, and Arabella burst into the tower brandishing a piece of paper. "Four hundred and seventy-two thousand dollars?!"

Runa jerked upright. "What's going on?"

"Nothing," Bern told her. "Go back to bed, baby."

"Are you kidding right now? Is this a joke?" Arabella waved her arms.

Bern squinted at Arabella. "I told you to stop playing that gacha game. Spending real money on digital characters can only lead to trouble, especially considering the odds."

"It's not my gaming bill! It's the bill from the Office of Records!"

Ouch.

"I'm going to kill Leon," Arabella growled.

Bern put on his noise-cancelling headphones and stabbed his finger at the meeting room.

"Let's talk in there." I headed to the gaming room, texting Leon as I walked.

"Four hundred and seventy-two thousand dollars!" Arabella snarled.

Leon shrugged. "I thought it was rather reasonable."

Arabella stared at him, and I wondered if her head would explode. My sister's volume control had suffered a critical malfunction. She seemed to be communicating in declarative statements only.

"Look," Leon said. "Twelve cars, two broken light poles, and a chunk of the parking lot that has to be repaved. We're paying replacement cost for the cars based on the current market value. We're giving them an option of taking a lump sum or a replacement vehicle. Most of them want the lump sum, which actually favors us . . ."

She planted her arms on the table and leaned forward. "That's not the point."

"They could have charged us for the building," he said in his most reasonable tone.

"We shouldn't be paying any of these costs. We did not cause this damage. Xavier, Gunderson, and Arkan are the ones who wrecked everything."

"I checked with Sabrian," I said. "We can sue Gunderson's estate, but they would likely turn around and sue us for wrongful death. They won't win, but it will be long and painful and will drag on forever, at the end of which we will be left with a bunch of legal fees. Unless we can get House Gunderson to pay them, but according to their credit reports, their financial situation could be better, so even if we did win, it would take years to—"

"We don't have to sue Gunderson. Let the Keeper sue Gunderson."

"It's really difficult to talk to you when you're like this," Leon said.

"It's very important that we maintain a cordial relationship with the Office of Records," I said.

"Which person in this family is responsible for finances?" Arabella asked.

"You are," I told her.

"Great. I'm so glad we got this cleared up. We are not paying this bill."

"Yes, we are," I said.

"It's not our responsibility!"

"Mom was in danger. She went to the Office of Records. They kept her safe until I got there. Then we had a giant fight in the parking lot and the cars belonging to the employees of the Office of Records were damaged. Someone has to make them whole. Xavier and Gunderson aren't going to do it."

"Not our problem," Arabella said. "The Office of Records should have protected Mom. It is their civic duty. They don't get credit for not being assholes."

"It's like talking to a wall," Leon said.

She turned her head and hit him with a death glare. "Did you even try to negotiate?"

"I did."

"How did that go? Walk me through it."

He shrugged. "I went in and met Michael. A somber looking dude. I told him that I was there on behalf of House Baylor to take care of the damages. He gave me a list. I looked at it. It seemed reasonable. I offered our apologies and told him we would handle it."

"And what did he say?"

"Nothing. I think he might be mute."

"He isn't," I said.

Arabella straightened. "I'm going to take that list, roll it into a tube, and shove it up Michael's ass."

"No!" Leon and I said at the same time.

"Yes."

"Don't do this," I told her. "That is a direct order."

"I don't care."

"Arabella, if you try to fight with him, he will kill you. He scares the shit out of me. He's death and darkness."

She raised her chin. "Good. I could use the exercise."

Oh God. I knew that look. She wouldn't listen to me. She wouldn't listen to anyone right now. I needed serious backup.

I grabbed my phone and dialed Nevada. She picked up instantly. I switched the call to FaceTime. My sister was in the car, in the passenger seat.

"Arabella's upset about the bill from the Office of Records and wants to confront Michael," I snitched.

Nevada leaned into the phone. I flipped it, so the screen faced Arabella.

"You can't do that," Nevada said.

"Watch me."

"If you do this, you will put the whole family in danger."

"What is the Keeper going to do? Assault us? He'll have to get in line."

"Listen to me." Nevada's voice vibrated with authority. She sounded almost like Mom. "You're having an emotional moment because you're still upset about Mom being hurt and Linus falling into a coma. You want to punish someone for it, but the Keeper of Records can't be that person. He didn't hurt Mom. Michael didn't hurt Mom. Michael actually saved Mom. And Catalina, and Cornelius. You aren't being fair."

"Well, it's not fair that Mom got hurt, is it?" Some of the heat went out of Arabella's voice.

Mom loved us and she was the ultimate authority when we were kids. But for most of our adolescence, Nevada took care of us as well. She ran the business that fed us and kept a roof over our heads, and when we had problems we didn't know how to handle, we went to her first and Mom second.

"We need to take care of this," Nevada said. "Right now this is a problem that can easily be solved with money. If you escalate it, we won't be able to fix it at all. Do you need money? Because I've got loads, and I don't mind at all making sure that the people who saved Mom are not left holding the bag."

Oh, that was smart.

Arabella drew back. "Keep your money. We have our own."

"Bug is looking for Xavier," Nevada said. "We will find that asshole, and when we do, Connor will squish him like the cockroach he is."

"Yeah, yeah, whatever." Arabella waved her hand.

I ended the call.

"You are not wrong," Leon said. "But you know we're right."

"Yes," Arabella growled. "Thank you for taking care of the bill and the negotiations. I'll issue the payment."

"You're welcome."

She got up and went out. Well, that had gone better than expected.

Leon put a long object wrapped in a towel onto the table. "For you."

I pulled the towel aside. Linus' null sword. Oh my God. It had survived.

"I pulled it out of Rhino's wreckage," he said.

"You are the best!"

"I am," Leon said solemnly. "It's the heavy burden I bear."

Bern waved at me through the glass wall.

"I have to go," I told him.

"I'll come with. I want to see this."

The big monitor showed the inside of Lenora Jordan's office, a space of oversize bookcases, red drapes, and Persian rugs. Lenora Jordan, a black woman in her forties, sat behind a heavy desk of reclaimed wood. She wasn't just the Harris County DA, she was its paladin, resolute, incorruptible, and unyielding. She wore a grey power suit, but it might as well have been armor. The Houses of Houston recognized the need for law and order, and they chose her as its enforcer. Lenora Jordan didn't know how to be intimidated.

Her face was impassive. She was looking at the laptop in front of her. On the other side of the desk, Alessandro and Konstantin sat in large leather chairs. Konstantin had shifted back into Smirnov. He was tall, dour, and stooped, and he fidgeted as he sat. I'd never seen him do that so far, so it must've been one of Smirnov's mannerisms.

A careful knock echoed through the room. The door must have edged open off-screen because Lenora looked up and nodded. Matt entered the room. The last time I'd seen him, when he came to pick up Alessandro, he'd worn a dress shirt with rolled-up sleeves, his hair was a mess, and his face had sported two days of stubble. Today he wore a black suit, his hair was brushed back, and his tan face was clean shaven. He looked like what he was, a young successful attorney.

He strode into the room and stopped in the middle of the rug in front of Lenora's desk. "You wanted to see me . . ."

He saw Smirnov. In a split second his expression tore like a flimsy mask. His hand went into his jacket.

Alessandro shot across the room, insanely fast. He gripped Matt's arm, twisted, and a gun fell onto the carpet. If I had blinked, I would've missed it. One moment Matt was reaching for his gun, the next he was bent over, his arm clamped in Alessandro's fingers.

"Thank you, Prime Sagredo," Lenora said. "I'll take it from here."

Alessandro released Matt and stepped back.

Thick chains burst from the rug, spiraling around Matt in a flash. In half a second, they gripped him in a magical fist, lifting him off the ground two feet into the air. His glasses sat askew on his nose, but they did nothing to diminish the defiance that twisted his face.

He looked down at Lenora and sneered. "Ah. I always wondered what this felt like."

"You betrayed this office," Lenora said.

"Yes."

"Why?"

"Money, of course," Matt said. His expression turned harsh. "Do you even know what my starting salary was? No, of course you don't. Sixty-four thousand dollars. I've been here for three years. Now I make sixty-eight."

Lenora remained unmoved.

A little color came back into Matt's face. He kept going.

"I graduated from Columbia with one hundred ninety thousand in law school debt, and that's on top of the hundred grand I still owe to Baylor U for my bachelor's. My apartment costs three grand a month, and I hate it. Every day I deal with Houses and Primes, whose brats get busted for underage drinking and DUI in their Mercedes and Audis, while I bust my ass so I can drive a Honda. I have to buy my suits on credit, just so I won't be laughed at."

"Is that so?" Lenora tilted her head. "One hundred and seventy-two dollars."

"What is that?"

"The monthly food stamp allowance my mother was receiving the year I graduated from high school. Tell me again about your suits. Are they nice?"

Matt blinked, then recovered. "You know what, whatever. You are a shitty boss, Lenora. You don't take care of your people, so I found someone who does. Whatever you're hoping to get out of me, forget it. The hex in my head is better than anything you can throw at it."

Matt twisted his neck to glare at Smirnov. "And you? Your days are numbered."

A door swung open, and Nevada walked in and stood beside Lenora. Matt's face blanched.

"Mr. Benson," Nevada said.

Matt didn't answer.

Nevada picked up the corners of the rug and folded it in half, exposing the dark floor underneath. The chains slid out of her way, shifting Matt aside, and straightened again.

"Last night Xavier Secada put a chunk of metal through my mother's leg," my sister said.

Matt swallowed and licked his lips. "I'm sorry to hear that."

"So was I." Nevada took out a piece of chalk. "I think you and I should have a nice long chat."

My phone rang. An unfamiliar foreign number starting with 351. Now what?

I waved at Bern. He muted the feed, and I took the call on speaker.

"Prime Baylor speaking."

"My name is Christina Almeida, Prime of House Almeida."

Female, young, slight trace of an accent, not Spanish, not Italian, something else.

Bern's fingers flew over the keyboard. The search engine spat the results. House Almeida, a Portuguese House, old nobility, rich, made money from rubber and cork . . .

"How can I help you?"

Another page of results. Christina Almeida, Magus Praelia, Prime. A warrior mage. Like Buller, who conjured armor, praelia conjured weapons and they used them with deadly skill.

"I've come to retrieve my fiancé," Christina said.

"Who would that be?"

"Alessandro Sagredo."

What?

A text popped up with GPS coordinates.

You have questions. That's understandable. Meet me at this location in one hour. Let's talk.

I showed the coordinates to Bern. He plugged them into the search engine and Google Maps obliged. A park, ten minutes down the road from us.

Arkan made his move. That was so fast. How did he know?

"Will you come?" Christina asked.

An hour was tight, but it was enough time.

"I'll be there," I told her.

"Good. I am looking forward to our discussion."

 **Chapter 11**

"A s your cousin-brother, I feel compelled to point out the utter fuckedupness of this situation," Leon said as I took the turn onto the side road.

"I thought we agreed you wouldn't use that term."

"Fuckedupness?"

"Cousin-brother. Pick one, not both."

The area around the Compound was still mostly rural, with the city encroaching like an urban octopus stretching its tentacles. Fields rolled on both sides of the road, with a farmhouse here and there and small businesses like car repair shops and veterinary clinics sprouting up by the road at random. The armored troop transport rocked as it rolled over haphazard bumps in the road. It was very well protected but far less comfortable than Rhino. I missed our tank-SUV.

Leon checked his SIG Sauer. Runa had heroically offered to go with me on this adventure, but she could barely stand. Besides, Leon had mentioned he "needed comfort" again, which in Leon speak meant he wanted to be useful.

"Is this fiancée even real?" he asked.

"Probably."

"How?"

"I suspect that's something his family arranged. He's been getting phone calls."

"What kind of phone calls?"

"The kind he takes in private. He speaks in Italian, and they make him irritated."

The Sagredo family had been overextended for generations. They dragged a mountain of debt behind them, and they expected to sell Alessandro for a pretty penny. They had arranged three engagements for him, and Alessandro had torpedoed every one of them. Trying to sell him for a fourth time didn't seem like much of a stretch.

Leon frowned. "Correct me if I'm misunderstanding this, but he's been excised. They disowned him."

"Yes."

"So how could they be arranging marriages for him?"

"If something happens and you are excised, will you stop caring about your brother, or Arabella, or Nevada?"

He grimaced. "So it's emotional blackmail."

"Probably."

Our childhood shaped us in deep, fundamental ways, and Alessandro's childhood was all about taking his rightful place as the Head of the family, carrying on the Sagredo name, and marrying well to stave off creditors so House Sagredo could survive for one more generation. At heart, Alessandro was a protector. That part of him never disappeared; it only grew stronger, except now my family and I were the focus of that protective urge. Before he'd left with Konstantin, he'd kissed me and asked me to stay in the Compound until he returned. If he found out I left on this little expedition, he wouldn't be happy.

Unfortunately, it couldn't be helped. I needed to ascertain the scope of this threat.

"It's a messed-up family," I said. "His grandfather runs it, and neither Alessandro's grandmother nor his mother can stand up to him. He wants him to marry an heiress."

"He has a grandmother? And what, we're not rich enough?"

"It's not just a matter of money. It's about generational guilt and lost noble titles which shouldn't matter but still do. He wants Alessandro to get a rich wife, come back to Italy, and then sit on his hands for the rest of his life. Because that's what he and Alessandro's father did. It's kind of a family tradition for the men in his family. If Alessandro goes out and decides to make his own money, it will invalidate his grandfather's entire life. He doesn't want him to be successful, Leon."

"So it's his version of 'I suffered and lived in misery, so everyone else has to'?"

"Pretty much."

"Never understood that," Leon said. "If you suffered, wouldn't you want your grandson to have an easier time?"

"You and I would because we are not assholes." I made another turn. "The timing on this is fishy. We grab Arkan's snitch, and suddenly Alessandro's fiancée shows up."

"I don't like it," Leon said.

"Neither do I."

In the past six months, Alessandro and I had made arrangements to limit the potential damage his grandfather could do, but no preparations could account for all of the possibilities.

He didn't talk to me about it.

"They can't honestly think he will put his tail between his legs and crawl back to them," Leon said.

"That's exactly what they think."

The field on the right side had ended. A new subdivision was going up, bordered by a stone wall, half-finished roofs peaking above it. Signs dotted the side of the road.

The Estates at Brushy Creek.
From the low $400s
NEW HOMES
First phase available
WELCOME HOME
Turn left

The entrance to the subdivision waited ahead, bordered by curved stone flowerbeds. I steered the transport into it. We rolled past the model houses doubling as sales offices.

Ahead the four-lane street split, flowing around an island of green lawn that offered a playground and a large covered pavilion with picnic tables and barbecue grills. The houses closest to the entrance had been mostly complete, but here the construction was still in full swing. Skeletons of future homes rose on both sides, as building crews carried lumber and sank nails into the wooden frames. A big blue taco truck had stopped on one side of the park, serving tacos and sandwiches to the construction workers.

I eyed the truck.

"PTSD?" Leon asked.

"Yep. Wondering if it might explode."

I looped around the island, parked on the other side of it, facing the way back to the entrance, and shut off the engine. Despite the controlled construction chaos on both sides of the street, the park itself was deserted.

"You know that I wasn't a fan of the guy when the two of you started," Leon said. "He did stupid shit, and he hurt your feelings. However, I changed my mind. The man works hard, covers his bases, and he loves you with fairy-tale love."

I raised my eyebrows at him.

"The kind of love that you're supposed to find but most of us don't. He isn't going anywhere, Catalina."

"I'm not worried that he'll leave me, Leon. I'm worried they will hurt him."

I opened my door and stepped out. Leon got out of the transport and the two of us took a spot on a bench by the table.

Bern had run a quick background check on Christina Almeida while I was trying to get all my ducks in a row for this meeting. House Almeida was the seventh richest House in Portugal, and Christina was the youngest of the current generation. By all indications, she was adored by her family.

House Almeida mostly stayed out of the limelight. The Magus Praelia area of magic covered a lot of ground. In general terms, it meant a mage who used melee weapons, summoned or real, and altered their bodies to make themselves better killers. Some praelia made themselves faster or stronger, others boosted their reflexes. Some were capable of unleashing bursts of magic with their weapons.

The taco truck opened its window. About a dozen construction workers lined up to order.

"Incoming," I told Leon.

He smiled a slow dreamy smile.

A silver Audi slid to the curb across the street with a soft whisper. A tall, lean white-haired man got out of the driver's side and went around the car to the rear passenger door. His skin had an almost ochre tint, and his features were sharp, as if struck from stone by an impatient sculptor. I couldn't tell his age from his face or the way he moved. Somewhere between thirty and fifty.

Leon whistled the opening tune from *A Fistful of Dollars*.

The white-haired man opened the car door, and a woman stepped out. She was a year older than me, with pale skin and long dark hair, a cooler brown with carefully chosen highlights. Tall, about five ten, maybe a hundred and thirty pounds, long waisted, long legs, long arms. And she walked like a fencer, balanced and light on her feet. Her dark pantsuit fit her perfectly but was loose enough to let her move freely.

Huge grey eyes on an oval face, straight nose, a large mouth she toned down with pale pink lipstick . . . She was quite beautiful, in that upper-class slightly generic way. If you googled *European heiress*, you would find a slew of girls just like her, with big eyes, lovely smiles, and perfectly applied makeup designed to elevate their features rather than emphasize them.

She walked over and sat across from me. The man took position behind her. I sent my magic out. It spiraled from me, carefully slipping around Christina to the man behind her. Not a mental mage. His mind was unshielded and vulnerable. Probably an aegis. That's who I would bring.

"I'll get straight to it," Christina Almeida said in her accented voice. "Alessandro's family and my House have made arrangements. We are able to meet their financial demands."

They sold him. Again. As expected.

I let a single tendril of my power gently brush against Christina, its touch featherlight. An antistasi wall.

Interesting.

"How much did you pay for him?" Leon asked. "Just wondering what a good-looking Prime antistasi goes for on the open market these days."

Christina ignored him. "Your feelings for him and his feelings for you are immaterial to this arrangement. This is about family, obligation, and children."

She wasn't as strong as the basalt rock that was Alessandro's mind. She must've ranked lower, probably a Notable. Antistasi plus a Prime praelia. Summoned augmented weapons, maybe?

Christina leaned back, raising her chin slightly. "His family will never accept you."

"Not the greatest argument considering they excised him," Leon said.

"It's not just a matter of money but of class and pedigree. You have neither. Furthermore, you have no idea how to handle a Sagredo or how to navigate their family dynamic. His grandfather is an insufferable, toxic man."

On that, we agreed.

"If you marry Alessandro and travel with him to Italy, his grandfather will make you miserable until you either quit or die by his hand. If you marry Alessandro and keep him here, his excision will become permanent. He will lose all contact with his mother and sisters. The guilt will eat him alive. We both know duty to his family is his Achilles' heel and the benefits of a pretty face and intense sex only last so long. No vagina is magic."

Leon smiled.

"Unlike you, Ms. Baylor, I have the leverage to free Alessandro from his grandfather while preserving his other family ties. I will give him what he truly requires—a family with status and powerful children. My line is compatible with antistasi magic. My grandmother was one. I am also one. Feel free to test my mind."

Heh.

"Our children will be powerful, and their future will be assured, because my House will commit all of its resources to their training. They will be worthy of the Almeida name. Your children with him would struggle even if by some genetic miracle, they were born with some talent. Let him go. Let him live the life he pretended to have all these years. If you love him, help me make this as painless for him as possible. We both know he doesn't belong here."

I glanced at Leon. "Did you catch the 'my House will commit all of its resources' bit?"

"Mhm," he said. "They're planning to play ball until the old buzzard dies and then they'll try to absorb Sagredo into their House."

"I will win in the end, one way or another," Christina said. "I've viewed the recordings of your power. You require an arcane circle to be effective and your command of the blade is rudimentary. You are no match for me physically, magically, or in terms of family resources. In the interest of resolving this matter quickly, I'm willing to negotiate. Name your price and we can conclude this unpleasant business. Don't look at it as a bribe. Instead look at it as an extension of assistance from someone who understands the emotional toll of sacrifice."

She was a child.

"Okay," I told Leon. "I've learned everything I needed to know."

"I'm being extremely generous," Christina told me.

"Of course you are. I'll return the favor. You've landed in the middle of a vicious House war. You are being used by our enemies as a distraction. Alessandro isn't leaving with you. He refused three marriages before you, and he isn't the type of person to allow anyone to force his hand. He isn't going to meekly depart with you because that's not the way adult relationships work."

An angry flush bloomed on her cheeks.

"Get back in your car, get on a plane, and go home. You're in over your head, and I cannot guarantee your safety if you stay. All of our resources are focused on protecting our House. I can't spare anyone to guard you."

"I don't need your protection," Christina ground out. "I'm a Prime!"

"So is everyone else involved. I don't have time for this." I looked at the white-haired man. "Take her home. She is not safe here, and this is not her war."

"In that case we will settle this here and now." Christina rose.

"There is nothing to settle. Alessandro Sagredo would know the moment I touched his mind," I said. "I've been rummaging in yours since you arrived."

Three things happened almost at once. A golden rapier materialized in Christina's hand. The white-haired man leaped into the air, his hands shifting into huge claws. Leon fired a single round.

The man crashed onto the table, clutching his side. Blood wet his fingers.

Christina took a step back.

"He'll live," Leon said. "If you get him to the hospital in the next hour or so."

Christina's eyes went wide. She finally realized that the man had been facing us when he attacked. He should've been shot from the front. Instead, he was shot from the back. I had no idea what Leon bounced the bullet off of, but it was damn impressive.

"Let me make this clear," I said, and this time, it wasn't my Tremaine voice. It was me, Prime Baylor, the Acting Warden. "This is my territory. If you leave here alive it is because I allow it. Look behind you."

Christina turned slowly.

Everything had stopped. The construction, the noises of human voices, all of it was silent. The two dozen construction workers and the woman inside the taco truck stared at us. They were all wearing my face.

Christina opened her mouth. Nothing came out.

"Go home," I told her. "I won't ask again."

Two workers, still wearing my face, walked over, picked the white-haired man up, and carried him to the Audi. A third burly construction worker came to stand by me. We watched the two guys pack the injured man into the car. Christina looked at them, looked at me, looked back at them. One of the workers opened the driver's side door and invited her to it with a sweep of his hand.

"Please," the worker said in my voice.

Christina's sword vanished. She gave me a look of pure hatred, ran to the car, and jumped behind the wheel. The Audi took off at a breakneck speed, looped around the picnic area, and shot out of the subdivision like a silver bullet.

"From the back?" I asked Leon.

"I was feeling fanciful," he told me.

The burly construction worker's body collapsed into a slimmer, elegant shape.

"I thought it went rather well, all things considered," Augustine Montgomery said.

# Chapter 12

Alessandro was waiting for me in front of the office with his arms crossed over his chest. He must've checked with Bern, and Bern told him exactly who I went to meet but not where, just like I asked him.

The best defense was a vigorous offense.

I parked the car, walked over to him, and brushed a kiss on his cheek.

"I'm not mad about your fiancée," I told him and walked past him into the building.

It took him exactly three seconds to recover. By the time I sat down behind my desk, he was in the doorway of my office.

"You left the Compound." He walked in and shut the door.

"I did."

"I asked you to wait, and you left. And you didn't take a protective detail with you."

"I took Leon, Augustine, and about twenty MII employees. They secured the area prior to my arrival."

I had discussed hiring MII with him while Konstantin had called home requesting permission for our deal with the Imperium. Originally, I wanted MII so we could pull all of Arkan's hidden informants off the street at the same time. It was an operation that required manpower we didn't have. Asking Augustine to put on a show for Christina's benefit was last minute, but he enjoyed demonstrations of power and he was so good at them.

Alessandro shook his head. "That's not the point. I didn't want you involved in this."

"Well, in that case, you should've told me. You never said, 'Don't go to meet my secret fiancée,' Alessandro." I spread my arms.

"She is not my secret fiancée," he ground out.

"You may want to tell her that. During one of your secret phone calls, perhaps."

He cursed in Italian.

"Why didn't you tell me?" I asked.

"Because it's my mess. My baggage. I never wanted the two of you to meet. In fact, I specifically told both Christina and my mother that she was not to come to the US." He ran his hand through his hair. "I won't allow my family's scheming to affect what we have. I will handle it. She won't bother you again."

I rubbed my face. I didn't even know what to do with that.

"I have no plans . . ." he began.

"You've been working yourself to a stupor for months so we could buy the Compound and then make improvements to it. This is my so-called baggage. This whole conflict is my baggage, because if I wasn't the Deputy we wouldn't be in this mess. So, you are allowed to carry my baggage, but I'm not allowed to carry yours."

"That's different," he said.

"How?"

"It just is."

"Well, let me know when you think of a way to explain it to me so my little brain can understand."

"It won't be an issue again."

I wanted to shake him. "I'm mad at you."

"I know."

"I want it officially noted."

"Should I prepare a document signed by two witnesses to acknowledge you being mad at me?"

"No, you should tell me when your family forces things on you. You should tell me when you're having a hard time, because I love you and I know when something is wrong, and I worry. I didn't go to meet her because I thought you were going off with her. I went there because we grabbed Arkan's informant and she popped out of nowhere with an 'I'm here for my fiancé' announcement. I went to assess a threat. I had no idea—I still have no idea—if she is here because it's a coincidence or because Arkan found a way to pressure your family and her presence is the result of a long chain of events he set in motion. You didn't tell me anything. I get it that you think it's beneath you to ask me for help or to accept help from me since I must be utterly useless and incompetent, but could you at least inform me of this kind of shit out of courtesy?"

He took a step back with his hands in the air in front of him.

My phone rang. I took the call and did my best not to snarl. "Yes?"

"The Spa called," Patricia said.

The Spa, otherwise known as the Shenandoah State Correctional Facility, a white-collar prison for the rich and famous. Ice slid down my spine.

"There's been an incident. Your grandmother was hurt."

I marched through the central hallway of the Spa like I owned it. People saw my face and got out of the way. In all honesty, it probably wasn't me. It was Alessandro looming next to me, looking like he would run over anyone who got in our way.

I'd called back to the Spa and had a conversation with a somber deputy warden which had taken twice as long as it should have because she was choosing her words like she was picking out the best apples at the market. My grandmother was attacked and injured. She was taken to the infirmary. She was also a little *upset* by the incident, so the Spa would be happy to waive the normal visiting procedures for my arrival. Translation: Victoria Tremaine is furious, so please, please, please hurry up and soothe her before everyone's brains start leaking out of their ears, thank you.

I had hung up and announced I had to go to the Spa. Alessandro decided to come with me. We dropped our fight, grabbed the Bus, two Humvees, eight soldiers, plus Leon, and came here. Leon was currently staying with the convoy just outside the prison gates both because it needed guarding and because the Spa gave him "the creeps."

Konstantin also wanted to come, but I nipped that in the bud. I wouldn't put it past my grandmother to lobotomize him. I could just imagine the conversation with the Russian Embassy. *Here is your prince. He can't speak in complete sentences anymore, so dreadfully sorry . . .*

We made a turn and walked into the infirmary. A prison guard stepped in our way.

"Prime Baylor to see Prime Tremaine," I snapped.

"Second room on the right."

We turned right, and Alessandro swung the second door open. My evil grandmother sat in a hospital bed. A bandage wrapped her head. Her makeup was flawless, her white kaftan blouse and white trousers pristine, and as she glared at me, her eyes were sharp and hard like two pale blue diamonds. Trevor, a human guard dog in an expensive black suit, stood by the bed, his face impassive. If you needed a faceless government agent with a short haircut, shades, and an unreadable expression, you needn't have looked further.

"Do I not warrant knocking?" my grandmother demanded.

Alessandro turned and knocked on the inside of the open door.

"Yes, very clever," Victoria Tremaine said.

Her eyes were clear, but her voice had lost some of its crispness. The attack shook her.

This was my fault. I had become so used to thinking of her as this terrifying, unassailable bastion of power that securing her safety had slipped right under my radar. That was what I had forgotten and so desperately tried to remember back in Bern's Lair. My grandmother was a magical powerhouse. Looking at her now, I didn't see that. I saw a woman past seventy who had been hiding her fragility for way too long.

Guilt gnawed at me. I had pulled my horrible aunt who didn't give a damn about us off the street all the way in Mexico, but I had forgotten about my grandmother who was an hour away and actually cared if we lived or died.

I pivoted to Trevor. "What happened?"

"She was attacked in the garden," he said. "A female guard hit her with a baton on the back of the head."

"And her body is now cooling in the morgue," Victoria said. "Problem solved. There was no need for them to contact you or for you to rush over here."

I had thought Christina showing up was Arkan's retaliation for us apprehending Matt. I was wrong. This was it. He'd targeted Victoria. He must've had it preplanned. It would've taken a single phone call and if the guard had been just a little bit quicker or hit a little harder, my grandmother would be dead right now.

I knew my grandmother. She had squeezed every drop of information out of her attacker before she crushed her mind. She wasn't asking me questions, which meant the guard didn't know much. She might not have even known who hired her. Right now, Victoria was likely trying to figure out which of her many sins had caught up with her.

I had to take her home.

"Grandmother, it isn't safe here."

Victoria scoffed. "Don't be absurd."

My phone chimed. A text message from Sabrian, our lawyer.

It's done.

"We are taking you out of here," I said.

"You forget yourself," Victoria snapped. "Nobody takes me anywhere. I make the decisions, and I've chosen to stay here."

She was betting that whoever hired the guard would try again. She wanted a second attack so she could figure out who was behind them.

"Signora Tremaine."

Alessandro had slid into the Italian form of address, his voice considerate, firm, and reasonable. He must have decided that she would respond better to a formal approach and was using all the powers at his disposal.

"We are being targeted by Ignat Orlov," he said. "This is not about you. This is about House Baylor. You are a vulnerability."

Victoria pinned me with her stare. Her magic clamped me in a vise. "And why exactly is a former Russian assassin targeting your House?"

"That's a private conversation, one I will be happy to have with you when we are safe in the Compound. Our lawyer has made arrangements for an emergency medical release."

It took a lot of pulling, but she only had six months left on her sentence, and I had anticipated something like this. All the paperwork had been prepped, so plugging in the specific details took almost no time. The Spa was only too happy to get her off their premises.

"We have an armored vehicle," Alessandro said. "We will transport you with minimal discomfort. As long as you remain here, you will be in danger and House Baylor can't afford to lose you. We will not survive without your wisdom and guidance."

The vise around my mind tightened. My grandmother's eyes bored into mine. Holding her gaze was like trying to stare into the sun. It would burn your mind right through your eyes if you weren't careful.

"You did not answer my question," she said.

"Grandmother . . ." I started.

She leaned forward, looking like an ancient predatory raptor. "What are you hiding?"

She'd left me no choice.

"Trevor, Grandmother is in danger."

Magic shot out of Trevor like an invisible fist and walloped Victoria. Her eyes rolled back into her skull, and she slumped onto the bed. Trevor scooped her up. The tendril of magic that connected us pulsed as I fed him a little more reassurance.

"Follow me please."

We walked out of the infirmary, Trevor with my grandmother in his arms following two steps behind. The guard stood aside, averting his eyes, as if we were carrying a plague victim.

"You cooked Trevor?" Alessandro muttered in Italian.

"Yes."

"When?"

"I did it little by little each time she sent him to talk to me."

"There will be hell to pay when she wakes up."

"I'm ready for it."

I walked into my office, shut the door, sat behind my desk, and took a deep breath. We had settled Grandmother Victoria in a bedroom upstairs. She was still out. I was ready to resume our discussion about baggage and secret fiancées, but Patricia came and got Alessandro because there was some urgent security issue that required his attention.

That was fine. I could use some time to cool off.

I stared at my screen. So much had happened this morning and I'd had no time to process any of it.

My gaze snagged on the scented candle on my desk. Serenity and Calm. Yes, I would like some of that. I rummaged in my top drawer for the candle lighter until I found it, lit the candle, and stared at it. Normally the calm candles smelled of lavender, but this one was vanilla with a hint of cinnamon, a soothing warm aroma that made me think of baking and Nevada.

Nevada . . .

I tapped the keyboard and initiated a video call. I could've just used the phone, but despite replacing it, I was still wary. Not that calling through the computer was any safer, it was the same . . .

Nevada appeared on the screen. Her hair was in a loose braid. She sat on the large couch in the situation room on the second floor of their house. The computer screen offered me a nice view of her and a small slice of the coffee table. She must've taken the call on her tablet.

Somewhere out of view Bug was likely perched in front of a cluster of monitors. Arthur had fallen asleep next to Nevada, and his dark head was on her lap. Someone had put a soft crocheted blanket over him. Connor's mother made them for her grandson. He had one in every color.

"Hey," my sister said.

"Is now a bad time?"

"Not at all. Bug is the only one here, and he has headphones on." She raised a mug to her lips and sipped from it.

"What are you drinking?"

"Milky oolong. It's soothing. You would like it. I'll bring some over once this thing is done."

"Thank you for your help with Matt."

"You're welcome, but you don't have to thank me. I like to make sure the DA office owes me. Keeps them out of trouble."

"Did you get anything good?"

Nevada smiled her scary truthseeker smile. "The man was a treasure trove."

I had run out of neutral things to talk about. It was time to get to the point.

"Linus is still unconscious."

Nevada sighed. "He is a tough man. As long as he's still breathing, there is hope."

"He left a USB. One of those 'If you are watching this, I am dead' recordings." Which was currently cooling its heels in Bern's dehydrator, because I was stupid enough to drown it.

"Mhm," Nevada said.

"He says he's our grandfather."

Nevada sipped her tea.

"You don't seem surprised," I pointed out.

"I thought he might be."

"Because he paid a lot of attention to us without any logical reason?" She shook her head. "How well do you remember Dad?"

I was twelve years old when our father died. "What do you mean?"

"Do you remember his face?"

I tried to recall it. I remembered his presence, I remembered what it felt like when he was in the room, his blond hair, but his face was . . . smudged. Guilt bit at me. I had forgotten my dad's face.

"On the server, there should be a folder under Photos that says Mom and Dad's Wedding," Nevada said.

I split the screen in half, searched for the folder, found it, and opened a slideshow. Mom, smiling, in a white dress, so young looking. She looked like a kid, like she was one of us. For some reason that was slightly disturbing. And Dad next to her, blond, almost pretty rather than handsome, grinning. The memories came flooding back from my childhood. I remembered his face now.

Nevada shifted forward slightly, reached for her phone, and messed with it.

My phone chimed.

Arthur stirred. The remote on the coffee table rose into the air. Nevada plucked it, put it back, and stroked my nephew's hair, soothing him back into sleep.

"He still manipulates objects in his sleep?"

"Yes. He stopped throwing them, for which I'm grateful. Look at your phone."

I checked the text. She'd sent me an image, a photograph of a young dark-haired soldier grinning, a strange firearm in his hands . . .

"Linus!"

Nevada nodded.

The resemblance was unmistakable. Dad looked like Linus 2.0, the blond edition. A little shorter, a little more delicate in the face, but the same eyes, the same nose, the same grin.

"I came across it two years ago," Nevada said. "Linus and Connor are two of the main donors for a veterans' charity. The charity had a project they wanted to discuss in person, so Connor and I went, and while there, they showed us a wall of pictures from donors who had been in the service. I was looking at it and here was Dad with dark hair. It was such a weird moment."

I stared at the image on my phone. So it was true. Part of me had doubted it and low-key hoped that Nevada would tell me it was ridiculous.

"Why didn't Linus tell us?"

"I don't know. He must have his reasons. Dad's birth was complicated."

Victoria Tremaine couldn't carry a child to term, but she desperately wanted one. She had to rely on artificial insemination and a surrogate. According to her, she paid a Prime to serve as the father, but was unable to find a Prime willing to serve as a surrogate, so she committed a monstrous crime. She had the embryo implanted into a comatose Belgian woman, the original Beast of Cologne who had lost her mind during her last metamorphosis.

Our father carried the biomarkers for four sets of magic: the truthseeker from his mother, the siren and hephaestus talents from his father, and the Beast of Cologne metamorphosis from the surrogate in whose womb he grew. Feto-maternal microchimerism was the reason for Arabella's powers.

Complicated didn't even begin to describe it.

"There is another aspect to all of this." Nevada reached over behind the tablet and held an object in front of the screen. Part of it was a wooden contraption that looked familiar.

"Is that a yarn swift?"

"Yes. The core of it is."

The yarn swift was a modified wooden umbrella that held the skeins of yarn so they could be wound into balls. But this one had coils of thread, and some weird wire bent into hooks, and more weird rainbow thread stretched in loops over the hooks.

"Arthur made it," Nevada said.

"What?"

"We were busy discussing something, and he was in his swing right next to us. He stole his grandmother's yarn swift and her craft box while we were talking, and then Connor noticed him building this thing in midair."

Well, it was certainly colorful.

"He's built things before. Small things that made no sense."

She didn't sound right.

"And this thing makes sense?"

"It functions," my sister said.

"In what way?"

Nevada raised the mutilated yarn swift straight up and squeezed a part of it. The band of blue thread snapped into the air. The yarn swift turned, firing the thread loops at an alarming speed.

It wasn't thread. Oh. Oh!

"Are you telling me Arthur built a rubber band machine gun out of the yarn swift and some thread?"

"And some pushpins."

Linus had to physically assemble the weapons. Yes, his magic made components snap together but only in a very narrow range. If he was truly a hephaestus mage, Arthur would be able to levitate parts to him . . . Oh my God.

"Are you okay?" She didn't look okay.

Nevada pondered the rubber band gun. "No. It's the pushpins that did it. They are sharp. He isn't supposed to have them. He bent them into little hooks, see?"

"At least he didn't use them as ammo." I probably shouldn't have said that.

"My son can barely speak, but he built a working firearm with tensile release and moving parts. We've got the telekinetic part down. We know what milestones to look for. We know the danger signs. We don't know anything about hephaestus magic. Linus needs to wake the hell up. Soon. For his sake and ours. And when he does, you can't kill him, Catalina."

She looked really frightening for a second. I pulled back from the screen on pure instinct. "Why would I want to kill him? Are you hiding things from me?"

"Are you hiding things from Arabella?"

Touché.

"Sometimes older sisters have to keep things to themselves for the greater good. Promise me that you won't kill Linus. I need him to help my son."

"I promise not to kill Linus when he wakes up."

Nevada nodded, satisfied, and put the rubber band gun down.

We looked at each other.

"But jokes aside, should I tell Arabella about the grandfather thing?"

My older sister sighed. "Why?"

"I feel like she should know."

"What's worse, losing a family friend or losing a grandfather you never knew and living with a lifetime of regret and unanswered questions?"

I thought about it.

"You're right," I said. "It just feels like lying."

"Arabella is still trying to deal with Mom getting hurt and the night-bloom. It's a lot."

"How do you know about the nightbloom?"

Nevada leaned closer, her eyes intense and wide, and whispered, "I know everything."

The screen went black.

I jumped out of my chair and headed straight out the office door and toward the main house. I needed to cook something in the worst way.

I popped the tray of chicken thighs into the oven. I had marinated them in a mixture of soy sauce, the juice of two limes, my homemade sweet chili sauce, and some spices for an hour. Most people thought that a proper marinade only happened overnight. In reality, for most meats, an hour was plenty.

Around me the kitchen of the main house was quiet. Kitchens were my sanctuary. And I really needed a sanctuary right now.

I washed the heirloom tomatoes, put a cutting board on the island, and took out my favorite cleaver.

My phone rang. Agent Wahl. Finally.

I took the call.

"The Bureau took this case as a favor," Agent Wahl said.

Straight to the point.

"So far, I've had to process a dummy crime scene and then give a dummy press conference about it. In the past forty-eight hours, I've been glamoured, blown up, poisoned with toxic air, and cussed at by my partner."

"You also stopped breathing for a bit."

"Tell me something good, Prime Baylor, because my patience is wearing thin."

"Would you like to get even?" I pulled up the draft of the email I had written this morning and sent it.

"I don't get even, Prime Baylor. This is not a schoolyard fight. I'm an agent of the law. I detect illicit activity and stop it."

"Have you checked your inbox?"

There was a long pause. I put the phone on speaker and started chopping my tomatoes.

"Is this legitimate?"

"Yes." I had just handed him half a billion dollars' worth of illicit activity. Arkan's US accounts complete with evidence of money laundering, tax evasion, and payments to and from people on international watchlists. Konstantin delivered and then some.

"Do I want to know how you got hold of it?"

"Let's say it was an anonymous tip. If you scroll down, there are notes at the end of the file. Point three is of particular interest."

If you followed the trail of financial bread crumbs outlined in point three, you would find a record of payments from Arkan to Luciana Cabera.

There was another pause.

"Explain this to me."

"How secure is this line?"

"As secure as it can get."

That was debatable but I had to cooperate with him to get what I needed. "Five years ago, a group of Primes financed Arkan's theft of an Osiris serum sample."

"Go on."

The tone of his voice told me that he understood the gravity of the situation. Anything regarding this theft had to be handled with kid gloves. The National Assembly and the US government had never acknowledged that the theft had taken place because the international ramifications would be disastrous. This was a massive show of trust on my part, and he understood and appreciated it.

"Luciana Cabera was part of that group."

"Okay, I see where she sent him several payments years ago."

She had done it very carefully, but Arabella and Bern were very good at untangling complex financial threads.

"I also see the trail of payments to her from the same account. What are those?"

"Dividends."

Arkan had shared profits from his sale of the modified serum. He had five investors total. Connor and Nevada unknowingly took out two when they destroyed the conspiracy several years ago. Linus, Alessandro, and I removed two others. Cabera had been the only remaining investor.

"Can you freeze these accounts?" I asked.

"Yes. Yes, I can. It will take time and the right people."

"How much time?"

"To do it carefully? Two days, maybe three. If you want it done ASAP, twenty-four hours."

"I would take option #2 if possible. Will you tell me when it's done?"

"Of course, Catalina."

Catalina, even. First-name basis.

"You'll need to prepare," he warned me. "Arkan's reaction will be significant."

"That's the plan. Also, MII is working on pulling the rest of Arkan's moles off the street. They are planning a coordinated strike. Would you like to assist?"

"Let me make something clear: the FBI will not be assisting MII. Montgomery International Investigations will be assisting the FBI with this matter. We will take the lead on this. I'll keep you in the loop."

There was a tiny pause.

"Also," Wahl said. "In the interests of trust and continued cooperation, there has been an event in Alaska."

What did that mean?

"Take care."

He hung up. Okay then.

Did he mean Sanders? That was the only operative Arkan had in Alaska, and we already knew that Arkan had pulled him out. Sanders was on his way here, and he had personal reasons to want Alessandro and me dead.

I dumped the chopped tomatoes into a bowl. Yellow tomatoes were next, followed by minced onion, cilantro, salt, and a bit of lime juice.

Arabella walked into the kitchen and plopped into a chair. "I came to tell you that the payment to the Office of Records has been issued."

"That was fast."

"It was only fourteen separate cases. I contacted everyone, wired the money, and had them sign off on it absolving us of all responsibility. The parking lot repairs will be handled by the Office of Records directly, so I issued them a lump payment."

When the occasion called for it, my sister could be so efficient, it was scary.

"Also, imagine my surprise when I went to check on Linus and found our evil grandma passed out in the next bedroom. Trapped in an arcane circle. It was very considerate of you to give her access to the suite's bathroom."

It was a very elaborate arcane circle. It had taken forever to develop it, and I had tested it on both Nevada and Alessandro along the way. Everything in that suite had been designed to contain my grandmother. I even had a dumbwaiter installed two months ago during the latest round of renovations so we could feed her.

"I'm sorry. There wasn't time to tell you about it."

"You asked me to defend the Compound. You can't put a dragon in the spare bedroom and not tell me about it."

"Again, I'm sorry."

"Are we going to be having soft tacos?" she asked.

"Yes."

"Will there be steak?"

I opened the fridge, took out the giant marinade container, opened it, and showed her several pounds of skirt steak soaking in my patented fajita marinade. It involved onion, pear, spices for a bit of heat, garlic, Worcestershire sauce, lime juice, and a dash of soy sauce, all put through a blender.

Arabella's eyes lit up. "You're forgiven."

"How badly did that bill hurt our budget?"

"It's a significant unplanned expense, Catalina. Our emergency fund is wiped out. We don't have to go on a ramen diet just yet. Maybe a baked potato diet."

"Potatoes are cheaper than ramen."

"Not if you factor butter, salt, cheese, and preparation time into it."

I split my pico de gallo into two bowls and started on peeling mangos. The family was evenly split on mango pico. Half of them loved it, the other half claimed it was an abomination, and both halves would be upset if their needs were not met.

A distant explosion of barks floated to the kitchen.

Arabella groaned.

The barks got closer, then died. Konstantin strode into the kitchen and landed in the chair next to Arabella, his expression tortured. Rooster padded close to him and lay down at his feet. The prince put his hand on his face. Even exasperated, he remained shockingly handsome. If Grandma Frida was around, she would be snapping pictures left and right. For "posterity."

"Welcome, Your Highness and Faithful Hound," Arabella declared.

Konstantin gave her a dark look.

Rooster wiggled on her belly, scooting a little closer, her gaze fixed on Konstantin's face.

"This infernal dog," the prince growled.

"If you don't change shape, she'll stay quiet," my sister told him. "In your place, I would be grateful. She's the only one here who likes you."

"I didn't try to change shape. I brushed my hair out of my face."

"Uh-huh." Arabella rolled her eyes.

Konstantin turned toward her. "Why is it you don't like me?"

"Aside from my mother getting hurt, and my sister being hurt, and my grandmother being hurt, I have four hundred and seventy-two thousand reasons. Also, you think you're better than everybody. Maybe at home you are, but here you don't hold a candle to Augustine."

Of all of us, Arabella ended up interacting with MII most often. Occasionally we passed cases to them, and they reciprocated. She was the one who handled the administrative and financial arrangements, and she had developed a certain respect for Augustine and his deep-water shark ways. They shared an instinctual understanding of money and power and the best ways of using one to get the other. Augustine treated Arabella as a promising younger sister.

"This Augustine, is he an illusion mage?" Konstantin asked.

If he had done any homework at all on us, he knew exactly who Augustine Montgomery was.

"Yes, and he is better than you," Arabella said.

Konstantin shook his head. "No illusion mage alive today, anywhere, is better than me. That's not arrogance, that's a fact."

"Augustine can turn invisible," Arabella said.

"Impossible," Konstantin said.

"No, I've seen it," I told him. "So to speak."

Konstantin frowned.

"Let's see it." Arabella planted her elbows on the table and rested her chin in her hands. "Do it. Turn invisible."

The prince narrowed his eyes.

Leon floated into the kitchen and smiled, his face happy and dreamy. "What smells so good?"

"Sweet chili chicken."

The smile on Leon's face grew wider. "Soft tacos?"

"Soft tacos with sweet chili chicken and skirt steak, regular tacos with marinated shrimp and beef chuck, queso, hot and mild salsa, pico, both kinds, sautéed bell peppers, grilled corn, salad, rice, beans, and chips."

Leon rubbed his hands together. "Serious question: On a scale from one to ten, how upset are you? Is it about a seven or eight?"

"Eleven," I told him.

"Fantastic."

Konstantin looked at him. "Why does it matter how upset she is?"

"She cooks to relieve stress," Leon told him. "Eleven means we're going to get all the food."

I handed him the steak container. "Go make yourself useful."

Leon saluted, did an about-face, and headed outside to the charcoal grills.

A sharp wail of outrage tore through the house.

Arabella rose. "That's my cue."

Konstantin glanced at me, a question in his eyes.

"Our evil grandmother is awake," I told him.

"I'm going to talk to her," Arabella said. "She likes me. All grandparents like me."

"Don't let her out of the circle," I called after her.

"Catalina, I wasn't born yesterday." She walked off, humming to herself.

"You put your grandmother into an arcane circle?" the prince asked.

"Yes."

The kitchen was quiet again. Just me and Konstantin. I finished the pico and put it in the fridge. I would need a dessert of some sort. Something easy. A pie. An apple and maybe a chocolate. Alessandro loved chocolate . . .

"One thing puzzles me," Konstantin said.

"Mmmhmm." Did I have any heavy cream in this fridge? And if I did, how old was it?

"You can have your pick of men. Any House, any country. Why Alessandro? What's the attraction?"

I took the container of heavy cream out, set it on the island, and retrieved Granny Smith apples from the fruit drawer. This was a dangerous question.

"Why do you ask?"

"I find it puzzling."

In my mind, Konstantin and I crossed our verbal rapiers.

"A few years ago, Alessandro was the god of Instagram. He is incredibly handsome."

"He is," Konstantin agreed. "And charming."

"That too. Maybe I'm just smitten."

"I don't think so."

Konstantin had rearranged himself in the chair. His pose was languid, yet elegant, and at the same time alluring. There was nothing specific in the way he sat that communicated seduction. It was the air around him. If Gustave Courbet was resurrected in this kitchen, he would've demanded canvas, paint, and brushes and refused to leave until the painting was complete.

This wasn't a coincidence. He didn't just happen to sit like that. Konstantin was a Prime and his appearance was as integral to his magic as my songs were to me. He wanted me to think of sex when I looked at him. It could have been simply habit. It could be calculated, or it could be vanity. Perhaps getting me emotionally engaged served as additional insurance. Perhaps he really was planning to recruit me to the Imperial side. That last thought was alarming.

"You and I are similar," Konstantin said.

"How so?"

"We are both planners, forced into it by both natural inclination and circumstance. Our families have a similar structure. My older brother is a lot like your Nevada. Smart, competent, slightly scary, with a strong sense of responsibility. Arkadiy fully committed himself to becoming the next Duke. He is our father's creature through and through. If he had any thought of taking the wheel and steering his life in any other direction, it has long been smothered by duty and destiny. He loves me and cares for me. Although I don't know if he does it out of genuine affection or because that's what an older brother should do. Arkadiy strives to be exemplary in every aspect."

I had no doubt that Nevada genuinely loved me and Arabella and not out of obligation. But this wasn't about me. This was about gathering as much information about Konstantin as he was willing to give.

"And your younger brother?"

The prince smiled. "He is very much like your Arabella. Mihail never met a rule he didn't want to rebel against."

He pronounced the name as Mee-high-eel and as he said it, a little distaste slipped through. *Not on the best terms with the younger brother, are we?*

"Sometimes his rebellion is justified; other times I think he does it because he's bored, or because he has fallen into a pattern and that is the way he is comfortable interacting with life. He has a temper, a real one, and the longer he holds it in check, the more violently it eventually explodes. He is two years older than you, but if our parents, Arkadiy, and I perished, he would run our House into the ground in six months."

Arabella did have a temper, but she was also willing to listen to reason.

"And you?" I asked.

"I'm the mediator. I intercede and soothe. I listen, I flatter when I must, reassure when it's needed, I threaten, I plan, I take steps, and so on."

"So what does any of this have to do with Alessandro?"

"Like your family, mine is loud and filled with strong personalities. We function as a unit because once a plan is laid out and agreed on, all of us stick to it. Even Misha, despite his relentless fight against all orders, does as he is told in a crisis. I've worked with Alessandro before. Alessandro rejects all plans except his own. He doesn't rebel, because to rebel against authority one has to recognize it exists in the first place. My distant cousin is an army of one, a world unto himself. He might put himself on a leash for a short while, but he will never let you hold it, and when he decides to charge, all bets are off. In short, if I had to work with him on a daily basis, he would drive me insane within weeks."

"But you did work with him." Not that Alessandro told me anything about that—yet another thing we would have to discuss. It just seemed like the logical assumption.

"Briefly, three years ago." Konstantin leaned forward. "I'll be blunt. The Imperium would move heaven and earth to recruit a Prime of Alessandro's caliber. Yet, we've made no effort to do so. He's a liability."

He was making Alessandro sound like an irrational, petulant man-child. That was so wildly off the mark, it wasn't even funny. Alessandro was perfectly willing to follow Linus' orders. He'd changed after Arkan almost killed him, but it was mostly about setting his priorities straight, not altering the core of who he was. There was more there that I would have to dig up.

"So, I ask again, what's the attraction? Help me solve this puzzle."

I shrugged. "You saw the Alessandro he wanted you to see and drew the conclusions he wanted you to draw. I see a different Alessandro."

"How do you know the Alessandro he shows you is the real one?"

Because he loves me. I smiled at him. "I trust him."

"That's not an answer."

I ignored him.

"He is so much trouble, Catalina. Is he worth it?"

"Yes," I told him. "He is."

You could always tell how good the meal was by how much talking was done at the table. The family stayed quiet for an entire ten minutes, so the dinner was a resounding success.

Now everyone was on the second helping or the fourth taco, if you were Leon, and the conversation slowly restarted.

"You hired Augustine?" Mom asked.

"We hired MII," I told her.

"Oh, how the tables have turned." Leon bit into his taco.

"It's coming out of the Warden budget." I glanced at Arabella, hoping to prevent another explosion of financial outrage. "Hopefully."

"I think that's a wonderful idea," Arabella said, giving Konstantin a dirty look.

"These tacos are delicious," the prince said. "The chicken especially."

He rolled some shredded cheese into a ball and dropped it on the floor for Rooster. She snarfed it off the tile without ever taking her eyes off him.

"Rooster will not respond to bribes," Cornelius informed Konstantin. He had been trying to rest and recuperate from his injuries. His color was good and Matilda at his side was smiling.

"Pass the mango pico, please," Runa asked.

"Blasphemer," Grandma Frida told her. "Pico is pico, it's not a fruit salad."

"Can we not start that again?" Mom asked.

The conversation floated around the table like playful currents clashing and winding around each other. In this happy little pond, Alessandro was a dark gloomy rock jutting next to me. The waters of banter flowed around him, while he remained silent. It didn't stop him from consuming a record number of steak tacos. They were his favorite.

Augustine Montgomery walked in. He was wearing his normal persona, a marble demigod in his early thirties, tall, lean, with perfect features and light blond hair. Konstantin glanced at him. The two illusion Primes stared at each other.

Leon whistled a vaguely Western tune.

"Nice scar," Konstantin said.

"So is yours," Augustine told him.

Arabella got up and pulled a chair out for Augustine. "Please join us, Prime Montgomery."

"I'd be delighted." Augustine sat down and began loading his plate. "It's done. The FBI was positively giddy."

Great.

"What's done?" Mom asked.

"We've removed all of Arkan's operatives embedded in the state," I said. "He is flying blind. Konstantin provided the intelligence, Matt the snitch confirmed it, and the MII and FBI jointly apprehended everyone."

"The FBI called it Operation Beartrap." Augustine rolled his eyes and bit into his taco. "The food is delightful as always, Catalina."

Konstantin looked at me. "Does everyone come to your house to eat?"

"Sometimes," I told him. I had made enough to send plates to our guards. When I'd told Leon that my upset level was at eleven, I wasn't lying.

My phone vibrated. I glanced at it. A text from Patricia.

We have a guest.

A video followed. I muted the phone and tapped play. Julian Cabera, the younger of Luciana Cabera's brothers, in our office. A slack expression claimed his face. He'd clenched his hands into a single fist, staring at the floor.

"Problem?" Alessandro asked.

I showed him the phone and turned to the family. "Something's come up."

Alessandro rose.

"Leave the plates," Arabella told us. "We'll clean up. You cooked. It's only fair."

"I didn't know you helped with dinner, cousin," Konstantin said.

"No, but he made it possible," Leon said.

Bern turned to Konstantin. "You should speak less."

"The lack of respect for the crown is appalling." Konstantin grinned. "I love it."

His smile was bright, but it didn't touch his eyes.

We hurried out of the house and down the path. The heat of the day showed no signs of abating. The air was still and ominous somehow, the way it felt before a thunderstorm.

We found Julian in the conference room, alone. Patricia favored a specific method when dealing with Prime visitors. She led them into a building, locked it, and watched them through security cameras. It minimized casualties.

Julian jumped off his chair the moment we walked through the door.

"I'm sorry, I didn't know where else to go." He looked frantic. "I called the FBI, and they sent me here. They said you would handle it."

"What's going on?" Alessandro asked.

"It's Kaylee." Julian dragged his shaking hand through his hair. "I think my niece has lost her mind."

Just what we needed right this second.

"What happened?" I asked, keeping my voice soothing.

"Four hours ago, Maria called from Sunnyside."

"What's Sunnyside?" Alessandro prompted.

"Um, it's an estate, my parents' estate, out in Sugar Land."

Sugar Land was one of many small municipalities swallowed by Houston as it expanded, about twenty miles southwest of the city center. It started out as a sugar plantation in the nineteenth century and slowly grew into an enclave of affluent mansions and spacious upper-middle-class houses offering suburban bliss at a premium price.

"This morning, Kaylee left to visit her grandparents. We thought it would help her with her grief. Maria said that Kaylee went into the study with her grandfather and grandmother. After half an hour she went to check if they wanted anything, and the doors were locked. Maria went to knock and saw Ahmad, he's my father's nurse, slumped on the floor. He wasn't breathing. She said there were thick black veins on his face . . ." Julian clenched his hands into fists.

Kaylee had attacked again. I expected to grab her once Arkan's siege of the Compound was over, but she wasn't giving us a choice.

"Then Maria knocked, and she said it was like her brain had exploded. She saw a sharp light and her ears started bleeding. She remembers someone laughing and she thought it was Kaylee."

Julian drew a long shuddering breath and stared at me. "I've sensed her mind before. Something is very wrong. She doesn't feel like a halcyon. She doesn't feel like anything I know."

"What happened next?" I asked him gently.

He swallowed. "Yes, um, I told her to get everyone out of the house. Elias decided to drive down and see if he could reason with her. He called me three hours ago and told me he was in the driveway and then the call cut off. I've called his cell, I've called the house, there is no answer. I don't know what to do."

He slumped back into the chair, defeated. "I don't understand. She was never a mean child. She had no magic. We all knew it, but Luciana didn't want to discuss it, so we just didn't. She was so loved by everyone, the whole family. And she loves her grandparents. When Mother was in the hospital for a heart bypass, Kaylee stayed with her in recovery. And then a month ago Luciana announced that Kaylee had awakened. We were all so happy for her . . . how did it come to this?"

"Please excuse us for a moment," Alessandro said.

We walked out into the hallway, shut the door, and walked to the other end, out of Julian's earshot.

"He isn't lying," I said. "His hands are sweating, he's breathing rapidly, his voice is elevated, and he keeps losing his train of thought. He is in genuine distress."

"Agreed. However, it's still a trap. He may not know it, but this is a setup designed to draw us out of the house. You, specifically."

"I don't follow."

"Kaylee didn't just decide to attack her ailing grandparents out of the blue. Her grandfather is on oxygen, and her grandmother uses a walker to get around. They're both halcyons and aren't a threat to her in any way. She went over there and took hostages, because you are our best chance at getting the hostages out alive. She's trying to lure you to that house."

Because with me there, we wouldn't have to shoot our way in. I could sing the hostages and their takers right out.

The last two times I tried to use my wings, they came out black. What if I couldn't sing again? What if instead of beguiling, I would screech and rip through their minds the way I had done with Gunderson?

I should have gotten that USB back from Bern. It had to be dry by now, but there was no time.

"What do you want to do?" he asked.

"We can't ignore it. Julian might not know it, but he just made an appeal for help to the Office of the Warden. We are duty bound to offer assistance."

"True," Alessandro said.

"You are my Sentinel. What's your assessment of this threat?"

"If we go, Kaylee will try to kill you," he said. "She will have backup, although I don't know who. Likely someone who can counter me."

"How likely is Arkan to attack the house looking for Smirnov while we're gone?"

"Very."

I took a mental roll call of our available fighters. "We will need Cornelius and Matilda to contain Konstantin if he goes rogue, so Cornelius is out. Besides he is still recuperating. Involving Augustine means negotiations and waiting for his people to return from dealing with Arkan's moles and that will take too long. Besides, this is a Warden matter. Do you want to take Leon with us?"

Alessandro shook his head. "No. I watched him grill the steak. He almost dropped the meat twice. He is hiding it, but those arcane vines he pulled off the car poisoned the hell out of him. Dr. Patel pumped him full of antivenom and you know what that does to the body."

"And Runa is still half asleep."

Alessandro nodded. "Arabella is the only one operating at full power."

We fought and we won, but everyone was hurt and tired. We'd paid a toll. We would likely pay another before this was over.

"It's you and me," I said. "It will have to be enough."

"It always has," he agreed.

 # Chapter 13

"W^{alther} Q5 Match SF." I lifted the gun from its spot and showed it to Alessandro seated across from me on the bench. "Blue trigger. 9 mm. 17 rounds."

"Walther Q5, blue trigger, 17 rounds," Alessandro repeated.

The cabin trembled as our vehicle rolled over some pothole in the road. Scarab 17, one of the latest in Grandma Frida's line of armored personnel carriers, didn't provide the smoothest ride but it would roll over a mine like it was nothing. The inside of it resembled the Bus: two long benches attached to the walls with a weapon console between them, which I was currently mining.

I slid the Walther back into its spot and picked up the next gun. "Duncan Arms Little Brother, red trigger, 9 mm, 17 rounds."

"DA Little Brother, red trigger, 9 mm, 17 rounds."

"Maximum Defense PDX." I lifted the light machine gun out. "Tan finish, 7.62x39 mm, 21 rounds."

"Excuse me," Julian said from his spot to the left of me. "Why are you doing this?"

"It shaves off time from the manifestation," I told him. "It will help him summon weapons faster."

It also helped when the specs of the firearm were said out loud. For some reason, Alessandro retained it better, and by now we had gotten the system down to an art.

Bladed weapons didn't require a review. They were simpler. When Alessandro needed a blade, he called up something narrow and fast or something heavy and wide and the exact length or weight of the blade didn't really matter. But the firearms were more complicated, so we assessed them to make sure he could replicate them fast. Once Alessandro summoned something, he couldn't summon it again for at least twenty-four hours, so selecting the right guns required a balance between too many options and not enough versatility.

"Got it," Alessandro said. "Next."

"Mossberg JM 940, 12 GA, 10 rounds."

Technically it was 9 rounds but when Alessandro summoned guns, they popped into his hands with a round in the chamber already. The beautiful thing about this shotgun was its speed. In the right hands, it fired almost as fast as a semiautomatic rifle.

"Winchester 1895." I didn't need to go through the specs. He knew the rifle.

Julian blinked. "It's an antique."

"Newer isn't always better," Alessandro said.

"What does it even fire?"

".30–40 Krag," I told him. "Next, Duncan Arms, Big Brother."

I tapped the section of the console and it slid straight up, displaying the machine gun. It weighed eighteen pounds and I didn't feel like taking it out.

"338 Norma Magnum, maximum range 2,300 meters, 700 rounds per minute."

Arabella had christened it the Six Thousand Dollar Gun. Linus gave it to us for free, but the ammunition it ate cost $8.50 per round. It cost us about six grand to fire it for a full minute.

Julian stared at the machine gun as if it were a striking cobra. "Is this necessary?"

"We won't know until we get there," Alessandro said.

"This is my family." Julian clenched his fists.

And this was exactly why I never took clients with us. Unfortunately, Julian had insisted. If we didn't take him with us, he would follow us in his car. I could compel him to stay if I disclosed that I was the Acting Warden, but I didn't trust him enough. Right now, we were just FBI consultants riding to the rescue.

"ETA five minutes," Brittney called out from the front passenger seat.

Brittney was one of our private guards and the only aegis we managed to get on our payroll. The aegis mages were hideously expensive and very selective about who they worked with. Brittney was a Notable, meaning the magic shield she projected would stop an average handgun and absorb quite a bit of rifle fire, but a sniper bullet would go straight through it.

I glanced at the screen embedded in the hull above Alessandro's head. It showed the feed from external cameras. We were driving through an estate neighborhood, a weird hybrid of rural living and suburbia. Huge houses sprawled on two- to three-acre lots, set way back from the road and protected by walls and gates. An affluent neighborhood. Their biggest battles were likely with their HOA and herds of marauding deer.

"This has to be a big misunderstanding," Julian said, and I couldn't tell if he was trying to convince us or himself. "I can't imagine Kaylee would hurt her grandparents. It's just not in that child's nature."

Human nature was a tricky thing. Five years ago, all I'd wanted to do was to scurry unnoticed through life, never causing conflicts, never getting into fights. Never drawing attention to myself. Yet here we were.

I had to make sure I didn't screech.

Alessandro was watching me.

"She has a big heart," Julian continued. "She was always a good girl. She wouldn't do something like this."

I didn't ask him what "something like this" meant to him. He was too scared to go there. But I did need to redirect him, or he would become a distraction.

"Mr. Cabera, have you checked on your other family members?"

He gave me a startled look.

"You have a large family. We know where your parents are, and we think we know where your brother and your niece are. What about the rest of your relatives? Somebody just targeted the Head of your House."

The Scarab turned. We were almost there.

"I don't . . . I don't know." Julian's eyes went wide.

"Please make some calls," Alessandro said. "You can do this from the safety of our vehicle."

"But don't you need me?"

Normally I would have jumped at a chance to use an upper-range halcyon in a fight. But Julian's hands kept shaking. Right now, he needed his own halcyon just to slow his breathing.

"We can fight," Alessandro said, his voice firm and sincere. "But we can't track down your family. You know them best. It would help us tremendously."

"If you're sure . . ." The relief in Julian's eyes was painfully obvious.

"Absolutely," I told him.

He took a deep breath. "Okay."

The Scarab stopped.

I opened a small box attached to the wall of the cabin, took out two pieces of chalk, and stuck them in my pocket. I doubted they would give me an opportunity to draw an arcane circle, but it was always better to have the chalk than to not.

The view on the screen showed a paver driveway. Kaylee wouldn't let us get through the doors of the house. She'd want a spectacle in front of an audience and whoever was with her likely preferred to target us in the open. The pavers of the driveway lay close together but not close enough for an arcane circle. The line would be broken. I'd need the screen.

Alessandro unlocked the rear door. Heavy metal clanged and the ramp slid to the ground. Brittney came from the front, dressed in full tactical gear complete with a helmet and bulletproof vest.

"Stay with Mr. Cabera," I told her.

"Yes, ma'am."

I undid the Velcro straps securing the roll of the screen to the hull and slid the cloth handles onto my shoulder. Made of dark plastic with several layers, the screen resembled a giant yoga mat, six by six when laid flat. It took the chalk like a dream. Circle mats like this one had existed forever, but common wisdom said that only circles drawn directly on unmoving surfaces, solid ground, the concrete roof of a building, and so on, were actually useful. Drawing a circle on a mat broke the magic continuity and failed to anchor it to the ground. Without that anchor, the circles were just chalk drawings. I had tested it myself, and the drop in power with an unanchored circle was dramatic.

However, last year I saw a recording of a powerful psionic using a mat on the grass. He'd managed to draw a House level circle on it, and it worked well enough for him to frighten hundreds of people into a blind stampede. I'd researched it, and Linus and I made appropriate modifications. The tube under my arm now was prototype #8. It worked, but it weighed almost fifty pounds.

I picked up Linus' sword. The blade felt clunky in my hand but reassuring all the same. It was also the only weapon Alessandro couldn't summon. The same inlay that enabled the weapon to generate a null field when primed with magic also short-circuited Alessandro's powers. He could replicate it, but only as an inert hunk of metal.

I hefted the blade in my hand. Good to go.

Alessandro and I walked down the ramp. He held out his hand. I gave him my yoga mat—arguing with him about it was pointless—and we approached the gates.

The house, a two-story Texas Mediterranean, rose in front of us at the end of a long driveway. It could have been on the cover of a luxury real estate publication in any of the state's large cities. Houston, Austin, San Antonio, Dallas, it didn't matter. Rich Texas was rich Texas. You could drive through any millionaire neighborhood and find a monster just like this one: thirteen thousand square feet and way too many bedrooms and bathrooms mashed together by beige stucco walls under a red tile roof.

This particular variation featured a Roman style portico with columns protecting glass-and-wood double doors and a short turret to the right of the entrance with a wrought iron Juliet balcony. The driveway ended in a roundabout with a massive fountain in the center of it, its spire the same height as the house. An iron gate stood wide open at the mouth of the driveway as if daring us to enter.

"Can you feel her?" Alessandro asked.

"Not yet."

We both knew Kaylee would zero in on me the moment I came into range. I was betting on a lifetime of feeling inferior. No matter how pretty and rich someone was, among the Houses, your magic was your primary asset. Kaylee had spent most of her life hiding her lack of magic power from her friends and her family. Crushing a mental mage would be the ultimate flex for her. Arkan must've told her about my powers and killing me would be doubly sweet. I was both a mental mage and a rival. I saw the way she had looked at Alessandro when he took my hand.

Nobody would be sniping us. That's why we had left our aegis with the transport, guarding our civilian ride-along.

We strolled up the driveway, taking our time, me on the right side and him on the left. The protective shell I'd been growing around my consciousness was almost complete. My mind floated in a tightly wrapped ball of vines spun from my magic. I'd begun building it the moment we decided on this trip. Maintaining it sapped my strength, but I had magic to spare.

Alessandro stopped and put his arm in front of me.

A creature perched at the top of the fountain, gripping its spire with oversize clawed fingers. Seven feet tall, it resembled an ape, slabbed with thick muscle under long nasty black fur. Its face was a horrifying meld of a baboon and a lion with a simian nose, massive jaws, and tiny eyes sunken deep into its skull. Sharp black quills thrust from its back, bristling like the needles of some nightmarish porcupine.

Revulsion hit me.

The beast stared at us. The quills on his back snapped upright.

Nausea swirled deep in the pit of my stomach and blossomed into fear. The urge to run gripped me, overwhelming my common sense. My body knew on a basic animal level that this thing was wrong and awful and the only way to survive was to run as fast and as far as I could.

Prime Nathan Sanders. A metamorphosis mage out of Alberta. Powerful, experienced, and nasty in a fight.

We had fought a metamorphosis mage before. Her name was Celia. Neither my magic, nor the bullets from the handguns Alessandro had summoned, worked on Celia after she'd transformed. My memory served up Alessandro splattered with blood, slicing a beast in half with a chainsaw. It had taken that chainsaw, a sword, and the world's most powerful hunting revolver shot into her mouth to take her down. Later we found that Celia happened to be Nathan's cousin.

A low growl sounded from my right. A larger version of the baboon lion waited under a tall oak. This one on all fours, bigger, thicker, with paws the size of dinner plates and claws like steak knives.

A third beast perched in the branches of the oak to Alessandro's left, smaller than the largest monster but larger than the one on the fountain. Its fur was a dark, dirty red mottled with black, its face more cat than baboon, its body completely quadrupedal. It gripped the branch of the tree with all four feet, its black claws hooked into the bark like sickles. A reddish mane framed its head and thick neck. If it had the ability to transform into a human shape, no signs of that remained.

Luke and Gabin. Sanders had brought his sons.

Alessandro slid the screen off his shoulder and unfolded it calmly. I sent my magic twisting to Nathan on the fountain. His mind was completely opaque, inert without any humanity left. The lights were on, but nobody human was home. Nothing I did to this consciousness would have any effect. House Sanders were holos-metamorphs. Once they changed shape, only the prey drive remained. They locked on a target as if their life depended on it, pursued their prey with single-minded ferocity, and didn't stop until they ripped them apart.

The beast on the fountain opened his mouth, showing us huge conical fangs.

I flicked my sword. The blade unfolded, snapping into shape. The sword generated its own null field. It would cut through anything as long as you fed it magic, but it burned through your power reserve in seconds. I had to use it sparingly.

The muscles on Luke, the largest beast, bunched. He gathered himself like a lion before a sprint. On the other side, catlike Gabin rose on the branch. The red mass around his neck, which I had mistaken for a mane, snapped upright like the hood of some crimson cobra.

Alessandro dropped the unfolded screen to the ground in front of me. I sent a pulse of magic through the blade. The organometallic inlay sucked it in, glowing, feeding off my power like a leech.

"I love you," Alessandro said.

"I love you, too. Take the sword."

"Keep it."

Nathan flexed and leaped off the fountain, a veiny, flesh-colored membrane popping open along his arms. Alessandro lunged left, while I dodged right. Orange sparks burst above Alessandro's hands, coalescing into a shotgun. The Mossberg thundered in a three-shot burst.

Boom-boom-boom!

The slugs hit the simian beast in midair. Nathan screeched, dropping, his trajectory aborted.

Luke charged toward us from my right.

I lunged into his path, feeding a wallop of magic into my null blade.

Alessandro spun toward Gabin still perched in the tree on the left and fired again.

Boom-boom-boom!

Luke barreled at me, fast, eyes shining with malice. I spun out of the way half a second before he would've hit me and sliced at his side as he tore past me. The null sword carved through ribs, muscle, and gristle like they weren't even there. The beast screamed, an eerily human sound coming from an animal's throat, and kept running, ignoring me.

Boom-boom-boom!

Alessandro sank a three-round burst into Nathan as he twitched on the ground, spun, fired toward Luke, and dashed to the side, as Gabin pounced on him. Alessandro backed away, dodging the claws like he knew where Gabin would strike before he even aimed. The cat's shoulder bled. Alessandro must have grazed it with that second burst.

Luke missed Alessandro and clumsily turned around. I had wrecked his insides with my slash. Even with the insane healing powers of the metamorphosis mages, it would slow him down.

Pain tore at my mind. The flexible shell of my magic blocked most of it, but what filtered through slashed me like a white-hot buzz saw. Kaylee.

I cut off the magic flow to the sword and strained, sending more vines to wrap around my mind. Her range was longer than mine. I could barely sense her to my right, somewhere in the house. I needed a boost to take her on. The mat was four feet away.

The PDX machine gun materialized in Alessandro's hands.

Kaylee struck at me, her magic a torrent of hatred. The world turned scalding white. The tatters of my magic slithered, trying to close the gap Kaylee had torn open. I went blind.

Gunfire erupted.

I kept moving, taking tiny steps in the direction of the mat. She tore at my shell, gouging chunks in my vines.

My foot nudged the edge of the mat. I took a big blind step onto it and stomped. A dry crunch announced the hidden reservoir on the underside of the mat breaking. The bottom part of the mat melted as the two chemicals mixed, and the liquefied plastic slipped between the pavers, anchoring the mat in place.

Kaylee cut through my shell. Pain scalded me. I wrapped more vines over the wound, pulled the chalk out of my pocket, crouched, and drew a perfect circle around my feet on pure muscle memory.

A short guttural grunt came from the left. Alessandro. He was hurt.

Kaylee hit me again. A burst of agony exploded in my mind. I gritted my teeth and added another circle to the main one.

She pounded on my mind. Cutting hadn't worked, so she'd resorted to brute force, raining blows onto me. Like trying to draw while someone smashed the back of your head with a baseball bat. I moved faster, the chalk gliding across the mat. The shell over my mind was paper-thin. A few more hits and I was done.

Punch. Rage sparked inside me.

Punch.

Punch.

You fucking bitch. You want my attention, I'll give you some.

I finished the last line, not knowing if it connected, straightened, and sank a pulse of my power into the circle. A geyser of pure magic burst through me, surging through my veins, purging pain, uncertainty, and fear. Only power remained, streaming through me like the current of a great river. I sent another pulse, and the circle responded. There was so much magic, I was drunk on it.

My vision cleared and I saw everything at once: the house in front of me, Kaylee grinning on the Juliet balcony, and Alessandro to my left, tossing an empty gun at Gabin. The feline monster and Nathan had boxed him in. Luke was limping over, trailing blood and pieces of his guts. Alessandro was trapped between them, and his back was red with blood.

The furious thing inside me howled, trying to break free and screech its fear at the world. They'd hurt him! They'd hurt him and I had to hurt them back! I would kill them. I would rip their pitiful minds to shreds.

I felt Kaylee gathering her power for another blast, her mind a brilliant white star.

Inside me dark wings flailed, straining, trying to emerge, their tips glowing with ruby red. They wanted to rip open my body and mind and burst forth like a butterfly from a chrysalis. They wanted to punish, kill, and protect.

No. I was in charge. I would decide.

The thing inside me clashed with my will, screeching to be let free. I grasped it and held it firmly.

I would not screech.

Wings opened at my back and for a torturous moment my feathers were a muddy grey.

I would not screech.

This was my magic. *Mine.* I didn't answer to it. It answered to me.

I opened my mouth and sang. Color burst through my feathers, bright vivid green and gold.

Gabin saw me and faltered from sheer surprise.

I held out my sword, drew more magic from the circle, and let the melody rise out of me. It was a beautiful song full of promises and forgiveness. It spread from me like a wave, washed over Kaylee's mind, and swept away her meager defenses. She knew how to attack but she had no idea how to defend herself.

Alessandro sprinted between two beasts with unearthly grace. His hand brushed mine, I let go of the sword, and he caught it.

My song soared, higher and stronger, spreading through the house.

The three beasts bore down on us, Gabin in the lead, his father right behind him, and Luke still staggering a few yards behind.

On the Juliet balcony, Kaylee wept like an overwhelmed child.

Alessandro slashed through Gabin's leg, whipped around, carved through Nathan's deformed skull, and then buried the blade in Luke's barrel chest. Nathan collapsed. Luke sagged onto his knees. Gabin ran, jerkily, picking up speed despite bleeding from the stump of his left paw.

My magic surged through the mansion, finding the bright sparks of other minds. I sang to them, promising safety, and kindness, and love.

Orange magic swirled around Alessandro. The Winchester appeared in his hands. He sighted the fleeing mage and fired. The three-legged creature dropped like a stone.

The front door opened, and people walked out, their gazes fixed on me. Elias, and an elderly couple, moving slowly, three middle-aged men, and one woman. Kaylee climbed over the iron rail and jumped to the pavers below. Her left leg snapped like a twig. She tried to stand, fell, and crawled toward me.

I needed to separate her from them. As long as I held her mind, she wasn't a threat.

Alessandro was walking toward me. His shirt hung in shreds, red gashes crossing his chest.

Black pulsed through my wings. I wrestled the control back, forcing the green to wash away the jet feathers, and kept singing.

A deafening metal groan rolled through the air. I turned toward where it came from and saw a giant metal cylinder rise above the tree-tops. It was thirty feet long and eight feet wide. It hovered in the air for a moment and spun. Blades slid out of the shaft.

The Grinder. Connor's House spell. Except this wasn't my brother-in-law, because Connor's Grinder had three cylinders, not one.

I had to get those people out of here. Where was safe? The Scarab wouldn't stand up to the Grinder. The house wouldn't either. If the Grinder didn't cut or crush us, the debris from the house would end us. We had to scatter, except everyone was bound to me. If I tried to run, they would just follow me like baby ducks and if I yanked my magic away, they would collapse.

The Grinder dropped, rolling forward. The trees between it and us snapped like toothpicks and behind them Xavier stood in the middle of a basketball court, a complex arcane circle glowing around him. He wore headphones. A deranged grin lit his face.

I reached toward him.

Too far.

Alessandro spun, snapping the Winchester to his shoulder. A shot cracked. Xavier laughed without making a sound.

Alessandro didn't miss. Xavier's circle had created null space. Our reality ended at that outer chalk line. The bullet didn't penetrate. Nothing would penetrate, not even a missile launch. As long as his magic lasted, he was invulnerable. The only way to survive was to get out of his range and line of sight.

Kaylee's elderly grandparents stared at me with adoration. They had no idea they were in danger. I had sung to them and promised them that everything would be all right. I could run away, but Xavier would kill everyone I'd beguiled.

The bladed metal cylinder rolled forward, spinning through the air three feet above the ground. Alessandro lunged to me.

The Grinder froze. It was still spinning, it just wasn't moving forward.

Xavier strained, his face a grimace.

The Grinder stayed where it was.

The trees on our right snapped and fell. Mad Rogan stood in the middle of a simple amplification circle drawn on the road. Nevada stood next to him. Behind them a tactical team sighted Xavier through the scopes on their rifles.

Mad Rogan's face looked like it was carved from granite.

Now was my chance. I stopped singing and smiled. "Come here."

They did, tripping over their own feet, trying to cluster around me.

"It would make me happy if you went to the bus," I told them.

They moved as one.

Alessandro picked the elderly woman up and carried her to the Scarab. Julian ran out and held out his arms. Alessandro handed the elderly woman to him, turned around, and walked back to where Kaylee was still clawing her way across the driveway.

The Grinder still spun in place. Alessandro walked six feet from it, unhurried, scooped up Kaylee into a fireman's carry, and leisurely strolled back.

Xavier let out a silent scream.

Alessandro gave Mad Rogan a wave and deposited Kaylee at my feet.

She hugged my legs, her eyes shiny and bottomless. "I love you so much, I'm so sorry. For everything. So sorry. Do you still like me?"

I patted her hair.

Alessandro hugged me to him like I was his greatest treasure.

Xavier's nose was bleeding. He clenched his fists, every muscle in his body rigid, straining. His mouth opened. He must've howled at the top of his lungs.

The Grinder didn't shift an inch.

The circle under Xavier's feet winked out like candle blown out by a draft. Xavier had exhausted his magic. There was no more power to fuel the circle.

He gaped at the Grinder in pure horror.

The Grinder turned, smoothly, as if it weighed nothing.

Xavier just stared.

The cylinder spun into a blur and streaked back toward Xavier. He threw his hands out in a futile attempt to stop it. It rolled over him.

There was no sound. No scream. Just red blood on the blades.

 # Chapter 14

I sat on the bed with my laptop in front of me. My wet hair spilled over my shoulder.

We'd come home an hour ago. Alessandro showered, and Dr. Patel treated two wide gashes on his back and the scratches on his chest. The wounds had bled all over the place but were relatively shallow. A couple of years ago the sight of them would've made me panic and now I was just grateful they weren't worse.

Konstantin was waiting for him outside the infirmary when we came out. I let them talk and went to our house. I was spent.

I'd yanked my magic from Kaylee quickly enough to stun her mind but not so fast that her psyche would suffer permanent damage. She would be sleeping for the next three days, possibly longer, which was fortunate, because I had no idea what to do with her. I needed to buy some time. Detaining her wasn't an option due to her power level. Normally Linus did whatever it was, and the National Assembly came and took charge of the criminal Primes. He didn't quite pass that part of the job down to me. For now, we stuck her in the infirmary. If the hostilities dragged on, we would have to induce a coma.

Before I broke free, Kaylee told me everything I wanted to know. Arkan had made her into a Prime. She had enjoyed her new power for almost four months when her mother came to her and told her they needed to kill Linus. Luciana had set up a meeting. They walked right into Linus' office, where Kaylee was supposed to attack Pete while her mother planned to pacify Linus with her halcyon powers so they could kill him too.

Except Linus never gave them the chance. The moment Luciana began building her magic, Linus took off. Her initial assault had barely grazed him.

Pete managed to pull out his gun, but Kaylee killed him before he could do anything with it. Luciana told Kaylee to run, picked up the gun, and went to hunt down Linus. Kaylee took off, and a few minutes later her mother carefully walked out of the house and joined her.

Pete's gun finally made sense. Luciana had picked it up and planned to shoot Linus with it, but she didn't count on the vault, and Linus, who was reeling from the mental assault, must've been slower than usual trying to get down those stairs, lock himself in, and activate the defense systems. It bought Kaylee just enough time to escape. Sometimes we overlooked the simplest explanations. Kaylee got out alive because she could sprint like a rabbit.

Untangling my power from the rest of the Caberas and their staff members took a lot longer and by the end of it, I was drained, both magically and physically. We had gotten most of the story out of them in the process. Kaylee had taken her grandparents hostage, killing two of their employees when they tried to intervene. When Elias arrived, she had lashed his mind as well. The only reason he was alive was because he had expected an attack and fortified himself. For all of her raw power, Kaylee had no idea how to fully penetrate the defenses of an experienced and well-trained mage like her uncle. He took a single blast and played dead.

The two Cabera brothers collected their parents and their staff, and Julian took everyone back to the Cabera mansion in River Oaks, while Elias stayed to supervise the cleanup of his parents' house and to make funeral arrangements. Neither of them expressed any desire to take possession of Kaylee. They would likely draft her excision documents the moment they got home.

When I went into our house, Linus' USB waited for me on the table. Bern or Runa must've brought it by.

Linus was still unconscious. It should've depressed and worried me, but I was too numb.

I had taken a shower, which made me feel a bit better, put on a long T-shirt and a fresh pair of underwear, and climbed onto the bed with my laptop. And then I stared at it for about five minutes.

I wasn't sure why I hesitated. I wasn't afraid. I was . . . weary and wary. Both.

Nothing good ever came from ignorance. I slid the USB into the slot, accessed it, and fast-forwarded the video to the point I remembered.

"Very shortly you'll be facing a crisis, if you aren't already. You've concentrated on only one aspect of your powers, but your magic is more complex than you realize. The black wings are the first manifestation of the problem, and it will become worse in times of emotional distress."

Linus leaned back. I recognized that pose. He was in his teaching mode.

"An ice mage attacks while hiding in a crowd. How do you find him?"

"He will be the one with the fever."

Magic altered the natural laws, but it didn't destroy them. An ice mage drastically lowered the temperature of the targeted body of water, and while magic dealt with most of the displaced heat, some of it slipped through. The air around the ice mage would become noticeably warmer. If they kept it up long enough, they would start to sweat, and their face would flush.

"We define ice mages as those who freeze, but we could also define them as those who inefficiently generate heat through displacement."

Where was he going with this?

"The siren beguiles and seduces. Our magic is named for her, but she also has a counterpart."

Alessandro slipped into the room and stopped. I paused the video and patted the blanket next to me. I didn't want to hide anything from him.

He approached, pulled off his boots, and sprawled on the blankets next to me. I scooted closer to him. He put his head on my bare thigh. I restarted Linus' magnum opus.

". . . she also has a counterpart. The harpy."

What?

"The harpy flies on black wings. When she emerges, she doesn't coax. She destroys."

"The harpy?" Alessandro murmured.

"Your magic is survival based," Linus said. "From the moment you were born, it began assessing the environment and attempting to eliminate those it perceived as a threat. From speaking to your mother, I know that you've encountered some people who have been unaffected, like your pediatrician. People like that truly had your best interest in their heart. However, they are very few and far between."

"Who else besides the pediatrician?" Alessandro said. "And me, of course."

"Cornelius and Runa are both immune," I told him. "It's strange, because the immunity developed gradually."

"Most people are fundamentally selfish. While they may not actively wish you harm, when given a choice between your survival and self-interest, they will choose self-interest. That's enough for your passive magic field to designate them as a threat. Your pediatrician, on the other hand, would literally die to keep you safe."

On screen, Linus took another sip of his drink.

"Through no fault of your own, you grew up terrified of your power, and you've exerted an enormous effort to keep it contained. Your control is outstanding. But to achieve that control, you've suppressed a lot of your emotional needs to limit other people's exposure to your magic. You didn't date. You didn't have friends. You denied yourself the web of human relationships that keeps us anchored among others of our kind. Humans are social animals, Catalina. We may choose to be solitary, but it comes at a cost.

"The last couple of years have brought a lot of firsts to you. First best friend. First opportunity to solely shoulder a heavy responsibility. First love. First heartbreak."

I ran my hands through Alessandro's hair.

"First deliberate decision to kill," Linus said. "Not because someone else said you should, but as a consequence of your own assessment. It's a coming of emotional age of sorts, much delayed. On a deeper level you welcome it and that's exactly what the harpy guards.

"It's easy to dismiss her as rage or fear. You can conquer both, yet you can't suppress the harpy. The harpy is love."

I paused the recording.

Love? The screeching enraged creature with black wings was love?

"I told you," Alessandro said softly. "You are still you."

I restarted the video.

"The harpy will protect those she loves at all costs," Linus said. "She isn't particularly efficient about it. She isn't complicated. She is an elemental force that screams and destroys her enemy's soul. Her victims still have an intact brain, but the complex tangle of thoughts and emotions that makes them who they are is destroyed. It is the permanent obliteration of the ego. If they can neither think nor feel, they can no longer hurt you."

That's what I'd suspected. By the time Michael's darkness had devoured Gunderson, he was already dead.

"Historically sirens attempted to find a balance between the two aspects, a middle ground between protecting others and allowing themselves a little selfishness in love. The ideal wing color was grey that lightened or darkened depending on which power was used. You have done the opposite. Your aspects are abnormally well developed. It makes you the most powerful siren on record, but it's a double-edged sword. You denied yourself for a long time, and the harpy is fueled by the fierce, unstoppable love for those you hold dear. To protect them, she will burn through all your magic, beyond the acceptable threshold, and then she'll cannibalize your mind so she can keep screaming. If that happens, you will die. We both know who the harpy's favorite is."

I knew.

Linus drew his hand over his face as if trying to wipe away some terrible worry. His eyes were haunted. "I don't know when or why you're watching this. I hope I've succeeded in neutralizing Arkan, but most likely I haven't because I would've destroyed this recording and we would be having this conversation in person. Catalina, it's essential that you don't allow the harpy to kill you. Even if he does what we all fear, you must survive. The future of your family depends on it."

Linus slumped in the chair.

"I am a terrible father, but I loved my son. It is my greatest regret that I never knew him. I love you and your sisters and your cousins. The five of you are precious to me. You are the heirs to everything I own and to my legacy. You must live, Catalina. That is my last request to you."

The video stopped.

Alessandro sat up, pushed the laptop closed, and looked at me.

"Am I the harpy's favorite?"

"Yes."

"What is he talking about? What will I do that makes all of you afraid?"

The fear inside me uncurled and raked me with its sharp claws.

Alessandro dipped his head to catch my gaze. "Catalina?"

I faced him. "You aren't rational when it comes to Arkan."

"What does that mean?"

"You've been trying to kill him for so long. You're obsessed. You will clash, soon. If you realize that the only way to kill him is to sacrifice yourself, you will do it. It terrifies me. My grandfather knows that I will do anything to keep you alive. I love you so much, Alessandro. He's worried that if I know you're about to die, the harpy will take over and burn through my magic and my consciousness to try to save you."

There. It was all out in the open.

He reached for me. His arms closed around my shoulders, and he pulled me to him as if I weighed nothing.

"I love you more than I hate him," he told me. "Killing him and losing you would leave me with nothing. If it was a choice between your life and his, I would let him go."

"That's not . . ."

"And if it was a choice between killing him or staying alive with you, I would stay alive. I give you my word I won't throw my life away for this revenge."

He hugged me tighter.

"If you want me to promise you that I won't try to fight him, I can't do that. I want to kill him. I want to see the life go out of his eyes, and I want him to know it was me who took it. But it will not be a suicide mission. I want to live well and be very happy, Catalina."

"Promise me."

"Te lo giuro."

I swear. He was saying all the right things, but I was still scared.

We sat for a while, him holding me. His scent was all around me, comforting and tempting.

"I should've told you about Christina," he said.

"When did it start?"

"Two months ago. My grandfather called me and told me it was time to put away childish things and come home. I would be forgiven. It was all very grandiose. He had arranged another marriage."

"What did you say?"

He sighed. "I was preoccupied at the time, so I told him exactly what I thought about it. He took offense and told me I had a responsibility to the family, I didn't like his tone, so I asked him if he thought about prostituting himself. I suggested that he should consider a discount since the merchandise was rather worn and in poor condition."

"Cathartic, but unwise." Alessandro was calculating in his responses, except with me and my family. His grandfather must've really gotten under his skin.

"Unfortunately, I knew he would take it out on my mother, and he did. That's when the phone calls started. I know that my mother is making them under duress. She's being supervised. First, she speaks in Italian. My mother always spoke English to us. Second, she sounds like she is reading a script. Usually, when parents tell you what a terrible son you are, they put more emotion into it."

"I'm sorry." I stroked his cheek.

He shook his head. "I know it's not her speaking. It doesn't hurt. Well, not that much. The point is, I should've told you. I apologize."

"Apology accepted. I wasn't trying to intrude."

He gathered me to him and squeezed. My back was pressed against his chest, his arms were around me. There was no place I would rather be than here, wrapped in him.

"I know," he murmured. "I was trying to protect what we have. Since it was coming from my side of the family, I wanted to take care of it. Your plate is already full. I didn't want to dump a slimy toad into it."

"Toads are not slimy. Their skin is dry. Frogs look slimy because of the secretions on their skin but they are not slimy to the touch . . . You really should tell me to shut up once in a while. Like right now."

"Shut up," he said gently, grinned, and kissed my hair.

He had taken care of most of his family's debt. About seventeen million dollars was still outstanding. A huge sum, but a fraction of what was once owed. He had tried to buy that debt using a loan Connor offered him. The creditor refused to sell. We had to settle for knowing that his mother and two sisters were taken care of. Alessandro sent them money every month on top of the nest egg he'd already built for them.

I shifted in his hold slightly. He leaned forward and kissed the bend of my neck. Mmmm . . .

"I'd like to meet the harpy," he said.

"You've already met her."

"But that was in the pool, in a public place." His lips traced a hot line along my skin. "I'd like to meet her here, in our bed."

"Why?"

"I need to know how much she loves me." He nipped my neck lightly.

A shiver dashed from the base of my neck all the way to my toes. Mine. *Mine, mine, mine . . .*

His arms were around me, carved muscle hard under the golden skin.

"You said I was her favorite." His voice was an open invitation. It caressed, it enticed, and I had no defenses against it.

"Yes."

I felt her rising in me, demanding, violent, and completely obsessed. He was the glowing core of her world. My world. She and I were one being and there was no holding myself back.

I pushed away from him and turned so I could see him. His face was uncompromising, his eyes hungry. I would've drowned the whole world just to have him look at me like that.

"Show me," he said.

"This is a terrible idea," I whispered.

He leaned closer, his face an inch away. "I want it. All of it. Everything."

"You don't know what you're asking."

"I do. That's why I am asking for it."

I smelled the light scent of citrus and sandalwood on his skin. He was so close. I knew every line of his face. His molten eyes, his harsh cheekbones, his strong nose, his sensual mouth, his chiseled jaw, and yet I stared as if we had just met, stunned and longing. Wanting something, needing something I couldn't explain. It was more than lust, more than sex, and it ate at me as if a gaping hole had opened in my psyche, and only he could make me whole.

My mind was full of dark feathers. They fluttered in my soul.

He leaned forward, close enough to touch. The space between us was so small, his voice was a breath on my lips. "Love me, my beautiful harpy."

I launched myself at him. He wasn't expecting it and I knocked him off the bed. Somehow, he sprung to his feet on the floor, taking me with him. My nails dug into the skin on his back, like talons. I locked my legs around him and kissed him, insatiable, furious that someone had hurt him and nearly insane with love and lust. I drank him in, swearing to love him forever, him and only him. He kissed me back, taking over, and thrust his tongue into my mouth, turning my assault into a pledge. It wasn't a kiss, it was an oath. And then I bit his lip and tasted blood to seal it.

There were brakes screeching in my brain, logic and reason, warning that I was teetering on the edge of a cliff. I shoved them aside, took a running start, and jumped, falling into the bottomless chasm. My black wings snapped open, their tips glowing with red, and I soared.

Alessandro stared at me for a shocked moment. I cupped his face between my hands and kissed him again. My wings beat around us. If they'd had substance, I would have pulled him off his feet into the air.

His hand gripped my butt, his fingers scalding hot on my skin. He grabbed my panties and tore them off. I spun off him onto the bed.

He barely had a chance to pull his pants off, and then I pulled him down, onto his back, and perched on top of him. His shaft was rock-hard under me. I yanked my shirt off.

He reached for me. I pinned his arms down and thrust myself against him. He slid inside me in a shocking burst of pleasure. It reverberated through me and erupted into a shout. The sound that left my lips was half song, half wretched cry, and the magic it summoned spun around us, conjuring distant echoes of salt spray and rough rock. He was the sailor I had stolen from the world and no force on Earth could compel me to give him back.

I leaned back and rode him, faster and faster, my black wings spread above us. His hands caressed my breasts and gripped my hips, pulling me harder onto him with every thrust. His magic whipped around us, a convulsing serpent of orange sparks. He arched his hips, matching my rhythm, his stomach flat and hard, the muscles on his chest tight with tension. There was so much power in him, in that strong body, in his eyes, in his magic. And in this moment, it was all mine.

Tension built in me, a storm on the verge of breaking. I wanted more, I wanted it harder. It whipped me into a frenzied rush.

He growled, his voice raw with need.

The storm inside my body shattered into ecstasy. Its waves crashed into me, so potent they almost pulled me under. I leaned forward and gripped his shoulders. His eyes were open, and I stared into them, mesmerized. He was so beautiful, and he was locked on me.

I would never let anyone hurt him again.

We hurtled into our own private typhoon. There was nothing hesitant or tender about it. It was a mad hymn, a violent coupling, and every moment of it would be seared into me forever.

Another orgasm gripped me, reverberating through me in an intoxicating rush. I arched my back, melting into it. My wings snapped wide as if catching a storm gust, and I sang out, a long wordless note that was less sound and more magic.

He strained beneath me, his body hard as a rock, his hands grasping me, and came. I licked the blood off my lips, feeling him shudder once under me, and collapsed next to him, spent.

# Chapter 15

I brushed my teeth and spat into the sink. It was morning. I had expected an attack in the middle of the night, but it never came. I got a blissful eight hours of sleep and now I was starving.

He should've attacked us. Why hadn't he?

"This is screwed up," I told Alessandro as we both pulled on clothes in the closet.

"What is?"

"I'm stressed out because he *didn't* try to kill us last night."

"He'll come at us in the next twenty-four hours," Alessandro said. "And he'll throw everything he has into it."

Keeping track of who Arkan had left was making my head hurt.

Our phones rang simultaneously. Argh. I stumbled back into the bathroom, grabbed my cell off the sink, and answered it, putting it on speaker. "Yes?"

"Christina Almeida is here," Patricia reported.

"Perfect. Just what we need."

"She's waiting for you. Leon is with her."

"You let her into the Compound? Why?"

"Because she brought a hostage," Patricia said.

"Who?" he asked.

"Countess Sagredo."

Cou—who?

"Where?" Alessandro squeezed through his teeth.

"I put them on the patio by the main house," Patricia said. "Mrs.

Baylor has a clear shot of Christina's head, in case any issues arise. Please hurry."

Countess Sagredo sat on a stone bench under a Mexican plum tree, an untouched glass of iced tea in front of her on a little table. This patio was the place we held family gatherings when the weather was good, and the heat was down. It was a beautiful, comfortable space, and Alessandro's mother sat as if the floor was lava, and her bench would sink into it at any moment. Two men flanked her. Both had the look of seasoned veterans, the kind who do bad things with professional efficiency and are not squeamish about it.

Christina stood to the left of the countess and her honor guard. She was glaring at Leon who sat on the stone bench at the other end of the patio entrance, his eyes closed, his face turned to catch the morning sun.

The countess saw me. Her face paled. From the background checks, I knew she was taller than me, but she seemed smaller, thinner, and she wore her fragility like a cloak, as if afraid she would take up too much space. She was beautiful, but her face was pale, her makeup failing to add any color or life to her features. Her dark hair, likely dyed because it showed no traces of grey, framed her face in a kind of loose updo that made her seem slightly frazzled. Her expression only reinforced that feeling of being out of place. She looked like a woman who wasn't sure exactly where she was or why she was there.

Christina, on the other hand, looked so pleased with herself, she was almost triumphant. She focused on Alessandro, slowly crossed her arms, and smirked at us as we approached. Alessandro marched to the patio so fast, I had to almost run to keep up. He stopped in front of his mother. The countess rose.

"Where are my sisters?" Alessandro asked. His voice chilled me to the proverbial bone.

His mother flinched.

"Is that any way to speak to your mother?" Christina asked.

"Be quiet." He dropped each word like a brick on her head.

Countess Sagredo flinched again.

Alessandro pivoted to her. "The girls?"

"Back at the villa," she said. There was a slight tremble to her voice.

"You left that old viper in charge of their safety, knowing he doesn't give a damn about them because he can't sell them yet."

The goon on the left, a huge broad-shouldered brick of a man, cleared his throat and said in Italian, *"Your grandfather says hello."*

Oh. So those were not Christina's goons. They were the grandfather's goons.

"Remember, Lilian," Christina said, "we talked about this. This is what's best for him. Stay strong."

She had no idea what kind of volcano was about to erupt.

Alessandro stiffened for a fraction of a second and slowly turned toward Christina. His voice was permafrost. "I told you to be quiet. Did you not understand me? Don't speak again."

She glared at him. "You don't have the authority to order me around. I didn't come here to entertain your infantile notions. Our Houses have a business arrangement, one a grown man would honor without being cajoled like a child. Your refusal to accept facts forced me to bring your mother here. The least you could do is treat us both with courtesy."

"It's good that you remember we are adults," Alessandro said. "Last time I checked, no one except me has the right to negotiate on my behalf. I'm not anyone's property. I'm not for sale. Whatever bargains you made with my grandfather have nothing to do with me."

"The payment has been made," Christina said.

"That's your problem." He turned away from her.

"Don't turn your back on me." Christina's voice rang out. "You will regret it. You are not the only Prime here. If you need help remembering your manners, I will gladly remind you."

And she'd graduated to direct threats. I pulled out my phone and texted Mom.

Please don't shoot her.

The Artisan smiled.

"She is rude, arrogant, and naïve," I said to him. "But there are worse things." *Come back from the killing zone. We have bigger enemies to take care of.*

Christina turned to me, clearly trying to think of a good comeback.

Alessandro tilted his head. "Make me regret it, Prime Almeida. Impress me."

Magic snapped around Christina like an invisible whip being cracked. She struck at him, a golden blade in her hand. He sidestepped, rammed his elbow into her face, knocked her leg from under her, and wrenched the blade out of her fingers as she fell.

Lilian gasped.

Christina scrambled to her feet, her nose bleeding.

Alessandro tossed the sword over his shoulder like it was trash. "Again."

She summoned another sword and lunged. He leaned out of the way, checked her extended right arm with his left forearm, grabbed her wrist, locked his other hand on her other wrist, crossed her arms, and twisted. She hit the floor like a sack of potatoes.

What the hell kind of move was that? I would have to make him show me later.

"Again," Alessandro snapped. "With feeling."

She leaped to her feet and spun like a ballerina. I felt her magic fire through her sword. It shot out in a crescent in front of her like a huge blade of golden light and missed. Alessandro had moved out of the way, twisted around Christina, and snapped a kick to her left thigh. She cried out and went down on one knee.

"Again!"

She rose, her face skewed by anger, and locked her teeth, her eyes blazing with rage.

He was being remarkably careful with her. All of it hurt, but none of it resulted in a permanent injury.

Christina flicked her wrist. Two golden blades appeared in her hands. She charged, slicing. He leaned back. Her golden swords carved the air half an inch from his face.

Alessandro snapped a kick to her other thigh. Chassé Italien, a powerful forward stomp, perfectly timed. Chamber the knee to the outside and drive the heel into the opponent's leg like a piston. Christina went down again.

I'd seen him cripple a man with that kick. If you delivered enough force in just the right place, you'd cause permanent damage to the kneecap.

Christina scrambled to her feet and screamed. It wasn't pain, it was outrage. He'd humiliated her, and he had done it unarmed.

At least she was still walking.

"Not good enough," Alessandro told her. "Whoever led you to believe you are ready to fight a real opponent has done you an enormous disservice."

"I hate you!" she snarled.

"Already? We haven't even walked to the altar."

He flicked his fingers. His magic twisted around him, delivering weapons into his right hand in a shower of orange sparks, a katana, a machete, Winchester, Little Brother, a tactical sword one after the other. He walked toward her, dropping the swords and guns the moment they touched his fingertips, leaving a deadly trail behind him.

His fingers closed about a short black blade. He'd summoned my favorite gladius. He spun it lightly, letting the blade glide over his fingers like it was glued to them by some mystical force.

"This idiotic nonsense is over," he said.

Of all the swords at his disposal, he'd chosen that one to end his engagement. I got the message loud and clear.

Christina took a step back. Tomorrow both of her thighs would be bruised, and she would need help to get out of bed. Her nose had stopped bleeding—Alessandro must've barely tapped it, but her eyes were still watering, and he'd thrown her on the ground none too gently. Right now, her whole body was in pain, but the sting to her pride was much worse.

The goon on the right with a ruddy thick face stepped forward. The bones of his skull crawled.

Lilian slipped off the bench and raised her arms in a smooth elegant move. Orange sparks clutched at her fingertips. Two guns barked in unison and the goons fell to the patio.

Leon fell off his bench. She was holding a SIG P226 in one hand and a Glock 17 in the other. She'd copied his guns.

Lilian glanced at the two men bleeding onto the stone. "I've waited a very long time to do that."

Um . . . What just happened?

Alessandro stared at his mother. Christina's mouth hung open.

Countess Sagredo arched her eyebrows at Christina. "You heard my son. Run along now."

Christina woke up, clenched her fists, opened her mouth to say something, changed her mind, and took off across the patio. One of our guards stepped out from behind the bushes and trailed her.

"Leon," I said. "Please give us some privacy."

"Nice guns," Lilian told him. "Thank you."

"You're welcome." Leon picked himself up and walked away.

Lilian gently lowered the two guns onto the stone bench and turned to Alessandro. "To answer your earlier question, your sisters landed in Chicago last night. Your grandfather has no idea where they are."

He just looked at her, mute.

"Well?" Lilian asked softly. "After all this time, do I not get a hug?"

Something broke in Alessandro's gaze. He stepped over the blood and hugged his mother.

Lilian sipped a glass of mineral water. She seemed different now. The meek air had vanished. Some of the fragility remained, but it was an entirely different kind of vulnerability. Lilian Sagredo was fragile like a very sharp stiletto. You could break it, but the blade would slice your hands to ribbons in the process.

Alessandro sat across from her, the wrought iron table between us. I couldn't tell what he was thinking.

"Would you like me to . . ." I started.

"Stay," he said. "Please."

Lilian smiled at me. "I don't mind. Go ahead, Alessandro. Ask."

"I don't understand," he said.

She sighed and traced the rim of her glass with her delicate finger. "I hoped to avoid this conversation because you worshipped Marcello.

A lot of little boys worship their fathers, especially if they are as cool as Marcello was. Your father could be breathtaking. I suppose it can't be helped."

She paused.

"Marcello was an attentive husband and a caring father. He showered us with attention, and he made us feel special. But when it came to the matters of money and succession, he had no thoughts of his own. He opened his mouth, and his father would speak through it. Franco Sagredo is a monster.

"The moment I landed in Italy, your grandfather took my passport for 'safekeeping.' The next time I saw it was two days ago. I was very naïve. My parents were older, and I grew up as an only child, cherished and sheltered. Franco seemed kind and caring, and his wife was this sweet lady who was always smiling. I thought I was lucky to have such kind in-laws.

"The first time I realized there was a problem, we were on a holiday in Greece. Marcello met some friends, another couple. We went shopping, and he bought me a beautiful necklace among other things. The next day his friends continued with their vacation, and Marcello gently explained to me that we would have to return our purchases, because it wasn't in our budget. I couldn't understand it. I had married into a wealthy House and brought thirty million dollars' worth of stocks to our marriage. We'd been married for less than six months. How could we be tight on money?"

Lilian's smile turned bitter.

"I convinced myself that Marcello was simply frugal in the way rich people are sometimes. After you were born, I wanted to visit my parents so they could see their grandchild. I was told it was unsafe. I attempted to access my accounts and found that I was locked out. I didn't know it at the time, but your grandfather had me declared mentally disabled. Franco had done a very thorough job of it, complete with medical opinions from two different doctors and eyewitness testimony. He was given complete control over my finances. He had my passport, he had my money, he had my husband in the palm of his awful hand, and you were barely two months old. I was trapped."

"And my father was fine with that?" Alessandro asked.

Lilian pressed her lips together, obviously choosing her words carefully.

"You know exactly what kind of man Franco is and how much pressure he could apply. You had me and Marcello for the first ten years of your life. We did our best to shield you and allow you to grow into an independent child. Your father had nobody. From the moment he was born, Franco dominated every minute of his life. Marcello was brave and kind, but if you tried to argue with him, he would simply fold like a wet paper doll. I had fallen in love with him, and I refused to give up. I naïvely thought I could pry him free. And then he died. He left us and the day after we buried him, Franco came to our side of the villa and took you away."

Lilian's voice caught. She cleared her throat.

"I fought for you. I was told that I was no longer necessary. The heir was born, and I had produced two daughters, who could be sold off to prop the family up. I was expendable. I needed to be grateful for being allowed the privilege of access to my children."

This was so horrible.

"I turned to your grandmother for help, and she pretended that she couldn't understand me. I was desperate, so I tried to kill your grandfather."

Alessandro drew back. "Mother! He's too strong."

"I found that out. I never had the kind of training he had. I did my best, but he nearly killed me. He may be old, but his magic has only grown with the years. I managed to escape that fight and I had disguised myself, so when he stormed into our side of the villa, I pretended I had no idea what he was talking about. He suspected me but he couldn't prove anything and killing me would be inconvenient. My parents are still alive, Alessandro. He wanted my inheritance. That's when he assigned guards to me to 'protect' me and the girls in case Marcello's killer came back."

Lilian looked down at her glass.

"I'd made a friend," she said. "A local woman about my age. Her name was Ginevra. She had two little boys. She was hired to clean and cook for us. Those two men killed her in front of me."

I didn't know what to say.

Lilian's voice shook with barely suppressed anger. "She had no magic, she was not a threat, she didn't provoke them in any way. They shot her in the head so I would stay in my lane."

Alessandro's face was a rigid pale mask.

"You know how little I saw you after that. Once a week if I was lucky."

"And every time I would come over, you would tell me how important it was that I went out with the right friends and attended the right parties." His voice was quiet.

"Your grandfather viewed it as a wedding advertisement, but I wanted the world to love you as much as I did. I wanted you to be famous and adored, because I knew that sooner or later you would rebel, and I had to make sure Franco couldn't make you disappear. If you had suddenly vanished because your grandfather locked you up, there would be a crowd of people looking for you and asking unpleasant questions."

Alessandro squeezed his hand into a fist under the table. I reached out and put my fingers on his.

"That night I begged you to leave with me," he said.

Lilian wiped a tear from her left eye. "If I tried to leave with you, none of us would escape. If I gave you any indication how things truly were, you would've stayed. You are so loyal. You would have never abandoned us. I saw a chance to save one child, so I shoved you away as hard as I could. I would do it again, no matter how much it hurt us both."

"I bought the debt," he said quietly. "Most of it. There's only seventeen million left."

"I know. I also know that you have supported us for years and how you did it."

"Bianca told you," he said.

Lilian sighed. "Sweetheart, you smuggled thousands of euros into the villa and entrusted them to a fourteen-year-old. She had no idea what to do with the money. I found it stashed all over her room, in her pillow, in sanitary products, taped under her dresser . . ."

Alessandro put his hand over his face.

"After Tommaso died and your sister took over as your broker, did you never wonder why Bianca was so good at what she did?"

Tommaso was Alessandro's first broker. He was the one who taught him the business side of assassination.

"No," he said.

"We tried our best to get you to quit, but you were relentless. You had this terrible need to punish murderers, so all we could do was make sure you did it as safely as possible. I'm so glad you stopped."

"How did you get out?" he asked. "Why now?"

"Last year you helped a man, Lander Morton."

The Pit affair. Lander's son was murdered, and we had solved that mystery.

"You've met Lander before," Alessandro said. "I remember seeing the pictures of you and Father on a yacht with him. He had a case of ginger ale delivered to you because you were pregnant with me and had morning sickness."

She nodded. "He reached out a few months ago. He is sick and worried about what will happen to his grandchildren once he passes. He has a great deal of money, and he uses it well. He did his research, realized the situation we were in, and he and I made a deal. He would provide me and the girls with false identities and help us escape, and in return, you will ally yourself with House Morton. I'm sorry I obligated you without asking, but I was desperate. Bianca is twenty-two, and Franco is shopping her around like she is a brood mare."

Franco Sagredo needed to die in the worst way.

Lilian leaned forward, her expression pained. "I delayed this as much as I could. I had her pretend to be sick. I used the money you sent to pay off a clinic to assess her as infertile and started a rumor about it, but this last winter he had her independently evaluated against her will and mine."

A typical trip to a gynecologist was not the most pleasant experience. To be dragged into an examination room against your will knowing that you will be sold right after . . . I clenched my teeth.

"He is moving forward with her engagement. I had to get her out," Lilian said. "We were scheduled to leave next week, but then Franco decided to fly me here so I could guilt-trip you. I had been meek and obedient for many years and since he had the girls, he thought I would do as I was told. We had to accelerate our plans. Morton's people got them out. By now Franco has to have realized it . . ."

Alessandro reached out and took his mother's hand. "It's fine, Mother. It will be fine. Why didn't you tell me?"

She looked at him, her expression soft. "Because you would try to kill him, Alessandro. He is very strong."

"So am I," he said.

"I can't take that risk. You were finally free of him. How could I drag you back in?"

Alessandro shook his head. "Somehow I have given the women in my life the impression that I must be protected."

I needed to change that subject fast.

"House Baylor has no problem allying with House Morton," I told her. "We will honor your commitment. It's a small price to pay for your safety. You are welcome to stay here as long as needed. I'm very glad you are here."

"Thank you," Lilian said.

They were so similar, Alessandro and her, both churning with emotions, sitting across from each other with guarded expressions on their faces. I needed to give them space. He said he wanted me here, but now he was using me as an excuse to not discuss things and they both had a lot to say to each other.

I stood up and smiled. "I have some things to take care of. Please excuse me."

I walked away before he had a chance to stop me.

What she'd gone through was awful. Franco Sagredo was truly a monster, as she'd said. But now Alessandro had a mother, who obviously loved him, and his sisters. I wasn't sure if I was angry, horrified, or happy, or all of them at once. It was too much at the same time. It didn't seem real, like when you barely avoid a catastrophic accident in traffic and a part of you refuses to let go of the adrenaline.

I walked into the main house and nearly collided with one of our guards.

"Prime Tremaine is asking for you," she reported.

At the worst possible time. I girded my loins and went upstairs.

Victoria Tremaine stood in the middle of a ridiculously complex arcane circle. Technically it wasn't a circle, it was an array, or rather a constellation encompassing two separate arrays with six power sinks and an off flow. It covered the entirety of the large suite, the bathroom, and the closet. I had utilized the walls and the ceiling. It took me two months to draw it and I had left it unfinished specifically so I could complete it fast. Once activated, the circle would eventually lose power and need to be redrawn, but I would get another week or so out of it.

The chalk lines pulsed with angry white. My grandmother was not pleased.

Victoria crossed her arms. "I suppose you think you're quite clever."

"Not at all, Grandmother. I'm only an amateur. I still have a lot to learn. Your example inspires me to try harder."

Victoria glared at me. I wondered if her head would explode.

"And now you're mocking me."

"I'm not. That is a true statement."

"You took Trevor."

There was no point in lying. "Yes."

"What else have you done? Out with it."

"The Empyrean Holdings. Also, House Belfair and the Finch, LTD."

Victoria's eyes narrowed. "How did you get to Albion Finch?"

"He has a daughter he's hiding."

Her eyebrows crept up. "Alesia? His niece?"

"That's the one."

"I should have replaced him five years ago."

"But you didn't, and now I have access to a third of your investments. Also, Bern loaded a fun little virus into your House network. You can't issue payroll to your people unless I authorize it."

"I'm so angry with you," she snarled.

"Of course. But you're also proud." I held my fingers close together. "Just a little bit."

She paced inside the circle. It flashed with white like a strobe show. Wow, she was mad.

I would've loved another three years or so to complete and adjust my elaborate trap. I had her temporarily contained but it wasn't enough. The plan had been to shift all of the moving parts into place, so if she ever crossed the line, I could neutralize her with a single blow. Instead, I'd had to resort to this half-baked arrangement, and now she was aware that I posed a serious threat.

"How long do you intend to imprison me here?"

"That depends entirely on you, Grandmother. Arkan is coming, and we could use your help."

Her gaze bored into me. "You never answered my question."

Here we go. "No, I didn't."

"Why is Arkan fixated on you?"

"You know why. He killed Alessandro's father. Alessandro has been annoying him for the last decade. He wants to remove him once and for all."

"You're lying."

"Your magic doesn't work past the circle boundary."

"I don't need my magic, you stupid girl. You're my granddaughter. I can see it in your eyes. Also, I have a brain. I know what that Russian butcher is capable of and how he thinks. He is risk averse. Your pretty boyfriend isn't enough to draw him out."

You know what, screw it. "You got me. I'm lying to you. But your lies are bigger, Grandmother. They're worse."

Her eyes narrowed. "What lies?"

"Linus Duncan is my grandfather."

She took a step back as if I'd punched her.

"You knew and didn't tell me. You allowed me to continue thinking he was just an inexplicably altruistic family friend. You, who always talked about how important family is and how vital the family ties are, how could you?"

She inhaled. "He told you, the sonovabitch."

"It doesn't matter who told me. I know."

She struggled with it for a few moments and raised her chin, her face defiant. "He doesn't deserve it!"

"What?"

"He left me and James. He abandoned us when we needed him and when James ran away, he helped him hide from me."

"Maybe it had something to do with the way my father was born."

She clenched her teeth.

"Grandmother, you implanted an embryo into a woman who couldn't consent to it and forced her to carry it to term. She was catatonic! I don't even know what that is. Is it rape, is it a kidnapping, is it human trafficking . . . ? You did something so horrible, there isn't a name for it."

"You are alive because of what I did!"

"Well, I can't exactly help that, can I?"

She clenched her fists. "Do you know what my family was like?"

"You never told me." I knew. I had done my homework.

"I was the youngest of seven children. I was beloved, Catalina. I was the baby with parents who adored me, five older brothers and an older sister, and in the span of three years, all of them were ripped away from me."

My great-grandmother had had difficulty carrying a child to term. It ran in that side of the family. She'd had one failed pregnancy after another, until her first husband demanded a divorce. She ended up marrying for a second time. Her new husband was a widower with six children, whom she'd loved like they were her own. When she gave birth to baby Victoria, it was a huge and joyous surprise. Victoria was the baby of the family. She was wrapped in love and affection until her family was destroyed.

My grandmother's voice was raw. "I was twelve years old when I had to kill for the first time. My sister sacrificed herself so I could live. I saw her die in front of me. House warfare took everything away from me. My parents. My siblings. My health. My happiness, my security, everything!"

The circle flashed with rapid pulses of white, reacting to her magic. I took a step back.

"All I ever wanted was to resurrect a little bit of that warmth. I wanted a baby, Catalina! A child I could love and raise. A family! Is that such a horrible thing? Yes, I wanted him to carry on our House name, because it would mean we won, but most of all I wanted him to be happy and safe. I had to sacrifice so much to bring your father into this world, and yes, I committed an atrocity, but I have been punished for it in the worst way possible. My son ran away from me. I loved him so much. I tried to make him strong because he had no magic. He was defenseless and I couldn't bear to lose him like I lost everyone else. But he hated me for it, and he ran away, just like Linus. I was all alone, always looking for him, always hoping for a tiny crumb of a hint that he was alive somewhere. I never saw him marry. I never got to hold you or your sisters when you were babies. That was the only thing I wanted, and I didn't get it. I will never get to hug my son again. He died without me by his side, and his daughters hate me. I know what you call me behind my back. You call me Evil Grandmother."

Tears wet her eyes. *Oh, dear God, what do I do now?*

"You think Linus is this sweet old man, but the things he has done would make you wake up at night screaming. He's worse than me! Somehow, he can swim through a lake of sewage and come out smelling like roses, and I ended up as this wretched witch whom everyone despises . . ."

The connecting door swung open, revealing Linus. He was slumped over, holding on to an IV stand to keep himself upright.

"Vicki," he said. "Baby . . ."

"Don't you call me that, you horrible shithead!"

My mouth refused to close. Was this even happening? What was happening? What . . .

"We had a deal," Victoria said, her voice bitter.

"I never meant to hurt you," he started.

"Spare me your bullshit! You knew what I was doing."

"I never thought you'd go through with it," he said.

Somewhere off to the side my brain processed the fact that Linus was awake and dispassionately noted that he was deflecting the responsibility off himself.

"Well, I did," Victoria snarled. "I spent years trying to atone for it. I took care of her family, I relocated them, I hid them, I supported them, I saved her sister from being kidnapped. I have done everything they've asked of me in that contract. None of it wipes the sin off my soul, I know, but I've tried. But how did you treat me, Linus? How did you treat your son?"

"Your granddaughters love you," Linus said. "Look, Catalina has been setting a trap for you for two years and she threw it away just to keep you safe."

"Don't patronize me." Victoria blinked. "Wait. Why are *you* here?"

"He was attacked and took an overdose of Styxine."

Victoria glared at him. "Have you lost your damn mind?"

It was my turn to drop a bomb. "Also, he is the Warden of Texas. I am his Deputy. Where else would he be?"

The room went as silent as a tomb.

Linus raised his right hand. "Vicki . . ."

"You bastard! You dirty sonovabitch!"

Oh-oh.

"Let's be rational about this . . ." Linus started.

"I'll fucking lobotomize you, you filthy prick. You made her into a Warden! She was mine!"

The door behind me swung open and Arabella stuck her head into the room. "What's with all the screaming . . ."

I pulled her in and clamped my hand over her mouth.

"You had two others to choose from," Victoria snarled. "You could have had the older one. She would've been perfect. She is just like you. If that didn't work out, you could have had the youngest one. She would walk across hot coals to get one of those kindly grandfatherly chuckles out of you. She adores you. But no, you took mine!"

"There were circumstances," Linus said.

"Fuck your circumstances. You can take your circumstances and shove them up your ass."

The circle pulsed with blinding light. If she had hit us with that much magic, our brains would have leaked out of our ears.

Victoria waved her arms around. "She stole Trevor from me! And I didn't know! The subtlety required, the planning, can your stupid old brain even imagine it? I taught her, I molded her, I made sure she could lead this family. I made sure to find her the perfect partner. Do you have any idea how difficult it was to maneuver the two of them together? I suggested to the Keeper that he should request that boy to come to her trials. I made her promise that she wouldn't leave the family for another House. I all but forbade her to love him, because forbidden fruit is the sweetest, and when she came to me, she was so meek and unsure, she would have fainted if he'd looked at her for two seconds. Their children will be invincible. And you ruined everything with your stupid plots and your inane nattering about duty and the greater good. Now she will die in one of your never-ending Warden schemes!"

Wow.

Linus opened his mouth.

"Don't you dare!" She pointed her finger at him. "I don't want your excuses. We had a deal. I held up my end of the bargain. I helped you with your idiotic Caesar plot! I became a criminal for you. I let them put me in prison. You promised me complete access to the children. You said I could pick one and you would not interfere!"

The circle pulsed. The floor under us shuddered.

"YOU LIED TO ME, LINUS!"

The chalk lines crackled with white lightning. We all stared at them until it faded.

"Question," I said.

My grandparents looked at me.

"Actually, I have several questions," I said, "But this is the most important one. Explain the idiotic Caesar plot."

Nobody said anything.

"Go ahead," Victoria said. "Tell your granddaughter about the mess you made."

"It's complicated," Linus said.

"He is Caesar," Victoria said. "The whole thing was cooked up by the National Assembly to dismantle that idiotic conspiracy, and your grandfather infiltrated it and got himself appointed as head idiot."

That was too much.

I covered my face with my hands.

"Catalina, are you okay?" Arabella asked.

"Yes. I'm fine. I can't kill him because he's my grandfather and I promised Nevada." I turned to her. "Can you please deal with this. I can't . . . I just can't right now."

"I've got this," she said. "I'll bring them cookies."

I turned around and marched out the door.

Chapter 16

I hid in my office. That seemed like the best place.

For a few minutes I stared at my email trying to read it. None of it registered. After twenty minutes I gave up and logged into the Warden Network.

It didn't take me long to find it. Some files, usually the ones dealing with past matters the Wardens have handled, required a higher clearance. They weren't available to me when I was a Deputy. But I was the Acting Warden now and the archives of the network were my playground.

Victoria was right. Linus was Caesar.

Two years before Adam Pierce blew up the bank that started our involvement, Linus was pursuing a complex corruption case and stumbled onto the Conspiracy. Two dozen powerful Texas Houses were involved, people with armor-clad reputations, strong connections, and staggering resources. It was too big to take down from the outside. After a consultation with representatives of the National Assembly, Linus made a decision to infiltrate it.

It took him six months. The conspirators needed a face, someone with an unassailable reputation they could use to inspire new recruits and reassure nervous members. Someone to shake their hand and promise with total sincerity that they were doing the right thing, that their cause was noble, and that future generations would celebrate their efforts and their sacrifice. Linus became that somebody. Caesar, a leader without power. An inspiration.

The notes were detailed in some ways yet cursory in others. He was frustrated at being constantly watched and monitored, but he also viewed it as a challenge. If Linus had a choice between direct interference and subtle manipulation, he chose the latter every time. I had seen him maneuver state agencies and prominent Primes like pieces on a chessboard without anyone realizing it.

The Conspiracy hadn't had a centralized hierarchy. Rather it was a gathering of power clusters, loosely united by a common goal. Sometimes they consulted him before acting, often they didn't. It must've been like trying to wrestle an octopus with each tentacle thinking for itself. Since they tied his hands, he'd needed a cleaver to do the dirty work for him. He decided on Connor.

His assessment of Connor was frank. According to Linus, Connor was stagnating after the war. Kelly Waller, his cousin, was already up to her neck in the Conspiracy, and she had brought her son in. Gavin was bouncing from one Conspiracy member to another, looking for someone to hero-worship and he'd settled on Adam Pierce. Linus expected Adam to spin out of control, and when he did, Gavin's presence would trigger Connor's involvement.

Nevada wasn't even mentioned.

When Adam was stopped and apprehended by Connor and Nevada before he burned the entirety of Houston to the ground, the leaders of the Conspiracy convened, and Linus convinced them that supporting Adam was too much of a risk. They abandoned him, and he won his first victory.

And so it went, a careful dance, a word here, a suggestion there. Little by little, step by step Linus worked to break the Conspiracy apart from within. As the events unfolded, his direction shifted. Knowing what I knew now, it was glaringly obvious. He was still focused on dismantling the Conspiracy, but he had acquired a secondary objective—protecting Nevada.

He'd stopped two assassination orders against my sister and personally killed the Prime who had been en route to attempt the third. He had taken great risks to keep her and us out of harm's way.

He'd also convinced the heads of the Conspiracy not to kill Cornelius in retaliation for Olivia Charles' death. He had been incensed by the death of Cornelius' wife, Nari. He was unaware it had taken place and blamed himself for his failure to anticipate and stop it. He'd thought Howling was devoted to him, but he hadn't accounted for the pressure Olivia Charles had exerted. The note in the file said, "Had I paid attention sooner, Matilda wouldn't have lost her mother, and a young woman who was just starting her life would be alive today. My hubris killed her." There was a whole thing with Sturm's illegitimate half-brother who was a member of a prominent House that we had known nothing about.

I thought I'd had a grasp on how the Conspiracy had unfolded. I'd barely scratched the surface. There were layers and layers I'd had no idea about. This was how the game was played in the big leagues. I had a long way to go.

Linus had taken so much responsibility and guilt on himself. He once told me that nobody who chose the life of the Warden retired with clean hands. I'd never truly understood it until now. In ten years, if another Conspiracy reared its ugly head, it wouldn't be Linus playing the spider and writing about his hubris killing innocent people. It would be me. If I learned well and worked very hard.

There was another file in there, locked behind a separate code. It was marked "Personal," but my code worked. Linus must've meant for me to see it at some point or another.

Cornelius had gone to see him after the firestorm from Olivia's death died down and we had neutralized Sturm, delivering what we thought was the death blow to the Conspiracy. It was just after Connor and Nevada's wedding. Cornelius told Linus that he came to kill him, but he was willing to listen to an explanation first. They talked. Cornelius left and both he and Linus were still alive.

Your family is my family. My sister and brother both feel the same. You, Arabella, and Nevada are the only older sisters Matilda will ever have. You never have to worry that I would harm any of you.

Cornelius knew. He must've forgiven my grandfather. He must've forgiven us as a family. And Nevada had known as well. She had interrogated members of the Conspiracy once it fell apart. They would've identified Linus. Nevada hated Victoria Tremaine. Our grandmother had put her through hell, and her hatred was justified. My sister refused to allow Arthur anywhere near Victoria. And yet Nevada had forgiven Linus, kept his secret, and let him be a part of her life. Was it because his goal was justified or was it because she learned how close to the edge he had come trying to keep her alive? Perhaps it was both. I would have to ask her once this was all over. This was a quiet conversation we would need to have in private over a cup of tea with lots of calming candles burning.

I wouldn't be surprised if she were the one who told Cornelius. Knowing her, she probably drove him to that meeting with Linus.

A big oddly shaped spider crossed my desk and stopped directly in front of me. Jadwiga and I stared at each other.

Slowly, carefully, I reached to the side, slid a drawer open, and pulled out a plastic container.

No sudden movements. I hummed softly, sending my magic out, and raised the container, holding it upside down.

"Hush little baby, don't say a word . . ."

Wait, what am I doing? She's a spider.

An inch. Another.

"Momma's gonna buy you a mocking bird . . ."

Jadwiga held still.

Maybe it's working.

The shadow of the container fell on the queen of spiders.

Jadwiga bolted across the desk and skittered down onto the carpet, up the wall, and into an AC vent.

Damn it. I tossed the container back into the drawer.

The sound of panting made me raise my head. Rooster sat in the doorway of my office, her gaze fixed on a point above her head.

Ah. "My sister got under your skin."

The empty air tore in random spots and melted into Konstantin in his sunny angel form. He was carrying Arthur's rubber band machine gun.

"It's the principle of the thing," he said. "As the best illusion Prime in the world, I have a reputation to uphold."

"Please, come in."

He entered, sat in my client chair, and put my nephew's contraption onto the table. "This awkward weapon came for you by drone. I volunteered to deliver it."

Nevada reminding me of my promise.

"Have you tested it?" I asked, nodding at the weapon.

He nodded. "Surprisingly it works."

Rooster put her head on his thigh and looked at me. He petted her.

"Traitor," I told her.

"It's not her fault. Dogs like me."

"How about spiders?"

He chuckled. "Not at all, I'm afraid."

"Of course now that I know you have subverted your guard, I'll need to replace her."

"No need." Konstantin scratched Rooster's ear. "Arkan landed in Houston twenty minutes ago under an assumed identity. I would guess we have until dawn. He likes to be dramatic. Also, visibility is particularly poor before sunrise. Dusk would also work, but he doesn't want to stumble around this massive house in the dark."

It was all coming to an end.

"A penny for your thoughts?" he asked.

"I've realized I'm a talented amateur who has a long way to go and I'm dealing with that."

"Ah. And here I thought you were brooding in here because Alessandro is talking to his mother. I stopped by for a few moments. It seemed very emotional."

I smiled at him. "I quite liked my future mother-in-law."

Rooster decided to lie down, and Konstantin put one leg over the other. "Oh? What is it you like about her?"

"She has excellent aim."

He frowned.

We sat in silence for a few moments.

"Arkan will attack tomorrow," Konstantin said. "Have you given any thought to what will come after?"

I had given all sorts of thoughts to what would come after, but my plate was rather full at the moment. "I don't follow."

Konstantin's face shifted.

The golden angel was gone. The man remaining in his place was handsome but very much human. He was still blond, but his skin had lost the perfect golden tan. His features were refined, but harsh. A square jaw, an uncompromising mouth, clear focused eyes under thick blond eyebrows. A scar crossed his left cheek from the temple down to the chin, just missing the corner of his mouth. It was almost the same color as his face, so it had to be old, but whatever had made it must have cut deep.

Rooster let out a soft woof. He bent down and stroked her head, and she went quiet.

"I thought it would be best to have this conversation face-to-face."

His voice matched the new him. Brisk, to the point, without his usual relaxed informality. He was showing me the real Konstantin and I wasn't sure if I was supposed to be flattered or alarmed.

"May I see the wings?"

He showed me his. It was only fair.

I let my wings out. They opened above my shoulders, a beautiful shimmering green. I pushed with my magic, and jet-black rolled over them from my back to the feather tips, turning them bloodred for a split second.

Konstantin raised his eyebrows.

I let the black color in my feathers die and shook the green feathers slightly, keeping all of my magic to myself. "Can you continue with the conversation, or would you like me to put them away?"

"Does it drain you?"

"No. The effort is in keeping them contained."

"In that, we're similar. Like you, I generate an excess of magic. Maintaining a slight illusion burns some of it off." He looked at my wings. "They are mesmerizing."

That's the idea. "What did you want to talk about?"

"You understand that Alessandro will die tomorrow?"

Anxiety pinched me. "You seem very certain of that."

"Have you seen the recording of Alessandro's father's death?" he asked.

"Yes."

Arkan's magic was unique and terrible. When he unleashed it, he stopped time. It couldn't be the true nature of his power, but that's what it looked like. He had gone to the wedding of Marcello's best friend to kill him, and when Alessandro's father put himself between Arkan and his target, Arkan had immobilized the entire wedding party. Even their wounds didn't bleed until the effect wore off. It wasn't something one would forget.

Konstantin was looking directly at me. He had a magnetic gaze, difficult to meet, but once you did, it held you like a tractor beam.

"Arkan's magic can't be countered. Five seconds of pure freedom to do whatever the hell he wants while everyone else stands petrified. His range is twenty-five meters. He can effectively immobilize a chunk of any battlefield. His magic has no name. He's one of a kind. None of his siblings inherited his power and neither did his son."

"He has children?"

"Had. A boy. He died. He looked a bit like Xavier."

"And you kept that fact to yourself."

He nodded. "You might have hesitated to kill him. We needed Arkan enraged. It's fortunate that Huracan lived up to his name."

"You plot too much, Your Highness."

"It's an occupational hazard. Alessandro can nullify all the magic around him. In theory, a perfect counter to Arkan. But Alessandro requires a circle to do his ultimate trick, while Arkan does not, and Alessandro won't use that circle tomorrow."

Where was he going with this? "How do you know?"

"It's omni-directional. His power cannot be aimed. He quashes all magic in an eight-hundred-meter radius, an equivalent of a magical EMP bomb."

It was nine hundred meters, actually.

"Your family requires magic to fight, while Arkan's people are trained killers even without their powers. If Sasha detonates his antimagic bomb tomorrow, you, your sisters, your cousins, your grandparents, all of you will become ordinary civilians, while Arkan will still have dozens of professional assassins at his disposal."

He thought Alessandro's power functioned like an environmental spell, affecting a certain area as long as you were in it. He was wrong. Alessandro's blast affected people within the area, but not the environment itself.

"Arkan is an excellent killer," Konstantin continued. "He was trained by the best in the Imperium. Sasha is a superb fighter, true, except he relies on his talent too much. He is younger and faster, but he alone won't be enough if the rest of you lose your powers. No matter where Arkan will be on that battlefield tomorrow, Alessandro would hone in on him like a guided missile. Whatever plans you've made, they will all go out of the window once the two of them see each other."

A few days ago I might have believed that was true. Even now doubt nagged at me. But Alessandro had made me a promise. Either I trusted the man I loved or there was no way for us to be together.

"You're probably thinking of your mother and her sniper rifle right now. It won't work."

I wasn't thinking that, but it wasn't a bad suggestion.

"What I am about to share is a state secret. Technically I'm committing treason." Konstantin gave me a narrow, humorless smile. "The petrification is Arkan's active talent."

Most mages had an active and a passive field. Active magical abilities required conscious effort, while passive powers were autonomic like breathing or sweating. My passive field evaluated strangers for threats and tried to make them like me on its own, which was why I had to constantly suppress it, while singing required a conscious effort and was therefore active. Konstantin's passive field let him see through illusions, among other things, but to change shape he would need to exert himself.

"Are you telling me that Arkan generates a passive field?" I asked. Nobody had ever mentioned it. Not the Warden Network, not Alessandro's spies.

"He does. It's approximately one quarter of an inch deep. No object can penetrate the field without Arkan allowing it to do so. Neither a blade nor a bullet can hurt him. He exerts conscious effort to put on clothes and brush his hair in the morning. He can drop the field long enough to get drunk, although if you tried to pour alcohol down his throat against his will, it wouldn't touch him. He has allowed himself to be cut on occasion, especially if he suspects he is being recorded and wants to protect his secret."

Was this real or was he lying? I wished Nevada was in the room with us.

"How does he breathe?"

"The field rejects objects depending on their density and threat level. Gasses are unaffected, liquids are affected somewhat, and solid matter can't penetrate at all."

"Then a venenata attack, provided gas is used as a delivery system, would work."

"Possibly," he agreed. "Although we are not certain. As I said, it's not density alone, it's also the danger that's a factor. He does get wet in the rain, but he has been repeatedly splashed with acid and it never burned him. Arkan doesn't have a single poison mage in his inner circle. He employs them but keeps them at arm's length. He prefers to prepare his own food with ingredients he gets from his own garden. He has a poison tester and travels with his own private shielder who guards his mind. The man is as unkillable as one can be."

"What about a fulgurkinetic?" I asked.

"Funny you should mention that. That was how we attempted to eliminate him the second time. The field negated the lightning. It also negates flames and enerkinetic fire, we tried that."

An icy tendril of frost crawled down my spine. "And Alessandro doesn't know?"

"No."

This was a game changer. The petrification power was the ultimate move, but it only lasted a few seconds and we counted on Arkan still being semi-vulnerable during it. We had a complex sequence planned including sniper shots, intersecting fields of fire, and poison delivery. That plan hinged on Alessandro not being within Arkan's range when he stopped time.

None of that would work now.

"Although of course you will tell him the moment we're done talking." Konstantin sighed. "It will change nothing. Sasha is an optimist. Must be the Italian side of the family, because in Russia we view pessimism as an Olympic sport. We will kill Arkan tomorrow. Either your brother-in-law, your best friend, or your younger sister will injure him. Perhaps you can sing him to death. Make him slit his own throat. But none of you will be fast enough. Sasha will get to him first, and Arkan will end him. Which brings us back to my original question, what will you do after?"

What would I do once Alessandro died? "I don't know."

"Would you remain in the house where you and he were happy?" He glanced around. "This place holds so many memories for you, of making love, of planning a future, of laughing together, and every one of them will be tainted, because he will be gone. Will you stay here, hoping for an echo of that warmth or would it be too painful?"

"What are you trying to say?"

"If the hurt is too much, come to Russia with me."

I had expected something like that but he still caught me off guard.

"I know it feels like a betrayal. After all, he's still alive, talking and breathing. You can still hold him. But tomorrow, when all of that is over, you don't have to face it alone. You can have a fresh start far away from all the things that happened before. No judgment, no guilt. A new life."

"Is this a formal employment offer from the Imperium?"

"It's an invitation from a prince of the blood to be his cherished guest," he said.

"Aren't the two synonymous?"

"Not necessarily."

I sighed. "Konstantin, we both know that if I came with you, sooner or later someone would suggest that I should do a little favor for my hosts."

"Nobody would ever suggest that. I would not permit it."

He didn't simply say it. He said it like he was ordering an ancient warrior to hold a bridge against an invading army. There was weight behind his words and complete assurance. There were very few places in the modern world a royal could say those words in that way and mean it.

"I would be lying if I said the Imperium wouldn't want your talent.

A mage of your caliber with your skill set would be a very desirable addition to the royal family's arsenal. That's not why I am extending this invitation."

"Your Highness, I'm confused." I'd managed to keep sarcasm out of the *Highness* somehow.

"I've watched a lot of Arkan's surveillance video. There were days when I did nothing but stare at the screen for hours to gather the intelligence I required. Strange as it seemed, I began to look forward to it, because sometimes that surveillance was of you. I saw you in the Pit singing to a man-made god. I saw you go into prison to visit your grandmother and be sick after. I saw you walk your dog in the rain."

I did not like where this was going. "It wasn't me, Konstantin. It was an idea of me. You were in a terrible place, surrounded by enemies, pretending to be someone you are not, and having to constantly watch yourself, and you were staring at screens for days."

He gave me a rueful smile. "This wasn't the first time I've been away from home. I've run this kind of operation before, more than once, more than twenty times, yet I've never developed an interest in anyone. Everything I've said since we met, the ridiculous conversation with Sasha in the car I knew you would watch, the time you introduced the dogs to me, our chat in the kitchen, all of it was designed to find some flaw, some reason for me to walk away. Instead, here I am, wearing my real face."

He knew we were watching him. Every moment had been calculated. Wow.

"I like the way you think. I like the way you smile. I notice how your face looks when the light from the kitchen window catches it while you chop vegetables on a cutting board. I look at you and I feel like a beggar, because I realize that half of my life something has been missing, and now I know exactly where it was all along. We are two of a kind. A matched pair."

I wished with all my heart that this was another ploy like all the other games he played, but it wasn't. He was completely sincere.

"I don't expect to win against Sasha. You love him. But tomorrow he will be gone. This will become a house of painful memories, an unbearable place. The Wardens can expect nothing more of you. You would have more than fulfilled your duty. Either of your sisters can easily pick up the reins of your House. And they might be better suited for it because you will be drowning in grief. Your younger sister is a calculating pragmatist. With Nevada and your grandparents to guide her, she would have no problem steering the family forward."

Strangely, he wasn't wrong about Arabella.

"If you choose to give me a chance, the Baylors will become untouchable. They will be guaranteed Imperial citizenship and protection, and even if they choose to remain in the US, they will enjoy special status. Your cousins and Arabella will be welcome at the highest strata of society. They will never have to fight another feud, because the might of the Imperium will loom over their shoulders."

He shrugged as if getting rid of a heavy weight.

"None of this will be the deciding factor, but there is one more thing I want to mention. When I told Alessandro that you are wasted on Texas, I meant it. Your stage is meant to be so much bigger, Catalina. Russia is vast and our interests are many. Some part of you must be tempted by the sheer scale of the playing field. You can test the limits and find out what you can really do."

"Perhaps I want a simple life," I told him.

His face blurred one more time. He was me. A little older, a little sharper, with a knowing look in my eyes. I wore a formal gown, deep green with a hint of gold. A golden tiara studded with emeralds rested on my hair. I looked beautiful, untouchable, and regal. That's how he saw me.

The illusion shattered. The real Konstantin smiled at me one last time, before redonning the flawless face he showed to the world.

He rose.

"Think about it."

The prince walked away, Rooster following him, a picture of canine devotion.

I stormed into the main house and ran up the stairs, brandishing Arthur's rubber band weapon. The grandparents' rooms were empty, Victoria's circle broken. Arabella had let her out. Of course.

Where would they go? Linus could barely walk.

Voices floated from the kitchen. *There they are.*

I ran down the stairs and headed to the kitchen through a short hall-way and almost bounced off Arabella going very quickly in the opposite direction.

"You do not want to go in there," Arabella hissed and took off.

Oh for the love of . . . I marched down the hallway into the kitchen.

Mom, Grandma Frida, and Alessandro's mother looked at me.

"Is there something you need?" Mom asked me. Her tone suggested that there was absolutely nothing I needed.

"Have you seen Ev . . . Grandmother Victoria and Grandfather Linus?"

"They are on the western balcony," Grandma Frida said.

"Thank you," I squeaked and escaped.

The western balcony was one of my favorite spots in the main house. It was on the third floor, a part of the same covered veranda that connected to Arabella's tower by a breezeway. Spacious and guarded by a thick stone rail, it was quiet and lovely, and offered a beautiful view of the rolling green that was southeast Texas.

Linus and Victoria sat in the chairs with a small table between them. The table held two glasses of iced tea and what was most likely a plate of Arabella's patented "vegan muffins."

Nobody was screaming. I took it as a good sign.

"There you are," Linus said.

I put the rubber band machine gun on the table and took the third chair.

"What is this?" Victoria asked.

"A projectile weapon." Linus picked it up and pressed the hidden trigger. The rubber bands shot into the air. "Rudimentary and clumsily made, but functional."

He ran his hand over the weapon. A hint of grass-green magic nipped at the modified yarn swift.

"Too complex for a toddler, too simple for a teenager," Linus said, putting the gun back on the table. "Who is our mystery hephaestus mage?"

"Arthur."

Linus spun around in his chair to look at me.

"He telekinetically assembled it in midair from his grandmother's yarn swift, thread, bands, and some pushpins. Nevada is upset about the pushpins."

"Of course she is," Victoria said. "They are sharp."

Linus picked the weapon up and held it gingerly as if it were the holy grail.

"Congratulations," Victoria said dryly. "You finally got one."

"Why is he building weapons?" I asked. "He can't possibly understand shooting someone."

"He doesn't know he's building weapons," Linus said. "His magic is informing him that some things in his environment can be manipulated. Rubber bands are stretchy, metal pins are stiff, thread can connect things, this wooden thing rotates. He is combining them in various ways to make things slide and snap. It's instinctive. He could make a moving sculpture next."

"So why is it called hephaestus magic?" I asked.

"Because making guns is the most fun," Linus said.

"Both of you lied to me," I said.

"We lie to everyone. Why should you be different?" Victoria said.

"Because I am family. I do love you, Grandmother Victoria. But that doesn't undo things that you've done. Setting aside how our father was born—because I don't even know where to start there—you put Nevada through torture. You concocted a huge scheme that would've branded Connor as a human trafficker and rapist."

Linus stared at her. "Victoria!"

"I had no intention of actually publicizing it," she said.

"But you let Nevada think that you would. I can't just sweep it under the rug. She knows. I know. You have to deal with it."

I turned to Linus. "I've read the Conspiracy file."

"Well, there is that," he said.

"You didn't tell me you were my grandfather. Why?"

He didn't say anything.

"He's afraid of rejection. He was an absentee father," Victoria said. "Now he's trying to be the benevolent grandfather. He was afraid that if the lot of you knew, you would shut him out of your lives."

"That's still a distinct possibility," I said. "Arthur needs you, but I don't. I can just quit being a Deputy Warden and a Tremaine, and never lose any sleep over it."

"You want something," Linus said.

"Arkan has a passive field."

"Do tell," Victoria said.

I laid it out for them, together with Konstantin's offer.

"The nerve," Victoria hissed.

"You can't hurt him," Linus told her.

"Never mind Konstantin. You are both horrible people, but you have decades of experience between you. I need to know how we can kill Arkan tomorrow. Brainstorm. Make some calls. Or he will kill Alessandro and I will run away to the Russian Imperium, and you will never see me again."

We all knew it was an empty threat, but I felt good making it and I sounded convincing.

Victoria looked at Linus. "Go ask him."

He growled and leaned back in his chair.

"You're being greedy," she said.

"I'm trying to protect them."

Victoria shrugged. "There is a difference between protecting and shackling someone. I know where that line is. I cross it all the time. You don't have to help. Just withdraw your opposition."

"Do you trust Arabella's judgment?" Linus asked me.

"In regards to what? Because she picks terrible cars."

"Men," Linus said. "Do you trust her to make the right decision for her relationships?"

"Absolutely." I didn't even hesitate. Arabella was a better judge of character than me.

Linus pushed out of his chair. "I'll make the call."

I unlocked my cell and handed it to him. He walked away with it.

"Is this something I'm going to regret?" I asked.

"No," Victoria said. "He thinks he knows better, but he doesn't always."

"Did he really promise you access to us?"

She snorted and somehow managed to make it sound delicate. "Of course. At first, before he knew you existed, he promised to help me find James. That's how he reeled me in. He said he was sure James was in Houston and he had seen him."

And she would know he wasn't lying. "And then?"

"As things with the Conspiracy progressed, he needed more help, so he told me that James died, but I could have my pick of the grandchildren."

I would be mad at Linus for a very long time.

Victoria turned to me. "Why, Catalina? Why the Wardens?'

"It was complicated."

"Oh, I know. He told me. But look at this mess we are in. This Warden thing threatens the survival of the family."

"Do you know you nearly broke Nevada with that horrible scheme? That was a bigger threat to us than this." I waved at the estate. "This is simple. We know who the enemy is. Nevada never expected you to stab her in the back."

Victoria heaved a sigh. "Is she happier now, being the terrifying truthseeker of House Rogan? Did I free her so she could be a wife and a mother?"

"You and I will never see eye to eye on this."

"And you think you will ever see eye to eye with Linus? This man has failed in every area of his life. He abandoned me and your father and went off to be a weapons merchant. Being a Warden is how he's trying to atone for his sins. He is fanatical about it. After I began my sentence, he came to see me in prison. I was shocked. I thought, 'Finally, a spark of humanity from that man.'"

"I have a bad feeling about this."

"He found out that one of the Houses involved in the Conspiracy planted a mole in prison to watch me. He wanted to flush them out. I met him in the gardens, and he started prattling on about building a new Rome, and hating to be bored, and how the cause wasn't dead."

I laughed. I couldn't help myself.

"I nearly strangled him. I should have strangled him. What would they have done, put me in prison? It is a miracle that man is alive. I get no credit."

She shook her head and sipped her tea.

Victoria Tremaine's battle cry. *I do everything and get no credit.*

"Why did he leave you and Dad?" I asked.

"I met him in a little coffee shop in New York. He'd had a fight with his grandfather and landed in the US with nothing except the clothes on his back. I had been looking for a donor for two years and I knew he was my best chance." Victoria sighed. "We met, we talked, we did things that two young people do when they find each other attractive. He agreed to the donorship. I didn't tell him the whole story about the surrogate, but he saw enough clues to put it together. Whatever his many faults are, your grandfather is not stupid. He chose to ignore it. Then when James was born, I brought our son home and Linus was over the moon. Your father was the most adorable baby in the world. For a little while we were a family."

She looked off into the distance.

She had told a version of this story to Nevada. Like most things she said, it was a half-truth. Truthseekers had to actively concentrate to be able to tell when another truthseeker is lying, and Nevada had believed her.

"I knew it wouldn't last. Linus had goals. He was ambitious. It was too easy, Catalina. Too nice and comfortable. He had a moment where he realized exactly how tempting it would be to stay with us and play house, and it must've scared him. He found the surrogate contract. He became upset. We fought. He left."

"What was in the contract?" That was the second time she'd mentioned it.

"Misha was a vegetable, Catalina. There were people hounding her family hoping to get their hands on the new Beast of Cologne. None of them had the magic, but it didn't matter. They had a child stolen. They consented to her use as a surrogate in return for protection."

I put my face into my hands. "It gets worse and worse."

"It's my sin, not yours. To them I was the lesser of many evils."

"Lesser evil is still evil."

She didn't say anything.

"Did you get their child back?"

"Of course I did."

Linus came striding back. "Get your guards. We have to take a road trip."

 **Chapter 17**

Arabella took a turn at thirty miles per hour in an armored transport not designed for it.

"I'm sorry about Pete," I told Linus.

I had finally given him a detailed account of everything that had happened. He had already heard the summary from Arabella, but there were things she didn't know about.

Linus didn't say anything. Pete had been with him for almost twenty years. He wasn't an employee; he was a friend.

"What about his son?" he asked.

"I had MII stash him in a safe location until this is over."

"That's good," Linus said. "Still angry with me?"

"Yes."

I was going to be angry for a very long time. I had compartmentalized it the way I compartmentalized my fear and outrage when I dealt with Victoria, my revulsion when I had to process a crime scene, or the deep anxiety I felt when Konstantin looked at me a moment too long with that longing in his eyes. I'd learned that I could do that. It was my super-power. But it didn't mean I forgave or forgot.

"You should've told us," Arabella said from the driver's seat.

"That I was your grandfather or that I was Caesar?"

"Both," we said at the same time.

"You were not ready for it."

"It's pointless," I told Arabella. "He thinks he is always right."

"No," my sister said. "One time he thought he was wrong, but he was mistaken."

"We could've really used a grandfather twelve years ago when Dad was dying," I said.

"I didn't know." Linus sighed. "After I left, I only saw your father once. I was coming out of a building and this young twenty-year-old kid bumped into me. I saw his face and it was like looking in the mirror. He said, 'I never asked anything from you. Keep her out of Houston.' That evening Victoria called me. She thought James was in Houston and wanted me to help her find him."

"What did you do?" Arabella asked.

"I manufactured a trail that led to Seattle and made sure she found it. I tried to find him, but I had nothing, not even a last name. Victoria had taught him how to hide. She was paranoid that if something happened to her, he might be targeted because he had no magic, and she made sure he knew how to disappear. When he did, she thought she could find him again, but he was smarter than both of us. I didn't realize who Nevada was until I learned she was a truthseeker and ran a background check. Your father's driver's license made things obvious."

The parking lot of the Office of Records didn't look nearly as bad as I thought it would. There was a crew working on the hole in the building.

"I was a lousy father," Linus said. "I'm working hard to be a good grandfather. I do love the five of you."

"Don't worry," Arabella said. "We love you too. Even if you are terrible sometimes."

Right now, the only emotions I felt toward Linus were anger and hurt. There were probably other things there, deeper under the surface, but those two blotted out everything else.

My sister parked, and we got out and walked to the building. The lobby of the tower was pleasantly cool. Linus spoke to the receptionist.

Arabella looked around. "Hm."

She had insisted on coming. I wanted to take Leon or Alessandro, but she was convinced that if she didn't go with us, something terrible would happen to "Grandpa." She had adjusted to his grandfather status awfully fast.

"Stay in the lobby," I told Arabella. "If someone blows up our car, don't try to save it."

"Yes, yes. Because armored transports grow on trees and are super cheap to replace."

"Linus is awake, he will deal with any damages."

"Uh-huh."

The elevator door whispered open, and Michael stepped out. His gaze slid over Linus and me and stopped on Arabella. She stared back at him, unperturbed.

A moment passed. Michael stood aside and indicated the elevator with his hand. Linus and I boarded, he followed, and we rode the elevator up to the fifth floor.

Déjà vu.

A couple of moments later we entered the round library. The Keeper met us by the couches.

"Prime Duncan, Prime Baylor. We are glad to see the Office of the Warden back to full strength."

"I come here today as a private citizen," Linus said.

The Keeper's black eyes narrowed. "How can we help you?"

"I need to know how an antistasi can kill Ignat Orlov."

"Please give us some privacy, Michael," the Keeper said.

Michael nodded and left the room.

"What do you want?" Linus asked, his tone blunt.

"You know my price." The Keeper's tone matched Linus'.

"Done. I withdraw my objection. I will not hinder but I will not facilitate either. It is up to them. This is my best offer."

"Perfectly satisfactory." The Keeper smiled and for a moment his teeth looked too sharp. "Wait here."

He disappeared into a dark alcove between the shelves.

"What just happened?" I asked Linus quietly.

"Nothing yet. This was not what I wanted, but this is the one time I cannot get my way."

"Can you just explain it to me?"

"No. You wanted to save Alessandro. This is the price. Trust me. I would never put any of you in harm's way."

The Keeper emerged with a stack of paper and a pen and handed them to me. "How is your command of arcane artistry, Ms. Baylor?"

"Expert." Now wasn't the time for false modesty.

"As I thought. Pay close attention, for I will explain this only once."

Darkness spiraled out of the alcove behind the Keeper, drowning the room.

"Don't move," I muttered.

"It tickles," Alessandro said.

"You are supposed to be a badass with iron discipline. Endure."

He sighed.

"Don't sigh either. Small shallow breaths."

I anchored my wrist on his muscular back and drew another tiny glyph in a complex pattern that spiraled around his neck, over his chest, over both arms, and onto his back. He stood in the living room in the house we shared wearing nothing except a pair of black briefs.

It was afternoon and the sun flooded through the windows. We returned from the Keeper of Records to some nasty news. The PAC, the mercenary company headed by Berry, Connor's nemesis, was on the move. House Rogan's contacts advised my brother-in-law that someone had hired Berry to attack his and Nevada's estate. They were mobilizing for a decisive strike, which was to take place first thing tomorrow.

Everyone agreed that Arkan was using Berry to tie up Connor and Nevada. Everyone also agreed that there was nothing to be done about it. Berry had numbers and skilled personnel and he was highly motivated. Apparently, the client had paid PAC a single dollar to ensure their participation. House Rogan couldn't ignore this. We were on our own for this fight.

My fingertips were going numb, and I still had half of his back and both thighs to go. It was him, me, my notes, and an art marker with Shadow as the audience.

"Ready?" Bern asked from the phone on the coffee table. I had him on speaker.

"Go," Alessandro said.

"Sample 1."

Arabella's voice came from the phone, haunting and persistent. "You're going to die. This is your last warning. Leave, and we will not pursue you. Save yourself."

"Sample 2."

A slightly different intonation. "You're going to die. This is your last warning. Leave, and we will not pursue you. Save yourself."

"Sample 3 . . ."

Apparently, my sister could sound remarkably menacing when the occasion called for it.

"The third one is the scariest," I said.

"The first one," Alessandro said. "She sounds like a younger sister guilt-tripping you."

"Our vote is for the first one as well," Bern said.

"It's your concert," I told him. "First it is."

He hung up.

I kept drawing. The glyph pattern wasn't difficult to understand. It was just hellishly complicated to draw.

"Konstantin was in your office for a while today," Alessandro said.

"Mhm."

"What did he say to you?" he asked.

"He thinks you will die tomorrow."

"I won't."

Damn right, you won't. That's why we were doing this.

"Anything else?"

He wasn't going to let it go. I knew that tone. "He thinks Princessa Catalina Jamesovna Berezina has a nice ring to it."

The muscle under my fingers went rock hard. My marker slipped.

"Damn it." I reached for a cosmetic wipe and scrubbed the ruined glyph from his skin. "Do you want to be here all evening?"

"Yes and no. I had plans for tonight."

Ah ha. "Were you naked in those plans?"

"Yes."

"Well, see, they came true."

I redrew the glyph and knelt to get better access to his side and hip.

"In my plans, we were both naked."

I glanced up at him. "Would you like me to take my clothes off?"

His eyes flashed with orange. "No, it might not be safe."

"You're doing your seductive voice again."

"I'm so sorry," he purred. "Is it distracting you?"

"A little bit."

"Clearly, I need to try harder."

"You need to hold still so we can finish this. Don't talk."

I redrew the glyph and kept going.

"Konstantin does bring a lot to the table," Alessandro said, as if thinking out loud. "He can look like anyone, which provides endless variety in bed. He is wealthy, powerful, and witty. Able to hold a stimulating conversation. And then of course, the perks of being a royal. The bowing, the rituals, the status. The family would benefit by association."

I stopped and looked at him.

He gave me that sharp and funny Alessandro smile, the one that made me stare at him like a lovesick idiot every time he did it.

"But to get all of that, you would have to put up with Konstantin every day. And that would be a fate worse than death itself."

"Are you done?" I asked him.

"Possibly."

"I'm so glad. Please stop talking."

"I love you, Catalina."

I growled at him.

"You are so smart and beautiful."

"Alessandro, shut up."

"Your wings are breathtaking."

I would punch him.

"You cook like a goddess . . ."

"Damn it!" I threw the marker on the floor.

He grabbed my hands and pulled me upright. His eyes were like molten amber. "Every time I wake up next to you, I feel like the luckiest man ever born. I can't believe you chose me. You have all of me forever. In this whole world, there is no one like you."

He touched my cheek with his fingertips and kissed me. There was so much tenderness in that kiss. It was made of love and hope, and it broke me. I had been trying to keep it together for so long, but no defense could've stood up to that.

He wiped the tears from my face with his fingers and touched my forehead with his. We stood an inch apart, the glyphs still drying on his skin.

"Don't die tomorrow," I told him.

"I won't. I promise."

 **Chapter 18**

$\mathcal{T}$he northwest corner of the wall widened into a patio originally designed to offer a scenic backdrop for wedding photos. The patio was crowned by a pavilion we'd dubbed the Wedding Cake because it was ornate and ridiculous. After buying the Compound, the Wedding Cake was converted into an observation post complete with reinforced walls and massive bulletproof windows. We still called it the Wedding Cake, despite all the renovations and the fact that its charming table and chairs had been replaced by a utilitarian counter offering a variety of cameras and binoculars.

I stood inside it now, drinking coffee from a white mug with golden lettering on it. The letters said, "You got this."

Dawn was breaking outside the ballistic window, the sky slowly flooding with red and orange. It promised to be one of those unforgettable Texas sunrises.

On the patio behind us, shielded from view by the Wedding Cake, Alessandro was drawing a complex arcane circle. I had a clear view of him through the open doors of the pavilion. He was dressed in black and my null blade rested in the sheath on his back.

Leon whistled a spaghetti western tune next to me.

"Shouldn't you be in your tower?"

"All in good time, ma'am. I'm taking in the sights and getting the lay of the land. A man only gets one Alamo in his lifetime. If he's lucky. I'm committing it to memory."

He was wearing one of the Scorpion ballistic vests and a helmet, just like me. Running in that getup to the tower wouldn't be the easiest thing in the world.

We had split our forces. We had two gates to protect, this one and the one in the south that faced Grandma Frida's motor pool. Arkan would be a fool not to attack from both points, so Grandma Frida, half of our guards, Runa, and Grandma Victoria took the south side. After some discussion, we all collectively decided that Arabella would join them. Nobody wanted to say it out loud, but both grandmothers had celebrated their seventieth birthdays some time ago, and while their magic was as strong as ever, everyone felt better knowing my sister guarded their backs.

Leon, Alessandro, Cornelius, and I took the north gate. Konstantin insisted on joining us, because, according to him, when Arkan finally knocked on our front door, he wanted to open it and say hello. We hadn't seen him since last night. We may have seen him and didn't know it was him, or he may have left. In any case, I couldn't spare any time to worry about it. Babysitting Russian princes was not on the agenda for today.

Mom positioned herself in her crow's nest at the main house. From there she had an opportunity to support both sides. Lilian went with her. My mother and Alessandro's seemed to have found some common ground. Lilian and I hadn't had an opportunity to really sit and talk, but she told me that her son was lucky, so I hoped it would go well.

Linus insisted on getting his mech out. We'd stored one of them in Grandma Frida's motor pool since we moved in. None of us could pilot it, and he shouldn't have piloted it either, not in his current condition. But we couldn't ignore the possibility that once the fights at the gates broke out, Arkan could sneak some of his people over the walls in random spots. The mech was light and mobile, designed for rapid response, and Linus was hell-bent on using it.

The distant rumble of artillery fire rolled through the morning air. Too quiet to have come from the south gate.

"The PAC is at Connor's house asking to borrow a cup of sugar," Bern said into my earpiece.

"Shouldn't you be drawing?" Leon asked me, mimicking my earlier tone exactly.

I looked at his feet. He glanced down. We were standing in an arcane circle. It would take me seconds to finish it. Grandmother Victoria and I worked on the design until almost midnight. It had to require a bare minimum of power. Neither one of us was happy with the power drain it would take to maintain it, but then we wouldn't have to keep it up for long.

"Touché," Leon said.

Cornelius strode into the pavilion. For some reason, the helmet and the vest made him look slightly ridiculous. It just didn't suit him.

"Something is coming," he said.

"Define 'something,'" Leon said.

"Something large."

"*Summoner portal,*" Bern said. "*Nine hundred meters out from the north gate.*"

They were just outside Alessandro's blast area. As if they knew his range. Hmm.

"*The portal has closed. Something is moving through the trees.*"

"Something large?" Leon raised his eyebrows.

"*Yes. Go to your tower.*"

The stone floor under our feet reverberated. Cornelius turned and ran out.

A colossal shape burst from under the trees at the foot of the hill. It was the size of an elephant, its thick lavender hide streaked with purple splotches. No, not splotches, armor, heavy bony plates stretching into spikes. Bony shields covered its broad head, bearing two large horns. It was shaped like a rhino, armored like an ankylosaurus, and it was charging toward us like a bull.

The floor shook.

"Time to mosey." Leon ran outside.

The beast thundered toward us, three pairs of small eyes gleaming in the skinfolds between the plates on its head.

"Brace!" I yelled and crouched down. I had no idea why I'd done that. It just felt right.

The arcane beast smashed into our gate with a deafening clang. The impact shuddered through the wall. Metal screeched.

I jumped to my feet and ran out onto the patio.

The creature slid to a stop in the parking lot, the wrecked gate stuck on its horns. It shook its head side to side. The gate went flying.

With one hit, it reduced our wall to nothing.

The beast bellowed and tore down the driveway toward the main house.

A short figure walked out from under the oaks and directly into the monster's path.

The beast bounded forward.

Cornelius raised his hand. His voice snapped in my earpiece. *"Stop."*

The dino-rhino braked with all six paws. He slid forward, comically landing on his butt, picked himself up, and trotted toward Cornelius.

"Significant, my foot," Grandmother Victoria said.

The rhino monster bumped its head against Cornelius' hand. Its skull was as big as Cornelius himself. Its long, spiked tail wagged.

"Incoming," Bern said.

I turned around and ran back into the Wedding Cake. Figures were emerging from the trees, running for the gap the beast had created. The four attackers in the front line shimmered behind the aegis shields.

"Good boy," Cornelius said. *"Go get the bad people."*

Arkan's people were almost on us. I could see them clearly now, dressed in identical tactical grey fatigues, odd helmets on their heads, covering the skull and the ears. Arkan had taken precautions against my siren song.

The creature bellowed.

"Go," Cornelius repeated.

A sniper rifle shot took a man down in the third row. The aegises stretched their magic shields, angling them up.

The floor under my feet shook again. The walls trembled, and the rhino beast hurtled through the gap it had made at full speed. The line of advancing soldiers scattered. Bodies flew, one of them desperately trying to adjust his shield against the impact.

The beast rampaged on the slope, running back and forth, stomping and goring anything in its way. It rammed one of the car wrecks we hadn't had time to clear and headbutted it like it was a toy.

"*Psychological warfare in three, two . . .*" Bern said.

Arabella's voice blared through my earpiece. "*You're going to die. This is your last warning. Leave, and we will not pursue you. Save yourself.*"

"Bern?"

"*Sorry. Had the speaker on.*"

Arabella's voice vanished.

On the field, one of the soldiers yanked his helmet off. Noise-cancelling helmets were fine and good, but you still had to transmit the orders to your soldiers. Bern had hacked into their communication channel. Right now, their ears were full of my sister's voice telling them they were about to die.

Loud booms of artillery bombardment came from the south.

"We have visitors," Runa announced.

On the hill, the attackers reformed into a column, the aegis mages in the lead, and charged the gap. A portal snapped open in front of the beast. It was galloping down the hill as fast as its legs could carry it and it had no time to turn. The creature vanished into the portal and the ragged dark hole collapsed on itself.

"Krause is in range," I called out.

"Good." Alessandro straightened in his circle.

The flood of Arkan's soldiers spilled inside the wall.

A rapid staccato of gunfire tore from Leon's tower. People dropped like flies.

The last woman through the gap stabbed the man in front of her with surgical precision, spun, sliced another attacker's throat, blurred into the man she just killed, and sank her knife into the third soldier's kidneys. Konstantin.

He was cutting them down like they were weeds, jumping from shape to shape as he went.

"*Stop it,*" Leon growled. "*I almost shot you twice!*"

"Any sign of them?" Alessandro asked.

"*No,*" Bern reported.

The real fight hadn't even started. These were the preliminaries. Neither Arkan nor any of his two remaining Primes and six Significants were on the field.

Arkan would have to provoke Alessandro. It was just a question of who he would use.

Konstantin and Leon were mopping up the intruders. If Arkan was going to push the go button, it would be now.

A woman strode into the opening at the bottom of the hill and jerked her hands up.

"It's Krause," I called out to Alessandro, covering my mike. "He's using her as bait."

"I wonder what she did to get on his shit list."

"Do you want to go for it?"

"She's not going to give us much choice."

I took my hand off my mike. "Please go to your designated circles."

A cascade of explosions came from the south.

I grabbed the tablet off the counter and pulled up the feed from the motor pool. The southern end of the property looked like hell on earth. Here and there asphalt burned with crimson magic. An oak crashed to the ground and caught on fire. The motor pool's roof in front of the camera looked like Swiss cheese.

Boom! Boom! Boom!

Across the wall, something exploded sending a geyser of dirt and fire into the air. A person howled in pain. Grandma Frida must have scored a direct hit.

Another mortar answered, splashing crimson fire against the motor pool. The front wall curved outward, bulged, and fell.

Magic cracked above my head.

"Bern?"

"She opened the portal directly above you."

On the tablet's screen, a tankette rolled out from behind the motor pool to face the southern wall. It was barely larger than the average full-size SUV. A 40-barrel stacked projectile volley gun rose from the tankette's roof. Unlike normal guns, stacked projectile batteries had no moving parts. Each of the barrels was stacked with bullets that had no casing and no primer. The bullets were fired electronically when a pulse was sent through the barrel. The rate of fire was insane.

The tankette brayed like a donkey, burping its entire arsenal in a fraction of a second.

This was the closest I had ever come to an actual war zone.

"Linus?" Grandmother Victoria said.

"I'll be there as soon as I can. I'm a little busy at the moment."

Cornelius ran into the Wedding Cake and came to stand next to me. Konstantin was close behind. I pulled the chalk out of my pocket.

At the foot of the hill, Krause was straining. I could see her arms shaking from where I stood. She had already opened two portals today and whatever she was pulling out of the third one was draining every last bit of her magic.

"I have the kids, Zeus and Sgt. Teddy," Runa reported. *"I'm activating."*

Magic flared in the distance, somewhere in the main house, a bright smudge across my mind that shone and vanished.

Leon jogged into the pavilion like he didn't have a care in the world. He hopped over the chalk boundary and landed by Cornelius. I crouched and finished the circle in two quick lines.

"We have lightning," Bern reported. Whatever she was summoning was about to come through.

"Today," Grandmother Victoria ground out.

"On my way," Linus said.

Something drummed on the Wedding Cake's roof like hail. Creatures fell into the Compound in a monstrous waterfall.

"If he isn't here in thirty seconds, go ahead and do it," Victoria said.

An acrid stench spread through the air. The roof to the right of me broke, and a creature fell into the pavilion. The size of a medium dog, it had no head or neck. Its body resembled a leathery sack, fish-belly pale, splattered with whorls of neon orange and turned on the side, so the opening served as its mouth. Four pairs of spindly long legs supported the sack, while two smaller limbs thrust from its belly, armed with three clawed fingers.

Leon shot it. It jerked and died.

"Arrived," Linus announced.

An explosion of blinding white burst in my mind's eye. Grandmother

Victoria, unleashing her power like a sun going supernova. She blazed and vanished.

I sank a punch of power into the circle. The chalk lines flared white and then all sound vanished. Another creature fell into the Wedding Cake through the hole and bounced off the invisible boundary of the circle. The four of us were cut off from reality by null space.

On the patio Alessandro's circle ignited with orange. A tornado of amber sparks spun around him. He jumped and hung suspended, the current of magic whipping around him. It suffused him, setting his skin aglow. He shone like a star.

This was the second time I'd seen it, and it took my breath away again.

Alessandro's eyes blazed with power. He looked like a god about to unleash his righteous wrath.

His magic detonated. The blast rushed from him in a radiant pulse. The creature scuttling around on the floor trying to bite through the invisible wall on null space died. At the bottom of the hill, Krause collapsed, screaming. I couldn't hear her, but I saw her straining.

Anyone or anything within a nine-hundred-meter radius of Alessandro had their magic ripped away from them.

Konstantin slow clapped. "Ever the showman, cousin."

"Three cars incoming," Bern reported.

We had given Arkan what he was waiting for.

I collapsed the circle. Keeping it up was like holding a weight, light at first, but growing heavier with every second.

Konstantin stepped out and twisted himself into Smirnov's shape. "So it's not environmental after all. Good to know."

We had just given away one of Alessandro's secrets to the Imperium. It couldn't be helped.

The cars disgorged their occupants. I tapped the tablet, zooming in.

Arkan. In the flesh. Average height, athletic build, pleasant face. Nothing at all remarkable about him. He could have been a businessman, a lawyer, a high school volleyball coach.

Another man got out of the car and came to stand next to him.

I went ice-cold.

A woman screamed into my earpiece, a sound of pure fury, and I knew it had to be Lilian.

Alessandro leaped out of his circle, wrapped in glowing magic, and strode into the pavilion. He stared at the two men, and his face was full of rage.

Franco Sagredo stood next to the man who had murdered his son. He wasn't restrained. Nobody was holding a gun to his head. He didn't look in distress. He stared in our direction, derision on his face.

Arkan waved.

"What a charming family reunion," Konstantin said.

"One more word, and I will shoot you," Leon said, not a trace of humor in his voice.

Franco raised his hands. Orange magic clutched at them, and he leveled a rocket launcher at us.

I ran.

We dashed out of the pavilion and down the stairs. Behind us the Wedding Cake exploded.

Leon sprinted to the other side, where the wall was still intact, pulling his guns as he ran. Cornelius took off toward the main house.

Alessandro turned and walked up the stairs back onto the wall. A hole gaped in the pavilion, but it was still standing. The reinforced walls resisted the blast.

The hill was a sea of flames. Someone was walking through them, like a ghost conjured from fire.

There was no pyrokinetic in Arkan's roster.

The wildfire parted and I saw the mage's face. Adam Pierce.

How? He was supposed to be incarcerated in an impregnable prison in Alaska. He was supposed to spend the rest of his natural life surrounded by ice and cold.

There has been an event in Alaska.

Oh my God.

Alessandro didn't even see him. He was looking at Arkan and his grandfather.

I took his hand.

"*È un uomo morto,*" the Artisan said.

Franco Sagredo was a dead man.

A wall of flames surged ten feet high and rolled toward us. The temperature spiked.

"We have to move."

He gave no indication that he heard me.

"*Mom, I need a bullet,*" I said into my mike.

"*I've tried. The fire is too hot.*"

How the hell was Adam generating fire hot enough to stop high caliber rounds? No pyrokinetic could . . .

He gave him the serum. Arkan gave the Osiris serum to a Prime. Holy shit.

The fire was roaring like a living creature, deafening. He would never hear me.

There was nothing we had to counter that. This was Armageddon.

A dark object arced through the sky. For a second, I thought I'd imagined it, but then my brain processed what I was seeing.

"No!"

Linus' mech landed on top of Adam Pierce. The two men vanished in a white-hot ball of fire. The blast wave of heat smashed into us, picked me up, and threw me against the wall.

It didn't hurt nearly as much as it should have.

I opened my eyes. Somehow, Alessandro had wrapped himself around me, his magic cushioning the blow.

Linus died. For real this time. Nobody could survive that.

"*What was that?*" Arabella demanded.

"*Nothing.*" My grief and fury jerked me to my feet.

The flames had vanished, and the mech was glowing red.

They killed our grandfather.

Static crackled in my ear.

"*Frida,*" Linus' voice said in my helmet. "*I need a bit of help. I'm stuck in my mech and it's quite warm in here.*"

Oh my God.

Next to me, the Artisan bared his teeth. "My turn."

"Go. I have your back."

He lunged through the gap in the pavilion and jumped off the wall, his magic flashing as he landed. I walked through the gap after him and stood at the edge of the ruined wall.

Franco scoffed and started toward his grandson, pulling two maces out of thin air. He didn't go for the guns. I knew what he wanted. He wanted to beat and humiliate Alessandro. Alessandro had disobeyed, and Franco counted on their family connection to either enrage his grandson until he became sloppy or make him hesitate.

He was wearing the headphones like the rest of them.

Another wave of Arkan's soldiers ran up the hill toward Alessandro. Magic sparked among them. Some of them sprouted blades. They were Arkan's best combat mages. He'd kept them in reserve for just this moment. Alessandro tore through them like they were paper dolls.

Franco was on a collision course, heading directly for him. They were like two knights sighting each other across a medieval battlefield. Nothing was going to keep them apart. Arkan was watching it like it was a movie.

There was no place to draw another circle. The wall was strewn with rubble. That was okay. I didn't need one.

Twenty-five yards separated Franco and Alessandro.

I took my helmet off and dropped it by my feet.

Twenty.

I sent my magic spiraling forward. Its tendrils found the impenetrable wall of Franco's mind.

Fifteen.

My magic wrapped around the old man's consciousness, locking me onto my target.

Ten.

Let me show you how much I love your grandson.

The black wings tore out of my back, and I screeched.

Not just the harpy. Me. The harpy and siren combined into one. I didn't hesitate, I didn't hold back. I gave him everything.

My magic bored into Franco's mind like a laser.

The granite crag that was an antistasi's mind resisted.

I kept screaming, the torrent of sound geysering out of me.

The granite quaked.

Soft fuzzy blackness crept on the edge of my vision.

You have all of me forever.

I fed the last drop of my power into my scream.

The stone mountain of Franco's mind cracked.

He fell to his knees, his eyes blank.

I was still screaming. His mind had vanished, but I couldn't stop.

I had to stop. I had to . . .

"I love you," Alessandro's voice said from inside my memories.

I grabbed onto the sound of those words and fell silent.

It was so quiet. The people had stopped fighting and running. They stared at me and some of them stared at Franco, kneeling in the grass with a blank look on his face.

In that silence, Alessandro and Arkan clashed, too fast to follow. They cut and carved at each other, striking, kicking, stabbing. The fight stopped. Everyone watched the two of them twist and spin. This was the point of the whole thing. This was exactly how it was supposed to end.

I walked off the wall, through the gap, and down the hill. Nobody tried to stop me. They parted before me like the proverbial sea.

Arkan was lightning fast despite his age, and he had decades of experience, but Alessandro was faster, stronger, and younger. Skill clashed with fury. Blood flew and I couldn't tell whose.

Arkan opened a gash on Alessandro's arm. Alessandro slipped around the blade, fluid, unbothered by the cut, and smashed his heel into Arkan's kneecap. Arkan's leg folded. Passive field or no, the raw force of that kick delivered enough impact. Like a suit of chain mail, Arkan's magic didn't permit a blade or a bullet to penetrate his skin, but it couldn't completely cushion him from a powerful blow.

Arkan slashed, protecting his injured leg, and Alessandro drove his elbow into the older man's face. The blow snapped Arkan's head back. Alessandro struck out, trying to trip him, but Arkan twisted at the last moment, and sliced at Alessandro's face.

A thin line of red split the skin below Alessandro's left eye. He grinned as if Arkan had given him a gift.

The resolve in Arkan's eyes broke. In that moment he must have realized that he wasn't good enough. He wasn't going to win this fight.

His mind lit up.

Magic crackled around Arkan. I didn't see it but in my mind's eye it was a black wave, dark and empty. It crashed against Alessandro and tore into me.

It was like someone had ripped me free of reality. I couldn't move. I couldn't breathe, I couldn't speak, I couldn't do anything except watch Arkan's mouth twist into a grim smile in slow motion. In front of me Alessandro stood frozen, his arm raised, his hand balled into a fist.

Arkan smiled wider.

Black glyphs appeared on Alessandro's skin, spinning over his arms and neck, and burst with brilliant light.

The magic gripping me tore.

It was a one-shot arcane circle drawn onto human flesh. Arkan's magic grasped all large objects within his immediate vicinity and froze them exactly as it found them. It was exceptionally powerful but very fragile. The circle I had drawn on Alessandro's flesh was designed to take that initial blast of magic and use it as a fuel to spin and slide across his form. That movement shattered Arkan's hold. His magic crumbled.

For a delicious second, Arkan's eyes widened. Fear slapped his face.

Alessandro pulled the null blade out of its sheath, activating it, and stabbed Arkan in the stomach.

The assassin stumbled back. His mouth gaped, in disbelief or pain, I wasn't sure.

Smirnov stepped out of the crowd. Arkan's gaze snagged on him. Smirnov twisted and became Konstantin again.

"The Imperium sends its regards," the prince said.

Alessandro freed the blade and swung. The top half of Arkan slid aside and fell on the grass.

It was over.

Finally, finally it was over. We had laid a trap and it had worked. It was okay to feel things now. It was okay to let go.

Alessandro turned away from Arkan's corpse and saw me. He crossed the space between us and hugged me to him. He'd lived. He'd survived. My knees shook all of a sudden. If he hadn't been clamping me to him, I would've fallen.

Konstantin turned to the remaining fighters. "Does anyone else want to challenge the Imperium?"

Arkan's people scattered.

Arabella ran out of the hole that used to be our front gate carrying a huge pincher-like tool. "Where is Linus? I have the jaws of life."

She'd left the grandmothers alone.

"Why aren't you protecting the south side?" I called out.

"Protect it from what? Sgt. Heart is there. There's nothing for me to do." She saw the mech still glowing. "Hold on, Grandfather, I'm coming."

Alessandro was staring at me. His face was bleeding, his left sleeve and the arm underneath it were shredded, and there was a strange look in his eyes. He looked a little deranged.

"Are you okay?" I asked softly.

"I've never been better."

The sound of a car's horn made me turn. A black SUV was making its way up our hillside driveway. It didn't look like FBI SUVs.

Konstantin frowned.

The SUV came to a stop. It had diplomatic plates.

Three men got out. The tallest of the three looked familiar. Athletic, handsome, dark hair, piercing grey eyes. Where . . . Mihail. Konstantin's brother.

Arabella pulled Linus out of the mech.

Alessandro's eyes turned dark. "We had a deal."

"I'll handle this," Konstantin said and started toward the men.

A quiet argument in Russian ensued.

Linus sprawled on the grass. Arabella heaved the jaws of life onto her shoulder and came over to stand next to me.

Mihail sidestepped his brother. Konstantin blocked his way. Mihail pushed him aside. Konstantin stumbled as if hit by a car.

Mihail marched toward us, his gaze locked on Alessandro. "Come with me."

"I affixed my seal," Konstantin growled.

"Yes, and our uncle changed his mind. His seal is heavier than yours, brother."

"What do you mean, come with you?" Alessandro asked.

"My orders are very clear. I am to come back with Orlov, and if you've killed him, I am to bring you in his stead. Come quietly. It will be easier that way."

Arabella stepped in front of Mihail. "I don't like that deal. How about you take this slightly damaged corpse instead. If you insist, I can throw in a brain-dead Italian count."

"Too soon," I told her on autopilot. They were out of their minds if they thought they could just take Alessandro.

Mihail stepped to the right.

She matched him.

He looked down on her. She was a foot shorter than him.

"Move," he ordered.

"Move me," she told him.

Mihail reached out and tried to gently push her aside. Only she didn't move.

"I don't know what you are, but I've had a bad day," he said. "Getting in my way is not healthy."

"Oh you had a bad day?" She pointed behind her at the Compound. "I live *here*. Look at my house. Now look at me. Turn yourself around, get into your car, and drive back to wherever you came from, and maybe I will let you walk away."

Mihail glanced at Konstantin.

His brother shrugged. "Those are your orders, not mine. I did my job."

The muscles on Mihail's jaw bulged. He raised his hand, very deliberately put it on Arabella's shoulder, and shoved her out of the way. Arabella took half a step, caught herself and shoved him, knocking him two steps back.

Mihail inhaled like an enraged bull. He swung at her. Somehow she dodged and slammed her shoulder into him. The prince flew back, landed hard, and rolled to his feet. Something hot and feral flared in his eyes.

"No, Misha, no," Konstantin warned, putting every drop of big-brother authority he could muster into his voice. "Not here."

Mihail's face trembled.

"She's a civilian. Misha!"

Mihail's body tore. An enormous monster spilled out, shaggy, ursine, with massive horns crowning his head. It just kept going and going, expanding, huge, enormous, enraged.

My House has a long affinity with bears. You might say we're practically family. Oh no.

Konstantin swore.

Arabella laughed.

The colossal bear creature opened his maw and roared.

Arabella's body erupted, and the Beast of Cologne surged out and roared back.

Konstantin gaped, his mouth slack.

They were the same size. Arabella was a little taller, but Mihail was thicker and heavier.

I turned to Konstantin.

He raised his hands. "My brother. The Bear of Kamchatka."

I looked at Alessandro. "Did you know?"

He nodded. "I didn't think he'd show up."

Monster Arabella took a running start and slammed into the Russian Bear. The ground shook. They rolled down the hill, ripping, biting, clawing.

Linus got up and walked over to us. His hair was smoking a little bit and his skin was very flushed.

"Well," he said. "That's something you don't see every day."

"I know we were going to wait," Alessandro said, watching my sister trying to stomp on the bear. "Let's not do that. Let's get married."

"Right now? It's been a long day."

"Not today. But soon. Will you marry me?"

"I already told you I would."

"Do I get to walk you down the aisle?" Linus asked.

"I haven't decided yet. I'm still mad at you and Benjiro Heart is very nice to me."

Alessandro laughed. I wrapped my arm around his waist, and he put his good arm around me.

Everything was going to be all right.

 # Epilogue

I lay on the grass and stared at the sky. It was very blue. The grass was itchy, and I was naked, but I didn't have enough energy to get up, so I just lay there trying to catch my breath.

The Russian prince panted next to me, also naked.

We had brawled for the better part of an hour. Maybe longer. I wasn't sure how long, but Catalina and Alessandro got tired of waiting and went inside. I was pretty sure the other Russians had also gone inside, too.

We should have stopped before both of us ran out of magic. I had never fought that hard for that long before. Apparently when I ran out of anger, I reverted to my human shape. Good to know for the future.

It was starting to get really warm. If I didn't get a move on, I would get sunburned on my boobs. Most of me was tan, but my natural skin color was somewhere between mozzarella and snowflake.

I groaned and forced myself to sit up.

The prince was looking at me. I could either demurely clutch my chest to cover up or look back. I decided to look back.

Okay, so they built them really well in Russia. Like, *really* well.

"You didn't win," I told him.

He just kept staring like I had grown a second head. All things considered, a second head would have been less shocking. He must have thought he was the only giant in the world. Ha!

"You're lying next to a fire ant hill," I told him. "Roll left when you get up."

I climbed to my feet, a little unsteady, but upright, brushed the dirt off my naked butt, and started toward the wall. Knowing my sister, she would have left a robe or a blanket out for me.

Our home was smoking, and there was a big crack in the wall, which would be expensive to fix. Later on the so-called authorities would show up and want things explained but none of that was my problem. I had done my part. Arkan was dead, my sister and Alessandro would get married, Grandpa Linus was officially part of the family, and nobody I cared about died in the final battle.

Now we just had to fix the gaping hole in our wall. Money didn't grow on trees, but it did crawl somewhere in our office, and I had two hundred and fifty thousand reasons to find it. Jadwiga and I had a date.

It promised to be another beautiful day.

 # A Happy Goodbye

The autumn night was warm, the heat of the day a distant memory. Fairy lights shone in glowing strands all over the main patio, and in their soft light, Bern and Runa danced to slow music. Runa's long shimmering dress floated like a white cloud around Bernard, dressed in black. Her red hair fell on her shoulders in beautiful waves. It was magic. I don't think the two of them even knew that the three hundred of us were here, seated on the periphery of the dance floor at small tables.

Runa's bouquet lay on the table in front of me, a big bundle of fiery orange celosia. The florist had suggested golden roses, but she told them it would give Bernard the wrong idea about their marriage. Roses were elegant and calm, and she wanted to let him know he should expect fireworks. I did my best to get Mom to catch it, but somehow it landed in my hands.

The family looked on, murmuring to each other in soft whispers. On the far left, Connor and Nevada sat with Connor's mother. Mrs. Rogan swayed gently to the music in her wheelchair. Connor and Nevada sat close. I was pretty sure they were holding hands. Arabella sat with them, baby Arthur asleep on her lap. She had informed me that I had zero chances of being his favorite aunt. She was probably right. That spot was clearly taken.

Runa had chosen a beautiful sage green for the bridesmaids' dresses and from this angle both of my sisters looked remarkably similar. Arabella was shorter, her hair was much paler, and she didn't look like Nevada, but there was something so alike about the two of them.

Across the dance floor, Victoria Tremaine and Linus Duncan sat at a table together. I was still mad at the two of them, Linus especially. Runa and Bern both wanted them in the wedding, so Nevada and I solved that problem by pretending our grandparents didn't exist. We would sort this out eventually, but meanwhile making the two most manipulative people in our lives sweat was quite satisfying.

Benjiro and Mom sat at the next table. They were sipping wine and holding hands. Benjiro Heart had announced his intention to retire. Arkan attacked us on short notice—the nerve—and Sgt. Heart hadn't been able to disentangle himself fast enough for his liking to rush over to take care of Mom and the rest of us. He decided to find a permanent solution to the problem of being always busy. Mom didn't say anything about it, but I knew she was happy. It was obvious. Mom deserved all the happiness.

Grandma Frida sat at the table with Leon and a tall blond girl he brought as his date. She was gorgeous, but after five minutes of conversation I knew it wouldn't work. Leon was . . . Leon. He needed someone who could keep up.

Ragnar also brought a date, a very serious, dark-haired boy with impeccable manners. He introduced him by first name only, but the way his date held himself was a dead giveaway. I didn't know who he was or which House he belonged to, but there was a House there, and I would know by tomorrow. They danced together and it was adorable. Now they sat at the table with Alessandro's sisters and Halle. Lilian had rented a house in Houston until they figured out what they wanted to do, and we saw a lot of them.

I liked Bianca instantly. We hit it off without a problem. The younger sister, who wanted to be called Lia, was a little more standoffish. She was clearly uncomfortable, which was understandable, but she was slowly thawing out. Last I checked on her, she was explaining to everyone at the table how authentic Italian food was far superior to American Italian food.

I looked to the left where Cornelius sat at the table with his daughter, sister, brother, and surprisingly Augustine Montgomery. I was hoping Cornelius would bring a date as well, but he hadn't. I wanted him to meet someone, but there was nobody like Nari. An animal menagerie, including Sgt. Teddy, Zeus, a small pack of attack dogs, a few birds, and three cats napped behind them.

There were so many people who were important to us here. We had gathered for the wedding, and I kept expecting some horrible shoe to drop, some disaster to strike, but everything was peaceful and warm. We had ended Arkan. We had fended off the Russian Imperium and sent the princes home. We had won and succeeded. This was what I wanted for us.

A hand brushed my shoulder. I turned. Alessandro slipped into the seat next to me and gave me a brilliant smile.

"Where did you go?"

"I was saying goodbye to my mother. They are going to visit my grandparents in York and they might stay in the UK for a while. She wants the girls to see the country."

"It sounds like a great plan. Are you sad?"

He shook his head. "No. I had them all to myself for a while and besides, I can see them again any time I feel like it. My mother is finally doing what she actually wants to do. She is accountable to no one. It's a happy goodbye."

I smiled.

He leaned over and whispered in my ear, "Speaking of happy goodbyes . . ."

"Oh?"

He flicked his fingers and showed me two plane tickets.

"Barcelona?"

"To start with. I want to show you the Mediterranean. Come with me."

"Right now?"

He nodded. "The plane leaves at four in the morning. No responsibilities. No relatives. Just you and me."

I glanced at the grandparent table pretending to be casual. Linus was watching Bern and Runa.

"Can we get away with it?" I whispered.

"Of course, we can. We are awesome."

"I'll need to pack."

"You are packed. The bags are in the car." A little glowing light played in his eyes, happy and slightly wild. "You can call the family from the road. Come with me. I promise you won't regret it."

I put my fingers into his and we slipped from the table into the night. We walked off just far enough to not be noticed and sprinted down the main driveway to the gates.